TO TRACK A TRAITOR

THE LANE WINSLOW MYSTERY SERIES

A Killer in King's Cove (#1)
Death in a Darkening Mist (#2)
An Old, Cold Grave (#3)
It Begins in Betrayal (#4)
A Sorrowful Sanctuary (#5)
A Deceptive Devotion (#6)
A Match Made for Murder (#7)
A Lethal Lesson (#8)
Framed in Fire (#9)
To Track a Traitor (#10)

IONA WHISHAW

TO TRACK A TRAITOR

A LANE WINSLOW MYSTERY

TOUCHWOOD

TouchWood Editions
touchwoodeditions.com

Edited by Claire Philipson
Cover illustration by Margaret Hanson

CATALOGUING DATA AVAILABLE FROM LIBRARY AND ARCHIVES CANADA
ISBN 9781771513876 (softcover)
ISBN 9781771513883 (electronic)
ISBN 9781771513890 (audiobook)

TouchWood Editions acknowledges that the land on which we live and work is within the traditional territories of the Lkwungen (Esquimalt and Songhees), Malahat, Pacheedaht, Scia'new, T'Sou-ke, and W̱SÁNEĆ (Pauquachin, Tsartlip, Tsawout, and Tseycum) peoples.

We acknowledge the financial support of the Government of Canada through the Canada Book Fund and the Canada Council for the Arts, and of the Province of British Columbia through the British Columbia Arts Council and the Book Publishing Tax Credit.

PRINTED IN CANADA

27 26 25 24 23 3 4 5

To Rhona,
in memory

PROLOGUE

August 1917

I HAVE KILLED HER. SHE STOOD in the doorway asking me what I was doing there. Me! She was always a mistake, from the very beginning. I only meant to strike her so she could understand what she'd done but then I felt a blackness come over me. I don't think I even thought. When I looked down, she was dead. It was done. I beg your forgiveness. I know I must turn myself in, but it is possible I will not survive the next battle. That would be best, I know. Remember me as I was.

The letter fluttered to the floor face up. Though he could still see the words, he stared uncomprehendingly, as if the document itself were an alien presence. He closed his eyes, moving his fingers convulsively as if trying to understand why they stopped working, why they were unable to hold even a slim piece of paper.

CHAPTER ONE

May 5, 1948

EVEN FROM A DEEP DREAM of a phone ringing, Lane knew the call to be for them. Two longs and a short. Pitying the two other households on her party line who had to wake up only to find the call was not for them, she dragged herself awake and looked toward the slightly open window. The chill night air was seeping in, and she saw that it was still dark. What time was it? She cast an accusatory glance at Darling, apparently in the grip of a profound and undisturbed slumber. Who would call at this time of night but someone alerting him to an emergency? Two long rings and a short, repeated the phone in the hall.

She threw the blankets off, not bothering with her dressing gown—she would shortly wake her husband to deal with whatever it was—and went into the hall to pull the earpiece off the hook of her ancient phone.

"KC 431, Lane Winslow speaking."

"You have a long-distance call. Please hold."

Shivering and puzzled, she leaned against the wall, looking toward the bedroom where Darling's bedside lamp had suddenly come on. The floor was freezing. Long distance wouldn't be for him. Feeling some regret at the lost opportunity to make him get up in the cold, she waited.

"Go ahead please, Scotland," said an operator, who, for all Lane knew, was somewhere in the middle of the Atlantic.

"Laneke? Is that you? It's Grandmama."

Lane felt a surge of worry. What time would it be over there? Why would she be going to the expense of calling? "Grandmama, hello. Yes, it's me."

"Did I wake you? I'm so bad at the times."

"You can wake me any time. It's almost morning. Is everything all right? How is Ganf?"

"Well, that is the thing, my angel. He's fine now, but he's had a little heart attack. They have him in the tiny hospital in the town for a few days. Dr. Mwangi has him well in hand. I didn't want to worry you, but I thought you should know."

Lane ignored her grandmother's wishes altogether. She was worried. "Oh, you should have called! We could have fretted together. When will he be able to go home?"

"The doctor says he can come home on Friday. You really mustn't worry. I can hear it in your voice. He'll just have to be a little careful now. Take his pills, not dig in the garden, stop shouting at the wireless, that's all. I think I'm calling you for moral support, really. He's going to be a beastly patient and will not do anything he's told. You know what he's like."

3

"Poor Grandmama! I expect you're right." Lane felt her anxiety subsiding a little. Surely plenty of old people lived with dodgy hearts. "But do you have anyone to help you? You can't manage an obstreperous man like that completely on your own."

"I've got Fiona. She's a big strapping girl, and she worked in a field hospital. He'll be no match for her. And..." she hesitated. "Diana is here."

Frowning at this hesitation, Lane said, "Diana?" Her sister was in South Africa. But, no, after almost ten years she had suddenly turned up in Scotland, apparently. "I had no idea. Will she be staying long?"

"She's planning to stay at least a couple of months. I hope she won't be too bored. I'm afraid we haven't much to entertain her. She's gone off to Aberdeen to visit friends. She didn't write to tell you?"

Having no idea anymore what would entertain her sister—but thinking ungenerously that giving a lot of trouble to everyone would be most amusing to her—Lane said, "Not a word, I'm afraid. Listen, Grandmama, hang up and I will call you back. You mustn't go to this expense. Then you can tell me everything."

Before she placed the call, Lane went back into the bedroom and got her dressing gown under the puzzled gaze of Darling, who was now fully awake. He was half sitting with his hands folded on the outside of the covers. The clock next to the bed said 4:12.

"What's happened?"

"It's Grandmama. Ganf has had some sort of heart attack, but he's going to be all right, she says. More mysterious

4

is that Diana is there, after all these years, only she's not, of course. She's no sooner arrived than she's gone haring off to visit friends. It sounds like a long story. I told her I would call her back, so I'm suiting up to do that. You can go back to sleep."

"You're going to call at this time of day?" He glanced at the clock.

"It's lunchtime in Scotland," Lane pointed out.

Darling took up his bedside book. "I will stay here, alert and potentially helpful. If you faint from dismay, or there is any other sort of emergency, I will be right on hand."

Lane smiled and leaned over to kiss him. "You are a love. I wouldn't dream of being such a nuisance."

"It would be the first time, then," he called after her as she went back to the hall.

Wishing she'd made herself a cup of tea, Lane waited in the hallway for the call to be put through. Finally, there was her grandmother's voice, made slightly hollow and tinny by whatever mechanism made an international call possible.

"Laneke?"

"All right. Now tell me everything. Diana is there, you said. When did she arrive?"

"Yes. Well, I mean she was here. She came a week or so ago, just when your grandfather was taking a turn for the worse. I think she just wanted to stay out of the way, poor dear."

Lane was surprised. She may have held jaundiced views about her sister, but she, like Lane, doted on their grandparents. It surprised her that her sister would dash off to visit friends when Ganf was sick. "How long will she be away? She could be helpful when he is out of hospital. You sound a bit worried."

"No, no. I mean, not much. It was such a surprise to suddenly see her. She didn't even wire us that she was coming."

"I wonder if she is all right. How did she seem?"

"Oh, you know Diana. Always cheerful and energetic. I almost wonder if all that activity in the house didn't make things worse for Ganf. Perhaps that's not fair. He started showing signs of a dicky heart a couple of years ago. Anyway. She is much like her old self. A little older, of course, and perhaps a bit too thin. I'm not surprised she went off to see friends. This place must seem like a morgue to a young girl like her."

Lane considered. She had not seen her sister since before the war, when she went off to South Africa, but she had certainly been someone who liked to be the life of the party. Nursing an invalid, even a beloved grandfather, might not be her cup of tea.

"Now listen, Grandmama, you have enough to worry about with Ganf coming home. Is there anything you need?"

"No, darling girl. Dr. Mwangi has given us a complete list of instructions, including what he must eat. Broth, lean meat, plenty of vegetables, and no drink, no sweets, not that there's much else on offer with rationing. And he has to go for sedate walks. He's not going to like it much, I'm afraid."

"Don't let him bully you!"

Her grandmother laughed. "The worst of it is that I suppose I will have to go on his eating regimen as well, for solidarity. But what about you, my darling. How is your fetching husband?"

"Very fetching. He sends his love. Listen, go get Fiona to make you a slap-up lunch with everything you won't be able to have when Ganf is home. Everything will be fine. You'll see."

"I'll let you know as soon as I hear anything from your sister."

WHEN SHE'D RUNG off, Lane snuggled next to Darling to recoup the warmth she'd lost standing in the hall.

"So?" he asked.

"My poor grandpapa is doomed to a life of roots and berries. He'll have to be careful. Grandmama feels she has to join him in his suffering. She sounds worried and I think, though she didn't say so, it is the mysterious behaviour of my sister that is troubling her. I must say, I find it puzzling too. Why has she suddenly turned up there after all these years? She is supposed to be staying a couple of months, and the first thing she's done is scarper off to visit friends in Aberdeen."

"Is any of it something that needs to be resolved just this minute?" He pulled the chain on his lamp and then brought her close to him. "Take some deep breaths and let's go back to sleep till it's respectably light outside. No, not the feet, I beg you!"

WHEN DARLING HAD disappeared up the road for his long drive to Nelson, the nearby town where he was the police inspector, Lane sat at the little cast-iron French table on the porch looking out at the lake. The air was filled with the myriad damp, promising smells portending greener days wafting from the surrounding trees. From somewhere in the forest, she heard the piercingly sweet cascading song of a thrush. She closed her eyes and then opened them again. It was no use; it was impossible not to worry.

Her grandparents were in their late seventies. A weak heart was not a good thing. She tried to cling to the disappearing delusion that everything stayed the same, that they would live forever. And then a much more practical worry made her sit up. What if Ganf died before she had a chance to see him again? Should she go over? Her grandparents had for all intents and purposes been her parents since her mother died when she and her sister were tiny and her father had been either distant toward her or absent on his spying missions. And what the blazes was going on with Diana? She felt a pang of anger. It was patently unfair that they should have to worry about her on top of everything else.

Closing her eyes, she let the warmth of the morning permeate her. She knew she was being unfair to her sister. It was unseemly to let these childhood hostilities and jealousies continue to affect her even in adulthood. She knew absolutely nothing about her sister—what Diana had endured during the war, what her life circumstances were. They had never been close, and almost never corresponded. The last time she'd seen her was when Diana had been sixteen years old, and they'd spent the entirety of the war in completely different worlds, Lane working for the Special Operations Executive in intelligence in Europe and Diana, presumably, living happily with her friend in South Africa. Lane assumed Diana was reasonably well off; they had both received a modest legacy from their father. But for all she knew, Diana could have married and her husband could have perished in the fighting. It stung her now to think Diana wouldn't have told her if she'd married, but then to be fair, she'd never written to tell her sister when she and Darling had married. She had meant to, but somehow the long years of silence between them had set the course for their relationship, she supposed. But now, here Diana was, back in Scotland. Perhaps Diana had dreamed of taking refuge in the love and comfort of their grandparents, as Lane herself had often thought of doing in the aftermath of the war. Maybe something of the sort had driven her sister there now. She really had no business making any sort of assumption about her sister, she knew that. And anyway, the one thing she was sure of is that they were both equally fond of their grandparents, and that was something. With this exercise in being a better person, Lane got up and stretched. She hadn't gone back to sleep, in spite of Darling's best efforts, and she did feel a little unrested.

Kenny and Eleanor Armstrong, who ran the post office in King's Cove, the tiny hamlet where Lane and Darling lived, might offer some perspective. It promised to be a warm day, early in May as it was. She could hear the coughing of Robin Harris's tractor grumbling to life down the hill from her. It was the comforting noise of King's Cove starting up its morning.

She tucked her moss-green wool shirt into her trousers, slipped her feet into her plimsolls, and made for the two mossy planks that served as a bridge over the little treed gully between her house and the post office.

DARLING ENJOYED THE drive into town. He had never imagined how lovely all the seasons could be out in the country. Since he had been in Nelson, apart from his years overseas during the war, he had only lived in his little house up the hill from the police station. Of course, a beautiful morning in May was plenty nice everywhere, but out in the lush quiet of King's Cove, it was expansive, full of birdsong and the lovely turning of deciduous trees from a pale yellowy green to the full-dress colour of their summer garb.

He was brought back to reality with a thud as he arrived at the ferry and saw that it was just setting off to the other side of the lake. He turned off the engine and listened to the boat churning away toward town. The thought he'd been staving off came into full focus: Lane would want to dash off to Scotland. He knew this as certainly as he knew it would be the right thing to do.

He tried to imagine spending their first summer as a married couple alone. In truth, he had not visualized what the summer would be. He was the head of the Nelson Police Station. He'd hardly be spending his summer like a school kid, swimming about and building fires on the beach, but still, he might at the weekends, if swimmers and boaters could keep themselves from drowning. Should he move back into town? He'd kept the house to use as a *pied-à-terre* when he had to work late.

Deciding to cross that bridge when he came to it, Darling settled in to wait patiently for the ferry to wend its way back for him. He'd come to quite like this little interlude just before he arrived in town. The cable ferry went back and forth all day and all night, as people were coming into and leaving town at all hours, but somehow it always seemed to be heading away when he arrived. Waiting the fifteen minutes for it to come back gave him time to gather his thoughts, though, in truth, he didn't much like the thoughts he was gathering this particular morning.

ALEXANDRA, THE ARMSTRONGS' Westie, rushed toward Lane and greeted her as if she had been absent for a year, and was rewarded with an affectionate scratching behind the ears. There were several people enjoying the mild morning and waiting for the post office to open. Alice Mather was talking earnestly to Gwen Hughes outside the post office door.

"It'll be a bad one this year, you mark my words. Hot weather brings them out like fleas on a dog," Alice warned in her strident voice. She was dressed as she always was when she made an appearance, in a pair of faded blue overalls with a worn wide leather belt cinched around her small waist. Her thin grey hair was rolled into a messy bun at the nape of her neck.

Gwen said, "Hmm," in a noncommittal manner and then smiled when she caught sight of Lane approaching.

"Good morning. Mabel is expecting you at eleven. You haven't forgotten?"

"Good morning, Gwen, Alice. Of course not. A lesson on how to make a proper chocolate cake is hardly something one is likely to forget!"

"I was just saying," Alice said, turning to her, "cougars bound to be bad this year. Heard on the wireless just this morning that a pup was snatched up in Revelstoke. Too late for householder to rescue it. Dreadful business." Alice always spoke as if she were dictating a telegram. She was, everyone knew, prone to "turns."

"How awful!" Lane exclaimed, casting a nervous eye for Alexandra, who was now sniffing suspiciously around the edge of the root cellar. Realizing she had not seen Alice for some time, Lane added, "It's nice to see you, Alice. I imagine your garden is coming along nicely." Usually Alice's swaggering husband, Reginald, made the trip to the post office because his wife was refusing to leave the house, and it was a relief not to have him to cope with this morning. Alice had periods of brightness, and this must be one of them.

"Deer ate what tulips we had coming up. That brings them around too."

"Tulips?" asked Gwen, who was only half listening.

"Deer!" said Alice, as if Gwen were soft in the head. "Cougars."

The screen door of the cottage opened, and Kenny Armstrong put his head out. "She's ready for you."

Lane waited outside, basking in the sunshine and watching Alexandra, thinking again how lovely it might be to have a dog, but in the next instant, the thought that she might have to go to Scotland intruded. She couldn't leave poor Darling to deal with a dog on top of abandoning him.

Alice came out of the post office first, holding some letters, a couple of newspapers, and a little greaseproof paper packet of, no doubt, some of Eleanor's magical cookies. She had her walking cane over her wrist by the crook, and strode off without using it, leaving Lane to wonder if she didn't just carry it for show. Or to fend off cougars. Or to bludgeon Reginald, she thought uncharitably.

Gwen followed, similarly laden with letters, newspapers, and cookies. She stopped and held up the packet, smiling. "Mummy always asks why Eleanor bothers, but then secretly devours most of them. These are the treacle and ginger. I'm hiding them so she doesn't get at them See you at eleven!"

Inside the addition to the cottage that comprised King's Cove's tiny post office, Lane saw Eleanor through the window organizing something in the mailboxes. Kenny drove his bright red truck down to the wharf every morning to meet the paddle steamer sternwheeler that carried goods and people up and down the lake. He collected the canvas bag of mail and any orders coming in from town. The mare, whose office it used to be to pull a small wagon down to the wharf, was at the fence looking with hopeful interest at the people gathered in front of the post office. Someone usually brought her an apple. Kenny, as was his custom in the mornings, left the socializing to Eleanor, and went about the work of the garden and keeping the stove supplied with wood.

Smiling at the poster for the Calgary Stampede from 1946 that still decorated the dark wood of the walls, Lane called, "Good morning!"

"Ah," said Eleanor, with her magnificent toothy grin. "You have an interesting letter today, my dear. Have you time for tea?"

"I have."

"Go around, I'll close up for the time being. I'm not expecting Angela or Robin till later." Eleanor slid the wooden window down with a clunk, and Lane went back outside and around to the cottage door, where Alexandra again greeted her like a long-lost friend.

Inside, Lane settled down at her place on a rattan chair full of squashed-down pillows and looked through the mail Eleanor had handed her. She saw immediately what Eleanor meant about an interesting letter. Looking somewhat worse for its travels was an airmail letter with a stamp from Suid-Afrika, with her name, Mrs. Frederick Darling, written in a most familiar hand.

"You'd think they'd put a zebra or something on their stamps, instead of the same old royal family," Lane said, putting the letter firmly down on top of her copy of the *Nelson Daily News*. She would read it later. It had better have an explanation for her sister's peculiar and irritating behaviour. Of course, Eleanor was quite partial to the royal family, Lane knew. George VI occupied a prominent place on the wall of their kitchen.

"It is a nice picture of the princesses, though," Eleanor said. "Don't you have family there?"

Instead of answering, Lane peered at the frank. It had started its journey a full month before, on April 5. "It's been a good while getting here," she commented. "It's from my sister, and she's not in South Africa, she is in Scotland, supposedly visiting my grandparents, but she no sooner got there than she's gone off to visit friends."

CHAPTER TWO

———

"**GOOD MORNING, SIR,**" **SERGEANT O'BRIEN** said as Darling came through the door of the station. He accompanied this with a brisk nod, perhaps the only brisk thing about him.

"Good morning to you," Darling responded in a way that told O'Brien that, if not actually cross, his boss was already exercised over something.

"You're in early, sir."

Darling rejected a deluge of sarcastic remarks and limited himself to "Early to bed, early to rise, Sergeant. Anything?"

"No, sir. Your criminal is doubtless late to bed and late to rise."

"Well, that's something anyway."

The telephone jangled and O'Brien answered it. Darling did not wait to hear about it but went upstairs to his office to contemplate his domestic situation. He hung his hat up and saw the file he'd left out as a reminder to complete his notes about a disturbance he'd gone out on the day before. He sat down and shook his head at the file. It had been an older couple, in their sixties. The shouting that had progressed to loud banging had finally caused the neighbour to call the police. She had been afraid someone was going to get hurt.

Darling had arrived to find the dispute mostly over. The husband was sullenly standing out on the little front porch of the ill-kempt house, smoking a cigarette. He had a bruise on his cheek. Darling had expected to find the wife in tears inside the house, but she was energetically sweeping up broken crockery, muttering, "Bloody bastard!" over and over; she did not stop until he cleared his throat. They always saddened him, these examples of marital disharmony. He thought of what it must have been like when the couples were young and had first fallen in love, a future of seething unhappiness unimaginable to them.

He took a deep breath. Neither he nor Lane had the disposition for tossing dishes, but they both had a slight tendency to independence that could edge toward a kind of reserve. If they weren't careful, it could create distance. Going to Scotland could create distance, too, he thought glumly.

The phone rang, interrupting these reflections. "Sir, that was a call from across the lake at Six Mile. A Mrs. Arden says her husband is missing. Went out in his boat last night, boat found this morning, no man. Sergeant Ames just came in. Shall I send him out?"

"No, you can send us both out. I'll be right down." It would be a distraction. And it was interesting. He imagined a rowboat homing, like a horse that had lost its rider.

"You sure you're all right to drive?" Darling asked Ames, standing before the station's maroon Ford.

"Got to start sometime, sir." Ames, who was recovering from a bullet wound he'd gotten a month and a half before, no longer wore a sling to protect his left shoulder, but he still held his arm carefully. He'd come back to work as quickly as he could because he'd grown restless under his mother's fond attentions, and his doctor's injunctions to take it easy.

They found the lakeside house easily. It enjoyed a little peninsula of beach and a narrow dock built out toward deeper water. A rowboat bobbed placidly in the morning sun. Ames knocked on the screen door, and the inner door was flung open. They could hear the quiet hum of an outboard motor chugging along somewhere on the lake.

"Oh, thank God! I've been desperate!" Mrs. Arden was in her forties, Darling estimated. He wondered if there were children. Perhaps they were at school. There was a school, he knew, nearby at Willow Point. It was plain she'd been crying.

Seated at the kitchen table, Mrs. Arden twisted a hand-kerchief in her hands and explained in fits and starts that Benjamin Arden had gone out around ten o'clock the night before in one of their rowboats and had not returned. The boat had been found by the neighbour, beached near his property. He'd brought it back to her and asked her if she'd like him to call the police, but she'd said she would.

"Was it usual for him to go out at night like that?" Darling asked.

Mrs. Arden hesitated fractionally and then shook her head.

Ames, pencil and notebook in hand, noted the hesitation.

"No. I asked him where he thought he was going. He just said, 'Never you mind.'"

"Had you had an argument?"

"No, not at all. It was just out of the blue!"

Darling glanced out the window toward the lake. "Was he despondent at all? Troubled by something at work, maybe?"

Mrs. Arden frowned. "Oh. Are you asking if he went out there and took his own life? What a horrible thing to say! We have two children. He's devoted to them. Would he do something like that to us?" She looked down at her hands, as if trying to take in the enormity of that idea.

Darling nodded. "I understand. We have to explore every possibility. Where does your husband work?"

"At the Kootenay Feed Store in town."

"Has he any health concerns? Heart and so on?" Darling asked.

Mrs. Arden shook her head. "Just the normal ones, I suppose. He gets stiff knees, his back hurts more than usual after he's been in the garden. It's the job. He has a lot of heavy lifting. I think he might have mentioned he has slightly high blood pressure. He's almost ten years older than me. He never likes to talk about his visits to the doctor."

Did this suggest he was hiding something from his wife? Darling wondered. Could he have had a heart attack while he was on the lake? But then he would most likely have been in the boat floating about till it made it to shore.

"If it is not usual for him to go onto the lake at that time of night, might he have been meeting someone?"

18

Her face flushed. "Well, I don't know what you mean by 'someone.' If you mean a woman, that's ridiculous. Who else would he meet? Someone from work? One of the guys is young and has his own friends, and the other one is Owen. We have dinner sometimes, or beach barbecues, if they come here. Owen is not the sort of man who would go out at night in a rowboat." There was another silence. "Oh, I'm sure he has a wandering eye like all men."

"Were there any signs of something unusual—even unexpected daytime trips out onto the lake, unusual letters, anything?"

She looked distractedly out the window and then shook her head. "No, nothing like that."

Ames wondered why she went straight for the idea that he might have met a woman. Was it something she worried about?

"Did your husband serve in the war?" asked Darling.

"Yes. Oh, not this last one. The Great War. Princess Pats. Why?"

"No nightmares or that sort of thing? Episodes that might keep him awake at night?"

Mrs. Arden looked down again. She seemed to be staring at her knees. There was a long silence. Darling waited patiently, his arms resting on the kitchen table. Finally, she looked up. "He doesn't talk about it, Inspector. I did sometimes wonder. But it's been a long time. We met after. Owen Barnes served as well, and he talks about the war all the time. Where they went, what they ate, silly things the other men did, even some of the battles. You'd think it was the best time in his life, the way he carries on. Ben never talks about the war at all. I mean, I guess I'm saying I don't really know. But I will say this: I never saw any signs of it. He always seems happy enough to me. He likes going to work and plays with the children, maybe even more than some of the other fathers. I guess at his age he appreciates them more, especially because it took us a long time to have them. We'd nearly given up. I was already over thirty." She put her hand to her mouth as if to stifle a sob. "He's been teaching Ben Junior to fish. I can't tell you how I felt seeing the boat empty like that."

Scribbling, Ames was aware of the sound of his pencil sliding along the paper in the silence that followed this.

"Mrs. Arden, usually we wait twenty-four hours when someone appears to be missing, but given the unusual circumstances, I will open a file and involve the RCMP as well. If you find anything or recall anything that might in any way shed light on why he might have gone out last night, please telephone right away. If I may, I would also like to talk to his doctor, and I will go and speak with the people at his work. Can you tell me who his doctor is?"

Mrs. Arden put her hand to her mouth, worry reflecting in her eyes. "Oh, but then people—"

"I don't think this is something you will be able to keep quiet, Mrs. Arden. It is better for us to have a complete picture so we can act quickly."

"Oh, yes. Of course. It's Dr. Epstein, in town there."

"Thank you. How old are your children?"

"Little Ben is seven and Audra is almost thirteen. Oh, God! What am I going to say to them?"

"Can we call someone for you? Mrs. Barnes?"

Mrs. Arden shook her head. "Oh, I'm sure I don't want to bother Cynthia. She lives in town. She won't have a way to get out here." But Darling could hear what sounded like hope in her voice.

"Why don't you telephone her, and I will have someone bring her out. Is that the boat your husband went out in moored outside? I'd like to have a look at it."

"Oh, no. We have two. My neighbour dragged it over and I pulled it up onto the beach." Mrs. Arden stood up and pointed down to a growth of bushes that marked the end of their stretch of lakefront. Darling had stood up to see where she was pointing.

"Sergeant Ames, can you go have a look, make any notes? I'll just get Mrs. Barnes organized."

AMES WENT OUTSIDE and walked down along the side of the house toward the beach. The air was fresh and cool, and he was relieved to be away from the stuffy kitchen and the anxiety and unhappiness of Mrs. Arden. He found the rowboat partially pulled up on the gravelly sand. It was a faded blue with a much-scuffed flat bottom that still contained an inch or two of water. As he peered cautiously at it, he realized he'd been holding his breath in case there was blood. Relieved at seeing only bilge water, he exhaled and looked for any signs of the missing man. Both oars appeared to be gone. So, a man and two oars. But then he saw the oarlocks were missing also. Perhaps Arden had just used an outboard motor and Mrs. Arden had removed it. He walked slowly around the prow and then to the other side of the boat, looking for any sign of new damage. The boat had been well battered with use, and judging by the other rowboat bobbing on its rope against the wooden pier, this was the older one. Shaking his head, he went around to the front of the house to retrieve his camera. He was going to have to pull the damn thing all the way onto dry land to get a look at the stern. Before he went back down to the lakeside he knocked and then opened the front door. Darling and Mrs. Arden were sitting at the kitchen table again, she with a handkerchief up to her nose.

"Excuse me, ma'am, but did your husband take a motor? I don't see any sign of the oars being used."

"Oh," she said, and then frowned as if she was trying to remember. "It's funny, I can't remember that. We'll have to look in the shed. That's where we keep the oars and a couple of engines."

The boat shed, tucked right along the property line at the north side of the house, contained several sets of oars, a couple of small khaki life jackets, and one outboard motor, mounted on a bracket on a two-by-four stud. Mrs. Arden pointed into the semi-darkness of the shed.

"The oars are here, but only one motor. We have two." She turned away and looked out across the lake as if she expected her husband to come putt-putting back. "It's so extraordinary that I didn't hear it. You know that loud buzzing it makes when you pull the starter cord to get it going."

"But the oars normally used for this boat are here?" Ames asked.

She turned back and pointed to the oars on the racks along the wall above them. "Yes. Right there. He usually takes oars even with the motor, in case it dies. It's so odd." Ames looked to where she pointed and on a lower shelf noted a battered cardboard box containing a combination of brass and partially rusted iron oarlocks. He glanced again at the engine in its rack.

"Did he take anything with him?" Ames looked up, pencil in hand.

Her eyes flitted to the left and back. "I don't know. I'll have to look, I guess."

Darling nodded. "Constable Terrell will be here soon with Mrs. Barnes. In the meantime, you might check his belongings to determine whether something is missing and if he had anything with him."

"WHAT DO YOU make of all that, sir?" Ames said as they drove back to town.

"I'm not hopeful," Darling responded.

"I noticed that she went right away to refusing the idea that it could be a woman."

"Yes, that was interesting. I noticed how red she got. I can't help feeling she is keeping something back."

"That's not very helpful. Maybe she's embarrassed about it. I admit, it made me wonder if there's a history of some sort of philandering. I mean, it's the sort of thing that happens to people that age, isn't it?"

"Really, Ames, you do think in clichés. I suspect you read too many of your mother's women's magazines while you were convalescing."

Ames said nothing. He had read a great many magazines while he lay on the couch, and it was one of the things he'd read about. They did a lively traffic in stories about men straying. He'd seen it called the seven-year itch, if he recalled right. To supplement his steady diet of women's magazines, he'd also been given books by Tina Van Eyck, the mechanic who'd taken over much of the work at her father's garage when she'd returned from England after the war. He'd had a woeful history of dating, but with some precipitous ups and downs, his relationship with Tina, the only one of Ames's girlfriends his mother liked, seemed to be holding. She'd been intent on improving him while he was captive to his injuries, and had supplied serious novels and even a repair book. He'd found the magazines preferable to the manual for the police force's Ford motor car. It had reminded him forcefully that he had no mechanical aptitude. He still cringed at the memory that she had once had to drive out to where he'd had a puncture to help him change the tire.

"Still," Darling said, "it's a thought. We might learn more when we talk to Barnes, if he confided in him.

"If it was a woman," he continued, "who was she and what has she done with him? It is quite conceivable he's had a fling with someone. He's had plenty of opportunity, I suppose, working in town, his wife tending house up the lake, but I can't make it play out. They meet somewhere along the lake and run off together? I can see an affair, but would a man in his position run off with someone? Perhaps O'Brien will have received a phone call about a missing woman by the time we get back. Or he might simply have had a heart attack and toppled into the water." Honestly, Darling thought, I have heart attacks on the brain since Lane's grandmother called.

24

"If he was trying, let's say, to get away from the noise of his children or a bad day at the feed store, he would have taken oars. Gone for a quiet little row in the moonlight, that sort of thing. But the fact that he took the outboard makes me think he had a definite purpose for going onto the lake. He had to be going somewhere," Ames said. "And, for that matter, if the boat drifted back, where is the motor?"

"That is a pretty good observation," Darling said. "If you have any more like that, send them along in triplicate."

"Well, sir, I also was surprised that she didn't hear it. I mean, it must be pretty quiet out there at night."

Darling nodded thoughtfully. "She could have had the wireless on."

"Except haven't they just had an argument about him going out? In fact, when I think about it, they have the argument, he storms off, and she goes outside to watch him leave because she doesn't understand what he's up to."

"You're smarter than you look. It's something to think about. But let's take her at her word. They have the argument, and he storms out. In a fit of pique, she turns on the wireless and sits fuming in the kitchen."

"Now I wish we'd asked her why she didn't hear the outboard motor. And about the radio. The only way I can think she might not have heard it is if he'd rowed some way into the lake before starting it, but he didn't have the oars."

By the time they pulled up in front of the station, Ames was feeling that it was good to be back at work, in spite of the pain he still felt in his shoulder.

"I'll get these photos attended to, sir." He'd focused a few shots on where the outboard motor ought to have been fixed. He looked for signs that it had been knocked out, maybe if the boat had run aground against a rocky point or been hit by another vessel.

"Yes, thank you. Let me know if you see anything else," Darling said, nodding. "Terrell get off all right to get Mrs. Barnes up the lake?" he asked O'Brien as he came through the station door.

"Yes, sir. I lent him my car since I didn't think Mrs. Barnes would like to ride pillion on the constable's motorcycle. It's not for everybody, that sort of transport."

"When you've deposited that film, Ames, we'd better get down to the feed store to have a chat with Mr. Barnes." He could have sent Ames on his own but keeping busy was going to stop him from thinking about Lane in Scotland.

LANE MADE HER way back through the copse of birch trees to her house. It was warm enough now to leave the doors open. She contemplated pulling her folding chair off the porch and moving it under the weeping willow next to the small unfinished pond, but then decided it was not yet too hot to sit on the porch. Ignoring the nagging of the break-fast dishes and the unfinished pond, she put the newspaper and cookies on the kitchen table and opened the French doors wide. On the porch, she sat resting her arm on the little cast-iron table they would soon use for their tea and coffee on warm mornings, holding the unopened letter from her sister in her hand.

Finally, turning her gaze away from the lake, her centre of calm, she looked at the envelope. When had her sister last written her? Almost two years before? She could feel the beginnings of anxiety gnawing at her stomach. She wondered if it was a premonition and then pulled herself together. She didn't believe in nonsense. With determination to get the worst of it over, she slid her finger under the flap of the airmail envelope and pulled out a single sheet of paper.

> *Dear Sister,*
> *I hope this finds you well. I heard from Grandmama that you married, and I am sorry for these late well wishes. I'm afraid I have no such news to offer. Things are more complicated since the end of the war, and so I have decided to return to the old country. I will of course go to see Grandmama and Ganf at their cottage in Scotland. I wonder if they have become used to it?*
>
> *I will write again when I am settled somewhere. Perhaps you will invite me to come out to Canada for a visit.*
> *Your loving sister,*
> *Diana*

"*Loving sister?*" Lane exclaimed out loud. Frustrated at the sheer lack of information, Lane read the letter again. She saw at once that what was buried between the lines told volumes. She was being made to feel guilty right in the second sentence, with its unsaid accusation that she hadn't told Diana herself that she was getting married. Never mind the greeting, "Dear Sister," as if she couldn't bear to write her name. There was also a shortness, or even anger, in the next sentence. She could hear Diana's voice in it. Had she had an unhappy affair? Was she envious of Lane? And that was followed by things being "complicated" since the war. That could suggest any number of difficulties. The unhappy affair, perhaps with a married man? That would certainly be complicated. No. There she was being uncharitable again. She remembered how utterly broken up she herself had been over Angus Dunn, her wartime lover. She didn't wish such pain on anyone. Perhaps it was something to do with politics. Had she become involved in the resentments between the Dutch and the English that no doubt simmered since before the Boer War? Had she joined some sort of organization that supported the African population of South Africa? She couldn't imagine her sister being altruistic enough to involve herself in political affairs.

And then she finished off with another bit of guilt. "Perhaps" Lane would invite her out to Canada, suggesting that hell was likely to freeze over before Lane issued any such invitation.

She turned the paper over, and then back again. Nothing more to be had from it. If she brushed away all her own resentful thoughts, there was something urgent about the brevity and tone of the letter, as if Diana had had to leave in a hurry. Was it anything to do with the conditions in the country? What she knew about South Africa she'd gleaned from the papers and an airman she'd met during the war. She remembered him saying things were very tense just prior to the war while the country was trying to maintain its neutrality. In the lead-up to the war, the Dutch Afrikaners had had sympathy with the Germans.

That must have created enormous pressures when South Africa declared war on Germany. And who knew where this tension between European settlers left all the African people who'd been there before the colonial takeover of their land? If it was anything like what had happened in India or to the Indigenous people when Europeans flooded all over North America, then it did not bode well for the Africans.

She stood up and folded the letter and put it back in the envelope. The truth was that this letter was all apiece with the other few letters she'd ever had from her sister. Short and to the point, revealing not very much at all. "Right. Work," she declared aloud. She'd tidy up, and then it would be time to go learn how to make chocolate cake.

"SIR," TERRELL SAID, knocking on Darling's office door. Darling looked up. "I dropped Mrs. Barnes off at the Ardens', and I guess Mrs. Arden had done more looking around after you left. She wanted me to tell you that some clothing and a rucksack are missing. More importantly, she found that her husband's Smith & Wesson pistol is also gone."

"Pistol? Why did he keep a pistol? A hunting rifle is the more ordinary weapon in the country."

"I asked her that, sir. Apparently, he kept his weapon, or somehow acquired one, when he was demobbed after the Great War. According to her, he has never touched the thing."

CHAPTER THREE

LANE'S FAVOURITE ROUTE TO THE Hughes house on the hill above the post office was the treed path that started just past Kenny Armstrong's garden and climbed up the steep hill in a long single switchback. She arrived at the top of the hill, already anticipated by the two spaniels kept by this enterprising family of mother and two daughters. The dogs hurried over, sniffed her shoes, and then gave a couple of barks to announce her. The sun flooded over the garden where the lupines and delphiniums were already budding. They would be a glorious sight in summer. Several beds of vegetables near the drive to the garage were full of promising and orderly looking lumps of green.

"Hello!" came the vigorous voice of Gladys Hughes. She was dressed in her usual gardening attire: faded blue trousers, Wellington boots, and rubber pads strapped to her knees. She waved a friendly spade from her position on her knees in one of the beds. The only sign of her being well into her seventies was the slight grunt she gave as she pushed herself upright.

"Girls are inside," she said, peeling off her gardening gloves. "I'm ready for a cuppa just about now."

"Good morning, Gladys. Your garden is a wonder, as usual. I do envy you!"

"Nonsense. A child of two could manage it," Gladys said breezily. "Here to make cake, are you?"

"I am. The inspector will be ecstatic. He loves chocolate cake."

"Mabel seems to have the knack. Both girls are pretty good at that sort of thing, but Mabel enjoys it more."

Lane smiled at the thought of Mabel and Gwen, both in their fifties, still being "the girls." "Well, let's hope I have the knack," she said.

There was time for everyone to sit down for a cup of tea before the lesson, Lane discovered. Mabel had a businesslike air about most things, and Lane had assumed she'd be set to work immediately. When Gladys poured the tea, and the plate of ginger cookies from Eleanor was set out, the Hughes girls asked Lane about the inspector. Then the conversation moved to Alice and her obsession with cougars.

Suddenly Mabel struck her forehead. "The pig getting out put it right out of my mind. When I was at the Bales store yesterday, I heard from that pert little number, Lucy, that Philippa Bentley from right there in Balfour ran out on her husband!"

"How the blazes does she know that?" asked Gwen.

"You know perfectly well. Lucy could blackmail half the local population with what she hears on the exchange."

31

"Whom was Mrs. Bentley meant to run off with?"

"Someone in town. She didn't say who," Mabel said, taking another cookie. "I've heard Mr. Bentley is a bit of a brute."

"I don't think he is," Gwen objected. "Isn't he the man who works on the steamer?"

Gladys sniffed and gulped down the last of her tea. "What does it matter if a man is nice or not? He works hard, provides for his family. Didn't get that sort of carry-on in my day. Don't know what's the matter with people. I'm back off outside. Gwen, you'd better see to that gate. Can't have Porky running off again."

"You know, Mother, you did get that sort of carry-on in your day. Remember Adele Robinson? You told us when we were girls that her first husband left her and their little boy for a girl who worked at the cinema selling cigarettes. What was his name again?"

Gladys was buckling her knee pads back over her knees. "Oh, yes. Poor Adele. I should go along and see her. Haven't seen her since last Dominion Day. Second husband died a couple of years ago." Gladys spoke with the complacency of someone who knew nothing so untidy could ever happen to her. In fact, her own husband had died suddenly when Gwen and Mabel were still in their teens.

"Yes, you should go see her. You were quite friendly at one time," Gwen said, going out the door. "Honestly, you're becoming reclusive. You never want to go anywhere."

"Who has time to gallivant? There's the garden to be attended to," Gladys retorted.

When the kitchen had cleared, leaving Lane with her instructress, Mabel said, "Right. Cake. Mind you, I'm not sure how it will be when you try it on your own. You have that unreliable electric stove. I can't think the oven will keep the right temperature the way our wood stoves do. Now then, here's what we'll need." She went into her larder and came out with large tins of flour, cocoa, and sugar, and a packet of butter. A bowl of eggs stood on the counter near the sink. "Can you go in and get the baking powder and baking soda? Middle shelf, on the right."

Lane, not a little thrilled to get a lock into the Hughes larder, went into what was a sizeable closet, shelves neatly stacked with tins, jars, boxes of oatmeal and cream of wheat, and, if she was not mistaken, a tin of mixed biscuits. She smiled. It was quite possible that commercial biscuits were a treat in a community where homemade was the rule. She found what she'd been sent for and put the two containers on the table with the rest.

"Do you have cake tins and measuring spoons and cups?" Mabel asked, pulling these out of a drawer. The cat, lying on the bench under which stove wood was stored, lifted her head languidly to watch in case any of the activity would prove beneficial to her.

"I don't myself, but Eleanor and Kenny have told me to root around in Lady Armstrong's household items in the attic for things I might need."

Mabel was on the point of answering when the telephone sounded in the hall. "Damn." She put down the large mixing bowl she'd fetched out of a cupboard and waited. "Mine. Back in a jiffy."

Lane went to stand by the sink where a long, low window gave out to the surrounding lawn and garden, which were bathed in sun. Gladys was motionless with her hands on her hips, surveying one of the curved beds near the driveway. Gwen was just coming up from the pigpen and stopped to say something to her mother. Lane could hear Mabel's muffled voice from the hall. She sounded as if she was deliberately lowering it in a bid to calm the other person down. It was such a lovely quiet house, Lane thought. It had a kind of peaceful, sunny, eternal quality to it, as if the three Hughes ladies had always been here and always would be, making a world out of unremarkable everyday acts that somehow resulted in the beauty of life well lived.

She turned as she heard Mabel come back into the kitchen. "Well, speak of the devil. That was Adele Robinson, absolutely beside herself. I'd better call Mother in; she'll want to hear this." Mabel went to the door in the mud room and pushed open the screen. "Mother, you'll never guess, Adele Robinson has just been on the telephone in hysterics."

Gladys turned and looked at Mabel. "Oh? That's odd, isn't it? We were just talking about her. What's going on?"

"You know how you were thinking you ought to go see her? Well, she'd like you to. It seems her son has run off in the night and left his wife and two children. Makes you think a bit, doesn't it?"

Gladys plunged her trowel next to a young dahlia plant and pulled off her gloves. Wisps of wiry grey hair had begun to escape from her rolled hairdo. "Now what's he gone and done a damn fool thing like that for?" She looked around the garden. "I've got masses of work to do. I can't go galloping off every time there's a little crisis in someone's life. Why doesn't she call the police? That's what they're for, isn't it?"

"Yes, Mother," Mabel said patiently. "If it's even a matter for the police. You'll have to change. You can't go into any civilized house looking like that."

Muttering a mild oath, Gladys went into the mud room and pulled off her boots. "I never thought much of the boy," she grumbled. "Not very bright, I'd have said. Took after his father. He was a colossal dimwit before he went and died. She always complained about her boy's difficulties at school. Mind you, I don't think that ass Robinson was any great help as a stepfather. But there you are, like father, like son. I don't know what I'm expected to do about it."

Gwen had been standing just outside the door smoking a cigarette. "You might try just being kind, Mother. Maybe that's all she needs. You are her oldest friend. I think it's rather sweet that you're the first person she called. I wonder where he's gone?"

"You're such a Pollyanna! You should go. Now, go get the car out of the garage while I change."

"HONESTLY," MABEL SAID, when her mother and Gwen had finally driven off on their errand of mercy, "I feel like I've avoided a lifetime of trouble by not being married. I don't have to be beholden to anyone, or obey anyone, or do anything but what I please."

The cake making could finally settle in and get started. Cake tins were prepared with butter and flour, and flour was sifted with baking powder and cocoa. Lane mixed the sugar and butter as directed with a wooden spoon until it was fluffy. The state of the mixture defied her understanding of "fluffy," but she carried on gamely, mixing in two eggs and beating until the whole thing appeared smooth and creamy and her arm ached.

"I hope all married couples need not expect one of them to run off," suggested Lane, resting her arm.

"Dear me, what a dreadful thing to say to a newly married bride! Of course not. And, in fact, my parents were perfectly happily married, though Daddy did die before it was convenient for anyone."

"No offence taken. In fact, I'm rather afraid I myself will be running off in a short time, leaving the poor inspector on his own. My grandfather has been ill, and I think I'm going to have to go off to Scotland."

"I'm sorry to hear it. Is it quite serious?"

"Heart. My patient grandmother is tasked with keeping him on the straight and narrow, in the matter of diet and exercise."

Mabel shook her head. "That's what killed Daddy, only no one knew anything was wrong with his heart."

"That must have been dreadful. You were in your teens?"

"That's right. Fifteen. Mother, of course, was a trooper. Chin up, have to soldier on, that sort of thing."

Mabel went to their tiny fridge, pulled out a bottle of milk, and poured it into the tin measuring cup. "All right. We are going to add the milk and the flour alternately in three goes, and we are going to fold it in carefully so as not to toughen the cake."

Lane, unaware that cake could be toughened, or of what folding was outside of the contents of her laundry basket, watched and imitated.

"Right. Into the tins, give them a good rap to knock out the air bubbles, and into the oven. We'll give them twenty minutes before we have a look. You can't open and close the oven door every five minutes to peek, and you definitely can't slam the oven door because your cakes will fall. Now, I suggest we go outside and make sure Gwen did an adequate job on the pigpen gate."

KOOTENAY FEED STORE was located on Front Street, an easy walk from the station, so Ames and Darling made their way there while Terrell went out on a noise complaint. A slat-sided truck parked by the front steps was being loaded up with sacks by two men. One of them saw Ames and Darling hovering at the bottom of the steps.

"Be right with you. Go on in."

Inside, the barrels and sacks of feed made the store smell pleasantly grainy, and Ames wondered at the way of life that would require bags of grain. Maybe if he moved out to the country he would buy something like this for, what, a cow? Some chickens? But, of course, Tina, with whom he was on a longish spell of getting along, did not keep animals. And neither did the inspector, as far as he knew, so it obviously wasn't a requirement of living outside of town.

"You don't keep any animals out there at King's Cove, do you, sir?" Ames asked, wandering up and down looking at the shelves with his hands in his pockets.

"I do not. Why, are you thinking of it?"

"Don't make me laugh. Can you imagine me with chickens?" He patted a bag of something just as the front door slammed.

"Now, what can I do for you?" The man they assumed to be Barnes had come in and was brushing his hands on the back of his overalls. "Bit short-handed today. Sorry about the wait."

Darling pulled out his warrant card. "Inspector Darling, and this is Sergeant Ames. Are you Owen Barnes?"

"I am. This is about Ben, I'm guessing. The wife phoned here earlier." Barnes removed his peaked cap, wiped his forehead with a grubby handkerchief, and set his cap back on his head.

"That's right," Darling said.

"I heard he got in a rowboat and disappeared. Is that right? My wife said Ben's wife, Maude, is pretty upset."

"What can you tell us about him?" Darling countered.

"Not much to tell. He's worked here for twenty years, been pretty reliable, honest, hard-working. Got lucky and has two little kids and a wife who came with a bit of money, so I would say he doesn't need to worry."

Ames took notes. Barnes had folded his arms and looked at them from under the brim of his cap.

"Did he seem troubled about anything lately?"

"I don't know. He isn't a laugh a minute at the best of times, but no. We both served in the Great War, and it took him harder than it took me. I gave him the job because he couldn't get anything else. Are you suggesting he did himself in? 'Cause I don't think that would be like him at all."

"He disappeared last night around ten and took a pistol with him. His boat was found empty. Did he mention anything that might explain this?"

Barnes sat heavily on the counter. "A pistol?" He shook

his head. "I don't believe it. I just can't see him going off like that to kill himself."

"So, he didn't seem to you to be unhappy?" Darling asked again.

"Like I said, not more than usual. He's been a bit moody since, oh, early winter. In fact, I'd say he was in a better mood than usual. Almost chatty. Doesn't like the winter much, so I figured he was cheering up with the longer days. Is his wife all right? My Cynthia is pretty close with her. Thanks for taking her out there, by the way. I'll pick her up at the end of my day."

CHAPTER FOUR

GLADYS WAS FINDING THIS OBLIGATORY visit to her friend Adele Robinson unsettling, and so she was feeling testy. Adele lived in a cottage perched up on a hill about three miles north of Nelson, with a driveway that was rutted and narrow and difficult to negotiate. Gwen stalling the car on the hill had not helped Gladys's mood, and she was cross by the time they arrived. Adele, who in every way was Gladys's opposite—plump and short where Gladys was lean and tall, and querulous where Gladys was decisive—stood anxiously at the front door as they alighted. The distraught woman appeared at first to still be in her night things, but in fact was wearing her dressing gown over a green flowered dress.

"What's happened, then?" demanded Gladys by way of greeting.

"Thank you for coming," Adele said, clutching Gladys's hand and nodding at Gwen. "I'm beside myself! I don't know where to turn."

"Never mind all that. Let's get inside and get Gwen to rustle up some tea. Have you had anything to eat today?" Gladys pushed Adele back into her house, gently enough, but with the air of someone putting an animal firmly back into its pen.

"Well, no...I...I can't seem to..."

"Right. Gwen. Get that tea on, see what she's got in the larder. Toast if you can manage it." Gladys got her friend seated in the little sitting room and sat down opposite her. "Now then."

Adele picked at the faded knobbly green material that upholstered her armchair. Finally, she spoke. "Maude phoned this morning, after the police had been. She said Ben went off last night in one of their rowboats. Boat washed up on the neighbour's beach, only Ben wasn't there." She began to cry, sniffing into the sleeve of her gown. "I don't know what to do."

Gladys whipped a handkerchief out of her pocket and handed it to her friend with a shake of the head. "I don't know what you imagine you can do. You can hardly dash off up and down the lake looking for him. I'm sure the police have it well in hand. They'll find him, you'll see. He'll have gone off and camped across the lake and lost his boat."

Adele fell silent, plucking at the upholstery, and wiped her nose with the handkerchief. "But he went off at ten o'clock at night." She hesitated, looking imploringly at Gladys. "And he took his gun."

This caused Gladys a moment of surprise. "Perhaps he was planning an early morning hunt."

"No, but you see, not his rifle. His revolver. I'm...I'm so afraid he might have done something foolish."

Thinking that rowing onto the lake at night with a revolver was already quite foolish enough, Gladys shook her head. "Now then. You mustn't fill your mind with nonsense. The man has a wife and children. He's hardly going to do away with himself."

This bald stating of Adele's secret fears made her squeak in dismay. "Oh, you don't think he'd—"

"No, I jolly well don't," Gladys said firmly. The two women fell into an uneasy silence until Gwen came in with a tray holding a teapot, three cups, and a plate of buttered toast. She put the plate beside Adele. "Here. You must eat. You need your strength," she said as kindly as she could manage. She found Mrs. Robinson tiresome in her helplessness. "What do you take in your tea?"

"How can I sit here eating and drinking while my boy might be drowned, or worse!" Adele wailed, with a sudden burst of energy.

Gladys leaned forward. "Mustn't get carried away. Gwen's right. You're no good to him if he is in trouble and you don't eat."

The next few minutes were spent coaxing Adele to eat some toast and watching her slurp tea, which she grimaced at because Gladys had added a good dose of sugar. Just as well, Gwen thought. Sweet tea would be just the thing for shock. She glanced at her mother, who had leaned back on the couch and was sipping her own tea.

"Right," Gladys resumed. "Was he upset about anything? Money troubles, that sort of thing? Troubles with his wife?"

She wondered if Ben Arden would even confide in his mother if he were in trouble.

Adele sniffed disapprovingly. "Maude was hardly the right woman, was she? I was against him marrying her right from the start. She's much too bossy. A man needs to have the upper hand, doesn't he? She's always starting rows."

If Ben were henpecked, that might be a reason for him to leave, Gladys thought. From what she remembered of Ben, it was quite easy to imagine any woman running rings around him. He had been, she felt, far too attached to his mother, and she to him. It wasn't normal. The sudden memory came to her about how free Ben had been with girls during his teens. "Maybe there's your answer. Perhaps he's gone off just to get away."

This idea seemed to take hold of Adele. Her face cleared slightly. "That will be it, of course!" She shook her head. "I remember him sending me letters from England, during the war, you know. He talked about a girl he'd met. She sounded so sweet and just doted on him. I assumed he was going to bring her back. I was so disappointed that he'd left her behind. Said she couldn't leave her family. He waited almost fifteen years before he thought of marrying again, and he went and chose Maude. I tried to warn him."

I bet you did, Gladys thought, pushing herself off the sofa. "Can't do much about what our children choose to do with their lives," she said decisively. "We'd best be off. You mark my words. He'll turn up." Thank God I had girls, she thought, settling into the passenger seat for the ride home.

"VERY NICE," DARLING said, surveying the cake. "I see you got a head start." He reached for the knife that sat, gooey with chocolate icing, on the plate.

"I wouldn't do that if I were you. You'll ruin your dinner."

"Will I? I can't think of any dinner that could be ruined by chocolate cake. What are we having?"

"Chicken soup. Out of a tin, I'm afraid," Lane said, smiling ruefully. "I've been busy making cake all day."

"There, you make my point. In fact, on reflection, it might be the other way around. The soup might ruin the cake. Should we just go straight to the cake?"

"I would like nothing more," Lane said. "However, I don't think we should support each other in falling into a life of dissipation. I am going to heat up the soup, use that nice new toaster to make a nourishing piece of toast to go with it, and then we can have cake."

"Thus speaks the woman who's already had a piece," Darling said, shaking his head. "Fine. I will fall in with your plans. I have had a busy day myself, and I will need my strength for tomorrow."

"Why? What's happened?" Lane asked, handing him a can of chicken noodle soup and a can opener.

"I actually like this stuff," Darling said, holding the can up to read the label. "Mrs. Anderson used to make it, and my father did too, for that matter, after my mother died." He applied himself to his task. "We got a call that a man got into his rowboat at ten o'clock last night and disappeared. Boat came back empty, sans man, and interestingly, sans outboard motor." He handed the opened can back to Lane. "And he took a pistol with him. In fact, right up your alley.

You found a dying man in a boat. Perhaps you can do something with this."

Lane dumped the soup into the pot, added a can of water, and stirred. "Can you handle the toast? You're getting quite good on that machine. As you know, I specialize in actual bodies. An empty rowboat can hold no interest for me. I'm afraid you're on your own. Could you set the table?"

The soup served, they slurped companionably together for a few moments, then Lane rested her spoon in her nearly empty bowl. "What is the man's name?"

"You say that in a tone that suggests it might be of interest after all. I sincerely hope not. I've been dying for a little private case of my own, with no interference from you. Arden. I shouldn't be telling you, but the cake is exerting a powerful influence on me. Benjamin Arden. Chum of yours?"

"Oh," Lane said, slightly deflated. "Only Gladys had to rush off to see a friend of hers who telephoned her in a panic because her son had left his wife and two kids. Her name wasn't Arden, though. Robinson, I think. That was it. Adele Robinson. It's funny, though—how many disappearing husbands can you have in one day? I can see how you might have several in a bustling metropolis like London, but how many people live up and down this lake?"

Darling put down his soup spoon, wiped his mouth with his napkin, and was about to speak.

"And that's not all," Lane interrupted. "According to Mabel, Lucy overheard a conversation about someone else running off—a woman. Something with a B."

"I can see at once that my dream of a happy little case of my own is not to be realized. Already the jungle telegraph of King's Cove has nosed out all the principal players and is no doubt well on the way to a solution. I would like to drown my sorrows in cake now, if you don't mind."

"You can laugh," Lane said, getting up to fetch a couple of small plates, "But..."

"I'm not laughing, I assure you. I'm inconsolable. This had better help." He held his fork upright like a pitchfork in readiness for his cake. "It is fully as good as that one we had on the train in Arizona," he said after a few moments. "I congratulate you."

When they had washed the dishes and tidied up after dinner, they took their whiskies into the sitting room. The air had chilled considerably, and they built a fire in the Franklin.

"Are you really going to do this?" he asked, reaching for her hand. "I don't know how I shall bear it."

Knowing he meant Scotland, she felt an acute pang of missing him already. "I don't know what else to do, darling. If he were to die...but I will promise not to stay long. If I go now, soon, I can be back by the beginning of July, and we'll have the whole summer."

MAUDE ARDEN HAD dropped the children at school and was making her way into town. She had a vague feeling that she ought to put things in order somehow, though she quailed at it. But still. She had children, and they needed stability. She would start at the bank, organize the money. Ben had done all that sort of thing. Men did. She felt her heart contract and clutched the steering wheel with both hands to hold herself steady.

Should she have told the police officers about the telephone call? But there'd been nothing in it, and it had been almost six months before. Best not confuse things. Now, though, it seemed as though it might be useful. They'd been sitting at the kitchen table having a late breakfast when the phone had rung. He'd gotten up and gone into the hallway and said, "SM 229, Ben Arden speaking." Her son had asked her if they could go out to the dock, and she'd been about to answer when she'd heard the receiver slammed down with unusual force.

Why did that strike her now? Because of the violent way he'd slammed the receiver. It had made her anxious at the time. When she'd asked him who it was, he'd shaken his head. "Wrong number." But he'd looked drained of blood and had almost collapsed in his chair. And that invitation. Well, it was all pointing to his secret life, wasn't it?

The sun danced along the ripples of the lake, and Maude had a moment of feeling elated by it, by the turn of the year toward summer, and in the next instant felt guilty. She pulled up at the ferry line and waited behind two other cars. Cigarette smoke poured from the open windows of both and wafted back toward her, reminding her of Ben. Thinking of him now, smoking in the living room of an evening, she reminded herself that she'd always felt uneasy about him. As if he was not what he seemed. Though he had never raised a hand to her, and he was gentler than many other fathers toward the children, she sensed a familiar dark current of unresolved feeling somewhere. Rage? Fear? She hardly knew, but she somehow was not terribly surprised by anything he did. If she'd known then what she knew now...

With a feeling of trepidation, as if she were trespassing in a place she didn't belong, she asked the clerk at the first teller window if she could see the manager and then sat down on the wooden bench to wait. She looked at the polished wood and gleaming brass of the bank's marble atrium. There were two men at one of the circular chest-high desks surrounding two of the pillars, signing cheques, and she was mildly surprised to see a woman at the second one. She crossly wondered why it should feel wrong for her to be in the bank. The bulk of the money they had was hers, after all. Well, obviously not "hers," she corrected herself mentally. "Theirs." They were a family, after all. Had been. Before that... and then her thoughts were interrupted.

"Mrs. Arden?" An impeccably dressed man of middle years stood before her. His finely crafted moustache hovered above nearly pursed lips, as though he were preparing to put her in her place. "I'm Mr. Sheffield, the manager. About what do you wish to see me?"

She looked around nervously as she stood. She couldn't explain it out here in the open. "It is a private matter," she managed in a near whisper, looking hopefully toward the door he'd emerged from.

With the slightest touch of impatience, he said, "Certainly. Please come this way." They settled at his vast oak desk. "Now then," he said, folding his hands on the large green blotter pad.

Mrs. Arden, suddenly faced with having to state out loud that her husband had disappeared, found herself unable to find words. "You see," she finally began, "my husband, Benjamin Arden, has, is...ah. Well, he's not available just now, and I need to look into our money, ah, financial affairs."

"Not available? Is he ill?" Mr. Sheffield was trying for something like sympathy, but his mind was running ahead to try to work out what this was all about.

"No. No, not ill. He's gone off somewhere. He appears to be missing." She leaned forward and said hurriedly, "Oh, I have consulted the police. They are investigating."

"I see." The bank manager frowned. This was well out of his normal experience. The police being involved suggested a level of urgency he'd not anticipated. He pressed an intercom button on the tidy desk. "Get me the Benjamin Arden file, please," he said to a raspy inquiry.

"You will want to be authorized to deal with the banking during this period, I assume?" He hesitated over the word *period* because he'd been about to say *crisis*, but of course the man would be found.

"Yes, that's right," Mrs. Arden said with relief. "There are the children, you see, and bills and so on. My husband handles all that sort of thing. He just gives me the house-keeping." She stopped. "Oh dear, and the car, the regular repairs, and so on. But I can cross that bridge when I come to it."

There was a discreet knock on the door, and a young clerk put his head through. "The file, sir."

Sheffield waved it over, and when the young man had left, he opened the file and adjusted his glasses. He ran his fingers down a ledger paper, turned it over, went on to the second page, and then closed the file. Rising, he said, "Excuse me for a moment, Mrs. Arden." He walked around the desk and, with a slight nod at her, left his office and closed the door, taking the file with him.

Feeling a stab of panic, Maude Arden clutched at her handbag and stared at the portrait of George vi, looking imperiously down at her. It had a stabilizing effect. Of course, in the well-ordered world of a bank, nothing could really be wrong. After another lengthy passage of time, she looked at her watch, and the alarm began to return. What were they doing? She began to formulate angry retorts to possible impediments the manager might present.

Finally, the door opened again, and Sheffield was back behind his desk with a muttered apology, the file in hand. He looked down at it where it rested under his hands for a long moment. "Mrs. Arden, are you aware of any financial difficulty your husband, or indeed your family as a whole, has been experiencing?"

With another rise of alarm, Mrs. Arden shook her head, more in confusion than negation. "Difficulty? No. What do you mean?"

He cleared his throat. "Well, I mean, extraordinary expenses, for example."

Something in Maude Arden snapped. She leaned forward and put her hand flat on the desk. "Look here, Mr. Sheffield. I don't know what you are hinting at. We have had no 'extraordinary expenses,' whatever they are. Please stop beating around the bush. I have quite enough to cope with at the moment. I have a right to know what you are implying."

Sheffield looked almost relieved at the prospect of being more direct. "The truth, Mrs. Arden, is that your accounts are nearly empty. Your chequing account has less than a hundred dollars, and your savings account is completely depleted. My records show that regular sums of money have been taken out in unusually large amounts, and very little put back."

Mrs. Arden felt herself blanch, felt the blood draining away. It surprised her that the feeling was accompanied by a loud ringing in her ears. She collapsed back into the chair, unable to fully take in what she was hearing. She focused now on one thing he'd said. "What? Very little put back? I don't understand. He took the money?" Her voice sounded high pitched and panicky to her. How was it possible that she had missed this? "But my husband's paycheque from the feed store—he has deposited that every month, surely?"

He shook his head. "Not for some months, I'm afraid. The last deposit"—he opened the file and adjusted his glasses again—"was November."

"November? Why do I know nothing about this?"

"Well, of course, Mrs. Arden, we assume that your husband, any husband, would be confiding some details of the family finances to his wife."

"He gives me housekeeping money once a month. That's the confiding I get," she said, angry now. "What about the savings? I had money when I came into this marriage, and that was put into savings for the children's education."

He shook his head. "I'm afraid there is nothing there now."

"But that was MY money!" Mrs. Arden said, furious tears beginning to slip down her face. "You people have done something, you've made a mistake."

"I'm afraid not," Sheffield said more firmly. He really could not have a woman in hysterics in his office. "The records show that he has regularly moved money out of the savings account into the chequing account and then has been withdrawing it, usually in amounts of $150 to $200 to as much as $500 on several occasions. In fact, I see that he also applied for a loan. In light of the steady depletion of funds and no incoming monies, this was refused by Mr. Stevens when I was away in February."

"Five hundred dollars?" she said weakly. "What does anyone need with that kind of money?" It was more than three months' salary, gone all at once.

"It is not our policy to question our clients' use of their own money," the manager said. However, he was visited by the uneasy feeling that he had failed. In fact, it was very much the policy. If the bank believed funds were being drained at an extraordinary rate and not replaced, he would have called the client to account with a visit to his office. And then he remembered. He *had* acted on the Arden file. He had phoned the man at work on…he opened the diary on his desk, turning the pages quickly, running his fingers along the appointment list. Yes. There it was, December 17. He'd been concerned by Mr. Stevens's report, he remembered. He struggled to remember the call. His face cleared.

"In fact, I did speak with him, Mrs. Arden. I telephoned him at his work, and I believe he told me you had purchased a small plot of land and were building a house on it, and that the outflow would be corrected when your current property was sold. That seemed in order to me. That, I expect, will be the explanation." He had not checked since.

"I'm afraid," Maude Arden said, using the bank manager's favourite phrase, "that will not be the explanation. We haven't purchased any land, and we are not building a house." She stopped, tried to think of what to do, what to say. She felt herself in an unassailable position suddenly. It gave her strength. "I want you to lock him out of our account. I don't know what he's been doing with it, but he's not doing it anymore. No, I can see you warming up to protest and tell me you can't, that as the wife I don't have the authority." Her voice had become almost shrill again as she got into her stride. "When I leave here, I am going straight to the police station to tell them about this. Somehow you have been hoodwinked by my husband into letting him do whatever he wants with the money, leaving me, and his children, in the cold with nothing. I don't know how the law allows for this. I imagine that inspector, Darling, or whatever he said his name is, will be interested in that part of it as well." Mrs. Arden stood up, pulled at the wrist of her gloves decisively, and turned to go.

"Wait, Mrs. Arden. If there is anything we can do—"

"I think you've done quite enough, don't you?"

DARLING LISTENED TO Mrs. Arden. He was pleased to see she had moved from the sort of bewildered passivity of his interview yesterday to anger. It was the right response. Whatever her husband was up to, it was clear he had used her very ill. The inspector thought of the possibilities. Had Arden developed a gambling habit? He knew there were one or two clandestine gambling establishments run out of houses and the basements of stores. It was the regularity of the withdrawals—$150, $200, $500, sometimes twice a month—that struck him, though. Someone gambling would be losing money more intermittently. Was he supporting another woman? Or a drug habit? Was Arden being blackmailed about any or all of these?

CHAPTER FIVE

L ANE WAS CONSCIOUS OF DRAGGING her feet through the morning cleanup. She stood at the sink, fiddling with a breakfast plate immersed in the hot water. Washing dishes after breakfast suddenly seemed the most gratifying activity. It meant that she and Darling had sat together over toast and scrambled eggs, that he had kissed her goodbye and she had watched him drive off up the lake. This morning ritual was at the centre of their lives together, its sheer ordinariness making it a touchstone. In a short time, he would be here on his own, missing her perhaps, or thinking ahead to his day. Or perhaps he would simply shut the house up and move back into town.

She finished the washing-up, dried her hands, and went to the bedroom. Darling had made the bed, as he did every morning, so she could now concentrate on going through her clothes, deciding what to take. Scotland would likely be wet and cold at this time of year. She peered into the drawer containing her long woollen underwear. This cold?

Damp, certainly, and the cottage had no central heating. On the other hand, they would take up a lot of room. No. Wool stockings and a pair of trousers and her tweed skirt. A light frock in the unlikely possibility of something like a summer day. Then she would drive into town and sort out the travel arrangements.

The act of packing for springtime in Scotland reminded her of how lovely it was, right now, in her own yard. Throwing down the pullover about which she was being indecisive, she slipped on her plimsolls and went outside to survey her little vegetable garden for weeds. But she could not turn her mind away from her trip. Of course, she knew she could do nothing to be of any real help to either grandparent. Moral support, she supposed, as her grandmother had said. The possibility of seeing her sister after all this time began to loom larger. Would it be a chance to repair a relationship she had long ago given up on?

Oxford, 1939

"WELL, NOW YOU'RE here, what would you like to do?" Lane sat in the well-used armchair in her room. Diana had thrown herself on the bed and was surveying the room with distaste.

"It's very small. And you don't have any view." She looked critically toward the window, which opened out onto the quad, two floors below.

"It's not meant to be a beach resort, Diana. It's a college."

"Well, I don't think much of it. In Marisa's house in town, I had a massive room to myself with a view right onto Grosvenor Square."

Lane sighed. "It is not given to all of us to have friends in Mayfair. Now you're here, what do you want to do? I have a lecture in half an hour. Afterward, we could go for a punt and then have something to eat in town."

"Don't you want to know how Daddy and Ganf and Grandmama are?" Diana sat up as if she'd remembered something and pulled her suitcase up onto the bed with her and opened it. "I nearly forgot, Grandmama sent you this." She brought out a flat parcel in brown paper and tossed it over to Lane.

"Thank you," Lane said, laying it on the table that functioned as her desk and was even now covered with open volumes and notebooks.

"Aren't you going to open it? She went to a lot of trouble to get it for you."

Lane bristled at this suggestion that she was ungrateful, especially coming from Diana, who took every advantage for granted and every luxury as her due.

"Daddy's away again," Diana continued, reaching now for her handbag and pulling out cigarettes and a silver lighter. "It's a frightful nuisance. He'll be gone for a good long while, I expect, with Herr Hitler and his bag of tricks. He's making life absolute hell for the German Balts. Hitler, I mean, obviously, not Daddy." She pulled out a cigarette and lit it, looking around for an ashtray.

"For God's sake, Diana, you're sixteen! Where did you pick up that filthy habit? I'll ask you not to smoke in here." Lane watched her sister get up and stride angrily to the window and grind the cigarette out on the outside ledge, only after taking an enormous draught and releasing it theatrically out the window. "Why did you come here, anyway? Aren't you expected back for school?" Lane asked, trying to quell her irritation.

"Almost seventeen. I'm not going back," Diana said simply, dropping the remains of her cigarette into the round trash can by the table.

For a wild moment Lane imagined she was going to have to host her sister in her tiny room at Oxford. "What do you mean? There's going to be a war. You should go home."

"Should I?" Diana asked, challenging her sister now, almost smug, much more grown up than her sixteen years. "Well, I'm not going to. I'm going to South Africa with my 'Mayfair' friend. She has an uncle there. Her parents want to get her out of the way of the war, and they've invited me along. Grandmama and Ganf particularly wished it, as it would get me out of danger as well."

Lane was silenced by this. Her chit of a sister was proposing to set sail all the way to South Africa. It came to her how utterly alien two people from the very same parents could be. She knew absolutely nothing about what motivated, pleased, or inspired Diana. She had spent her whole life, practically since Diana was born, reacting to her. She couldn't remember a single moment when they played together, or laughed at the same thing, or read the same books.

She remembered the wonder she had felt when Diana was born, but it was not possible to extricate that from the towering blow of her mother's death so soon afterward. She struggled now to locate that wonder, and yes, love. It is intrinsic to children to love, and she remembered that she had loved Diana, had been overwhelmed by it.

"Of course, I'm glad to know you'll be going somewhere safe. But do you know enough about these people? Does Daddy know them?"

Diana looked at her impatiently. "Oh my God, stop fussing. You never stop trying to interfere, do you? It's *fine*." She dragged the word out. "I knew Marisa at school. Anyway, Daddy wants me to go. He wrote to them. Of course, I'd really rather stay on where the action is, wouldn't I? But I could hardly turn her down. I'll only stay for a year. If there's a war, it will be over by then. Maybe I'll come to Oxford and live in one of these poky rooms." She ran her hand along the ledge and then leaned out the window and watched the gowned students hurrying along the walks below.

Lane, momentarily rebuked by her sister's accusation, took the opening. "What would you read? What interests you?"

Diana shrugged. "Why aren't there any boys here? It must be so dull."

"They are at the men's colleges. It's quite busy. There isn't really time to be dull."

"It's dull right now," Diana said with an exaggerated sigh. "You promised me a punt and a meal. I suppose we'd better go do that. I'm leaving tomorrow to go back to London. We're sailing in a week."

Remembering her grandmother's present, Lane pulled it forward, untying the string. It was a silk scarf in greens and gold. "Oh, that's lovely! How wonderful of her to remember my favourite colours."

"I don't know why you're surprised. You *are* her favourite."

Lane stood up. "Don't be silly! You know they both dote on you. Now, I have to go to my lecture. I'll be back at three, and we can go for that punt."

"I hope we see some boys," Diana said, throwing herself back down on the bed.

REMEMBERING DIANA'S VISIT to Oxford, which was the last time she'd seen her, Lane thought about Diana's remark that Lane had been their grandmother's favourite. Wasn't it the same thing Lane had always said about Diana and their father? Had Diana felt slighted at the idea that Lane was the favourite? Or was she so secure in her father's favour that she could make this observation without any loss to her own self-esteem? She looked at Darling's maroon paisley dressing gown hanging on the hook on the door. The thing is, she wondered, did any of it matter now? By some miracle that she had yet to understand, she, after what seemed a lifetime of feeling second best, had landed on her feet. She had not achieved it by nursing imaginary grievances against Diana, who could no more help her father's behaviour than she could. Lane had found her way by carrying on with her own life and finding her own strengths. When she saw her sister again, she would be generous and loving. One of them had to take the lead, and it would be she.

October 1947

THE DIFFICULTY ABOUT the St. Saviour's Anglican Church of Nelson flyers wasn't caught until nearly all of them had been distributed. They'd been put up cn notice boards and distributed to shops and the library and the Legion, and anywhere else they were bound to be seen. It had been Mrs. Spinks, the vicar's wife, who had caught it.

"Look at this, Donald, they've only gone and put the wrong time on the notice. I said eleven in the morning. They've put pip-emma. That won't half confuse all the dear old things."

The vicar looked up from his desk and removed his glasses, rubbing his eyes. He didn't like to tell her he was having more and more difficulty seeing properly. She'd only fuss. He took the flyer she handed him and put his glasses back on, surveying it closely. There it was: "Bazaar doors open 11 PM."

"That's not really going to put anyone off, is it? No one in their right mind would think a church bazaar would start in the middle of the night."

"I suppose you're right. I've a good mind to march down to the printer's and get them to change it. We paid good money for these." She put the flyer down and, in her turn, removed her glasses and chewed thoughtfully on the arm, looking out the window. "I do hope this weather holds! It would be so lovely if it were a warm day like this. We'd raise a good deal more money."

"Unless everyone thinks it's in the middle of the night." The vicar smiled, and then, seeing her worried look, said, "We can put a correction in the paper, and we can announce it this Sunday. Everything will be absolutely fine."

"It's not the first time, though, is it? It's like the invitations we had printed up for Jessica's wedding."

The vicar frowned. "There was something wrong with the invitations?"

"Yes, don't you remember? There was the beautiful invitation and then right under the RSVP was the number two hundred. I couldn't make out what it was supposed to be. Harry even asked if it was meant to be a hint about the size of the wedding gift. Most unlikely! Luckily good sense prevailed, but even though he's your brother-in-law and I know he was only joking, I felt a bit embarrassed, in case anyone else thought the same thing. Of course, I didn't find out till later it was only our invitation and Harry's that had the mistake. Everyone else's were fine."

Patting his wife's arm, the vicar got up and stretched. "Any chance of a cup of tea? I can't think of what to focus on for the sermon. Honestly, if I'd really thought about being persecuted by this everlasting demand for an amusing, instructional, uplifting sermon every single week, I'd have gone into shoes."

"I'll get you that cup of tea, and then I am going to see the printer. I'm not bothered about the mistake; everyone will understand, but I just think they should know, don't you?"

May 6, 1948

LANE'S DRIVE INTO town to see the travel agent had a nostalgic quality to it, as if she were already in Scotland remembering this drive, on this day. She had the window rolled down and was taking deep breaths of air laden with green spring smells. She was brought to reality with a bump when she came round a bend and found herself slap behind a caravan of cars that was, no doubt, being led by a logging truck. She wouldn't miss this inconvenience, at any rate.

She ran again through her list: tickets, traveller's cheques, gifts, including one for Diana, though Lord knew what she could possibly like, and a trim at the beauty parlour. She'd not had her hair attended to since her wedding, and she didn't want to arrive in Scotland looking like something from a shipwreck. Perhaps she ought to stop in and see Lorenzo and Olivia Vitali. They had just finished redoing their restaurant after a fire that nearly took Lorenzo's life, and she would like to see the renovations and ask after Lorenzo's recovery.

The logging truck had slowed her down all the way to the Harrop ferry, so she was running late for her three o'clock appointment by the time she finally got to Nelson. She parked the car and waited impatiently for the trolley to go by, then hurried across Baker Street. She hated being late for things.

"I'm sorry, Lottie," she said, bursting through the door. "Logging truck." It was an excuse everyone understood.

Lottie, who had been sitting in a chair with her feet up having a cup of tea, smiled and waved her hand in a "think nothing of it" gesture. "It's given me a chance for a little sit-down. What will it be today?" She showed Lane into a chair and lifted a fine veil of hair and let it fall. She looked in the mirror at their reflections, thinking how truly lovely Lane was, with that rich auburn hair and green eyes and that extraordinarily warm personality. That inspector was a lucky man.

"Just a bit of a wash and a trim. I'm off to see my grandparents, and I wouldn't want them to think that Canada has turned me completely wild."

"You could never look completely wild, my dear, no matter how hard you tried. Where do they live?"

"Scotland."

"Goodness. That's a long way to go. Hello, Mary. Come on in. Have a seat; the teapot still has something in it," she called at the sound of the bell and the shop door opening.

Lane looked over and smiled at the newcomer. "Sorry. It's my fault. I was late."

"Think nothing of it," said Mary, settling in with a magazine. She closed it again after a few moments and watched Lane having her hair washed. "You know that Ben Arden, who works down at the feed shop? His wife comes here sometimes."

Lottie said she did.

"Well, you'll never guess. He's only gone and left her and the kiddies!"

Lottie stopped her lathering and said, "What?"

"What indeed! His poor wife. I heard from Mrs. Barnes— you know, her husband owns the feed store. She says there was something not quite right about him. Arden, I mean. I think they were in the same unit in the Great War, and he was quite the womanizer. Even had a go at a commanding officer's wife during a leave, I heard."

"I'm sure he's not the first man in the world like that," protested Lottie. "He's quite good-looking still. I imagine he was a knockout when he was twenty. Of course, that doesn't explain his running off like that now."

Mary sniffed. "A handsome man makes a wife's heart ache, my mother always said. It doesn't surprise me that he's been at it this whole time behind her back."

Lottie stopped mid-lather again. "Really? Now wait, did I hear something about that? It'll be a few years ago now. Damn! I wish I could remember." She shook her head and began to rinse. "Was that Arden? The woman was someone up the lake somewhere."

Mary perused the magazine again thoughtfully. "Marriage vows don't seem to mean anything nowadays."

Lane was transferred to the cutting chair, her hair wrapped in a pink towel. Lottie pressed Lane's hair dry and took up a comb. "Are you sure you wouldn't like a short bob? Everyone is getting them. So easy to care for. Especially if you're travelling."

Lane was not tempted. She smiled and shook her head. "Just a trim to keep it at my shoulders. I think I'd feel naked with short hair."

Mary glanced up from her magazine. "Aren't you the police inspector's wife?"

"That I am," Lane said, smiling and skewing her eyes sideways because Lottie had her head in a firm grip.

"I think it's nice that you're keeping your hair long. Everyone is so quick to jump on these modern trends."

Lane smiled again. She wondered momentarily if Mary was implying she was old-fashioned. She gave a mental shrug. Perhaps she was.

Lottie was in mid-snip when she stood up straight. "It was one of those names that's a man's name, only made into a woman's. Not Johnna—what a travesty that is!

Michaela? No. No doubt chosen by a father unhappy his baby wasn't a boy. It had an *f* in it. No, I mistake me. Not an *f*. A *ph* ... Philippa ... that's it!" She returned to cutting. "I remember at the time it was a bit of a scandal. It seemed everyone knew except his poor wife."

CHAPTER SIX

LANE, HER HAIR DONE, MADE her way to the travel agent. It would take some time for him to put together all her tickets for the trip to Scotland, so she decided she would stop by and see Darling. On the way she thought about the whole business of marriage, and Mary Whatever-her-name-was's contention that marriage vows mean nothing nowadays. No doubt she meant that hers had meant something, but you couldn't trust anyone else's. She imagined Darling leaping into a torrid affair with...she looked about her on the street and picked a likely looking young woman just going into the bakery. She began to giggle. She just couldn't see it. She supposed she ought not to shortchange him, but she knew his enormous reserve would make such a thing nearly impossible. And anyway, it would be all over town in no time, if Mary and Lottie were anything to go by. In fact, he'd narrowly averted a scandal, not of his making, not a month before when a rumour had gone around that he was on the take.

Pushing open the door of the station, she smiled broadly at the front deskman. "Good morning, Sergeant O'Brien," she said. "Is the inspector available for a quick word, do you think?"

"He has someone with him now, but she's been a good while, so I'm sure it won't be long, Mrs. Darling." Pleased by her respect for his position as gatekeeper, he picked up the phone.

Lane saw Constable Terrell at his desk at the back of the room and gave him a wave. He nodded and smiled.

"I've let him know you're here," O'Brien said. A woman in a pale blue dress and green jacket was coming down the stairs, her eyes red, and her jaw set in an angry line. She clutched a handkerchief in her gloved hand. She didn't seem to notice the gate had been opened for her, nor did she acknowledge O'Brien's little nod.

O'Brien jerked his head in the direction of the stairs, indicating Lane should go on up, and then he went to open the front door for the distressed woman.

Darling was writing something on a notepad when she knocked. He rose and kissed her on the cheek and motioned at his spare chair.

"You look very nice," he said.

"No need to sound so surprised. I've been to the salon, actually, to be trimmed up a bit. And now I'm waiting for Brown down at the travel agency to assemble some sort of travel itinerary. I don't think I fully realized how difficult it is to go anywhere from here."

"No one wants you to go anywhere."

"Yes, darling, I know. I wouldn't if I could avoid it.

As lovely as it is to be admonished for leaving by a man with such a pathetic hangdog, pleading look as yours—a look against which I have set my heart and mind, by the way—I've come to tell you something I've just heard at the salon. It might have some relevance to this case of the missing man. Who was that poor distressed woman I met on the stairs just now?"

"Wife of the missing man." He closed the door behind her and shook his head. "Before you accuse me of making her cry, she's just discovered her husband has spent most of the last year cleaning out all the accounts; she and her two children have been left with nothing to live on." He sat down with a tired thump and took a deep breath. "So, even on the way out the door, you want to get your oar in. You take the cake, you do." He took up his pencil and paused, looking at her with exaggerated attention.

"Poor woman! How could she not have known?"

"Because he did all the banking. It sounds like the bank manager was reluctant to tell her even that much."

"Typical antediluvian male nonsense. If all the finances in all the families were given over to the woman of the house, the world would be better off."

"You're probably not wrong there, given what I've seen in my professional life; however, not all men are bastards, so there's that little ray of hope. Now then, what critical information have you got, without which I will never solve this case?"

"If you'd rather I didn't meddle, I can tell you where to get the same information. Just pop down to Lottie at the beauty parlour and wait. People will talk. Now, mind you,

I'm not sure they would talk freely in front of a man, a man who is also the head of the police. You might be able to disguise yourself as an aspidistra, and with any luck they won't notice you." She smiled brightly.

"Yes. Very amusing. I'll miss this when you're gone, no doubt. Well?"

"I was late getting there, so the customer right after me came in and had to wait, and she filled the time with idle and, I think, useful gossip. It is apparently all over town that Ben Arden has gone missing. It appears he has a reputation for womanizing, and there was a hint that he's been at it the whole time he's been married. This same unimpeachable source, called Mary, by the way, said she had heard that he was quite active during his time in the Great War, and even made a play for his commanding officer's wife.

"This is, perhaps, par for the course, as gossip goes, especially as everyone searches to explain something as intriguing as a nighttime disappearance, but a very specific woman was named, and it happens to be the same woman I heard about at Gladys's yesterday. Your man is the son of a friend of hers, and his mother is distraught. In fact, Gladys and Gwen rushed off to offer comfort and succour while I was still there." Here she paused to collect her thoughts.

Darling, who had made some point-form notes, waited.

"When I was with the Hughes girls, one of them mentioned that Lucy, of Balfour telephone exchange fame, had passed on that a woman called Philippa Bentley had upped stakes, packed up the child, and left her husband, presumably a Mr. Bentley. Now, Lottie at the beauty shop remembered that Arden's name had been linked to a Philippa some years ago. Of course, if it was a long time ago, it might not be relevant, but as you know, I thought it quite singular that they should both disappear at the same time."

"Yes, you did." He rolled his eyes for her benefit, but he was nevertheless very interested in the information. They had little enough to go on. "Now I will have to go to the trouble and expense of sending someone out to interview this possibly abandoned man, Bentley, and Arden's poor mother. Did any of your gossiping ladies mention where the Bentleys might live?"

"Now wait: Mabel said, 'From right here in Balfour.' So, not so expensive; he's right nearby," she said cheerily. "You can send Terrell out on that fabulous machine of his. Oh, and he works on the steamer. Bentley, I mean."

"I, of course, welcome any insights you may have, but I draw the line at you allocating my staff for me."

"Of course, darling. I wouldn't dream of interfering." Lane smiled brightly and got up. "I don't want to keep you from your work."

Darling shook his head. "Incorrigible. It's too bad Lorenzo isn't open yet. I could use one of his comforting lunches. As it is, it's the café for me. I couldn't treat you to a grilled cheese?"

"Nothing I'd like better, but I'm actually on my way to see how the Vitalis are getting along, and then I'll have to pick up my travel things, find a few gifts to take along, and get home. There's one good-sized piece of chocolate cake left, and I want to get at it before you."

"I hope it chokes you," he said mildly. "I guess I'll see if Ames would like to lunch with me. Say hello to the Vitalis.

See you back home. I'll probably have to stop in Balfour on the way back, thanks to you." She smiled and opened the office door. "One moment," he said, closing the door gently and taking her in his arms. "I love you, you know that?" he said after a few moments.

"Yes, darling, I know." Perhaps she shouldn't go to Scotland at all.

August 1935

BEN ARDEN WAS singing "Yes Sir, That's My Baby" in full voice, relishing the warm summer air swirling in the cabin of his truck from both open windows. If he'd been conscious of his own state of mind, he'd have said he was savouring a sudden respite from the oppressive dread that seemed to be his constant companion. It was the war, and he knew it. No matter how far it receded into the past, it was still there, a black and terrifying void sitting right on his chest. In the truck, on a sunny day, he felt he could outdrive it.

He bumped along the road to the farmhouse, preparing himself for the meeting with Doug Bentley, who invariably seemed to be in a bad mood. When he stopped at the gate, he saw that Bentley's own truck was nowhere to be seen, and breathed a sigh of relief. He could just leave the bags of chicken feed with the wife. He imagined her as a frayed, exhausted woman with greying hair, worn down by marriage to the bad-tempered Bentley.

He pushed open the gate, mounted the steps to the little porch, and rapped on the door, still singing under his breath. A woman's voice called, "Coming!" There were hurried steps, and then the door opened.

"Yes?"

Arden was momentarily speechless. The young woman, some dark flaxen hair coming out of the roll at the back of her neck, her skin something, he decided later, between pinkish and golden, stood impatiently waiting for him to answer. Her eyes were the dark blue of a troubled afternoon sky.

"I've brought the feed. For your husband," he added as an afterthought.

He watched her dark eyebrows, so stunning in contrast to her golden hair, gather momentarily in a frown and felt the breath stop in his chest somewhere. "It has to go out to the shed," she said.

She stepped onto the porch so that she was only inches away from him. It took him a moment to step back, but in that moment, he had breathed the warmth of her skin, the smell of Palmolive soap.

She pointed to the side of the house. "Over there. I'll go open the latch for you." She wiped her hands on her apron, waiting for him to vacate the porch so she could go down and along the path to the shed.

"You're Mrs. Bentley?" He tried to keep the surprise out of his voice.

"Yes. Is it some concern of yours? Is my husband the only one who can accept a delivery?"

Arden smiled broadly and shook his head. "No, ma'am. I'd rather deliver to you any day of the week. Ben Arden."

"Well, Ben Arden. You can get the hell out of my way and bring the feed out to the back."

All the way home he felt his heart burning. Mrs. Bentley. Those eyes. In that moment, he could not remember wanting any woman more. His mood slid from elation to resentment as he got closer to where he'd be turning off to his own house at the end of the day. He wasn't ready for a kid. His mother had been right. He should never have married bloody Maude. She was a demanding shrew, as if her pregnancy gave her every right to make his life hell.

May 6, 1948

LANE PUSHED THE restaurant door open, calling, "Hello?" A sign on the door said, "Grand Reopening May 7." She and Darling would be at tomorrow's opening. She could book a table now.

Lorenzo came through the swinging door, his arms outstretched, beaming. "Signora! Thank you for coming. What do you think?" He looked around at the refurbished dining room and then back at her. "Come, you will see everything."

He still limped, she saw, and an angry-looking burn scar was evident on his left hand. One eyebrow had a gap where his face had been burned. She followed his gaze. It really was remarkable, she thought. The fire that had nearly killed him had gutted the kitchen and filled this room with acrid, choking smoke that had seeped into every tablecloth and every curtain. Now the dining room radiated the kind of cheerfulness that Lorenzo himself exhibited. New white tablecloths covered all the tables in the still-chairless room, and three new light fixtures hung from the ceiling. The new curtains, an attractive pale charcoal colour, contrasted with the newly painted white walls. The baseboards were black, as were the window frames. The whole thing looked understated and very elegant.

"It's just about the best thing I've ever seen!" Lane declared.

"Chairs still being finished. They are sanded and painted, now have to dry," Lorenzo explained. "But I think it will be finish on time for opening tomorrow. You will come, yes, with *Ispettore*? Is special, for thank you to so many people. Come. You must see kitchen. Olivia will be so happy to see you."

"I wouldn't miss it. I was going to book a table," Lane said, following Lorenzo through the swinging door.

"No booking table. You are a guest of honour!"

Olivia Vitali was stirring something red and smelling of tomato and oregano in a large pot on the brand new stove. She perched the wooden spoon across the pot and wiped her hands on her apron. Even working in the kitchen, she seemed to Lane to be the picture of elegance.

"Signora Lane! How good of you to come! You see?" She turned around in a circle with her hands out, showing Lane the kitchen. "Is beautiful, no?" She kissed Lane on both cheeks.

"It is beautiful, indeed," Lane said. "And I see you are making a lovely sauce. I cannot wait to try some. The inspector and I are planning to be here for your opening."

"If you don't come, I will be very upset!" Olivia said. "And what do you think of him?" she said, pointing at Lorenzo. "He okay too, no? Not as good as new kitchen, but still, I can use him." She smiled.

"I think he looks splendid. It must be all those Chamber of Commerce meetings."

"Ha!" said Olivia. Lorenzo had had trouble getting into the Chamber of Commerce because there was still some lingering prejudice against Italians after the war, but since the fire that had burned out their restaurant, good sense had prevailed and he had been invited to join. Olivia Vitali had never really got over their initial rejection. "But is okay. He is happy. Anyway. So many people help, and now we have a restaurant again."

Lorenzo shook his head. "Only thing, no more any wine, even 'under table.' Is crazy law, but what you can do?"

INFECTED WITH THE happy optimism of the Vitalis, Lane pushed the door open at the travel agent.

"Ah, Miss Winslow. I have everything ready for you. Please, sit down," Mr. Brown said.

Lane sat, her stomach beginning to knot. When she was young, going anywhere was exciting. As a child it had meant being away from her oppressive house. She and her sister had finally moved permanently to their grandparents' home outside of Riga, but the trips to the seaside, or into Riga, were exciting just on their own. Now she felt that same excitement, but it was mingled with anxiety and unhappiness about being away from Darling.

Brown had a pile of papers before him. "Now, I've booked all the way through to Croydon, and the return dates are open, as you requested, and booked through Trans-Canada Air Lines. You will have to make sure you contact the airline to get your seat on the date you want. Plane travel across the Atlantic is becoming very popular since the war ended. Here is your train ticket to Lethbridge, Alberta. Here is your flight ticket from Lethbridge to Montreal, and here is your flight to Croydon. You'll have a stop in Gander. It is a long flight, but it beats being a week at sea. I assume you can get yourself to your final destination. I had difficulty contacting the rail system in Britain. It seems to be under new management and they're still sorting themselves out. I did speak with one party who said there's nothing easier than getting tickets once you are there."

Lane looked at the various tickets in their little pocket folders. A week at sea was something she particularly liked, she thought wistfully. Perhaps, if time allowed, she would take a boat back. "Thank you, Mr. Brown. I don't know how you do it. I should have been weeks trying to sort all this out on my own."

He smiled happily. "It's what we are here for, Miss Winslow. Any questions?"

"Well, yes, actually: If I did decide I wanted a week at sea on the way back, could I cancel this open ticket and just sail back to Montreal?" She could see that Brown was very bullish on modern air travel.

He sighed and rubbed his chin as if it were a complex problem. Perhaps it was. Finally, he said, "You will have to cancel with Trans-Canada and then book your own passage. If you think you're going to do that, we ought to do it now."

"Oh. Well, the thing is, I don't know just yet. How long ahead would I have to cancel?"

"I'm not actually sure. But since the ticket is open, it shouldn't be a problem, I suppose. In fact, if you can ring through to me from over there, I should be able to do it at my end."

Lane could see he looked a little disappointed, but she was grateful nonetheless. "Thank you, Mr. Brown. That is wonderful of you."

He smiled. "I just am not a big lover of a sea voyage. We had a terrible crossing going out in '42, and terrible weather coming back in '45. I'd just as soon get the whole thing done in twelve or fifteen hours."

Out on the street again, Lane thought about air travel and saw its advantage: she would be home sooner with Darling.

CHAPTER SEVEN

DARLING PULLED UP IN FRONT of a white cottage that was his first stop on the way home. It had seen better days. What must have been a lovely garden was showing signs of long-term neglect, and the paint along the handrails and the trim was peeling. He was saved the knock on the door by the appearance of a stout older woman from around the side of the house. She was wearing a voluminous flowered housedress and a beige cardigan with a long, grimy apron tied over both. Her salt-and-pepper hair was pulled back, giving her round face and downturned mouth a fretful look. She frowned, looking momentarily past him at the car.

"I heard you drive up. Are you the police?"

"Yes. Inspector Darling of the Nelson Police." So, she was expecting a visit, Darling thought. "Are you Mrs. Robinson?"

"Have you found him?" Her voice shook. She nervously put down her trowel and walked slowly toward him, wiping her hands on the back of her dress, her knees stiff.

"No, I'm afraid not as yet. I've just come up to see if I can get a bit more information about him. He's your son, I believe? Benjamin Arden? Can we sit and talk for a moment?"

Mrs. Robinson turned toward the stairs without a word and began what looked like a painful climb to the front door. She leaned on the banister, almost pulling herself up. Inside, she fell into one of two kitchen chairs and took a handkerchief out of the apron pocket and wiped her forehead and the back of her neck.

"He used to come and give me a hand. Not much lately. No doubt that wife of his keeps him busy." She said this with bitterness. "She telephoned me, you know. He insisted I be on the telephone, though I never did have any use for it. He told me I could talk to my grandchildren whenever I wanted. Neither one of 'em has bothered. She told me he got into a boat and disappeared with some clothes and a revolver. As if I could do anything about it at my time of life! First time *she* ever got on the phone with me, I can tell you. I knew something was wrong the minute I heard her voice."

"It would have been unusual behaviour for him," Darling suggested.

"Of course it was unusual! He is a good boy. Fought in the Great War. Wonderful war record. He got a medal for gallantry."

She turned and pointed toward the mantelpiece in the compact sitting room. Darling could see, front and centre, a small glass-fronted box, the light from the window reflecting off it. He assumed the medal was in it. He wondered why Arden didn't keep it in his own home.

"It always used to be there on the mantelpiece, but he told me it was embarrassing; he's so humble, and he made me put it in the attic, but as long as he's not around, I have it where I can see it. It reminds me of what a fine boy he is. Always looked after me, until she came along." She sounded aggrieved.

I'd better check that war record, Darling thought. Medals for gallantry were not handed out every day. "Was the revolver something he'd brought back from the war, do you know?"

"I don't know," she said. She'd produced a handkerchief from the pocket of her housedress and was twisting it anxiously.

"Do you know of any friends or perhaps war comrades he might have visited along the lake anywhere?"

Mrs. Robinson hesitated for so long that she gave the impression she was struggling with something. "He is a grown man. I don't know all his friends and the like. Do you think that could have something to do with it?"

The fifty-something-year-old Arden had been a "good boy." Now he was a grown man. What did that suggest? "I'm not sure, Mrs. Robinson. We have to look into every possibility. Did he have any romantic liaisons, say, before his marriage?" Or during it, Darling thought.

Her face reddened and she made a jerky little movement with her head. "I don't know what you're suggesting," she said, looking down at the table.

"Mrs. Robinson, I am trying to gather any, *any* information that might help us locate your son. The smallest thing might be useful. It is unusual for a man to leave his home at that time of night, and it is worrying that he has not returned. If there is anything you can tell me about his habits or his life, it might be helpful."

Clamping her mouth tightly shut, Mrs. Robinson stared down at her lap, her hands busy pleating her apron. Finally, she said, "Twelve or so years ago, there was someone. He met her before the children were born. I'm not saying they were up to any hanky-panky. But that was a long time ago."

"Do you know what kind of relationship it was?"

"I told you. I'm sure it was nothing, but he did go visit her several times just around the time his wife got pregnant. I don't blame him. His wife was being difficult. Using her pregnancy to be demanding. Of course, it was intolerable."

Darling, wondering at the "of course," said, "How did you learn about his visits to this woman?" It seemed very odd to him that an adult would tell his mother this sort of thing.

She sniffed. "We were closer then. He confided in me. He told me she was nice, gave him tea when he made deliveries. You could see he was regretting his marriage. I knew she cared about him. You could see he missed her terribly when they ended it."

There had been an affair. "When was that?"

"Just about the time Audra was born, and that lady knew he had to be free to look after his own. I'm sure she missed him, but she got pregnant herself, so they would have broken it off anyway. Mind you, I'm not saying they might not have talked from time to time."

"And has he been seeing her more recently?"

Mrs. Robinson looked away sharply. "Of course not! He is devoted to little Ben and Audra. You can ask anyone."

This fatherly devotion, at least, had been confirmed by the children's mother. "Did he tell you her name?"

Mrs. Robinson's hand flew to her mouth, and she uttered a little "Oh. No. I mean, not actually." Then, collecting herself, she said, "It was just like him to be considerate like that. He wouldn't want to sully her name."

Oh, what a good boy, indeed, Darling thought repressively. He wondered if the woman Arden had been seeing was, in fact, the missing woman, Mrs. Bentley. He still had Mr. Bentley to visit. Perhaps there was no connection, but it was hard to imagine there wouldn't be. "And can I ask, to your knowledge, was your son engaged in a building project anywhere? Perhaps planning improvements to your cottage?"

Here she frowned and looked at him directly, clearly puzzled. "No, not as far as I know. Certainly nothing here. Not that I haven't asked him to do some repairs here. He always tells me there isn't the money right now. A likely story. That wife has plenty of money and I bet she has a death grip on it. She never was a generous sort of person." Her mouth turned down again, giving her a look of the truculent teenager.

Darling stood up, feeling he wasn't going to get much more out of her, and said, "If he contacts you, or you remember something that might be of help, can you call the station? Just ask the exchange for the Nelson Police Station. If I am not there, you may give your information to anyone who answers."

Bumping back down toward the main road on the steep and little-used lane, Darling thought about Mrs. Robinson. A kind of ghastly combination of defensive and aggrieved. He understood a mother defending her son, but it surprised him that even a mother could approve of the kind of behaviour he exhibited. Ben Arden seemed to him to be becoming more and more unattractive as the inquiry went on.

Using the instructions that Sergeant O'Brien had provided, Darling found the Bentley house, lakeside in Balfour. The expanded road connected to the new ferry terminal had physically divided the community. The properties on the south side were more well-kept and almost affluent, if anyone along the lake could be called affluent, but on the other side of the terminal, to the north in the King's Cove direction, the properties were smaller and dingier. He finally found the place down a narrow, heavily treed road. A battered green truck of some twenty years' vintage was parked in front of the house. A wooden fence enclosed a patch of turned-over earth at the side of the house that he assumed was a vegetable garden. The house was well maintained but somehow managed to appear neglected. It had a forlorn air.

He knocked on the front door and heard a mutter and the scraping of a chair inside. The door was pulled violently open by a man perhaps in his early fifties, dressed in oil-stained coveralls. The man seemed irate.

"What?"

"Inspector Darling, Nelson Police." Darling held out his warrant card. He was about to ask if the man was indeed Mr. Bentley, when the man leaned on the door frame, his face suddenly drained.

"You found her? What's happened? I knew that bastard would do for her."

"Are you Mr. Bentley?"

"Yes."

"We've not found anyone. I've come by to ask a few questions. We are pursuing a missing person inquiry and we are looking into information that your wife might possibly know something. Is she away?"

The man stood back to let Darling in, and then proceeded to an armchair in the dark sitting room and collapsed into it. Darling sat in its mate, wishing they were sitting in the kitchen because he had sunk further than he expected into the sagging armchair and felt vaguely at a disadvantage. He waited.

"Would you look at that—you have 'information.' Looks like everybody in the world knows my business. She's away, all right. I come home from my shift on the steamboat and find nothin' but a note: 'I'm leaving with Eddy. Don't look for us.' That's my boy. I won't, believe you me. I know more'n to try to keep a woman that don't want to stay."

"You referred to a 'bastard' earlier. Who do you mean? Have your wife and son left with someone?"

"That I couldn't tell you, but it stands to reason, doesn't it? She's gone off with that bastard Ben Arden. They were at it like rabbits years ago. I forgave her, more fool me, and she come back, all right, but it wasn't never the same. It seems they never stopped. I don't even know if Eddy is mine."

"Your son. How old is he?"

"Twelve. The older he gets, the less of me I see in him." Bentley shook his head and looked down at his shoes. "But when he was born...well...you get attached to a baby, don't you? I had my doubts, but it didn't seem to matter."

"Has she been in contact with Arden recently, do you know?"

Bentley shook his head. "How the hell would I know what she gets up to when I'm at work all day?"

Darling gave the room a quick look. "Did she know Mr. Arden before you were married?"

"Nope. They met when he was delivering feed. We used to keep chickens. Doesn't that beat all? She goes off with the milkman. Feed-man. Same difference." He looked at Darling. "Good riddance, as far as I'm concerned. I thought you come to tell me she was dead or something. And before you ask, I don't know where they'd go. He has a wife and kids as far as I've heard. You can waste your sympathy on them."

"Mr. Bentley, you said earlier that you knew he'd finally 'do for her.' What did you mean by that?"

The aggrieved husband leaned forward, his arms resting on his knees, his hands clasped. "I met him back then because he did all the deliveries. Smooth bastard. I didn't like him. I met guys like him in the Great War. Too eager to fight, eyes too shiny. Too anxious to get at the enemy. Do you know what I mean?" He glanced up at Darling.

"Yes," said Darling. "I think I do. You felt somehow he was dangerous?"

"That's it. Like you couldn't trust him not to go crazy. Of course, the wife needed a good smack from time to time, but a man like that? You make him mad and there's no telling."

Darling, stilling his revulsion at this talk of periodic smacking, thought instead about the picture Bentley was painting of Arden. It was like having a pile of jigsaw puzzle bits dumped on the table that were supposed to assemble to make Arden, the man. But they appeared, so far, to make three different Ardens: the mama's boy, the loving father, the womanizing chancer with a dangerous temperament.

"So, it is some time since you and your wife got along well?"

"You could say that. Like I said, good riddance. I miss the boy, is all. She left me for a few weeks about twelve years ago now. Said her mother was poorly. I thought then she'd run off with him, but he never budged. She was all right for a while when she came back. Turned out she was pregnant. Then they musta started up again sometime. Like I said, I'm not going to fight a battle I can't win. Now if you haven't got any more questions, I'd like to get on with making something to eat."

"You think she might have gone to her mother now?"

"Her mother's dead. But if she's gone off with him, good luck finding them."

Darling rose. "Thank you, Mr. Bentley. I'll be in touch if I've any more questions. Your normal shift is during the day on the steamer?"

Bentley frowned. "Yes, it is, if it's any of your business. You don't come bothering me at work. I want to keep my job, if you don't mind."

DARLING DROVE OVER a slight hill and around a bend. He gazed at the long, curved sweep of the cove, nature's soothing elegance, and thought grimly about its opposite: men like Bentley. Good, honest, working blokes who genuinely thought it was their right—hell, they probably felt it their duty—to give the wife a good slap from time to time. He reminded himself fiercely that he'd met many a good, honest workingman who thought no such thing. And he'd met highly educated men who also believed it their right. He wondered if the beleaguered Mrs. Bentley had simply left on her own and was even now staying with friends in Vancouver or somewhere, her disappearance unconnected to Arden's. Unfortunately, their disappearance at the same time was extremely suggestive, and one thing it suggested was that they would likely be very hard to find.

The charm of the lake in the evening light was lost as soon as he made the turn up to King's Cove. His own wife even now was no doubt packing for her departure. It was still a couple of days away, and they did have an invitation to Lorenzo's reopening. But far from cheering him up, he imagined this would have all the doleful character of a goodbye dinner. "Well," he said out loud, as he turned down the last hundred yards to his gate, "there might be a scrap of chocolate cake to be had, I suppose."

Oxford, 1939

LANE GOT BACK from her lecture and called out, "I'm back. We can go now."

Diana was lying on the bed, one arm behind her head, a cigarette in the other hand, one of Lane's saucers on the bedside table holding ashes and a dismaying number of cigarette butts. Immediately Lane's temper rose again. She'd told her not to smoke in her room.

"Oh, good. I was going *mad* with boredom," Diana said, grinding her cigarette out on the saucer. "Sorry. I couldn't think of anything else to do. You've absolutely nothing to read in here, and no wireless for a bit of music."

Lane held her tongue. There were piles of books on every surface. No point in getting into a donnybrook with her sister. She'd be gone in the morning. She put her books down and took off her academic gown and hung it in her wardrobe. "Right then. Are you wearing those shoes?" She pointed at the red pumps with the Cuban heel that her sister had kicked onto the floor when she'd come in.

"Yes, why not?"

"They're not very practical. Have you nothing flat?" She pointed down at her own flat lace-up Oxfords.

"I wouldn't dream of having anything so unfashionable. I assure you, I'm quite adept at not falling over on these *massive* heels."

"Suit yourself. Do you at least have a jumper? It can get cool in the evening."

"God, you're like some nightmare nanny! I have travelled on my own from Riga, you know!" She slipped on her shoes and buckled the strap and then stood up to straighten her stockings. She rustled around in her small overnight bag and pulled out a red cardigan and held it up. "There, happy? There had better be some boys punting!" She tied the cardigan around her neck over an attractive red and blue scarf already knotted there and stood by the door, waiting.

Lane gathered her handbag and cardigan, and they went down the stairs and out the building onto the walk.

"What sort of lecture did you go to, then?" Diana made an effort to sound interested but was checking her handbag to make sure she had cigarettes and lipstick.

"I'm reading languages and history. It was about the Civil War. Causes, long-term effects, that sort of thing."

"Gripping."

At that moment, Lane felt she understood very well how civil wars started. She led Diana out the gate and past the Ashmolean. "This is a very famous repository of books and historical documents," she said, doing her best as a guide.

"I'll be happy when you show me to a very famous repository of drinks at the end of this."

"You are too young to drink alcohol in this country, I'm afraid. It'll be barley squash for you. I'll drink squash too, in solidarity. How's that?"

Diana rolled her eyes. "Daddy always lets me drink at home."

"Well, Daddy is not in charge of the drinking laws in this country." What she wanted to say was, Daddy always lets you do anything you want, but mindful of civil wars, she resolved to hold her tongue and have fun.

They arrived at the edge of the River Cherwell, where a small shed was occupied by the man who let out boats and punts.

"Afternoon," he said. "Quiet just now. Should be pleasant. Just the two of you?"

"Yes, please," said Lane.

"You've been before," he said, coming out of the boathouse and walking with them onto the dock. "You know what you're doing. I never forget a pretty face."

"Thank you," Lane said, nonplussed. She was still not used to the male attention she seemed to garner when she went out of the college.

She settled her sister in the prow and pushed off. Diana leaned back and trailed her hand in the water. After some time, she said, "This it, then? Ducks and water?"

"Yup. Ducks and water. People come from all over the world to do this."

"That's a surprise. Where are they then, all the people? You promised me some boys."

"I did not promise you some boys. I promised you a punt and a pub supper."

Several boats passed them, one with what looked like four drunk undergraduates from one of the men's colleges. They leaned over, nearly upsetting their boat.

"Hey, lovelies. Should you be out on your own? Join up with us. We'll look after you!" One of them called, waving a champagne bottle at them.

Lane looked firmly ahead, but Diana giggled, glanced at Lane, and then called back, "What's the point? That bottle's empty!"

The young men laughed, and one of them pulled up a new bottle and said, "We've got more!" One of them winked broadly at Diana.

When they had passed, their laughter fading farther up the river, Diana turned to Lane. "You're certainly no more fun than you used to be. What would have been the harm? Oxford men. Boys from good families."

"You'd be amazed, my dear, what boys from good families can get up to."

CHAPTER EIGHT

"CONSTABLE, SINCE YOU APPARENTLY HAVE idle time on your hands, look up the war record for our missing man, Benjamin Arthur Arden. Not this last one. Great War. Princess Pats."

Terrell said, "Right away, sir," and folded the letter he'd been reading back into its envelope.

Darling had already asked O'Brien if any calls had come through from someone finding a body. None had. He thought about the miles and miles of lake, the forests cascading down the mountains, growing right to the edge of the water, and the tiny pebble bays that dotted the eastern shore. Only a couple of small communities and the railway, which hauled ore off barges brought from the recently restarted Bluebell Mine. The rest was wilderness. If Arden had run off with Mrs. Bentley, why take a gun? If, on the other hand, Arden had had an assignation that required a gun, he, or someone else, could be dead anywhere along there and they'd never be found.

He gave a small sigh as he started up the steps to his office. At least it was extremely unlikely that if Arden was dead, Lane would find the man's body. This thought plunged him into gloom. He'd really rather she found people dead every day of the week than take herself off to Scotland. She was coming into town later in the evening for the opening night at Lorenzo's, and he could sense already he was going to be unhappy about the whole thing. He knew he was being churlish, and it made him feel small that he should selfishly wish Lane here with him, rather than attending to her beloved grandfather. Consequently, he was in a barking mood when he saw Ames come out of his office and hover near his door.

"Well?"

"Good morning, sir. Good drive in?"

"Are you hotel reception or a police officer? What do you want?" Darling asked irascibly.

"Mrs. Arden called the station first thing, sir. She found something she thought you ought to know about."

Darling threw his hat accurately onto the top of his coat stand and sat down, raising his eyebrows expectantly.

"Yes," Ames said hastily. His boss was in a mood. He opened his notebook to double-check. "She said she found a parish jumble poster and a wedding invitation pushed into the inside pocket of one of his jackets. She'd been going through his things, you know, for any clue about where he's gone."

"A wedding invitation? I'm shocked to my core. That should just about wind things up. Put it in the 'solved' column and we can all go on holiday." He almost said "to Scotland," but refrained.

Ames, used to his boss's sarcasm—though it seemed heavier than usual this morning—was about to plough on when Darling spoke again, astounding him completely.

"Sorry, Ames. I'm not in the best frame of mind. Sit down. Tell me about the invitation and the poster. It must be unusual, or Mrs. Arden wouldn't have called."

A bit dumbfounded by this apology, Ames sat. "That's all right, sir." He wondered if he should say more, and then decided against it. Another good moment for his mother's favourite adage: Least said, soonest mended. "She did find it unusual, sir. It was for a wedding held last October, and they don't even know the people. It was in an envelope addressed to Mr. Arden. She didn't recognize the handwriting, and he never mentioned it to her. They certainly did not attend a wedding in October. And they never went to jumble sales."

It was odd, certainly. It added to the impression that Arden had a secret life. "Was there anything unusual about the invitation itself?"

"She didn't think so. She has to come into town, so she is going to drop it off here."

Darling put his hand to his chin and thought for a moment. "Go get your notes from our visit and make sure Terrell gets up here the moment he's got the information I asked him for." There wouldn't be much in the way of fingerprints on the invitation, he thought, if the invitation was even relevant. The poster could have been picked up anywhere, from a pile in the café for all he knew, and would be of little use as a source of fingerprints.

Ames jumped up, causing the chair to slide noisily, which

in turn caused Darling to wince. Ames put his hand on it, as if to urge it to keep quiet. "Sir."

While he waited, Darling took up his writing pad where it was placed neatly in his wooden "in" tray and picked up one of the pencils lined up tidily beside the tray. He wrote out the notes from his conversations with Mrs. Robinson and Mr. Bentley.

AT BREAKFAST THAT morning, Lane had seen at once that Darling was still unhappy, and she knew her leaving was the cause of it. He had put on a brave face, asked about what she'd do with her last day, kissed her, and said he looked forward to dinner at Lorenzo's, but these niceties were subdued. She'd followed him out to the car, where he'd stood for a moment with the door open.

"Oh, darling, I am sorry," she'd said, putting her arms around him. "I wouldn't go unless I felt I absolutely had to."

"I know that," he'd said, holding her close, resting his chin on the top of her auburn hair. "It's just that I'll miss you. I've lived my whole life never knowing you even existed, and now I can't imagine you not being here."

"I can't imagine not being with you, either, if it's any consolation."

"Not very much," he'd said, and then kissed her.

She'd opened the gate and watched him back out and drive up the road, a flurry of dust marking his progress. When he'd turned down the hill toward the road to Nelson, she listened to the receding car until she could hear only the light rustle of the leaves and the high-low tweet of a chickadee somewhere in the forest.

"WELL, MY DEAR. Are you excited?" Eleanor Armstrong asked. Lane had taken her disquiet over Darling's unhappiness and her part in it across to the post office in the hopes of some cheerful distraction. They were standing outside where Lane had found her neighbour just returning from the root cellar with a basket of eggs. Alexandra was in Lane's arms, trying to lick her face. She wasn't really a young puppy anymore, but she still behaved endearingly like one.

Lane put Alexandra down and shook her head. "I always used to be excited about going somewhere. Now, I confess, I feel a bit sad. I hate to leave here, really. Poor Frederick is being plucky. I hate to think how he's treating his team. I should phone ahead and warn them."

Eleanor smiled. "I'm sure they are quite used to him. They never look very cowed by him when I've seen them. I'm sure Kenny would be just the same if I ever had to go off anywhere. Luckily in these thirty years it's never come up. I don't really have anyone in the old country anymore. You'd better come in and have some tea. It's such a lovely morning that we'll set it on the veranda out back. Kenny's in the garden. It will be quite uplifting to watch him toil while we drink tea. You can tell me how the whole business of that disappearing man is going."

Lane doubted that Kenny would continue his toil for one minute extra if there was tea and an update on the latest case going, and she was right.

The back porch was one of the loveliest places one could be, she thought, when the tea was on the table and they were all sitting around it. They sat facing the lake, which sparkled tranquilly below. It reminded her of the veranda at her grandmother's house; when she and Diana were children, tea was always taken on its wide expanse in the summer. It ran the full length of the house, open on three sides and protected by a long roof from both sun and rain. It looked out onto the lawn and garden and had been full of potted palms, rattan chairs, and little tables. It filled her with a momentary nostalgia that almost choked her with longing.

How foolish nostalgia is, she thought, fighting it back, when I am here in this beautiful place right this minute, with these wonderful people. "I was just thinking how much this lovely veranda reminds me of the veranda at my grandmother's house. It was just like this: open, sunny, full of comfortable furniture. We took tea there all the time. And now it belongs to the Russian overlords who tossed them unceremoniously into one room for the whole duration of the war and made no compensation when they finally moved out. It shows you, like nothing else can, that nothing lasts forever. Oh, gosh. Look at me being glum. I am sorry."

Kenny nodded. "I know what you mean. I sometimes have some glimmer of a memory of the house I was born in, and I feel myself pining, like it was some beautiful Eden, but I'm sure it wasn't. Just an ordinary house. It's funny how we colour our childhood memories."

"Well, while you two are wandering down memory lane, I'm waiting to hear what's what with the missing man. Gladys was very forthcoming about her visit to the man's mother. She certainly doesn't think much of him, nor, by the sounds of it, of her. Says he's a mama's boy, and it's Mrs.

Robinson's fault. Never let him go, she says, even though the boy neglects her and treats her rather callously. I guess that's a sort of nostalgia as well, remembering how sweet your little boy used to be and not being able to let go, no matter what sort of man he's turned into."

"He can't have been all bad. Had a medal for gallantry in the Great War, according to his mother. But there are some twists and turns." Lane knew she shouldn't tell them what Darling had told her the night before, but, she reasoned, they were all part of the same extended lake community. They all met at the church bazaars, Dominion Day picnics, Bales's little gas station and store. Anything she said could trigger some memory that might be of use. And, she reminded herself, Darling knew perfectly well that whatever she found out was likely to find its way to the Armstrongs, even without her. She stopped at repeating anything he told her that came from direct investigation. "Gladys's story about him having had an affair with a woman in Balfour a decade ago is interesting, and there is also a rumour, which I heard at the hairdresser, that he even tried it on with his commanding officer's wife during the war."

"I wonder why his commanding officer's wife was over there during the war," Eleanor commented. "She could have been nursing, I suppose."

"Yes, of course. I hadn't thought of that. It must have been unusual because there was a rule against married nurses. I was a little surprised that he had a medal. His behaviour, if the rumours are true, does not indicate a man of honour."

"Ha!" Kenny said. "It doesn't surprise me at all. All

kinds of people got medals in combat who were beastly in civilian life."

Lane was thoughtful. "I suppose it's something to do with taking risks. Going after other men's wives is risky behaviour. I can imagine such men throwing themselves at a pillbox full of German machine gunners."

Kenny shook his head and poured tea into his saucer. "I think it's a crying shame people like that came back covered in medals, when good officers never made it back. Now, take John Battersby: he lives across in Riondel now, but he was a Balfour boy. Friend of mine from school. His commanding officer was a bulldog, but brilliant. John says he wouldn't be here now if it weren't for him. Men hated him but trusted him completely, if you know what I mean. Shot just on an ordinary little reconnaissance. Always led from the front. The way John tells it, that bullet was meant for him. Almost no one from the party made it back. Renshaw, that was his name. I think he was from Slocan somewhere. His father was from a rich family down east that became a family of bigwigs here. I've heard they lived in a palatial house up Slocan way. Anyway, my point is, a man like that should get to come home. Instead, it's people like this Ben Arden."

The bell sounded in the post office cubby and Eleanor got up. "Funny old time to come here."

While she was gone, Kenny and Lane sat contentedly looking out over the lake. The tops of the birch trees with their delicate new leaves rustled like tiny birds.

"I don't suppose the inspector will have much time to deal with the gardening," Kenny said.

"No. Gosh, I hadn't thought of that. It's planting time, isn't it? I'll be back, of course, in a month, but by then it will be too late." Last time she'd had to go away she'd come back to find all her vegetables planted by her earnest neighbours. She certainly could not put them to that sort of trouble again, though she knew they were likely to do it, even if she strictly forbade it. She turned to Kenny with an idea that she thought almost ridiculous.

"What if I asked the Bertolli boys to do it? Would you be willing to guide them? I bought a lot of seeds before I knew I'd have to leave."

Kenny scratched the back of his neck. "They're awfully young and a bit of a handful when they're all together. But I suppose you'd have some chance of getting the odd carrot at the end of the summer. The thing is, the peas have to go in smartish, or it gets too warm for them. Go on, then. Ask Angela if she can lend me her boys. It might be fun." He chuckled from somewhere in the back of his throat, as if he was already imagining the tricks he might play on them.

"Well!" declared Eleanor, sweeping back onto the porch. "You'll never guess!"

The interested silence of her listeners assured her that they never would.

"Gladys has had a phone call from her friend, her 'tiresome friend,' she calls her. The police came around yesterday afternoon to ask whether her son had been planning some renovations on her cottage, and immediately after they left, Mrs. Arden called her in a state to tell her Ben bled all the bank accounts dry and has left them with nothing. Not a brass farthing! Apparently, Mrs. Arden more or less blamed

Adele, demanding to know what she knew about it."

And there it is, thought Lane. "Well, that's a turn-up," she said innocently. "It doesn't sound like Mrs. Arden gets along very well with her husband's mother."

"According to Gladys, there was never any love lost between them. But it sounds like he's played them both for fools," Eleanor said. "According to what she told Gladys, he'd been siphoning money in quite large sums since November. Two and even five hundred dollars at a time."

"Blimey!" Lane said. "For what, I wonder?"

"Plain as the nose on your face," Kenny declared smugly. "Blackmail."

MAUDE ARDEN STOOD looking out the window at the lake, repeatedly tapping the top of the armchair beside her with the fingers of her right hand. Her lips were pressed tight. She felt as though she was trying to hold herself together and release her pent-up angry energy at the same time. She could never have bargained for this, and she could not imagine how they would cope. How had she not known? His beastly mother wouldn't help, that was for sure, even if her own grandchildren were to starve in front of her eyes. She'd made that perfectly clear. In fact, the old bat had seemed almost triumphant that her son had left. She'd laugh out of the other side of her mouth if she knew all the things her precious son had been getting up to! She wanted to turn away from the lake, to get on with doing the washing, tidying the house. Life must go on, she told herself. But her mind kept going back to that afternoon in December.

"**YOU DON'T OFTEN** come in, Mrs. Arden," Lottie said. She'd been very busy with the Christmas rush, but there was only one customer waiting after Mrs. Arden, and she was feeling cheered by the idea that she'd be getting home soon to put her feet up.

"I just thought it might be a little treat. My husband's boss has invited us for dinner. I thought I should spruce myself up a little bit, anyway."

"Oh, that's nice. I do like those smaller Christmas gatherings," Lottie said when Mrs. Arden was settled for her wash. "You can talk to people, can't you? Is that too hot?"

"No, it's perfect," Mrs. Arden said, closing her eyes and giving herself over to the luxury of having someone look after her for a change.

The other customer, an older woman who clung obdurately to the 1930s in her choice of hairstyle, sat watching the hair-washing proceedings, a magazine open, but unread, on her lap.

When the hair washing was finished and Mrs. Arden was sitting in the chair waiting for the curlers, the older woman cleared her throat. "You're Mrs. Arden, aren't you? Ben Arden's wife?"

Maude Arden turned and looked at her. She didn't know this woman. "Yes, that's right. How do you know my husband?"

To her surprise, the woman snorted, but Maude was not able to see the woman's expression because Lottie had firmly turned her head toward the mirror.

"No fidgeting," she said.

"Listen, love, it's none of my business, but do you know what he's up to?"

At this, Maude turned and scowled at the woman, yanking a strand of hair out of Lottie's hand. "I don't know what you mean." She turned angrily back to face the front, in time to see Lottie's face in the mirror giving the other woman a distinctly warning shake of the head. "What's going on?" Maude demanded now.

"I didn't mean anything by it, lovey, only it's not right you should be kept in the dark."

"Kept in the dark about what?"

"It's just all over the place that he's been seen with that Philippa Bentley from up the lake."

"Well, that's all right, then. That's old news." Maude Arden sat firmly staring at her own now-burning face in the mirror, and when Lottie seemed to have ground to a halt, she said, "Go on. I haven't got all afternoon." She wouldn't let them see her emotion. She tried not to think of the humiliation of discovering Ben had started up an affair with that floozie on his delivery rounds while she had been struggling through her first pregnancy. He'd come back in the end. She'd won. She had. She put that letter right out of her mind.

The woman with the magazine shrugged and turned her lips down, skepticism positively radiating off her face, and began to turn the pages of the magazine. Minutes of silence passed by while Lottie efficiently installed row after row of small curlers in Mrs. Arden's hair. Suddenly, the woman with the magazine looked up. "It could be wrong, what I heard. It was three days ago, on the Castlegar road. He stopped for gas, and she was with him. Her and that little boy of hers. Hislop—he's got the Esso station there, he's a friend of my husband—said they looked like they were fighting something awful. So, you're probably right. There's probably nothing in it. I just don't think it's right, though, you not knowing. If it were me, I'd prefer to be told, that's all," she finished primly.

"Well, thank you. You've done it. Now you can get back to your magazine," Mrs. Arden said. She stared only at her reflection and Lottie's as the curlers went in and the kerchief was tied. Once under the dryer, she couldn't hear what Lottie and the other woman were saying, Lottie looking urgent and disapproving. She could feel the heat of rage building inside her, hotter and more durable than the heat of the dryer she was under now.

CHAPTER NINE

"**S**IR," TERRELL SAID, LOOKING INTO Darling's office where Ames and the inspector sat with papers covering the desk. "It wasn't hard to find out, sir. Benjamin Arden, far from getting any medal, was presumed killed in an ambush that wiped out most of the scouting party he was part of. They never found his body, and if he did turn up, he'd face court martial for desertion. They were very interested to learn he'd resurfaced. They assumed he was dead all this time."

"Well, well," Darling said. "I wonder if he'd still face punishment after all this time?"

"And how did he sneak back to Canada? Surely if he'd boarded any ship his name would be on a list somewhere," Ames said.

"He could have lain low and then travelled back with a wave of enlisted men, or even long after the war. We are in the back of beyond here. What with one thing and another, especially if his regiment thought him dead, he could slip right back into his life, telling some fancy stories and no one would pursue it. I did see the medal, though, when I visited his mother," Darling said.

"That is a matter of concern, sir," Terrell said.

Ames jumped up. "I'll just go get another chair."

"Oh, thank you, sir. I can do it."

"Nonsense, take mine, and you just mull over that interesting observation."

Darling leaned back in his chair, one hand resting on the side of his chin. He made a little "will wonders never cease" gesture with his head. Terrell took the chair and pulled it up to the desk. "Thank you, sir."

"Think nothing of it," Ames said on his way out to his own office. "Just a little thanks for your constant attendance and keeping me up to date while I was home with this shoulder."

Darling waited for Ames to return, then nodded at Terrell. "We are concerned about the medal, why?"

"Didn't you say his mother said he'd been awarded a medal for gallantry? That's not really what they were handing out during the Great War—not called that, anyway. Now, perhaps that's what she translated it as herself, but it would be useful to get a look at the actual medal to see what it was. The next question has to be, how would he get hold of one if it isn't genuinely his? I know today you can probably pick them up in a pawnshop, or even in an antique store, but not right during or after the war. They would be very difficult to get."

"Could he have taken it off a dead soldier?" Ames asked.

"It's possible, but not so likely. I can't imagine people

went into battle wearing their hardware. They'd keep it safe, send it home to their mother and so on."

Darling, who suspected Terrell himself had received hardware and sent it home to his mother, but who would not dream of prying into the business of so private a man, nodded agreement. "That's true. It might be a bit of a business getting hold of one. So, this adds to the weight of Arden being a very dark horse indeed. Let's go over what we have. When we've done that, you and I will have to go out to Mrs. Robinson and break the news and get hold of the medal, see if there's any way to track it. Terrell, I expect Mrs. Arden will have dropped off the mysterious wedding invitation. I'd like you to go over it closely to see what you can see, then I want you to go along to the bank and make an official visit to the manager to get a closer look at the way Arden was emptying bank accounts."

"I THINK IT'S miserable that you are going away just at the most beautiful time of the year," Angela complained. She and Lane were sitting on the veranda at Angela and Dave Bertolli's beautifully appointed log cabin, the two collies snoozing nearby in a patch of sun.

"I know. I just don't see how I could not go. And I *will* get to see my sister. It's been almost ten years."

Angela twirled the ice in her glass of lemonade. "I thought you didn't get along all that well with her."

Lane nodded. "Yes, but that's me being uncivil, clinging to childhood prejudice. She was very young and rather overindulged by my father, and I think I resented it. She can't be blamed for that."

"Well," Angela said, shrugging, "you're a better man than I am."

"That's an interesting point, actually," Lane said. "Are men better at this sort of thing? One does hear of sisters not getting along, but not that often of brothers. The inspector has a younger brother, and he seems to get on with him. I mean, they are two completely different kinds of people, but there's certainly no animosity."

"I don't know that we can make generalizations, can we? Dave has a younger brother, and they might as well have come from different families. They have nothing in common at all. His brother fits in with the family view of life, which is 'business is king,' and poor Dave is a bit of a black sheep with his artistic bent and wanting to get away from all that family history. And look at Mabel and Gwen. They get along just fine. I mean, I suppose they have their little spats—Mabel can be quite domineering in that older sister sort of way."

Lane laughed. "Maybe that's it. Maybe I was just unbearably bossy. Whatever it was, I'll try to fix it. It's unseemly to carry childhood grievances into adulthood. But I do have something I'd like to ask for while I'm gone."

"Anything!"

"I was wondering if the boys, under the guidance of Kenny, would like to take a crack at getting my vegetable garden up and running. I'm leaving at the worst time for that, and of course Frederick will be dashing off to work every day and won't have time."

"What a wonderful idea! It will be very good for them. I'll ask them when they are back from school. They'd do anything for you, you know." Lane had taught the three boys briefly before Christmas at the local school, and she had achieved hero status in their eyes.

"Quite unwarranted, I assure you. But I'd be very grateful. I've set out everything just inside the garage. I've bought seeds, and there are some old but usable tools there. Kenny said he'd be happy to instruct and supervise."

HER PACKING DONE, Lane readied herself for the opening night dinner at Lorenzo's. She would drive in and meet Darling at six. With growing regret, she went onto the porch that faced the lake and leaned against the banister and closed her eyes, feeling the sun on her eyelids. Was she making a mistake? The truth was that she was powerless to do anything for her ailing grandfather, and she doubted, in spite of her brave words to Angela, that she could affect the damaged relationship between herself and her sister. There was certainly nothing in her sister's letter to indicate *she'd* undergone any transformation. In fact, Lane rather suspected that her attempts at some sort of reconciliation would be seen by Diana as just another way to boss her around.

May 1939

"LOOK," DIANA SAID, pointing across the garden where they were having their pub dinner. "Isn't that the man who came alongside us? He's very handsome. He's looking this way."

"If you fall for every man who flirts with you, you'll end up in a world of trouble. Your life will never be your own.

There's a good film on at the cinema. Why don't we go to that? Diana, I'm talking to you."

"All right. Keep your hair on. What sort of film? Probably some boring intellectual thing, no doubt."

"I'm sure *Goodbye, Mr. Chips* isn't either of those things. It just came out and it's got good reviews. I checked."

"Well, all right. I'm just off to the loo." Diana took up her handbag and settled her cardigan around her shoulders.

Lane watched her crossing the grass toward the pub door. She was making sure, of course, to pass near the man's table. Lane closed her eyes, drawing in a deep breath. She was, in Lane's opinion, overdressed with that silk scarf. No doubt she would restore the ridiculous red lipstick that had been removed by her fish and chips. It felt a massive and nerve-racking undertaking, keeping her sister in line until she could put her on the train back to her friends in Mayfair in the morning. Diana was, like Lydia Bennet, the most determined flirt who ever lived.

THE CURTAIN CAME down at the end of the film and the lights came on. Lane noted with irritation that her sister was not back from yet another visit to the loo, and that she'd missed the end of the film. She sat on, becoming increasingly angry while the cinema emptied. Where the bloody hell was she? Finally, she got up and walked down the sloping aisle and pushed open the door to the ladies' room.

"Diana, could you get a move on?" she called, but she could see already she was speaking to an empty room. Wondering if she had somehow missed her, but not understanding how, she hurried back up the aisle and then into the lobby. There were still a few people standing in clumps, smoking and talking, but no Diana. Perhaps she'd simply gone to wait in the street. Outside on Charles Street there were plenty of people, but no sign of her sister. It was dark out and Lane began to feel frightened. What had the girl done?

She rushed back into the theatre, looking for a manager, or anyone working there, and finally found a young woman who seemed about to enter the box office.

"Excuse me, I'm sorry. I seem to have misplaced my sister. Did you see a young woman, dark hair to her shoulders? She has a..." Lane struggled to remember, her mind confused by her growing fear. "A red cardigan and a red and blue scarf with sort of polka dots."

To her amazement, the young woman said immediately, "Oh yes. I remember that scarf in particular and that very crimson lipstick. Very pretty girl. She went out about fifteen minutes before the film ended. I think she was meeting someone outside in the street."

Aghast, Lane whirled around to look through the glass door and then back at the young woman. "Meeting someone? Who? I'm the only person she knows in Oxford!"

"Well, apparently not. She certainly seemed to know that man. They seemed very chummy to me. They kissed each other on the cheek and went off arm in arm."

Lane gave a little shake of her head, as if to clear her mind. "Man! What did he look like? Have you seen him before?" Lane could feel her voice rising.

"I didn't get a close look at him, no. He was standing just outside the marquee lights. Not old enough to be her father or anything, but he seemed older than her, I'll say that."

"Anyone is older than she is! She's sixteen! Oh my God!" Lane's hand flew to her forehead. Fifteen minutes before the end of the film? That was nearly twenty-five minutes ago. They could be anywhere. She stood, congealed with worry and indecision.

"I'm sorry, love," the ticket girl said sympathetically.

Lane nodded distractedly at her and hurried outside onto the street. Who was the man? If it was the man from the pub, perhaps someone there knew him. She retraced their steps in the direction of the pub, trying to recall what the man looked like, anything that would single him out. Then she stopped for a moment and tried to reason through what they might do. Would he hustle her sister immediately off somewhere to have his way with her? Or would they go for a drink somewhere first, observe some of the niceties? If he was a college man, it was unlikely he'd take the risk of trying to sneak her into his rooms. If he lived in town, he was probably under the thumb of some ferocious landlady who would not allow girls into her tenants' rooms.

She took a deep breath. The pub first. It was crowded and noisy, a pall of smoke floating above the din. She tried to look as though she was simply trying to find friends she'd agreed to meet. She wandered between the tables, looking for any familiar face. Finally, near the door, she did see a face she recognized. One of the men from the punt who'd been sitting near them during the dinner. She hurried over to the table and said, "Excuse me."

The man turned and looked at her, his face wreathed in an appreciative smile. "Who, me?"

His friends whooped.

"Can I talk to you?"

"Any time, love."

He was certainly not an undergraduate, Lane thought. She indicated the door, and he pushed his chair back and got up, following her into the garden. The night had cooled and there were only a few people sitting outside.

"We saw you earlier with three other men. One of them was..." Lane struggled. "He had dark hair, combed back, maybe, and a moustache. He was wearing a brown tweed jacket, I think. You'd been with him on the river as well. We passed you in the punt, my sister and I, I mean."

The man's puzzled frown cleared. "Oh, you mean Tommy. Tommy Clay. Repellent lip hair, I must say."

Relieved to have got this far—she had a name now—she went on. "What college is he in?"

The man barked out a laugh. "Tommy? Not old Tommy. I'm not even sure he finished. He went down last year. He's just up for a visit. Went back this evening. Say, is this about that pretty girl you were with? Though let me say, not a patch on you!"

Fuming, Lane said, "That 'pretty girl' is my sixteen-year-old sister."

The man whistled. "Sixteen! He is an old dog. But listen, I'm pretty sure they knew each other. He said she was staying with friends of his in town."

Lane leaned against the door frame, her arms crossed, looking at the ground, feeling completely defeated.

"Listen, I wouldn't worry. He's okay, is old Tommy. Maybe he's just run her up to town back to her friends."

Taking a deep breath, Lane stood up straight. "Thank you." She couldn't face going back into the pub with its carefree noise and smoke, and she made for the gate out of the garden.

"I say, why not come in and have a drink? You'd improve the look of our table no end," he called after her. But seeing her walk determinedly into the dark with not even a backward glance, the man shook his head, tapped a cigarette out of his packet, and went back to join his friends.

ON THE WAY into town to join Darling for dinner, Lane, who had dressed in the beautiful chinois evening dress she'd worn to a society party the year before, suddenly remembered the whole incident of Diana's visit to Oxford. "Absolute classic Diana," she said to a passing green roadster. She'd arrived back in her rooms and had found the note lying on the bed and wondered that she hadn't seen it as they were leaving for dinner. *No offence intended, dearest sister. I don't think I could stick a whole night in this eye-watering place. Don't worry about me. Thanks for the punt and thanks in advance for the supper.*

Diana had phoned and left a message with the porter the next morning saying she was back in town with her friend Marisa Fairfax. Lane had tracked down a telephone number and called. Of course, Diana was there, peevish at being scolded, furious at not being trusted. And then suddenly, into the angry silence, she'd said, "Listen, Lanette. Please take care. I think it's going to be an awful business, this war. And please don't worry about me. I'll be all right, I promise."

Lane remembered her tears even now, partly relief after her night of worry, partly something else, almost familiar, but unfamiliar to her: love for her little sister.

LORENZO BEAMED WHEN Lane and Darling came through the door. "Signora, Ispettore! Welcome! You look so elegant, Signora!" He vigorously shook their hands and showed them to a table by the window with a Reserved sign on it.

The restaurant had a warm feel, enhanced by a new carpet that moderated the sound and candles on all the tables. They were greeted cordially by the businessmen who had helped Lorenzo and Olivia Vitali after the fire, and Darling saw, in the rear corner, Mayor Dalton and his wife. He nodded in their direction as he took his seat.

"You've hired some help," Lane said, seeing a young woman carrying plates across the restaurant. "I'm so glad!"

Smiling, Lorenzo watched his new waitress setting plates before the Smiths, his nearest neighbours. "Yes. It's better. I can do some things, but not too fast. She is very good, too. She is called Betty."

He looked, she thought, a little unhappy about his diminished ability to move as he once did before the fire, but in a moment he was all smiles again.

"Today, no menu. Mrs. Vitali make whole thing. Full Italian." He leaned over and whispered. "No wine." He shrugged and made a face as if to say, What you can do? The law is an ass.

"He's right," Darling said wistfully to Lane. "You do look elegant. I remember the last time you wore it we had a falling-out, as I recall."

"There will be no fallings-out today. I feel as if the world has been restored to its rightful orbit, sitting here again, waiting for something scrummy to appear before me," Lane said happily.

"I think its orbit is wobbly, or have you forgotten you're disappearing into the sunset tomorrow?"

"I haven't forgotten, but I've prepared a little surprise for you."

"Whatever it is, it will not replace having you here," Darling said mournfully.

"You are a love," Lane said. She smiled and leaned across to kiss his cheek.

CHAPTER TEN

May 9, 1948

KING'S CROSS WAS BUSTLING AS Lane, feeling sleepy and disoriented, looked for the platform for her train north. Someone bumped her from behind and begged her pardon, and she nodded, attempting a weak smile. It hadn't been that long since she'd been in London. It was nearly three years since the end of the war, and the city still looked battered, but the speed and purposefulness of its inhabitants felt heightened. The city was hurtling forward, driving around the wreckage, as it were, as if determined to put the war behind it. Or perhaps, she thought, finally seeing the platform for the Flying Scotsman, it's because I feel like a wrung-out dishrag.

She was approached by a porter who looked past her quizzically. "Luggage, miss?"

"No, just this," she said, indicating her modest suitcase.

"You do travel light." He took her ticket and pointed. "There you go, luv, compartment three. You look like you need a kip, and then go to the dining car and have a nice lunch. Mind you do."

Lane nodded, managing a smile. Having her exhaustion pointed out to her made her at once more exhausted but at the same time mutinous. There'd be no kip. She'd read and then go for lunch and then spend the rest of the trip admiring the countryside, though what kind of lunch she could expect with rationing still on, she didn't know. There would still be travel to do getting from Edinburgh to Peebles and then Broughton, though thankfully not too much. And then a local bus.

She settled into a seat by the window, suitcase stored, and watched the coming and going on the platform. She was surprised to see many people still travelling with large suitcases and trunks that were being pushed along in carts by porters. She thought the war would have taught people to be more efficient in their travel. But perhaps she was the odd one out with her one suitcase. She wondered what the porter would have thought of her luggage if he'd known she'd come all the way from Western Canada.

She smiled at a woman of a grandmotherly age travelling with a small boy in school cap and shorts who took up the seat opposite her, and then pulled her book out of her handbag.

She awoke to the sound of a man's voice as from a great distance. "Miss, I'm sorry to wake you, but you will miss your luncheon."

Lane heard the full sentence, but dragging herself out of a deep sleep, she still could not assign any meaning to it.

"Luncheon, miss," he repeated.

She sat up straight, looked at him, and then smiled weakly. "Thank you so much. I didn't mean to doze off like that. Which way is the dining car?"

"Just on your left, miss, two cars down. There's a very nice bit of fish soup to be had."

When he'd gone, Lane composed herself. Her travelling companions must already have gone to lunch. Her book was next to her handbag beside her, and she saw that a piece of paper had been slipped in as a bookmark. She pulled out her compact, straightened her hat, and tucked an errant wave of hair behind her ear. Her eyes were a little red and she suspected the dark circles under them were not just from shadow. It would have to do.

In the dining car she caught sight of her fellow travellers and approached them. "Thank you so much for rescuing my book and the page. I should have had a time finding it again!"

"You looked all in, you poor dearie. I don't think you read a single word before you dropped off." The woman had a soft Scottish burr. "Here, you must sit down with us. We've only just started. This is Robby, my grandson. He's the one who rescued the book. I'm Mrs. Sinclair."

Lane gave him a warm smile. He was about the age of Rafe Bertolli, and she felt a pang of already missing King's Cove. "Thank you, Robby. What have you got to eat there? It looks very good."

The boy looked at her shyly. "It's fish soup, miss. There's rice pudding for afters."

"Splendid, I do love rice pudding!"

"Have you come from London for a holiday?" Mrs. Sinclair asked.

Lane explained, to oohs and aahs, about her trip.

"Are you one of those that married a Canadian and went out?"

"Not quite. I moved out to Canada on my own. But I did marry a Canadian, yes. A police inspector in our local town."

"Well, now!"

They chatted happily, and Lane, under the influence of lunch and lovely company, began to feel more human, as if she was no longer still lagging behind somewhere over the Atlantic.

Alighting in the late afternoon in Waverley Station in Edinburgh, she bid adieu to Mrs. Sinclair and young Robby, who were to travel on to Dundee. She walked into the main hall, not huge but magnificent under its beautiful Victorian glass dome, and began to look for where she might buy a bus ticket. She'd been a year before with Darling and remembered the ticket vendor was near the entrance of the station. She hoped she would not have to wait a long time for a bus, or worse, stay overnight to catch a bus the next morning. She was second in the queue when she heard her name called, but even then it took a moment for her to register. "Mrs. Lanette Darling?" It was a young man of about twenty, and he was holding a sign with her own name on it.

"Yes. I am she."

With a relieved smile, he said, "I'm to drive you to the cottage, miss. Missus. Let's have your bag."

"What luxury! Did my grandmother organize this?" Lane said, coming off the queue and relinquishing her bag with a burst of gratitude. She would be there in an hour.

"Aye. I work at the greengrocer. I have a wee van, so she asked if I'd fetch you."

"How heavenly! Thank you, Mr. . . ."

"Mark McRae, ma'am. Happy to do it."

They arrived at a dusty greengrocer's van parked just off Princes Street, and Lane settled herself on the lumpy passenger seat and leaned her head on her elbow, still not quite believing her luck. "I don't think I can thank you enough. I remember taking the bus during the war and it took ages to get there. This is such a treat."

"Oh, aye. It stops at every little village. We should be there in a little over an hour."

"How did you find me so quickly?"

The young man went slightly pink. "Your gran. She told me to look out for the most beautiful woman in the station. It wasn't hard." He collected himself for a moment. "Can you tell me about Canada on the way? I've a mind to go there."

"Happily!" said Lane. It was just what she was in the mood for.

"I'VE DUG A bit further, sir," Terrell said, poised outside Darling's open office door. "The man disappeared from his regiment in August of 1917, during the Passchendaele campaign. His commanding officer was a Major Richard Renshaw. Missing, presumed dead."

"Arden disappeared while Renshaw was still in command?"

"No, sir, not exactly. Thinking this Major Renshaw might still be alive, I thought to track him down to see what he could remember, but they told me he'd died in late August just before the Canadians secured the ridge. Arden was in that party, went missing around the same time. Apparently, most of the party died, but they never found Arden's body and he didn't resurface. They assumed he died." Terrell consulted his notes. "They were in the middle of a difficult campaign, so I'm not sure much effort was put into finding him."

"Ah. Well, here we are, thirty years later, trying to find him again. About Renshaw..."

"Yes, sir."

"My wife had it from one of the neighbours that they knew an officer named Renshaw who died in Europe. He must be the same man, I should think. He was a local man, evidently. Slocan."

"Do you want me to try to track down any relations, sir? Long shot sort of thing?"

Darling considered. "Yes, why not. Pop along to the bank first, though. I'd like to hear more about the disappearing money."

"Oh, and we heard back from Arden's doctor. He wasn't terribly forthcoming because of patient confidentiality, but he did say Arden did not suffer from any heart trouble."

MR. SHEFFIELD LOOKED askance at Constable Terrell, who had responded to his chilly greeting by nodding and holding up his warrant card and giving his name. They had met only once when Sheffield had approved Terrell's opening an account at the bank. He wasn't any warmer this time around. "How may I be of assistance?"

"I've come to talk to you about the account of Benjamin Arden. Is there somewhere we can talk privately?"

Once they were in Sheffield's office, the bank manager folded his hands and looked obdurate. "I am, as you may imagine, not at liberty to reveal the details of a client's financial transactions."

"The client's wife has already been around to see us with a report about her visit to your bank. She was pretty upset, as you can imagine. I've been sent to double-check what she said, in case, in her distressed state, she didn't fully understand what had happened. We"—he chose this instead of "I" to emphasize that the attention of the police was on the Ardens' banking situation—"understand that she learned her husband had completely emptied the bank accounts. She's wondering whether it's legal for a husband to take all the money, including that belonging to the wife. Would the bank not have become concerned by Arden's behaviour?"

"We did become concerned," Sheffield said tightly, lunging for the one point where he thought he, and the bank, might be most vulnerable to censure. "I did contact him to ask about his withdrawals. He explained that he had purchased a property and was building a new home, and that the money would be replaced when they sold the current home. I had no reason to doubt him."

"Mrs. Arden also said that she learned that her husband had not deposited his paycheque since last fall sometime. Did you ask about that, or contact Mrs. Arden?"

Sheffield raised his chin in a little motion that was perhaps a nervous tic but served to give him an air of defiance. "It is most irregular to involve a woman, a wife, in the financial dealings of her husband. As I said, we were satisfied with his explanation. He did recently ask to borrow money, and he was turned down by the manager who was standing in for me while I was away." He said this with satisfaction. They had been doing their job with due diligence.

"This request was made through a manager?" In Terrell's experience, bank managers watched the behaviour of their customers like hawks, and it appeared that Sheffield, at least, had let an awful lot go in the case of Arden.

"Certainly, yes. He was told that he did not qualify for the amount he was seeking. He seemed to accept it and did not ask to see me upon my return. Will there be anything else?"

"Just one more thing. I'll need the dates of all the withdrawals, and the amounts."

Sheffield again looked as though he would like to resist, but finally said, "I'll get those done up for you and send them around to the station."

"Certainly. If we could have those by this afternoon, that would be ideal." Terrell stood up. "Sir." Outside the manager's office, he put on his cap, nodding to a clerk called Williamson who had admired his Triumph one day when he was parking it on Baker Street.

Once back at the station, feeling a certain amount of satisfaction about his interaction with the bank manager, Terrell found O'Brien holding up an envelope and folded piece of paper.

"That Mrs. Arden dropped these off. The boss said you were going to do something with 'em."

Terrell nodded and took the envelope to his desk. He sat and looked at it. It was good, high-quality paper and was addressed to Mr. Benjamin Arden. Inside the envelope was indeed a wedding invitation. "Reverend and Mrs. Donald Spinks request your presence for the wedding of Miss Jessica Spinks to Mr. Timothy Varden," followed by the date, the previous December, time, address, and, in the lower left-hand corner, "RSVP" in the same fancy script as the rest of the invitation. Underneath that, centre, last line, on its own, the number two hundred.

Terrell turned the invitation over to look at its blank side, and then back again. It must have been a massive wedding, if two hundred invitations were issued. He could make nothing of it. He looked at the return address on the envelope. He would go to the printer, and then to the address to talk to the bride's parents. Mrs. Arden had said she didn't know the people who sent the invitation, and she didn't think her husband had either. Shrugging, he put the invitation on his desk and took up the small poster and looked it over. Typical parish jumble sale announcement. He was about to put it down when he noticed the time of the event: 11 PM.

"There's a mistake here, I'm sure," he said to O'Brien's back. "They must have meant 'AM.' I'm going to that printer up the street. I think they're the outfit that printed these. Maybe they can see something amiss in the wedding invitation. I sure can't. Judging by this announcement, they are pretty sloppy. Someone from the bank might drop off some paperwork I asked for," he said on the way out the door.

O'Brien emitted a low whistle when the door closed behind Terrell. He was very impressed that the constable had managed to get the notoriously forbidding bank manager to cough up any kind of paperwork.

April 1917

"THIS IS DISGUSTING," Arden said, grimacing at a tin mug of tea. It was lukewarm, had ash floating in it, and tasted nothing like tea. He was sitting on an overturned box along with the other soldiers in the murky pre-dawn. His stomach was churning. He knew it was fear and he hated it. He looked at the others, tin helmets on, tipped at various angles, rifles to hand. They all looked afraid, he thought. It was in their eyes and small fidgeting movements. He wondered if looking unconcerned would lessen the feeling. The mud-hardened sock on his right foot had bunched under his big toe and was causing irritation. He suspected his toe was bleeding. He felt a sudden desperate need to fix it, but knew he had no time. They'd been warned the whistle would be coming any second. He'd been over the top once before. It was where he'd learned to fear. He had spent much of his sleepless night in the pursuit of hopeless plans for escape. He saw himself moving the other way when an attack was ordered. He'd get lost in the rising morning and be unmissed and forgotten. The war would carry on without him.

The whistle pierced his thoughts and he lurched onto his feet with the others, waited his turn on the ladder, heard the instant burst of fire from the other side. Men were already down when he gained the top and he ran forward, trying not to fall over anyone, trying not to look to see who they were. He had no real idea of what was supposed to happen. He should run forward, pick out a Boche on a machine gun, and shoot him. But he couldn't really see with the moving mass of people in front of him, the dark, and the blinding flashes. He looked down at his right boot, conscious of his bunched sock, willing it to straighten out, and the next thing he felt was that he was rattling down a hill, tumbling head over heel, landing sharply on something hard.

The charge was above him, suddenly dreamlike, men pouring around, the shouting somehow echoing as if they were far away. He closed his eyes, thinking he'd been shot. After some time, he opened his eyes. Grey morning light illuminated the crater he was in, the half-buried bodies, the silence except for someone groaning. It took him a moment to realize the groans were his. He was lying against an abandoned 13-pounder, his shoulder screaming.

CORPORAL BEN ARDEN grinned at the nursing sister. "It's just a sprain," he said. It was something he said with almost giddy relief. He was not dead. He had all his limbs. He was sitting on a chair, not badly hurt enough to warrant a bed in the infirmary. His shoulder was hunched up and it hurt like the devil when he moved.

"I suspect you've done something to your collarbone. A doctor can wrench it back into place."

"Wrench! That's a harsh word!" He smiled again, pushing his cap back on his head so that it looked almost jaunty.

"Would you listen to yourself. I've men in there with their limbs blown off. How old are you, anyway?"

"Twenty-two. Plenty old enough." He winked, and then winced.

She ignored him. "You'll have to sit over there till someone can see you." She pointed to the edge of the tent where there was a row of chairs reserved for minor injuries. There were already three men sitting. They were slumped from boredom, or waiting, or pain, he couldn't tell which. Or exhaustion. Rain began outside, pelting against the tent at an angle. He could hear more seriously injured men groaning, calling for help, crying out. Some of them would be going home, he thought, shipped out to England, or back to Canada, too damaged to fight again. That was what he wanted. To go home. To get the hell out of here.

He wasn't sure how long he'd dozed, waking up several times when he'd slipped sideways and was woken by the pain in his shoulder, but he was roused finally by a shockingly familiar voice.

"Ben? Is that you?"

Arden opened his eyes and could scarcely believe what he saw. He felt his heart flip. "Franny! What are you doing here?" He sat up, grimacing and smiling at once. She should be back in Canada.

"I was sent to check on your shoulder, and, if it's not broken, pull it back into place," she said coldly.

"It'll be like old times, you with your arms around me." He tried to wink but found even that painful. "I can't believe you're here." He seized her hand with his one good one and winced again.

Francine hissed, "Shut up!" and yanked back her hand. "If I had my way, I'd break your collarbone and chuck you out. Just so you know, before you start any nonsense, I'm engaged to be married."

"No. Come on, angel. In this short time? What do I have to live for now? Who is the bastard?" He tried to keep up a tone of nonchalance, but he felt as though he'd been pierced.

"You will address me as Lieutenant MacDonald. My intended is really none of your business, but he's called Renshaw."

Arden felt a well of outrage rising. "My CO? You haven't gone and gotten engaged to Mad Dog! He's an absolute bastard. What made you do a stupid thing like that?" The fury was, he suddenly saw, because he hated Renshaw. But to his own amazement, he felt a kind of relief as well. He gazed at her, all the years he'd loved her tumbling forward. But the whole thing had become a little tiresome toward the end. He'd felt trapped, somehow. If the war hadn't come along...but he didn't really feel anyone else had a right to her either. Especially not his bloody CO. "How do you know him?"

"It will surprise you to learn I had a life outside of you."

"He's a monster. You should have thrown your lot in with me when you had the chance."

"If you don't be quiet, I'll throw you out like this. Don't think I won't!"

"Aw, you're just saying that. We got along fine, didn't we? Say, does your everlasting major know about those days?" He winked again.

Blanching, Francine took a step back and looked hastily around. The station was unusually busy with the wounded from Vimy pouring in. No one was paying any attention to the lightly wounded men. "You wouldn't," she hissed. "He's your CO. What do you think he'd do to you?"

"I wouldn't. Of course, I wouldn't. Don't get so excitable. I'm just fooling around." He pulled at her hand, putting on an imploring expression. "Come out with me, your next day off. We can talk about the old days."

"Sorry, I can't." She didn't sound at all sorry.

Ben leaned back on the bench, nursing his sore shoulder with his other hand, and looked at her. "Oh, we'll have a little time, I'm sure of it. I have to stay here a few nights, and you have to get time off to sleep sometime."

Later, Francine found herself feeling almost light-headed. She'd waited till he'd been escorted to the tent he'd spend a couple of nights in before he went back to his unit. Then she'd stood for a moment, gulping in cold wet air just outside the door of the casualty station. What if he did tell Richard? Things were already shaky in that department. She hadn't seen her fiancé for more than two months, and they'd exchanged few letters. Then she had her idea. She would meet Ben. She had an afternoon off just when he was due to be released. She would beg him not to say anything. Then a new fear made her almost double over. Would he try to blackmail her? She tried to tamp down this fear. If that's what he was planning, threatening to tell her fiancé about what had happened when she was young, she would tell him herself. Then he'd have no hold over her. She would break with Ben once and for all. Late at night, finally released from the rush of wounded, she collapsed on her bed. Betsy was already asleep, snoring lightly. She felt pressure on her chest, as if Ben himself were sitting on it. She'd always had the upper hand with him. When did that change?

August 1906

"I SAW YOU, you know." Franny sat next to him on the edge of the pier, her skirt hitched and her legs swinging above the water. Her shoes and stockings were piled next to her. "I want some." She held out her right hand.

Ben gulped and put his hand behind his back. "I didn't do anything." He could feel his heart beating fiercely. He looked behind them at the tackle shop from where he'd taken the gum, but Mr. Henry still hadn't rushed out shouting. Maybe it was going to be all right.

She pulled his arm away from his back and dragged his fingers open with painful force, revealing the packet of Juicy Fruit.

"Ow!" He tried to pull it back, but she had it now and she was holding it above his head.

"Do you always steal?"

"I didn't steal it. He gave it to me!"

"Nuh-uh. I told you—I saw you." She ripped open the package and sniffed it, her eyes closed. "I love how it smells." She pulled out a stick of gum and held it out to him. "You can have this."

He reached for the gum, and she pulled her hand back.

"First you have to do something. Let's see, jump in the water with your shoes on? Let me pinch your arm? I have to think of something good. I know! You have to kiss me."

131

Ben could feel his face get hot, but he didn't understand why. Something between shame and excitement.

"What about Billy?"

She frowned. "What about Billy? He's not here. No one is." It was true. The afternoon was heavy and quiet. Her brother was out on the lake. All the people who had come in the morning for supplies and bait were out on the lake somewhere. They were alone. There was only the gentle green ripple of the water under the wharf.

"But he might come back. He said—"

"Do you want this gum or not?"

"Did you ever kiss anyone before?" he managed.

"Of course I did. I'm two years older than you. What do you think?"

"Who?"

"None of your business."

Emboldened by a sudden powerful thought of beating whoever it might have been, Ben moved in her direction and held his face close to hers. He could smell the gum and her skin. She leaned in and put her lips on his and let them rest there and he closed his eyes.

And then she pulled away abruptly and stood up. She threw the entire package of gum at him. He missed it and heard the splash as it hit the water. "You don't EVER tell anyone, you understand? Specially not Billy!" With her shoes and stockings clutched against her body, she turned and ran up the pier. He watched her, his ten-year-old heart full of a longing he thought would never leave.

CHAPTER ELEVEN

"**N**EWS OF MY IMMINENT DEMISE is greatly exaggerated," Ganf said, taking Lane's hand. They were sitting in the garden where Fiona had set out tea, complete with quartered fish-paste sandwiches and some scones and jam, the sun having put in a shaky appearance after a morning of rain.

"You do look splendid, I must say. All fierce beard and flashing eyes," Lane said, leaning over to kiss his cheek. It may have been true about the beard and the eyes, but he looked pale, and she had not imagined his progress down the stone steps would be so shaky. He'd insisted on making the trip on his own, and had clung to the rail, frowning at his wife as she hovered beside him. She suspected he'd overruled everyone's advice in order to put on a show of health for her.

"But you must tell us about your trip. You got here very quickly. I was expecting you in a few weeks." He was reaching for the sugar bowl and then pulled his hand back when his wife gently slapped it. "Harridan!" he exclaimed. "You see how it is, my darling girl?"

"Poor Ganf! How will you cope?" Lane said. She moderated her own usual two full teaspoons of sugar to a scant sprinkle. The sugar bowl was full and gave the appearance of normalcy, but she knew sugar was still rationed. "I took an aeroplane most of the way. I got here faster, but I feel like a bit of laundry that's been beaten on a stone in a river. It was noisy and I was cold the whole way. I never remember feeling like this when I sailed. Frederick sends his love. No holiday for him, I'm afraid. He's chasing down a missing man."

"How absolutely remarkable! I still can hardly believe in all this flying across oceans!" Her grandmother shook her head, smiling. "How *will* the inspector cope without you? Don't you usually solve all his cases?"

"Dear heavens, Grandmama. If I've given you that idea in my letters, then I've vastly inflated my part. I was involved a tiny bit in a few because I happened to be on the scene. He needed me to translate, that sort of thing."

Her grandmother got up and pulled the blanket that had been sliding off Ganf's knees back into place. When she sat back down, her expression became troubled. "Speaking of solving, we are beginning to worry a little about your sister. It's been all of ten days now. Or eleven? I've lost track."

"You don't mean she hasn't contacted you in all that time?" Lane was astonished, and then in the next moment she was not. How like Diana.

"Not a word, aside from the second day after she left. She put a telephone call through to say she had arrived and asked after the patient. I know she's a grown woman, and quite free to do what she likes, but of course in the wee smalls I can't help thinking of dreadful things...accidents, kidnapping. You know how one does."

"I do indeed." Lane sat back, frowning. She battled back her initial angry response. Diana had no right to put people through the mill like this! But her own sense of Diana prevailed. She had never known her to be anything but kind and solicitous to their grandparents. Something was not quite right. "Who did she say she was going to stay with?"

Ganf shook his head, his lips turned down. "That's the thing. She never did say exactly. 'Friends' is all she said."

"How long was she here before she left?"

"Only two days," her grandmother said. "We hadn't seen her since she left in '39. Poor thing was only a child then."

A wilful, selfish child, Lane thought, remembering what she'd put her through on her visit to Oxford.

"Has anyone looked through her room?"

"Oh dear, no! She would think it unforgivable!"

Out of the corner of her eye, Lane saw that Fiona was in the vegetable garden, pulling some wintered-over carrots. She saw her straighten up and look toward the table, shaking her head with disapproval. She guessed Fiona thought no more of Diana's behaviour than she did.

"Well, I have no such scruples. Directly I've had my tea, I'll dig in and see what I can find. There may be a letter, a wire, something. I remember now she had friends who lived in Mayfair. She and the girl went to stay with an uncle in South Africa for the duration of the war. I'm trying to remember if she ever told me the family's name. She must have told you."

Ganf nodded firmly. He had the air of a man who was relieved that someone had come to take charge. Her grandmother was looking across the garden distractedly.

"I have it!" she said suddenly. "Marisa, she had one of those last names from a novel. Austen? Dickens? No, Brontë! Fairfax. That was the name." She sank back into her chair again. "But she didn't mention her as she was leaving," her grandmother said. "Wouldn't she have said something if she had come back with this Marisa Fairfax? And anyway, the girl lived in London, not in Aberdeen."

"Yes! That's right!" Lane said. "Good for you for remembering. I remember her mentioning the girl when she came up to Oxford to visit me just before she left. Now at least we have one little clue. Maybe Marisa did come back, either with Diana or earlier. The war has been over for almost three years. Perhaps there was no reason to stay on." What had been Diana's reason for staying on until now? Lane wondered.

Fiona showed Lane up to Diana's room while Lane's grandmother got Ganf into the bedroom off the sitting room to have a little nap.

"I made the bed, but I've done nothing else to the room." Fiona pushed open the door to a comfortable but small room at the top of the stairs. Yellow curtains were closed and the May sun filtered through, creating the oily yellow glow of a mica lampshade. The single bed occupied the middle of the room, parallel to the window, and a tall dressing table and washstand against the opposite wall sat tidily in the obscurity, looking as if the room had never been occupied.

Lane pulled open the curtains and looked around. There was a faded green armchair and ottoman in the corner, she could see now, with a small round table and a tall lamp behind it. A pile of four books sat on the table. She looked for a suitcase under the bed, but of course Diana would have taken that on her visit to Aberdeen.

So absorbed was she that Fiona's voice startled her.

"If there's nothing else, Mrs. Darling. Only I have to go get started on the potatoes."

"I am sorry. In a world of my own. No, please, do go. Thank you for showing me the way." Lane smiled apologetically. Was she always this oblivious when she was on the scent?

Fiona nodded and turned to leave, hovering at the door wondering if Lane would want it open or closed.

"Just leave it open, that's fine. Oh, and do please call me Lane," Lane said, understanding her hesitation. Only when Fiona was partway along the passage did she say, "Fiona, if you think of anything, anything she might have said to you, please let me know."

Fiona stopped and turned to her. "I'm quite cross, if you must know, that she'd put her grandparents through this worry, what with her granddad not well." She appeared to think she'd said too much, so she clamped her mouth shut and went on her way. Lane understood her answer to mean that she would most certainly let her know if she thought of anything.

Lane started with the drawers, pulling them open, reluctant to touch what did not belong to her. Only the top drawers had anything in them. The first drawer contained a few jumpers, some stockings and underwear. Diana hadn't taken everything with her, so she intended to come back.

The second had a pair of folded trousers, some jodhpurs, a brown riding skirt, and a beige crepe blouse. Lane felt gingerly under these, not really knowing why, but turned up nothing. The remaining drawers were empty. A pair of lace-up heeled Oxford shoes was pushed to one side of the armchair, as if Diana had pulled them off and tossed them aside after wearing them for a long day of travel.

She marvelled at the small ladylike size of the shoes. Just another reason she'd been jealous of her sister: her own feet were enormous by comparison. Everything about Diana was compact and neat. She dropped into the armchair, disgusted with herself, and worried that she had found nothing useful. She turned her attention to the books. Mystery novels. Agatha Christie. With surprise, she noted that the bottommost book was in German. *Roger Ackroyd und sein Mörder. The Murder of Roger Ackroyd*. So, she was keeping up her German. She thought about herself. There was so much to be kept up from their early education. French, Russian, German. Well, her own wartime experiences had certainly helped her keep up with her French. In the last couple of years in Canada, she mostly seemed to be keeping up with her Russian, helping Darling with translating during some of his cases.

She put the book down and gazed out the window. What had Diana done during the war? She'd barely turned seventeen when it broke out. Marisa Fairfax's family must have thought that they were sending the girls to a neutral country, but South Africa rejected neutrality and declared war against Germany just five days after the whole thing started. What had it been like there?

Wondering what more she could glean from the room, she picked up the German book and leafed through it, and then turned it upside down and shook it, looking for papers, notes, a letter, anything. Instead, what she found were some marked-up pages. Words written into the margins. She looked more closely, thinking they might be translation notes. Perhaps, after all, Diana had had to look up some German words in a dictionary. The pages of the book were yellowing, and the dark pencil markings were smudged with time, or with handling. But instead of English translations of underlined words, she saw what looked like dates. Next to the word *hütte* was not the English word *cottage* but rather "3/12 10p."

Intrigued, she leafed through and found three more pages with similar notations, only different numbers. On a hunch she turned ten pages forward from the first marking. There was another German word underlined, a notation in the margin. She got up and walked to the window, trying to avoid what she suspected. No, what she was certain of. She gazed down at the garden where they had had tea, the little table now empty, the cushions taken off the chairs and brought into the house. This was her side of a code. Somewhere, someone—a German, maybe—had had his or her own copy. What a family, she thought. She knew suddenly that finding Diana might be a good deal more difficult than anyone imagined.

Pretoria, March 1941

"WHAT DO YOU think?" Diana turned in front of the long mirror, trying to see herself from all sides. She was wearing a black cocktail dress with turquoise beading at the neckline and a peplum waist pleated at the back.

"You look very grown-up," Marisa said. She sat in her silk dressing gown waiting for her crimson nails to dry.

"I am very grown-up, you ninny. I'm eighteen. But I look at least twenty-one. I hope I do. That's what I'm telling everyone. I shall be drinking champagne all night long."

Taking off her silk dressing gown, Marisa pulled her own dress off the bedpost and slipped it on. A mandarin orange–coloured floral silk. "It amazes me that we can go to these parties and swill champagne whilst back home everyone is getting their one teaspoon of sugar a week, or whatever it is. We'd better enjoy it. Daddy is coming in a few weeks. He might not like us drinking champagne. Though it's perfectly legal now." She surveyed herself in the mirror. "I wish I could look older like you do."

"Never underestimate a little black dress. I wish the officers were a little younger. I hate being slavered over by some balding captain with a wife at home," Diana said. Marisa's daddy apparently wasn't going to object to his daughter being pawed at by officers.

"I'm afraid being slavered over is our bit for the war effort. British officers must be entertained," Marisa said.

"Well, as long as they keep their paws off me and keep my glass filled, I suppose they can be as old and ugly as they like. Is your uncle James ready?"

The party was held at the rambling and airy home of a junior official at the British High Commission. The vast sitting room was sweltering, and the veranda doors were thrown open. Partygoers had drifted outside and leaned against the balustrade of the porch that extended the full length of the house. The light from the sitting room spilled out the doors and windows, imparting a golden glow to those seeking to cool off outside in the soft darkness. Alas, it was not much cooler there.

Khaki and flowered dresses were the dominant theme, and shouted conversation and laughter coiled upward with the smoke, competing with the blaring music from a phonograph. Couples danced close together near the music, adding a pervasive odour of sweat and perfume.

Diana was outside, looking through the windows, scanning the mass of people for Marisa, but she was not to be found. Sighing, she pulled out her cigarette case and was startled by a lighter materializing beside her.

"Having fun?" The man who spoke was—she could tell because she had memorized every pip imaginable—an army major. He was in his thirties, she guessed, good-looking in a sandy-haired sort of way. Blue eyes.

"It's all right. A bit crowded. The bubbly is good, though."

"You don't appear to have a glass on hand. Shall I fetch one?"

"If you like." Diana drew on her cigarette and turned away to look down the length of the veranda.

When he returned with two glasses, he somehow manoeuvred her to the farthest outer corner of the porch, and they stood looking out into the city lights below them.

"What's your name, then?"

"Diana Winslow. Yours?" It was hard to tell how far he was going to take this. She put one arm across her waist in an unconscious move to protect herself. She didn't particularly want to be pawed, and it worried her that he'd brought her so far from most of the revellers.

"Major Tremaine."

"On leave?"

"You could say that." He looked at her speculatively, as if sizing her up. "I'd like to have a chat somewhere private."

Here it was then. "I suppose you have a wife somewhere, here or back home."

"I suppose I do. That's not interesting to me. I've learned something interesting about you, though."

With a sinking feeling she knew what he was going to say. That he had found out she had lied about her age. She glanced back at the heaving crowd inside and wondered if Marisa had already been asked to leave. She leaned back and looked directly at him. "Well?" She swigged her champagne and put her empty glass on the railing, steeling herself.

"No need to be alarmed. It's just that we believe you have something that could be of use to us."

"Who is 'we'? Obviously, I need not have bothered introducing myself. Do you spy on all the women who come to these things?"

"No. Just the German-speaking ones. You'll understand our caution."

Diana was silent, waiting. She had not expected the conversation to go in this direction. Finally, after watching him load his pipe and tamp the tobacco, she said, "I'm sure you couldn't throw a rock in here without hitting people who speak German."

"Not so, at least I hope not, or we've not been doing our jobs very well."

There was that "we" again.

"Oh, you needn't worry, we've had a bit of a look. We don't think you're working for the other side. But we do think you could work for ours."

Did this mean "we" also knew how old she was? "What sort of work?"

The major pulled a card out of the breast pocket of his tunic and handed it to her. "Tomorrow, shall we say nine in the morning? All will be explained. Oh, and don't mention this to anyone. You can tell your chum you've been offered a job in a typing pool."

"I don't type."

"Oh, we specialize in on-the-job training." With a wink, he turned to go, one hand in his pocket, the other cradling the bowl of his pipe.

Near Durban, November 1941

THE STOEP, EVEN under the shade of the long roof, was hot. Diana was thankful for a slight breeze that lifted off the fields, though it made no inroads on the humidity. The distant waters of the Indian Ocean looked almost unreal, like the blue ends of the earth, she thought. She heard her host's footsteps in the hall and readied herself. He would require handling.

Dijkman came through the screen door, letting it slam. "I've ordered some refreshment," he said as he settled his long, lean form into the chair opposite her. There was a low square table between them. "So, Fräulein Weber, you are the new girl, eh?" His German was clipped. Similar, she thought, to the English accent of the Afrikaners she had met.

"I am merely a messenger," Diana said. Her smile, she hoped, covered her loathing and wariness. He was spread out in his chair, filling space with his size and his authority.

"A very pretty little messenger."

Feeling suddenly very alone with this man, Diana calculated her ability to run to her car with him in pursuit. "You are most kind, Herr Dijkman, but if we are to make headway against the English, we must not waste time. Every time an Allied ship passes by out there unmolested, our war effort is impeded. I have brought what you need to communicate with us. Your only job is to let us know what you see and to harry their effort within this country."

Dijkman leaned back in his chair. "Ah. Here is the boy with our tea."

The "boy" was an African man, Diana noted, of at least fifty. He laid out the tea things without looking up. She wanted to thank him, but she did not want to alert her host to any sympathies uncharacteristic of a good Nazi. She gave a brief nod. The man gave an almost imperceptible nod back, and then hovered in case anything else was wanted.

Waving his hand in dismissal, Dijkman said, "You can go," in Afrikaans. He looked at Diana, appraising. "I harry the English whether you are here or not. The arrests have put us back. If I am to build a force, I will need resources. Here is a list." He handed Diana an envelope.

She opened the envelope and scanned the paper it contained, and then folded it back into the envelope. "Where are the others?"

Dijkman shrugged noncommittally. "I assure you, there are plenty who are waiting to do their patriotic duty." He leaned toward her. "We have to see what we are dealing with. *Who* we are dealing with." He sat back and nodded with a self-assured smile.

"Your caution is admirable. You're dealing with someone who will make sure you are supplied. However, while you evaluate me, British ships are getting through, the war machine is strengthened, and the power plants are humming." Diana fished in her handbag and removed a book and held it out to him. "When you have overcome your reluctance to be of use to both your own stated ends and those of the Reich, page 32. Do not use any other. You will contact me when you have a solid plan." She showed him how to use the simple code, and then stood up, looped her handbag over her left arm, and raised her right arm. "Heil Hitler. Good day, Herr Dijkman."

Without waiting for his reply, she turned and walked with deliberate slowness down the steps of the stoep and along the red dusty road to her car. When she was at the car, she turned back. Dijkman had got out of his chair and walked down two steps and was watching her, the book in hand.

"If you suspect this is some sort of test," Diana called, "it is. If you pass, I wish you luck."

"HE'S CAUTIOUS, NOT to say suspicious." Diana lit a cigarette and stood looking out at the path through the middle of the lawn. The flagstones were white in the sunlight. The safe house was a small, neat farmhouse on the side of a hill near Pretoria. "I felt that asking him too much about his compatriots at this juncture would put him on the alert. The arrest of the last lot also means they have to reorganize."

Her handler exhaled impatiently. "He may already suspect you, which will render you useless and possibly drive him underground."

"He is a man with a massively good opinion of himself. And I told him that this initial meeting is a test. He won't be able to resist showing off." She blew out a cloud of smoke and sat gracefully in the chair opposite the desk, crossing her legs and holding her cigarette away from her face. His doubt was irritating. She knew he questioned women being involved at all. "Give him a week. He will check my *bona fides* and contact me. In the meantime, I think we should work out what we'll be offering them."

"In the meantime, they'll be blowing up another railway," he said.

"If we do it my way, we'll catch them at it. But suit yourself, of course." She leaned over and stubbed her cigarette into the glass ashtray on the desk. "I can just as well go back to Blighty. I'm sure they'll find something for me to do there. In the meantime, I'm off home." She stood up, dusting her skirt.

"Sit down," her handler said. "Fine. We'll do it your way." He pulled the list toward him. "This is a ridiculous demand. We will give them a quarter of this. If the plan fails, they will use what we provide to sabotage our own war effort."

"You know, there is a whole population of people you could involve."

"What do you mean?" he snapped.

"The Africans. They hate the Boer."

"Don't be ridiculous! The Blacks couldn't manage this sort of job."

Diana raised her eyebrows. "When this war is over, the Boer will run this country. You may come to regret this waste of human potential."

"If I may be pardoned for saying so, you are naive. The Afrikaners are traitors to this country. They will be caught and punished and that will be the end of it. British rule here is unassailable. How old are you?"

"Twenty-one. What has that to do with anything?" She had been passing for twenty since she was seventeen.

"Well, that makes my point. You are too young to understand."

"But not too young to risk my life, evidently."

The handler shook his head as he watched her leave. Tremaine had been wrong about this one. Clever, to be sure, but too confident. Too stupid to know what she didn't know. It irked him that she clearly was someone who would not be told. He sighed and pulled some papers forward. It would, of course, all end in disaster. She would make a fatal mistake and cost them time and resources. At least he would have the satisfaction of having warned them.

CHAPTER TWELVE

"**C**AN YOU GIVE ME A list of his friends' names, perhaps people he served with overseas, especially any who live, or lived, in this area? Perhaps school chums who signed up when he did? At this point, we have to cover every angle." Darling sat, notebook in hand, while Mrs. Robinson clasped her hands together, fingers fidgeting.

The usual operator of the notebook, Ames, was wandering around the room looking at photographs, and working his way toward the mantelpiece. Mrs. Robinson eyed him warily and brought her gaze back to Darling.

"Well, I don't know, really. It's been years, hasn't it? There was Billy. I think they went together. I didn't want him to sign up, but he ignored me, went on his own. That's Billy there." She pointed at a yellowing photo of two boys sitting in a rowboat, both holding the sides and grinning as if they were going to rock it to tip it over. "I told Ben I didn't want him over to the house. God knows who his people were. The MacDonalds. Complete riff-raff."

Ames, who'd been almost at the mantelpiece, took the photo off the bookshelf and brought it over.

"They were about eight years old then, I think. Inseparable. I didn't approve of the friendship. Billy was a real hellion. Wrong side of the tracks, I'd have said. Very strange family. He had a sister that was no better than she should be, as my mother used to say. Any trouble my Ben got into was Billy's fault all through the years. I expect he's the one who pushed Ben to sign up. That's Ben there," she said, pointing at one of the boys. His hair was short and looked as though it had been glued to his head with brilliantine. Billy's hair flew in all directions. "But in the end, Ben had the last laugh, didn't he? He came home with a medal. Billy never did come home."

Ames went to the mantel and picked up the case with the medal in it. "This one?" he asked, holding it out to her.

"That's right," she said, taking it and looking at it wistfully. "He was so brave. He got it rescuing several men who were under heavy fire. Including that wastrel, Billy. Poor fellow probably died of his wounds." She said this as if his death were because of his own bad management.

Darling held out his hand. "May I see?" The silver medal, featuring a shield and military helmets but not the familiar figure of George V, had a ribbon of red and blue, and was pillowed in a bed of satin. "May I take it out of the box?"

Mrs. Robinson looked puzzled, then flustered. "Oh, I've never had it out of the box. Ben said I mustn't because the air will tarnish it. It's silver, you know." She leaned forward anxiously, in what seemed tacit approval, and watched as Darling unhooked the clasp that held the lid.

"We won't have it out for long." Darling pulled the medal carefully from the box, turned it over to show the victory wreath on the back, and then looked at the edge. "Three one nine eight six," he read aloud. The last number he wasn't sure about. A six? An eight? Ames, who was standing behind Mrs. Robinson, had pulled out his own notebook and now made a note of the numbers. Some of the other engraving had worn off, Darling noticed. There should be the recipient's unit and initials, or first initial and last name. He ran his finger around the edge, and then carefully replaced the medal into its satin bed and arranged the ribbon.

"You must be very proud," he said, handing it back.

At the threshold he turned back to Arden's mother. "Do you know either a Timothy Varden or Jessica Spinks?"

Frowning, Mrs. Robinson shook her head. "No. Should I?"

"They invited your son to their wedding last year."

"SHE'S DELUDED, SIR," Ames remarked as they bumped back onto the main road into town.

"All mothers are deluded," Darling said, but perhaps it was the bitter prospect of returning to an empty house speaking. "That's an odd-looking medal for the Great War. Most featured the King. I want you to find out whom that number belongs to. It was difficult to see if the last number was a six or an eight because it was worn away, as was most of the rest of the information."

Ames glanced at Darling. "Worn away? How so? It's been sitting in its comfortable little cloth-lined box since the war. It should look brand new still."

"Very good, Sergeant. It was relatively skilfully done. Made to look natural." Darling perched his right arm on the window ledge. "He's run away from the army, bags himself a medal, and alters it to look like it's his—or at least removes any trace of its original owner. Then he manages to get back to Canada unmolested, marries, and becomes an exemplary husband and father. Then, after a considerable length of time—beginning last October, say when he stops depositing his paycheque—he starts to drain the bank account. At some point he possibly takes up with an old flame, Philippa Bentley, though, meeting her husband, I'd say she might well have left him for her own good reasons. Then, a couple of nights ago, he climbs into his little boat with a backpack and a revolver. What does this suggest to you?"

"That all is not as it seems, sir?"

"Your perspicacity astounds me."

Undeterred, Ames added, "You forgot that he maybe goes to a wedding, or at least gets an invitation to go, from people his wife has never heard of."

"Yes," Darling said thoughtfully. "Or his mother, though that doesn't mean much. Get Terrell to track down the happy couple, Timothy and Jessica Varden, and find out how they know Arden. If not them, the bride's mother, Mrs. Spinks. She likely ordered the invitations."

"Sir."

Silence reigned for a few miles and then Ames spoke again. "Now that you're a bit of a straw widower, sir, my mother says you can come any time and have dinner with us."

"Thank Mrs. Ames for me. Unfortunately, I've been left in charge of a garden, and I only have the hours at the end of the day to tend to it." It was the best he could offer as an excuse, but then with a sinking feeling he realized it was true.

"Good for you, sir. Though you don't really seem like the gardening type."

"I'll thank you, sergeant, to keep your personal observations to yourself."

Passchendaele, June 1917

FRANCINE WENT TO her tent and sat on the cot, rubbing her forehead. Her abiding feeling was shame. She felt one of her headaches coming on. She lay back and closed her eyes. She tried to remember the last day she'd had peace of mind. Maybe back in Canada when she'd heard that he'd signed up. That had meant he wouldn't be coming around, that she would be rid of him and his constant wheedling. Toward the end she had begun to feel he might threaten her if he didn't get what he wanted. But to her shame, she knew it wasn't just him. They were bad for each other. Always had been. It had been a shock to see him sitting there, waiting for someone to fix his shoulder.

How had she fallen for him at all? How had she allowed herself to be overwhelmed with waves of unfamiliar physical yearning? God almighty, he'd still been a boy, really. The surprise of seeing him, that sly suggestive smile of his inducing a wave of fear and desire. She sat up again abruptly. It didn't matter anymore. She couldn't change what happened. She couldn't take the risk that Ben would keep his mouth shut. She knew what he was like. Impulsive. She'd given

Ben what he wanted—no, she supposed that wasn't fair; it had taken both of them. Now look where she was.

Christmas 1916

FRANCINE STOOD AGAINST the wall of the mess, a tin mug of champagne in her hand. There had been enough in the way of tins of cake and biscuits and chocolate sent to the nursing sisters that they had decided to dress up their usual rations with these gifts of food and invite a few of the Canadian officers. No one had sent her anything, and she felt vaguely dishonest taking part. The officers had duly arrived with bottles of champagne. How could they always get what they wanted? The nursing sisters certainly couldn't, not even things they needed for their work. Only seven officers had arrived, but they brought their batmen, which made up the numbers and gave the gathering a slightly raucous atmosphere that she felt shut out of. She watched them, intent on enjoying themselves, flirting with the sisters. Even under the gimlet eye of both Matron and their commanding officer, Major Richard Renshaw, they took liberties. She could hear giggles and male laughter.

She looked into her mug and gulped back the remains. She was tired and wanted to go to bed, but she didn't want to upset Betsy, who was having a good time by all appearances. She put her cup on the edge of the table and crossed her arms in front of her. The pretense of a good time did not take away or diminish the horror of their work. She almost wished they were at work, all mental energy extinguished but that required to tend to the wounded.

She didn't want to think about anything. That's when she saw him watching her—Renshaw, the commanding officer about whom she'd heard nothing but bad things. Men told her, laughing sometimes, desperate at others, about his ferocity and unbending sense of discipline. She looked across at him for a moment, wondering what kind of man made people feel like that, and their eyes locked. She looked away quickly, something inside her rising and sinking at the same time, as if a curtain had been momentarily pulled open on her own fate. The mess felt hot, and she wanted to go out and feel the icy winter air cool her face. She had just turned toward the door when he was beside her.

"You don't appear to enjoy this any more than I do," he said. He stood stiffly, one hand holding a bottle, but his other arm behind his back, as if he were a particularly correct waiter. He held up the bottle and reached for her abandoned mug.

She sighed and took the mug. "Thank you." Looking out at the laughing group, she said, "It doesn't change anything, does it? The Boche are still going to hammer us, and we're still going to be covered in blood by the end of the day."

She was surprised to see a smile flit across his face. He lifted his own drink. "To devotion to duty." The smile was gone as quickly as it appeared. "You are from somewhere near Nelson. I know of your family."

"I am sorry." It had been a pale attempt at sarcasm. She found herself unable to make out how to talk to this man.

"Why? They seem quite respectable."

She almost snorted. "Respectable? They're bohemian

to the core, all a bit unconventional, I'm afraid, and I'm the sorry result. The only one with any sense is my brother Billy, and he doesn't like me at all. Anyway, most of them are dead except my grandmother."

Renshaw had a sudden sense of unease at her words, at the mouth that said them, at the blue eyes that looked at him for only a moment, and then away. He could feel his face redden. He wanted to turn away, to leave her. He felt vaguely out of control. He put down his own mug, as if it might be to blame. Of course, she was wrong. He would put her right on that, at least. He had a fleeting thought that she was like a child and needed care.

"William MacDonald. He is in my command. He is a good soldier."

At the far side of the room someone began to play a waltz on the upright piano that had not seen a tuner for some time. An accordion joined in. They struggled unsuccessfully together for a common pitch. Couples began to dance. Renshaw put up his arm.

"Do you dance, Lieutenant MacDonald?"

"I'm surprised you do. If you like my brother, I assure you, you cannot possibly like me. I would reconsider, if I were you."

But he had taken her hand, put his arm around her waist, and led her around the dance floor. Someone had dropped a glass, and she became aware that his officers were watching him, astonished.

"You are very lovely, Lieutenant." He said this awkwardly, as if he'd been coached by someone. "I'm sorry you don't get along with your brother. We must fix that."

"I'm sure I'm not the first person who does not get on with a brother. It is of no consequence, really."

"It is of every consequence. I have an elder brother. We are loyal to each other because we are family. Family loyalty is surely the greatest virtue."

Francine felt a wave of sadness and exhaustion. Billy was certainly not loyal to her, nor, if the truth be known, she to him. She was there even now, being rude about him to his commanding officer. "I'm sorry. I'm being very offhand. I'm tired, I think."

His response was to press his guiding hand more firmly into her back, and she felt a jolt, her breath faltering. He leaned in and almost whispered, "I could look after you. Get you out of this."

Was it the exhaustion, the hopelessness of the endless stream of broken men her days were filled with? The unending struggle to keep a sense of independence from her brother? She felt at that moment that being looked after was the most desirable thing in the world. It almost overwhelmed her. She leaned into him, and felt his sigh encompass her whole being.

July 1917

THEY WERE TO be married in less than a month. She stared down at her writing box. She wanted to write her usual sort of letter, not confess that she and Ben had briefly become lovers again. She shuddered at the thought of what saying that would result in. No, maybe not that they were ever lovers. She could just say that she knew him before, back home. She had to say something. But her fiancé would wonder why she bothered telling him that. Would he guess there was something more?

The whole idea of her even having a fiancé had become somehow distant, with the scramble of her own work and the fact that she hadn't seen him for months. That was no excuse for her behaviour, she knew. She almost wavered, decided against saying anything, but the danger of Ben telling Renshaw, especially now, was too great. He could be crazy, Ben, if he lost his temper or got drunk or something. Or he could tell any chum of his. Anything would be better than this gnawing fear of what Renshaw might do if he heard it from one of his own men As it was, she didn't trust Ben not to gloat about it with his fellow soldiers. Renshaw would hear it sooner or later that way. It was amazing, she thought, how longing and fear felt so little different, one from the other.

She took out a piece of writing paper and placed it, with the small bottle of ink and the pen, on the closed lid of the box. Before she had time to change her mind, she opened the ink bottle and dipped the nib into it. She would not give it to him until they were married. "My dear, there is something I must tell you..."

DARLING ATE HIS lunch at his desk instead of with Ames and Terrell in the café. He was surprised to realize that he didn't feel like company. If he was going to be alone, he might as jolly well be alone. His bottle of Coke half gone and the ham and cheese sandwich dispatched, he was surprised that pining had not made a dent in his appetite.

Where were they with the missing Ben Arden? He moved the bottle aside and brought his pad of foolscap to rest in front of him and took up one of his perfectly sharpened pencils. The case reminded him of an overgrown pot of chrysanthemums. It had started out as a missing call and had exploded into a bouquet of contradictory views of the man himself and his behaviour. A possible blackmailing effort, or a suicide bid, an AWOL from the Great War, theft, adultery...could murder be far behind?

With a sense of his own silliness, he drew a pot of flowers on the paper and began to label each bloom with a possible aspect of the case. He drew frowning eyebrows on each flower for good measure. He gazed at his inexpert handiwork and threw his pencil down with a sigh. So, this is what pining did to him. He was about to turn and look out at Elephant Mountain when his phone rang, making him jump.

Seizing the handset, he barked, "Yes?"

"Dalton, sir."

"The mayor? Put him through."

"No, sir. He wants you over there in person."

DARLING, IRRITATED AND filled with trepidation, was issued into the mayor's office. Last time he'd made the trip, his career had very nearly ended. He wondered now what fresh horror was in store for him.

"Ah, Darling. Sit. No, no, don't worry, you're not here to be raked over. Listen, I've had a visit from Dominic Renshaw. You know the name. Mining outfit. Big contributors to civic life. Apparently his long-missing sister-in-law has been found outside of London somewhere in a bombed house.

She's called"—here the mayor peered down at some notes he'd scribbled—"Mrs. Francine Renshaw. He's putting rather a lot of pressure on me to have someone go over to look into it. I don't know why exactly. This Mrs. Renshaw obviously isn't the first Canadian to die overseas."

"She must have been the wife of Major Richard Renshaw, who was the commanding officer of the man who's gone missing. Our current case sir. A small world. As I understand it, our missing man and his commanding officer were on the same patrol and were ambushed. Nearly everyone was lost. My missing man was presumed dead by his regiment, but he's been living here quite comfortably since the end of the war, it seems."

"Very small world. Of course, when all is said and done, Nelson is a small town. People are bound to be connected in one way or another."

Darling began to wonder why he was in the mayor's office for what was beginning to feel like a chat. "Wasn't there a Renshaw on council at one time? I seem to recall him when I first came here."

"That's right. They are a sort of founding family. Fading a bit, but can still pack a punch, so I'd like to get this resolved. He's a bit difficult to deal with."

"How does this involve me?" Darling asked.

"As I understand it, Francine was one of two nursing sisters from Nelson to go over to France during the Great War, only she never returned. Her husband, Major Renshaw—that'll be Dominic Renshaw's brother—died in battle, and she just disappeared. Now Dominic Renshaw wants this looked into, personally. I'm not able to go over."

"I still don't see why anyone has to go all that way," protested Darling.

"I suspect there might be some sort of scandal about the whole thing. At a guess, he wants it tidied up and put to bed without the involvement of the papers. He says there were rumours at the time that upset his parents."

"What sort of rumours?"

"I don't know, do I? He said his parents were horrified by the marriage because the woman was a bit bohemian. That covers a multitude of sins. He wouldn't say more. Just that he wants someone over there. He found out about the discovery of the body from a British paper he gets. Didn't I hear your wife has gone over to Blighty? You could get this sorted and then join her for a holiday." He attempted a winning smile. "I'm sure you're owed one."

Darling, who had indeed begun to see the benefits of such a trip, said, "By the time I get there, I'm afraid she might be on her way home."

"You won't be lounging about on the *Queen Mary*, Darling. You'll have to fly. Bloody awful expense, but there you are. I'll authorize it. You can go get more details from Renshaw. Retired out to their farm near Slocan."

FARM DID NOT adequately describe the palatial house at the end of a very elegant treed drive. Darling stopped on the curved driveway near the front steps and looked across at a pristine lawn and the burgeoning spring growth in the flower beds surrounding the house. If Renshaw lived here on his own, he was certainly not letting the place go to seed. The front door was opened by a young woman in a white apron and a lace cap who gave a little bob.

"He's expecting you, sir. Through there in his study." She held out a hand for his hat and placed it on a table near a coat rack.

Renshaw's study looked out onto the lawn, and beyond it a bank of trees and then the river. It was darkly panelled and full of books. He expected to see a large desk dominating the room, but the desk was small and near a glass-front bookshelf full of what appeared to be war memorabilia. Darling could see photos of stiff men in uniform, a battered silver box, and several medal displays.

"Ah, Inspector Darling. Come in. Thank you, Bella, you may go. It's a fine morning, so I suggest we sit in these chairs and look out at the garden."

Renshaw was tall and slender, though a slight stoop to his shoulders revealed his age in spite of his military bearing. Darling wondered if it was the moustache that gave the impression of his being military. Renshaw indicated a pair of wingback chairs facing out toward the window onto the lawn. There was a small, dark wine table between them.

"Can I get you something?" Renshaw asked, waiting for Darling to sit before he himself did.

"No, thank you. You have a splendid view here," Darling said.

"Thank you. I'm the only one who sees it nowadays. Wife's gone. Son out in Victoria. Now then, thank you for coming out. It's..." Renshaw stopped and shifted in his chair, turning his gaze back to the window. "It's a delicate matter. It needs to be discreetly handled."

"Can you tell me about it? I only know that the remains of your sister-in-law have been discovered outside London somewhere, and that you'd like someone to look into the matter."

"It's an overlong story, Inspector. I'll say this much: She was serving as a nursing sister in France, she and my brother married there in 1917, and shortly afterward my brother was killed during a scouting mission. I had had a letter from him saying he was sending her home…" Here he paused again. "Sending her home. Nursing sisters could not be married. Only she never came, and then she vanished off the face of the earth. She was, er, with child. My late mother…well, that's not important. The important thing is that we tried every imaginable avenue to locate her, and it really was as if she'd completely disappeared. There were circumstances, but in the end we couldn't find her, so we assumed the business was finished. And now, after all this time, I read about it in the *Times* over my morning coffee. That she'd been found, I mean. Of course, I get the paper a couple of weeks late, so this discovery was presumably made earlier in the month."

"Have you been in touch with the authorities in England?"

"Yes." He paused again and looked down at his clasped hands. "Yes, I…I spoke with a Chief Inspector Sims at Scotland Yard. I asked if she could be buried in a Canadian cemetery over there and have done. He said that unfortunately it appears she'd been shot, and he's having to leave it open as a cold case." He turned to Darling. "I want someone over there on the ground with enough clout to move the business along and bury her decently. I really can't have this drawn out, risk more exposure in the papers. My brother had a distinguished military career, Inspector. He fought in the Boer War and even as a sergeant was decorated. I don't want his memory tarnished. Dalton said I could trust you."

Darling took a deep breath and tried to marshal his thoughts. Trust me to what, exactly? "I am in the middle of a case, Mr. Renshaw. I wonder that there needs to be such secrecy and urgency. I beg your pardon, I understand she is your sister-in-law, and you'd like it sorted out. But why not let the police take care of their end? That way you may discover what the circumstances of her death were."

Springing from his chair, Renshaw positioned himself close to the window with his back to Darling. "No, that's out of the question. She was my brother's wife; she did her patriotic duty, after all. She needs to have a decent burial so the book can finally be closed."

Does he want to involve me in some sort of cover-up? Darling wondered. "I think, sir, that you should tell me everything. I can see that you'd like the business concluded, but I can understand Chief Inspector Sims's point of view. He has a murder on his hands. He cannot just bury the victim and forget about it."

Renshaw wheeled on him. "I don't see why not. They'll never find who killed her after all these years." He shook his head. "But, of course, you're right. I should tell you what I can. Then you can help. Perhaps if they understood the circumstances..." He moved to a cupboard and opened it, revealing a small liquor cabinet, well stocked with bottles and glasses, and pulled the cork off a bottle of whisky. "Drink?"

Darling shook his head.

Renshaw splashed some whisky into his glass and walked back. He stopped for a moment as if undecided about something and then sat down. "Look, Darling, what I tell you can go no further."

"I can't absolutely promise that. I'm sure you understand."

"No, no, I do see, of course. But once you understand, you will see what I mean. It's like this: My brother was a career soldier. Splendid man." He waved toward the cupboard with the medals. "Got every medal going and sent most of them home to me. He didn't like a fuss made for what he considered just his job. He married the woman in the middle of the bloody war, in what I can only assume was a moment of madness. He discovered very quickly she was not the sort of woman who could make him happy. She grew up outside of Nelson and came from a fairly well-known family, not to say, as I soon discovered, infamous. Unfortunately, we did not know the family when we were young, but if he'd known more about her, he would have reconsidered. She was, I guess it's called 'bohemian,' in her ways. Not at all the right woman. Absolutely without social scruples might be more accurate. They were separated almost immediately after the wedding for some months. She should have been sent home then and there because she was married, but circumstances were bad at the front and she stayed on. She was pregnant. Not"—he cleared his throat—"not, I'm afraid, with her husband's child."

"How did he know this?"

"She wrote him, begged for his forgiveness. He was dismayed, of course, but there was a war on, and he was a major. He hadn't time for this sort of nonsense. He wrote me that he was sending her home, and I received the terrible news shortly afterward that he'd died in an ambush during a scouting sortie. Needless to say, she never made an appearance."

"I see. Have you told Chief Inspector Sims this information?"

"No, of course not. It will only make matters worse. That's why I need you over there. Persuade them that the case is too old. How are they going to find her killer after all this time?"

"Mr. Renshaw, I cannot understand why you wouldn't want the killer identified. And I can't go off to England to subvert the course of justice I think you are best to leave it to the police. Tell them about your concerns. Ask them not to let the papers get hold of it, if at all possible—that at least is fair—and await the outcome." He stood up. "I have a missing persons case I must get on with. Please let me know if there is anything more I can be of assistance with."

"EVERYTHING ALL RIGHT, sir?" O'Brien asked as Darling slammed into the station.

"No, Sergeant, it is not. What the hell is the matter with people?" Leaving this unanswerable question in the air, Darling made his way upstairs. He was about to shout, "Ames, where are we?" when his telephone rang.

"Yes?"

"The mayor, sir."

Now what? "Put him through."

"Darling, I'm disappointed."

Contemplating a response of "Me too," Darling said instead, "Sir?"

"Renshaw is not at all happy with the outcome of your visit. Now, you're going, and that's final."

Taking a deep breath, Darling said, "It's a waste of my time, sir, and your money. I know Chief Inspector Sims who's handling this case, and he's excellent. I recommend it be left in his hands."

"So much the better if you know the man. I've had my secretary arrange everything. You'll be leaving day after tomorrow. That leaves you the day to put whatever you're working on into the hands of Sergeant Ames and that Constable What's His Name."

"Terrell, sir. Constable Terrell."

"That's right. Don't bother objecting. You're going."

DARLING'S IRRITATED MOOD was again interrupted by the phone. "A long-distance call is being put through, sir, from England. Hang up and I'll send it on."

Lane! His heart did a little somersault. He stared at his phone expectantly and then looked at his watch and counted. It would be a little after eight in the evening there, assuming Scottish time was the same as English time. He imagined the scene: supper finished, Lane, Diana, and their grandparents sitting around the fire reading or chatting. He'd got some knitting needles into her grandmother's hands when the phone jangled again.

He picked up the receiver and said, "Hello!" Only to encounter the operator saying, "One moment, please."

More than one moment passed. Finally, a clicking sound

and a male voice saying, "Inspector Darling?"

Darling, his hopes dashed, cast an accusing look at the instrument and said, "Yes, this is he," in what he realized at once was an unnecessarily short tone. It also was dawning on him that he vaguely recognized the voice of the caller, but he could not draw the memory forward.

"Ah. Good. Chief Inspector Sims, Scotland Yard. You may remember me."

Of course! Darling sat forward. You're hardly likely to forget someone who charges you with murder and, as far as he was concerned at the time, interrogates you more than absolutely necessary. "Yes, of course, sir. Congratulations, by the way. Weren't you a mere inspector the last time we talked?" He had almost fond memories of Sims now because he'd been an honest policeman and had seen in the end that there was something very wrong with the charges laid against Darling. Then, for a wild and terrifying moment, he wondered if Sims was calling to tell him something had happened to Lane. But, of course, it wouldn't be that. It would be about the beastly Renshaw business.

"Good memory, Darling. Thank you. Listen, long distance and all that. I'll get right to it. I was told you'd be on your way, and I wanted to tell you how pleased I am. I think you know we have discovered the remains of a young woman in a bombed-out farmhouse outside of London, in Kent. The new property owners were clearing out the rubble to rebuild, and there it was. Our coroner tells us the victim was shot and left in the house as long ago as thirty years."

His irrational worry that something had happened to Lane dispelled, Darling said, "Yes, I have been told of it, and I feel I must apologize in advance. I'm being sent over quite against my will. I will try not to interfere."

"Oh, not to worry. I've got a lot on. If there's anything you can do to help, I'm grateful."

"How did you know the identity of the woman, by the way?"

"Leather satchel found under her head. Been lying there since the Great War. Turned out it's one of your lot. A young woman from Nelson, British Columbia."

"HE'S A LITTLE moody today," Ames observed, drinking the last of his coffee. "Should we bring anything back for O'Brien?"

"I don't think so, sir. I believe his wife keeps him pretty well supplied," Terrell said. O'Brien came into work each morning with an enormous metal lunch box that always contained several fat sandwiches, a Thermos of tea, and some sort of cookie or scone. It reminded Terrell of the lunches his mother used to pack when he went to school. He had a flash of memory of his excitement at opening his lunch box every day to see what it contained.

Terrell himself was not moody, exactly, but rather subdued. April McAvity, who usually dished up their breakfast and lunch, was off in Vancouver, attending a course at the Police Academy for a couple of months. Her replacement, Marge, was a woman of a certain age with a voice like a dragon with phlegm. She stood no nonsense and didn't smile, apparently as a matter of policy. He missed April more than he liked to admit to himself.

"What are you up to now? I've got to get hold of the

army to find out about that serial number on the medal. Can you imagine stealing someone's medal and calling it yours?" Ames was indignant.

"No, sir, I really can't." Terrell couldn't. The very thought appalled him. If there was one thing service in the armed forces should instill, it was a sense of honour. Someone had fought, sacrificed, perhaps saved others, and someone else—in fact, someone who had run away—had tried to steal the glory. "Right after lunch, I'm going to take the invitation Arden got to the printer, and then I'll see about the couple who sent it."

Ames lifted his chin in acknowledgement and then said, "Why bother with the printer? Why not just go straight to the couple? They know the guy."

"Yes, it is probable that would be enough, but I'm curious about one aspect of the card. I happened by the window of the printer and saw various samples of wedding invitations on display, and none had a number on the bottom. I just want to satisfy myself that that might be something to do with the number of people invited. If that is the case, it would potentially increase the number of people who knew Arden and could tell us something."

"Didn't you say that number was two hundred? That's an awful lot of people to have at a wedding, and way too many to interview."

"I thought the same thing, sir."

Ames got up, depositing some coins on the table. "Well, fortune speed your inquiries. I'll be hanging on the telephone all afternoon waiting to find out about that medal, no doubt."

"GOOD AFTERNOON. AM I speaking with Marisa Fairfax?" Lane was in the hallway, leaning against the wall. She knew her grandparents were listening hopefully in the sitting room. It had not been difficult to get the number.

"Yes, who is calling please?" The voice sounded young and slightly airy, which gave it a tentative quality.

"How do you do, Miss Fairfax. My name is Lane Winslow—"

"Oh! My goodness! Diana's sister. She told me so much about you. Where are you calling from? I understood you live in Canada."

"I do, yes, but I'm visiting our grandparents in Scotland." She wondered what Diana had told her friend about her. "Listen, I'm sorry to ring you out of the blue like this, but you wouldn't know where Diana is just at the moment, would you?"

Marisa Fairfax uttered a little breathy "Oh," and then paused.

"I understood she went to South Africa with you before the war, so I wondered if you were still in touch."

Marisa seemed to finally find words. "You see, I've been back since last autumn. Diana decided to stay on because she said there was still work to be done."

"What sort of work?" Lane asked this before she could stop herself. In spite of Diana's evident secrecy, the idea of her sister working at anything was still strange to her.

"I'm afraid I can't say." The breathiness was gone and replaced with something steely.

"Of course." There was no point in alienating the girl, though she wanted to reach down the telephone line and grab her by the collar and demand answers. Keeping her voice pleasant, she said, "Diana was here, in Scotland, and then she went off a couple of weeks ago to visit friends and seems to have disappeared. Would you know the names of the friends in Aberdeen she might be visiting?" Lane was beginning to realize this was hopeless. If what she suspected was true, and this girl was in on it, she'd get nothing. And quite rightly, she reminded herself, only now that she was confronted with this enforced War Office secrecy herself, it was utterly exasperating. She had begun to think of whom she might approach in government circles when Marisa spoke.

"Aberdeen?" She sounded surprised. "She was here for a bit over a week, ten days, I think. I don't know anything about Aberdeen. She seemed quite busy getting in touch with old friends. At least that's what she said." She was silent for some long moments and then spoke with more resolve. "Alex Tremaine, maybe. Look, it's all I can tell you. I hope you find her."

"Thank y—" Lane began, but the line went dead.

"Well, that was just about a bust," Lane said, throwing herself onto the sofa next to her grandmother. "She was...secretive, I guess the word is. Diana was with her for more than a week, apparently using her time to connect with 'old friends.' I can't think what sort of old friends, since she was away for the whole war. Miss Fairfax seemed...I don't know...a bit cagey. She seemed very surprised at my mention of Aberdeen. She abruptly gave me a man's name and then hung up. I shall follow it up tomorrow. I do hope Diana's not in some sort of trouble."

Ganf was dozing in his chair. "Secretive," her grandmother said quietly. "I'd say that Diana had that about her as well. She reminded me a good deal of your father. I put it down to a sort of family resemblance; you know how children can adopt the mannerisms of a parent. But perhaps it goes further than that. Your father used to drop you two off sometimes, when he hadn't sent you with the coachman, be as charming as can be through tea or supper, and then say, 'Well, I must be off. I have business in Archangel, or Petersburg,' or whatever they're calling it now. I don't know why he bothered pretending; we all knew." She folded her hands and gazed at the fire. "I remember when he first came and swept your poor mother off her feet, he told us he worked for the government, but never said what he really did. That was just before the Great War. He'd disappear for ages and then come back without a word of where he'd been. It surprised me, I must say, that he wasn't enlisted, an able young man like that. As the years went by, he remained secretive but became somehow harder. I don't think he ever really knew how to be social in the normal way with people, to start with. He'd come back from wherever he'd been, full of charm and presents, but it was as if he was pretending to behave as he thought normal people must behave. I think your poor mother's death in '26 was the final straw for him. He got more silent and brooding than ever, and he certainly hadn't the first foggy clue what to do with a couple of little girls." She lifted her shoulders in a great sigh and stared at the fire, the light of the flames animating her face. "That's exactly what Diana was like just now. 'Must dash, won't be gone long.' I'd say she's up to the same sort of thing."

Lane nodded. She'd already reached that conclusion. Her grandmother saying it out loud somehow confirmed it. She turned to her grandmother. 'Did she say a time she'd be back? How many days? Because I think that might be important. It will be all the difference between something small being amiss or her being in some sort of trouble."

"Oh, dear. You know, I don't think she did. Just that she'd be back soon, or at least wouldn't be gone long. She might have said something to Fiona. We can ask tomorrow." She shook her head, gazing at her husband. "Look at him. Such brave words about wanting to sit up and wait to see what you learned from that friend of Diana. Let's get him off to bed."

"Would you mind if I tried to call Frederick? I think he'd be about getting home now."

"No, you must!" her grandmother said. "Give him our love."

But there was no answer. Darling must still be on his way home. Lane lay awake long into the night, turning her mind back to her childhood. She had never spoken with her grandmother about the effects of her father's behaviour on them. Her childhood had just been what it was: stressful days in the care of their father and glorious days when they were handed off to her grandparents. Now she could see how important her grandmother's love had been to her own ability to love.

Her sister, though, had been closer to their father, had wanted to be like him. And now this. If her sister was in intelligence, how had she got there? And if it had started with the war, what was she doing now that the war was over? Her eyes flew open and she stared at the darkness that was the ceiling above her. If she had started during the war, she would have still been in her teens! Of course, she was behaving like a grown-up woman at sixteen, so she could have fooled people into thinking she was older. She turned onto her side, staring into the darkness. There the two of them were, following in their father's footsteps. It was hard to imagine it for Diana, in spite of her worship of their father. Flighty, haughty, spoiled, comfort-loving Diana. But she was equipped with the same skills Lane had, including a perfect facility for languages. And Diana was fearless. Much more than she was herself. Her sister could have thrown herself into a life of espionage without any sense of the danger, the way very young soldiers threw themselves at war, believing they were immortal.

The trouble with youth is that while one is fearless, one lacks any real judgment. Whatever Diana was doing, if she had expected it to take only a few days, she could be in danger. If the work had merely taken longer than she anticipated, Diana would have contacted her grandparents, Lane was sure of it. With a sinking heart, Lane knew absolutely that something was amiss. Spies kept the outer veneer of their civilian life organized. Nothing to see here! She had told her grandparents when she'd be back days ago. Something was definitely wrong. She could see already that, to find Diana, Lane might have to go back into a maelstrom of the old life she thought she'd left behind forever.

"DICK FRENCH," THE printer said, shaking Terrell's hand. He was standing behind the counter in the tidy, cheerful front room of the shop, where customers would leave or pick up their orders. There were two scrapbooks of card and announcement samples on the long counter, with an old-fashioned brass cash register at the other end. A long shelf behind the counter held samples of paper stock, a few catalogues from type foundries and ink suppliers, and some books on printing.

"Bill must have done these. Bill MacDonald, my assistant. It's funny," French said, looking at the invitation proffered by Terrell. "You're right to ask about this number. We don't usually put numbers like this on invitations. Let me have a look at some of the overruns. We usually print a larger number than we need in case things go wrong. They should still be around somewhere." He disappeared through a door into a back room, and then returned with two cards. "Here's what we would have printed up. As you see, no number on the bottom. He did these on the iron hand press, on this fancier paper. We do most of our other work on the vertical platen press. I can show you, if you like."

Terrell was ushered into the back room, which was stuffed to the rafters with paper, equipment, cramped workspaces, and three different sorts of presses. It would have been hard for Terrell to point to anything that looked remotely familiar to him.

"Wow," he said, and meant it.

"It is pretty tight." The printer smiled and shrugged. "Anyway, I can't see the point of adding a number like that to a card like this. They were done on this press here." He pointed at a press that looked to Terrell like old pictures in his school books of the Gutenberg press, except that it was made of iron instead of wood. "If you come over here, I'll show you an example of how we set up the letters and so on." He held up a rectangular iron frame that contained several lines of type in the centre. The type was held in place by strips of wood all around it, with what appeared to be metal wedges at the bottom and one side. "I won't bore you with all the names, but you see here? If I wanted to add something to this, like that number two hundred at the bottom," he said, laying the forme down on the flat surface of a table and picking up a T-shaped tool, "I'd loosen the wedges—we call them *quoins*—with this key, take out these two pieces of wooden furniture from the chase, replace them with the line with the numbers, and tighten up these quoins again. Then it would just be a matter of inking the thing and printing it. It looks to me like that's what happened here."

"I see what you mean. The numbers don't look different from the rest of the invitation."

"No, exactly. He used Caslon here, that's the typeface, because it's attractive for this sort of thing. And he'd have to have done this immediately after the run, before the chase was dismantled. We set all our jobs by hand, so he'd certainly not go to the trouble of resetting the whole thing. I'll have to have a word with Bill when he gets back. I already had a complaint from the vicar about a notice we printed up for him. Wrong time. That'll be Bill too."

"We have that church poster as well. Where's he gone?"

"On holiday. He has people in Alberta somewhere. Should be back next Monday. Before you go, let me show you the type case. It'll give you a better idea." French led Terrell to a frame of shallow drawers, one of which was resting on the top of the frame.

"This is the case of Caslon type Bill used for the job."

Terrell looked with interest at the case, divided into three sections, each section further divided into dozens of little boxes, and each box glinting with small metal pieces.

"Every one of these boxes holds a letter, or number or what have you. Each letter in a piece of printing has to be separately picked up and set into lines of type, like in this invitation."

Terrell, both bewildered and impressed by the finicky requirements of printing even a simple invitation, asked, "What happens if you run out of a letter?"

French flashed him a smile. "Well, each of these pieces is called a 'sort.' If you're missing one, you're definitely 'out of sorts'!"

"That's where that saying comes from?"

"That, and 'Mind your p's and q's.'"

"Well, how about that? Live and learn," Terrell said.

Once back in the front of the shop, Terrell asked, "How long has Bill worked here?"

"MacDonald? I hired him about three years ago. He'd been apprenticed to a printer in England after the Great War, and he knew how to use the old iron press, which I'm not so good at, as well as the regular platen press, so I was saved all the trouble of training. And it meant we could expand our work. We've done a few vanity books of poetry, for example. A small run for a local poet."

"He's English? MacDonald, I mean."

"No, no, Canadian. From right around here, in fact; he decided to stay on after the Great War. Married an English girl and didn't bring her back the way most of 'em did. When she died, he said there was nothing there for him, so he came back. Here, let me check on the original order for this job." French went to a wooden file cabinet and fished through tightly packed files until he found what he wanted. He pulled out the file, which was thick with orders, leafed through it, and found what he was looking for.

"Yup. Here it is. Spinks, the vicar of the Anglican church, up the hill there. Forty ordered, text wanted right here, you see? No two hundred."

Terrell wasn't looking at the text. He was looking at the address on Ward Street. He reached into his pocket and pulled out the envelope. The return address was not on Ward. It was up on Trevor Street. "You're sure about this address?" he asked.

"Definitely. We sent the invoice there and a cheque came back promptly."

"Hmm. It's not the same as the return address written on this envelope. May I copy the address you have?"

He might as well check with the Spinkses, so he made his way to the address French had given him, which was just up the hill. No answer. He pulled out the envelope and looked at the return address: 45 Trevor Street. He'd better find out from O'Brien where that was. He returned thoughtfully to the police station, feeling slightly out of sorts himself.

AMES, TRUE TO his prediction, had had a very long wait indeed for a return call from the Princess Pats. They were able to tell him that the soldier he named, Benjamin Arden, had been presumed dead; however, his body was never found. A telegram saying he was missing was sent after the war. Ames thanked him and was about to say goodbye when he asked, "Would he have won any sort of citation or medal?"

The man on the other end was silent for a moment. "I've just read through what we have. No record of any medal, but several references to discipline issues. It looks like he spent a couple of nights in detention. What's this about? Has he surfaced?"

"Benjamin Arden? Yes and no. It seems he's been living here peacefully since the end of the Great War, but he's disappeared."

"Seems to be his *modus operandi*. Well, if you find him, we'd be interested in a chat. He could be facing a charge of desertion if what you say is true."

"What sort of punishment would be involved after all this time?"

"Well, he wouldn't be shot at dawn, but it is something that would go on record. That could affect his civilian life. Certainly, a dishonourable discharge. Or, depending on circumstances, I suppose there might be jail time."

"I see," Ames said. "One more thing," he continued, "I have a medal here with some of the information rubbed off, but I have a number." Ames read off the number. "The last one might be a six or an eight. Is there any chance you could track down who the recipient was?"

The sigh at the other end of the line accompanied by a reluctant "I suppose it can be done" told Ames it was likely to be a time-consuming task for some underling.

"Thank you. Can you give me a call at the Nelson Police Station when you find out?"

After he hung up, Ames looked at his watch. He'd had experience being on the telephone to Britain on a previous case. In order to catch anyone in the middle of a working day, he'd have to place his call at the crack of dawn. He might as well find out how the others were doing, and then it would be time to go home. He still tired more easily since he'd been shot, and his shoulder was aching now. He put a hand to it, wondering if this was the sort of thing he'd be faced with for the rest of his life. He'd be like his uncle Alfred, whose war wound acted up every time the weather "turned." He couldn't even remember now what part of Uncle Al had been wounded, but it had also been occasioned by a bullet.

His musings were interrupted by the bark of the inspector from the next office. "Ames!" He stood in his boss's doorway. "Sir?" Darling seemed agitated.

"Don't hover, Ames, sit down." Ames sat, aching shoulder momentarily forgotten.

Darling squinted at him. "What's the matter with you?"

Ames shook his head. "Nothing, sir. Shoulder acting up a bit." Oh my God. He was Uncle Al.

Darling looked genuinely concerned. "I'm sorry to hear that." He picked up a little pile of papers, squared it, and dumped it into his inbox. "I'm going to have to pop across the pond."

Ames beamed. "To join Miss Winslow, sir? That's great. You never take a holiday."

"No, Ames, to join a man called Chief Inspector Sims. They've found a body belonging to us. Francine Renshaw. I've been more or less ordered to go by our good mayor. I'll have to go and see what's what. You'll be in charge of the Arden business while I'm gone. Think you can manage it?" The whole thing seemed like unnecessary madness to Darling, but it could mean a little holiday with Lane in England.

But Ames wasn't thinking about managing. His brow furrowed. "Renshaw? Arden's commanding officer during the Great War? That's a bit odd, sir."

"Your favourite word, Sergeant. Yes, it is. If I learn anything to purpose, I'll be sure to call you."

DARLING'S DRIVE BACK to King's Cove had been filled with conflicting thoughts. Britain was a long way, and he felt a little guilty about leaving the station on such a flimsy excuse. On the other hand, he hadn't taken a holiday for over a year aside from his short honeymoon the previous November. He allowed himself a moment of pleasure, thinking of holidaying with Lane in England. But, once there, would he even get to see her? Knowing Lane, it wasn't guaranteed. And now, yet another connection to the Arden case. Was this dead nurse the very woman Arden had reputedly made a play for? She was, after all, the wife of at least one of his commanding officers. Did he need to draw another chrysanthemum into his ridiculous picture? He must remember to get that out of his drawer before Ames found it when he took over the work of the station. With this slightly alarming vision of Ames wondering if his boss had gone around the bend, he pulled into the grassy yard and parked his car behind Lane's, already feeling downhearted about his solitary evening ahead. If Lane was too busy with whatever she was doing, it might be fun to get up to Scotland and enjoy Lane's redoubtable grandmother fussing over him.

Expecting a cold, empty arrival, he was surprised to see the garden, just visible around the side of the house, alive with people.

"Ah, Inspector," Kenny Armstrong said, when Darling appeared at the edge of the plot. "Just getting the boys trained up. Not there! See those tubers you're digging up? They're dahlias. Put them back!" He addressed this to young Rafe Bertolli, who was being particularly enthusiastic with a trowel. He turned back to Darling. "They should be proper gardeners when I'm done."

"Look!" Philip, the eldest Bertolli boy, said, pointing at a row of turned-over soil. "I did that. That's what you're supposed to do first."

"We helped, too," Rafe said resentfully, giving Philip an elbow.

"It looks marvellous. Let me put my things inside and get my boots. I'll come help," Darling said. He had envisioned a glum evening of cold supper and a lonely scotch in front of the fire, and instead his day would end with a burst of youthful and muddy banter.

"Thanks, Armstrong," he added on the way into the house.

Inside he changed his trousers and shirt and looked for his boots outside the kitchen door in the mud room. He could hear the children calling out and shrieking, punctuated by the low rumble of Kenny's voice keeping them, he very much hoped, under some control.

"Right. What's my job?" he asked when he'd got outside.

"You'll need to decide where you want the peas. They'll have to go in first, as they like the cool," Kenny said. He'd removed a gardening glove and was wiping his forehead.

"I don't think I know enough to have an opinion. They were over there last year," Darling said, pointing along the back of the garden plot.

A juvenile yell interrupted Kenny's reply, as a clod of earth hit Rolfie, the youngest of the three boys.

"Hey!" Kenny commanded. "I'll fire the lot of you, so smarten up!"

He turned back to Darling. "I arranged a salary scale with your good wife before she left. Now, then. The peas. If it were me, I'd put them along there. They'd get a bit of shade from the worst heat of the afternoon, but plenty of sun in the morning."

So, this was Lane's surprise! "Then let's do that. Right, you lot, we're going to have this end of the garden, from here to here, turned over." He walked to the end of the garden where the peas were to be and indicated a line through the middle of the area he'd pointed at and then came back. "Now, got your shovels? Follow me, men!" He marched them to the bottom of the garden. "Halt! This is my side, and that's your side. When Mr. Armstrong says 'Go,' you three start digging and I'll dig on my side. First side finished wins." He took up his shovel and stood ready while the children, who'd been equipped with the smallest shovels Kenny had been able to find in his garden shed, jostled each other for position. They readied themselves enthusiastically, though patently disadvantaged by the size of the shovels they were wielding.

Kenny pulled out his stopwatch and said, "Go!"

"THAT WAS AN extremely effective way to get the soil turned over," Kenny said later. He and Darling, having sent the children on their way home to much-needed baths and dinner, now sat in the kitchen with glasses of scotch. "It's not surprising you're the head of the Nelson Police. You are a natural leader."

"I just think of them as three little Ameses," Darling said. "That's actually quite hard work," he added. "I have a newfound respect for what you do, keeping your enormous garden going, along with all the other chores. I'm afraid my town upbringing has made me a weakling!"

"You did very well, for a weakling." Kenny leaned back and swirled the puddle of scotch in the bottom of his glass. "I've never really hankered after any other way of life. If I'd been brought up where I was born, God knows what I'd have done with my life. Served my time in a bank, sucking up rotten London air. I'd be dead by now. Instead, I live out in the most beautiful place in the world, breathe clean air, and spend my days with good, honest work."

"You came over as a child, then?"

"I did indeed. Father was a diplomat and Mother a minor aristocrat, Bloomsbury before there was any Bloomsbury. He was posted out here in Canada, and when he died, Mother and my brother John and I moved here. She absolutely loved it. She taught music and reading to the local children in that little schoolhouse up the hill. Of course, she always said John and I grew up like barbarians, but she was unconventional in her ways. I think she liked how free we were."

"She sounds like a wonderful woman."

"Oh, that she was. I'm sorry she's not left your house. I suspect she's very fond of your wife." Kenny raised his glass toward the attic, where the ghost of his mother was reputed to abide, opening the windows during the heat of the summer. "By the way, you're to come eat with us. Eleanor didn't think you ought to spend your first dinnertime on your own."

"Oh, I can't be mooching—"

"Nonsense. We won't pester you every night. Just tonight. And seeing as we've had our aperitif, we ought to get going, or I won't answer for the consequences."

"Actually, it transpires that I will have to be going over myself. It won't be for long. It's a police matter."

Home again, Darling thought he should busy himself packing, or tidying up the house so that it would be nice to come home to, but instead he stood moodily in the darkened sitting room looking out into the night. Her absence was a source of acute and, he felt, childish misery. He wandered into the kitchen and thought about making a cup of hot chocolate—her nighttime nostrum of hot milk had never been appealing—but instead of acting, he patted the top of her typewriter and absently pulled open the drawer on the little table she used for writing.

It was here, he knew, where her stabs at poetry came to rest, just as he knew, without having been told, that he was not really welcome to snoop about reading what she wrote. He always assumed that one day she would produce one of these with a flourish, saying, "I have finished this one! What do you think?" But that day had not yet come. With hardly a scintilla of guilt he took out the topmost page.

> *I am here, in and free*
> *And down the green-covered hill*
> *The murmur of water holds me*
> *On its lapping edge. Can they still*
>
> *be mine to hold,*
> *these handfuls of liquid grace?*
> *Is this the place I can unfold*
> *Or just a glorious hiding place?*

Smiling on the first read, he thought it was a nod to Yeats, her favourite poet. *I will arise and go now, and go to Innisfree,* also about a lake. But his second read caused him to toss the paper back into the drawer. "Serves me right," he said out loud. The disquiet he felt at this evidence of Lane's uncertainty about—what? Him? Living here? Her own place in the world?—would not be soothed by any amount of hot cocoa.

CHAPTER THIRTEEN

LANE SHOOK HER HEAD AND shifted on the chair she occupied between her grandmother and grandfather. Tea had been served on the veranda because it was overcast, but it was still warm enough for Ganf to be outside with his blanket on his knees. "I'm not having much luck. I checked that name, Tremaine, and there is no one in the Aberdeen directory by that name." She lifted her cup of tea and sipped it, wishing she could have squirrelled a little more sugar into it. "I'm afraid I'm going to have to go to London to follow up on Marisa's lead. It'll take a couple of days, I expect."

Grandmama shook her head. "Now we are losing you as well. What can she be playing at?"

What indeed? Lane wondered. If her sister was playing at espionage, she might be very difficult to find. "I'm just going to retrace her steps and check a few leads in the Foreign Office."

Ganf frowned. "The Foreign Office? What could she have to do with that?"

"Well, you know, Ganf, she speaks German and Russian. I'm not sure how she occupied herself in South Africa during the war, but I think it highly likely she could have become involved with the diplomatic corps." Better the diplomatic corps than what she really suspected. Her grandmother seemed to know already what Diana had been up to, but she didn't want to alarm her grandfather.

"Oh, dear. I never thought of that. But why would that take her away from us now? The war has long been over."

Why, indeed? "I'm sure it will be sorted out. I'll leave on the early train tomorrow morning." She looked at her watch. "I suppose I'd better telephone Frederick and let him know. I couldn't reach him last night. What's the time? Four. I'll wait an hour to be sure and catch him at work. Do you mind? It's an awful expense, but I promise to keep it very quick."

"Darling girl, you don't have to ask! Talk as long as you want. Poor man must be lost without you!"

Lane smiled. "He did very well without me before I came along. I'm sure he's fine! I'm sure he's had an invitation to dinner every night. People in King's Cove doubtless think he's absolutely helpless."

"Men are absolutely helpless," Ganf said. "Wouldn't last a minute without your grandmother."

"Ha. I doubt Fiona would let you starve," her grandmother said, rising and taking his arm gently. "Come on, up and into the house. There's a nasty breeze blowing up."

DARLING'S PHONE RANG at ten after nine. He was expecting the travel agent.

"Darling?"

It was Lane, at last! "Telephones down in Scotland?"

"I know, darling, I'm sorry. How are you?"

"Better now. Have I mentioned that I love you?"

"You have, yes, from time to time. Luckily, I love you too. Listen, I just wanted to say that this Diana business is a bit more complicated than I thought. I'm leaving to go down to London for a few days, so I didn't want you being disappointed if you tried to call here."

"What sort of more complicated?" Darling asked, filled with misgivings. For Lane to use the words "more complicated" meant it was a lot more serious than that.

"I can't really say over the line. In fact, I can't really say at all, if you take my drift."

Stifling what he'd like to say about her drift, he said instead, "Happens I'm on my way over myself. Perhaps we can meet for lunch, if you've a moment."

"Here? Are you? Have they given you leave or something?" This was surprising but very good news, though immediately she realized the Diana problem might keep them from having any sort of time together.

"Sort of. I've been ordered over by Mayor Dalton to look into a long-dead woman from around here. He's had pressure from some local Nawab the woman was related to. Remember Sims, that inspector from the Yard? He's involved, so I'll be seeing him. I don't, strictly speaking, need to be there, but what with you already there, I'm thinking of it as a holiday. A change is as good as a rest, after all. Ames can't wait to see me gone, I'm sure. Suspicious death, I gather. I may get to go look at the scene of the crime, and who knows, I may even bring her back to her relations, though that seems less likely. She might be considered a casualty of the war and be buried there. I think that's what they're hoping. The bigwig seems to be trying to avoid a scandal."

"How intriguing! Too bad I'll be all tied up looking for Diana. I could help."

"Very amusing. I'm setting off tomorrow—flying, if you can believe it—at the public's expense. I should be there the day after. I'll stay with Rudy and Sandra." Rudy Donaldson had been a fellow pilot during the war, and as close a friend as Darling ever had.

"I can't wait to see you. I miss you like nobody's business. I'll be staying at a little hotel near Victoria Station, the Imperial."

"It's nobody's business how much I miss you, nor what I have in mind when I see you."

"You'll be exhausted from the trip over," she said.

"I'll manage."

LANE SAT FOR a long moment when she'd put back the receiver. She was filled with warmth at the thought of seeing him again, so unexpectedly, and she chided herself for allowing this utterly selfish feeling to nose out her growing alarm about Diana. And anyway, perhaps there was no need for alarm. It was so easy to work oneself into a state without sufficient evidence. And that was the point: Normally she was cool and logical, could think things through, but when it came to Diana, she felt her thought processes muddled by... what? Love? Resentment? That seemed most likely, considering their history. But she had appointed herself Diana's guard an since they were very small. She used to stand over her like a vigilant wolfhound when Diana was still a toddler. That was certainly a kind of love. She could still remember the power of it overwhelming her when she had first looked into Diana's pram. She also remembered being shooed off by their nanny and belittled by their father, but perhaps that early passionate older sister feeling never really went away.

Feeling annoyed by this journey into the psychological twists and turns in her relationship with her sister, Lane stood up, making herself cut through all of it. She was worried about Diana, and that was that. And more importantly, she knew her grandparents were as well. She would do anything to alleviate their concern.

"You'll never guess! Frederick is coming over to London on business. He'll be there the day after tomorrow. He's only just found out," Lane said, rejoining her grandparents in the sitting room.

"But that is splendid, Laneke! You must bring him here. It will be lovely to see him again!"

"I don't know how long he'll be able to stay," Lane said ruefully.

"What sort of business?" her grandfather asked. "Police business to be sure, and nothing short of a dead body or a dastardly international criminal would cause someone to come all this way!"

Lane smiled. "I've got neighbours just like you, Ganf. Very nosy Parkers they are, too. It's remarkable how respectable people can eat biscuits and drink tea with insouciant calm in the face of murder and mayhem. If you must know, they have found the body of a woman, suspicious circumstances, before you ask, who happens to be from the Nelson area. There. That's as much as I know, so there is no point in any further grilling."

Her grandmother settled comfortably and folded her arms. "That's all right. You'll fill us in when you and your dishy policeman come to stay."

"I really don't know if he'll be able to. He may have to rush back in a day or two. And I don't know how long I'll be, for that matter."

"Nonsense. No one comes all this way for a few days! Remember when we were young?" She aimed this at Ganf. "We used to visit friends for a month or six weeks! It was an insult to stay for any less time."

"I suppose now that people can fly, they can pop over any time they want, though they'd have to be awfully rich. They don't have to burden their friends with long stays, eating them out of house and home. Anyway, early train, as I said, and I hope to talk to Diana's friend Marisa, see if I can shake a little more out of her." She could not tell her grandparents what her real plan was: to go to the War Office in search of Major Hogarth.

SHE FELT ALMOST lighthearted as she boarded the train the next morning, her grandmother waving from the platform as if she were going away forever.

Lane settled in, feeling the weight of movement as the train began to pick up speed, and thought about her next steps. She had liked Major Hogarth when she'd met her the year before, and there'd been enough in their conversation then to convince her she knew a good deal more about the now-defunct Special Operations Executive than she let on. And the best thing of all was that she wouldn't have to see her disagreeable ex-lover and handler, Angus Dunn, who had been precipitously retired the year before after botching the whole business that had nearly cost Darling his life. And, of course, she would see Darling himself. With this happy thought she turned to the copy of *Roger Ackroyd und Sein Mörder* to practise reading German and try to recreate the code that Diana had been using. The rumble and rock of the train made her look out at the passing countryside periodically and ponder how one could simultaneously entertain worry, anger, and happiness. The human heart was stretchy and remarkable.

HAVING SEEN DARLING off on the train to Alberta, Ames stood outside the station looking around, his hands in his pockets. As he always did when he was left in charge, he felt trepidation about his ability to make a mess of things, but he surprised himself with an additional layer of feeling, which he could only describe as confidence. After all, this was the third time that Nelson had effectively been his. And he had excellent help. Terrell was clever—cleverer than he was, if he were being truthful—and easy to work with. And O'Brien never changed for anyone or anything.

He imagined Darling coming back and finding the whole case of the disappearing Arden solved and shelved. It was this soaring vision that finally brought him back to earth with a clunk.

Arden had been a deserter, a womanizer, and a hero impersonator—and possibly a gambler, a drug addict, or the victim of blackmail. Sighing, Ames started back to where he'd parked the car. It didn't take much imagination to guess that this would, as his mother always said, only end in tears. The question was, whose?

"IT'S NOT THE same, is it?" Ames said dolefully when the gravel-voiced Marge had retreated to the counter. She'd plunked down their cups of coffee, demanding to know if they were getting pie, her tone suggesting it was a federal crime not to.

"She's a good saleswoman, though," said Terrell. "I don't normally eat pie at eleven in the morning."

"You know what I mean. April."

"Yes, sir. She's definitely not April." Terrell would admit to no more, though April was never far from his mind. "I wonder how she's doing."

"She's smart and personable. I'm sure she's doing fine. If she does any good at her initial training course, it'll be kind of sad, in a way, that she'll never get to show her full ability, what with her being a woman."

Terrell nodded thoughtfully. "Perhaps you're right, but it *is* 1948. Things are changing. Look at Miss Van Eyck. She is able to show her full ability as a mechanic. No one is standing in her way."

"Ha! I'd like to see them try!"

Marge appeared with peach pie, and while Ames agreed with Terrell that a large piece of pie at eleven, very close to lunch, was probably ill-advised, he nevertheless felt a little stir of happiness. Picking up his fork, he said, "About this case: we are working with air. We don't know where the man has gone and, if he's found, whether he could be charged with anything. I'm sure it is within a man's right to get into a boat and disappear if he's so inclined, even if he's leaving behind family obligations. It's also not against the law for him to have a fling with a grumpy farmer's wife. It's not even strictly against the law to take all the family money and leave the wife and kiddies high and dry, more's the pity, though she might have grounds to sue him for desertion."

"You're right, sir. And not just his wife. The army might want a word with him for desertion, and perhaps for passing himself off as a hero with someone else's medal, but after all this time will they even follow it up? I'm sure they have plenty of things to deal with from this recent war, never mind things left over from the Great War. He's certainly managed to get away with a lot over the years. It would be much easier if we had a body.

"Oh, and I haven't had time to tell you about my visit to the printer. It was very interesting. I bet you couldn't imagine all that goes into printing a little wedding invitation. That card Mrs. Arden dropped off was probably the only one with the two hundred on it. He found some examples from that run, and none of the other cards had it. He told me how it could be done quite simply."

"Who did it?" Ames asked.

"His assistant, apparently, Bill MacDonald."

"Well, well. That's the name of Arden's friend from the war. His mother told us. Could be one and the same? We should have a chat."

"We should, sir, except he's away on a holiday," Terrell said. "And, also interesting, it turns out that the return address on the envelope Arden got is not the same as the address of the vicar who ordered those invitations. The return address was on Trevor, but the Spinkses live up on Ward.

Ames frowned. "That's odd."

"Yes, sir. I'm planning to visit both addresses."

Ames nodded and pressed his fork into the remaining scraps of pie crust. "Good. If that Bill MacDonald altered the invitation..."

"To the tune of two hundred—might those be dollars?"

"Exactly. One of the amounts Arden was forking out. Then, he could be a candidate for the role of either gambling-debt collector or blackmailer." He dropped his napkin on his now spotlessly clean plate. "You know what this case needs? It needs a body."

"But whose body?"

"Exactly! Whose body—Arden's? Or, more likely, the body of the guy getting all the money, maybe this MacDonald guy, except he's alive and well and on vacation. Unless he's dead. You see, I was thinking about Arden, and he has the morals of a cobra. He thinks nothing of bankrupting his family, never mind desertion and all the rest of it. If someone is threatening him, I bet he would think nothing of doing him in. I think we should look for a body. How do you feel about being on the water?" Seeing doubt on Terrell's face, he continued. "Hear me out. Arden goes off in a boat. What if he's off to find his persecutor and dispatch him?"

Terrell nodded thoughtfully. "He's been asked to meet him, using their usual method of communication, whatever that is, to bring more money, say. Why the boat ride? How has the money been handed over all the other times?"

"Well, we don't know he hasn't gone off in the boat all the other times, though it seems like a lot of work when they could meet practically anywhere to hand off envelopes of money without being observed. Let's say this time he's had it. He's out of money and wants the whole thing to end. He tells his blackmailer he'll leave the money somewhere in the woods; this time he hides in the shrubbery, and when he sees the guy, he finishes him off."

"Why hasn't he come back?"

"He's killed someone, hasn't he? And he's out of money, so he can't show his face around the family home again. He's off to start again somewhere else."

"Perhaps in the company of the missing farmer's wife."

"Perhaps. Though she'd be a fool to link herself with a desperate, broke murderer. The more we learn about this guy, the more he has a character only a mother would love, and boy does she!"

"There is a problem with that theory, sir," Terrell said, raising a friendly hand toward Marge, who was standing in the doorway into the kitchen, smoking. After another puff, she tossed her cigarette behind her somewhere—into the alley, Terrell hoped, and not somewhere it would lie waiting to burn the café down—and ambled slowly toward them with the bill.

"Want anything else?" she asked, directing her question at Ames.

"Oh. No, thanks." Ames said, reaching for the bill.

"I'll get that, sir," Terrell said, snatching it away.

197

Out on the street, Ames asked Terrell, "What problem?"

"Bill MacDonald called his boss two days ago to say he was extending his stay in Alberta. Which means not only can we not interview him, he is unlikely to turn up dead."

CHAPTER FOURTEEN

L ANE STOOD AT THE FRONT desk at the War Office, waiting for the corporal in charge to finish talking on the telephone. She looked around, her memories flooding back. It amazed her to think about who she had been during the war, and who she felt herself to be now. It was as if that Lane were some other person, so completely transformed was her life and all that she thought important.

"Miss?" The young man had evidently already tried to get her attention.

"Oh, yes, sorry. I'd like to see Major Hogarth, please."

"Have you an appointment?"

"No, but I believe she will see me. My name is Lane Winslow."

The corporal busied himself with the telephone again, and eventually, clearly somewhat surprised, he told her to go to the second floor and turn left. The major would find her there.

Hogarth hurried into the hall, her hand extended in welcome. "Miss Winslow! I never expected to see you again.

Please come through." Major Hogarth was tall and lean, her businesslike exterior of uniform and sensible shoes softened by her delighted smile. "Now then, how can I help?" she asked when they were seated across from each other at the major's tidy desk.

"You were so helpful last time I was here, a year ago."

"At least now you don't have that stuffed shirt of a barrister in tow."

Lane laughed. "He wasn't so bad, really. And he did come to fully support my cause." She didn't elaborate on the desperate situation that had brought her here the year before, saving Darling from the hangman. Lane suspected with almost weary certainty that somehow Hogarth knew all the details. "I am here because my sister, Diana Winslow, seems to have disappeared. I'm afraid I have very few leads." She hesitated. This was dicey territory given the proscriptions of the official secrets, but it had to be attempted. "I believe she may have been in Special Operations, or something like it, in South Africa. She returned to Britain a little over two weeks ago and has effectively vanished." Lane described what she knew of her sister's movements.

Hogarth pursed her lips and leaned back in her chair. "I see. Tell me her name again?" She took up a pencil and wrote it at the top of a clean page in a notebook. When she'd finished, she said, "By the way, there's a new director, did you know that?"

Lane stifled a smile at this very oblique reference to Angus Dunn and then nodded. "I imagine a new director, and a new direction. All those wartime concerns swept away by the new world order of thwarting our old Soviet allies."

"Exactly. You see the problem, then. I'm certainly not familiar with this name. You have some reason to believe she was with the SOE?"

"Only very tenuous reasons. But I have to start somewhere."

"Of course, yes. The problem is that there have been massive changes since the war ended. People leaving, being reassigned, new people coming in. SOE's been scrapped. You see?"

"I do see, yes." Lane could, in fact, see several problems. One was that her sister could have been reassigned, in which case she was unlikely to learn anything; another was that if her sister had retired to private life after the war, the agency might be very concerned about her disappearance. The agency tended to keep tabs on retired spies to make sure they weren't getting up to anything beyond a quiet, private life. "Diana and I were brought up speaking French, German, and Russian. If she is no longer working, then it is quite possible she has disappeared for reasons of her own, but if not, I'm worried about her safety. She was staying with our grandparents. She's very close with them. I don't believe she would leave without contacting them. I was given this name." She pushed the paper with "Alex Tremaine" on it toward the major.

Hogarth took the scrap of paper and looked at it, her face revealing nothing. Then, pulling her notebook forward, she wrote it down. "I will see if there is anything I can find out, but I very much doubt it. Not really my department, all this sort of thing. Where are you staying while you're here?"

Lane nodded. "At the very inaptly named Imperial Hotel near Victoria. You can leave a message there." She rose and

201

offered her gloved hand. "Thank you, Major. Any amount of information would be of help."

Major Hogarth sat for some long moments after Lane had left, staring at the wall opposite her desk. Finally, she picked up the receiver and dialled Gregory Fairfax, upstairs. "Greg. It's Janet. Can you come down a moment? We might have a problem."

BACK OUT ON the street, Lane stood indecisively on Horse Guards Road. Darling must have arrived by now. Perhaps he'd already left word for her at the Imperial. The sky had a few patches of grey that could pose a threat later in the afternoon, and she could smell the coming rain, but the morning was mild. She had an appointment with Marisa on Brook Street at noon. It would be a short walk, so she had time for a cup of tea.

She found a little tearoom and settled into the last seat near a window, took off her gloves, and opened her handbag to extract a notebook and pencil. As friendly as her interaction with Major Hogarth had been, she was certain that for the tiniest fraction of a second Hogarth's face had registered concern on hearing that Diana had disappeared. In the next moment, though, her opaque expression had returned. She opened the notebook and then gazed through the murky window. The clearing of a throat interrupted her barely coherent thoughts.

"Miss?"

"Tea, please, and have you a scone?"

"We have, miss. With jam?"

"Yes, why not." Butter must still be hard to come by.

She thought about the richness and plenty of the food in Canada. With rationing still on here, it was certainly another world.

She picked up the pencil and found herself stymied right from the top. Had her sister been a spy? Yes, clearly, but for whom? All Diana's very closest friends in Riga had been German, and she had admired the Germans, from Bach to Nietzsche. Was it even remotely possible she would have been deluded enough to work for the Nazis? She shook her head. Diana had seen the beginning of the forced repatriation of Germans from Latvia to Germany. People who'd lived for generations in Latvia suddenly uprooted and made to go "home" to a country they had never known. She remembered an afternoon when Diana had stormed into the house. She'd been, what, fifteen? She'd been raging about her friend Gitta, whose family was being forced to sell up and move. The German family had been beside themselves, she remembered now, in tears about this forced exile. No, Diana would never have worked for the Nazis, she was sure of it. She could still hear her sister's rising voice, exclaiming, "It's so unfair! Why should they have to move away to satisfy that jumped-up little man? This is their home!"

"Thank you," Lane said when her tea was brought. The sugar bowl had very little sugar, but she rejoiced at being able to take more than a teaspoon. She stirred her tea and suddenly wondered if Diana had even spent the war in South Africa after all. But she was only sixteen when she left. She couldn't have been involved in anything at that age. Or could she? What kind of espionage would she be engaged in there? She knew that many Dutch South Africans, the Afrikaners, supported Germany and even engaged in the destruction of rails and other kinds of sabotage to thwart the British. Diana did not speak Afrikaans, but, and here Lane took a sip of tea, she could definitely pose as a German, perhaps feeding misinformation to rebel elements within the country.

The scone was a little dry, but was improved by the strawberry jam, and she chewed on it thoughtfully. Diana, stubborn, plucky, defiant, would no doubt have relished the role. And she would be doing exactly what her beloved father had been doing. Lane realized that she had never thought about how intelligent Diana might be. Her sister had had no interest in university, and this had perhaps coloured Lane's view of her. There was, of course, more than one way to be clever, and she saw now, given who Diana had been all her life, that her sister would certainly have the canny kind of brightness that would be exactly suited to espionage.

So, if you had spent the war spying on the Afrikaner resistance, what would you do after the war, if you didn't want to retire? There wasn't an easy answer. The new shout was the Soviet threat. Diana could use her Russian, or she could continue with the German theme, given the growing Soviet sphere of influence.

She dropped her napkin onto the table in frustration, gulped down the last dregs of tea, and left some coins by her saucer. The trouble was, none of those possibilities answered the question of where her sister was right now, this minute. Outside, she pushed her hands into her jacket pockets and relished the light breeze on her face after the stifling café. For all she knew, Diana's current whereabouts had nothing to do with spying. She could have gone for a hike with her hosts in Aberdeen after all, and they could have all fallen over a precipice and be lying dead, never to be found, she thought irritably. If only she'd told her grandparents who her bloody friends were!

MARISA WAS BLOND, delicately pretty, and dressed in a tweed skirt and a lemon-yellow blouse. She answered the door herself. "Miss Winslow. Delighted to meet you." She held out a limp hand and looked anything but delighted. "Please come through." She led Lane along a wide passage to a sitting room. Something about the room felt hollow to Lane, as if things were missing. She gave a surreptitious glance around. It had some very expensive furniture but little of it for such a large room. It was as if some designer had decided on an elegant but severely monkish style.

"Please sit down. Can I get you anything?"

"No, thank you, I've just had a cup of tea." She sat on one of two chairs in front of the unlit fireplace, and Marisa settled herself on the other. A silver-framed photograph of a couple, taken in the 1920s, was the sole ornament on a small round table between them. A glass ashtray with the remains of several cigarettes sat beside it. Lane had a sudden vision of this pale girl spending her whole time pacing this room and smoking.

"I don't know how I can help. I've not really seen much of Diana since she got back, aside from the time she spent here."

"And you said that was about ten days?"

"More or less, yes."

Ten days. That accounted for much of the time since she'd left their grandparents.

"Can you tell me a little about what she did during the war? I know you both were quite young, but did you engage in any sort of war work?"

Marisa lifted her chin and took a breath. "It wasn't right away, but after the first year we entertained officers—you know, went to parties to provide a bit of company. Oh, nothing sordid, in case you think that. They just thought some pretty girls would provide a bit of amusement."

"So that was it? Did Diana do anything else?"

Marisa got up abruptly and stood in front of the fireplace, her back to Lane. "I'm not supposed to say anything," she said at last. "But honestly, I was very cross with her." She picked up a gold cigarette case lying on a solitary occasional table, extracted a cigarette, and then held the case out in Lane's direction. "It's my one little luxury, this case. Daddy says we've lost all our money."

"No, thank you," Lane said, not knowing what to say about the loss of the family fortune. "Why are you so cross with her?"

Marisa lit her cigarette and inhaled and then blew the smoke out the corner of her mouth. "Because I invited her to go out to Africa to be with me, to be *my* friend. I was being exiled by my beastly father to the ends of the earth, and she was to be my salvation. Do you see?"

Lane nodded.

"And then the next thing I know, she meets this Tremaine fellow at one of these cocktail parties, and she bashes off with him. Goodbye, best friend. I had a good mind to tell them she was only eighteen." She came back to sit opposite Lane, where she leaned forward to angrily tap some ashes off her cigarette into the ashtray. "And the worst part of it is that she wouldn't tell me anything. She disappeared for days sometimes. I thought she was having an affair. The man was old enough to be her father, for God's sake! I was terrified my uncle or Daddy would disapprove and send her packing. Daddy does some sort of government work and came out several times, but they never did make her leave, and I couldn't make out why. I warned her once that she'd be up the spout if she wasn't careful, and she just got angry and said, 'It's nothing like that.' Then one time she came back from one of these jaunts with several books in German. That really put the wind up, I can tell you. I thought she'd gone over to the enemy."

Marisa had certainly gone from a refusal to tell her anything to a voluble relation of every nuance of how she felt about Diana's treatment of her. She feels betrayed, Lane thought.

"You must have felt let down," she said.

"I bloody well did! Then one time, toward the end of '44, she came back and tried to pick up like nothing had happened. But she was different, cagey. I asked her what had become of her boyfriend, Tremaine, and she told me I was never to mention him to anyone, that I wouldn't understand—that it was important that if anything happened to her, I was not to say a word." She snorted and stubbed her cigarette out. "Well, I'm being as good a friend to her now as she was to me then. I'm blabbing away to you."

She jerked her head defiantly. "Why shouldn't I? *I* didn't sign anything."

"I'm terribly grateful to you. I know it's been difficult. Did you come back before she did?"

"Yes, right after it was over. I told Daddy I'd had enough, and I wanted to go home. Diana said she would stay on. As I told you on the telephone, she had things to finish up. I really didn't care anymore. I know she stayed on at my uncle's for a period, but I don't know how long. And then suddenly, about twelve days ago, she turned up here. Would I mind terribly if she could stay a few days with me? I could hardly slam the door in her face. She is my oldest friend from school, so in she came. And then, without a warning or goodbye, she pushed off suddenly in the night, or early morning, I don't know which. I woke up and she was gone. That's all I know."

No wonder Marisa was angry. "How did she seem?"

"I don't know. Older. When you don't see someone for a while, you think they're going to be the same, like they were in school, but she's in her mid-twenties now and looks it. I'd say she was more serious, more sure of herself." She sighed. "I never had the knack for being sure of myself. But she seemed fine. Delighted to be back. We went out together to a little club, went shopping. I put on a lovely dinner party for her on her second night here and introduced her to a few of my friends. I thought a man more her age would get her away from that Tremaine, if they were still entangled. Daddy is away a good deal, but he came back during the week and wasn't all that happy to see her. I suppose he'd had enough of her living with us in Africa. She left a few days after that. He's been away, as a matter of fact." She said this last with an air of having been abandoned to deal with a diminishing life on her own.

"Had she got a phone call or anything?"

"Not as far as I know. Why would she?"

How to put the next question? "Did any of the people you had at the dinner party do the sort of work she did?"

"Well, you have me there, don't you?" Marisa said angrily. "I have no idea what sort of work she did. She never told me bloody anything. Just disappeared and reappeared and acted like everything was normal." She walked toward the tall window that opened onto a narrow balcony and stood. "I feel as if she's used me, if you want the truth. We were close at school, but I always felt she had the upper hand somehow."

In that moment Marisa looked so young and vulnerable that Lane felt quite sorry for her She knew a little about feeling used by Diana. She took out her notebook and wrote her address and telephone number at her grandparents', and then the name of her hotel. "It's kind of you to see me and tell me all this. It is certainly more than I had to go on before. If you think of anything else, here is my grandparents' address, and I'm at this hotel until perhaps the day after tomorrow." She tore out the page and handed it to Marisa, and then hesitated and took it back. "I can also be reached here. These are friends of my husband. Would it be possible for me to get hold of your uncle in South Africa if the need arises? He may know something about her movements after you left, if she stayed on with him."

Marisa shrugged. "Sure, if you like. His name is James Fairfax. Here." She held out her hand for the notebook, and then wrote down her uncle's address and telephone number. "You could reach him by calling the exchange in Pretoria, but I don't expect he will have changed the number."

She had walked Lane downstairs to the front door, and they stood for a moment in silence. "Look, could you let me know if you find her?" Marisa said finally.

"Yes, of course. Thank you so much, Miss Fairfax, for everything."

Pretoria, December 1942

THE CHRISTMAS PARTY felt subdued after the gaiety and near-abandon of the pre-war parties. Diana looked inside from her vantage on the veranda. She'd chosen the farthest corner to watch through the window. Someone was making an effort, anyway. The phonograph in the vast sitting room was being deployed, but they had chosen Glenn Miller's "I Know Why, and So Do You." They won't get up any enthusiasm with that dreary piece, she thought, but it was a perfect title for what most of them in the room did. We all know what we're doing, and no one says it. She turned away, sighing, and smoked into the night. She felt Tremaine's approach before she saw him, and her heart turned over. He leaned next to her, pressing his shoulder into her.

"I always thought you were a life-of-the-party type," he said.

She shrugged, feeling his weight against her. "There's a war on. Anyway, it's hard to get enthusiastic with that moribund music."

Quite suddenly he turned her toward him and took her in his arms. "Let's dance, then."

She could feel her breath almost stop, and she allowed herself to be pulled in a gentle circle. She opened her mouth to speak, but he shook his head. "Don't talk." Then he leaned in and kissed her lightly, his lips soft against hers.

"I know I have no right," he said when the music stopped and they stood facing each other. He still held her hand. "You asked if I have a wife. I do. She's a good person. I liked her at once. I still do, but I never loved her."

Diana smiled for the first time. "That is probably what they all say." She waved her hand to encompass all the officers inside, pouring drinks for women to whom they weren't married, she was sure.

He looked at the ground for a moment with a short laugh. "I expect you're right. In my case it happens to be true. We live quite separate lives."

She brought his hand up to her cheek and then kissed it. "As separate as all this?"

"I'm not entirely sure. Would it matter?"

"No," she said softly, and kissed him.

Pretoria, March 1943

"YOU GAVE US this," Tremaine said. He was angry but was trying not to show it. He held up a piece of letter paper with coordinates on it. "We were there, but your traitor Afrikaner chums from the Ossewabrandwag never showed up."

"Don't look at me, darling," Diana said, inhaling deeply on the cigarette she held in her beautifully manicured hand. "This is what I got, in the usual way. Maybe something held them up, or they changed their minds."

Tremaine slapped the paper on his desk and leaned forward, shaking his head. "Yes, but why suddenly? It's been like clockwork. They arrive, we arrest them before any damage is done, and Bob's your uncle."

"I imagine they're getting tired of having their people arrested. Or someone here has told them what we're up to. Oh. I see. That's what concerns you. Well, as I said, don't look at me."

"*Have* you been talking to anyone?" Tremaine, who'd been looming over her, sat down finally, much to Diana's relief.

She glared at him, hurt, infuriated. "Certainly not! You should know better than to ask." She could feel her heart banging against her ribs, fury and hurt assailing her.

"We can't afford to fumble the ball at this point. They're wreaking absolute havoc. I want them all banged up in prison for the duration of the war." He stopped talking and leaned back in his chair, looking away, his chin on his hand. "I'm taking you out of it for the time being. We can put you to translating at the War Office. And..."

And... what? Diana worked to contain the new rage she felt boiling up. Finally, she spoke, grinding her cigarette into the ashtray. "I live to obey. But you'll see. While I'm tucked up with the ladies at the typing pool, it will happen again. And again. Because, my dear Major, it's not me." She stood up, swept her handbag onto her wrist, and started for the door. Then she turned back. "By the way, I should remind you, I can't type worth a damn."

At home, torn between fury and anguish, she went to her bedroom and locked the door. She sat at her dressing table, angry tears spilling down her cheeks. She swept them away. It was the betrayal, she thought, the absolute betrayal. How could he imagine for a minute that she was a traitor? That's what his words amounted to. He was calling her a traitor. It infuriated her that she loved him, and yet he could sit there like a pompous ass, blithely proposing to "take her out of it" because she couldn't be trusted. She was sure he knew how she felt. She was sure he felt it himself, and yet the last few months apparently meant nothing. Well then. That was the state of things. She wiped her eyes and took a deep breath. Daddy had once told her that he loved her mother so much that when she died a part of him did as well. She knew Tremaine was the one, the one you take the chance on because there would never be another one like this. Obviously, it had not been true for him. Perhaps he only "liked" her the way he liked his wife. But even as she thought this, she knew it wasn't true. He must, she knew, be in agony too.

She took up her lipstick and applied it, looking at her blotchy face. She really didn't cry well. Marisa's father was over from England, so she couldn t go about looking like this. Fresh water had been put in her basin, so she took up the neatly folded linen towel and soaked it and wrung it out. She lay down on the bed and pressed the towel on her eyes, feeling some relief with the cool compress.

It was only then that she began to think. She had not betrayed the plan, so who had?

DIANA STOOD IN her bedroom, the door cracked open, listening. The silence in the nearly empty flat was almost hollow. Marisa and her father had gone out to lunch at the home of an old family friend. The housekeeper was, Diana was certain, out at the shops. It would have to be now. With her heart pounding, she moved swiftly to Fairfax's study and turned the handle. Locked. Looking quickly around, she pulled a pin out of her hair and bent it open. The door yielded easily. She hurried inside, leaving the door ajar so she could hear if anyone came into the house, and went to the wide, heavy desk that was positioned in front of a wall of nearly empty bookshelves. He must have sold off his library, as well, she thought.

Not really sure what she was looking for, she took a cursory look at the shallow middle drawer and found only what she expected: pencils, an expensive fountain pen, paper clips, rubber bands. She felt into the back corners of the drawer but found no papers. Shutting it, she glanced toward the door, and then opened the side drawer. There were files of correspondence. The first file revealed itself to be full of letters demanding payment for various things. "Not surprising," she muttered, replacing the file and pulling the next one. Notices from his bank, at least three of which were letters urging Fairfax to pay a visit to the manager. Two were demands for payment for loans. One indicated the manager regretted that he would not be able to extend the sum of three thousand pounds Fairfax had requested until he found himself able to settle his previous accounts.

Several more files revealed more personal letters, including several with a South African return address. These proved to be from a woman. The last one showed signs of having been crumpled and then smoothed out. The lady, who signed herself Sophie, was regretting things as well. She told him she would be unable to see him as she had become engaged to someone else. Fairfax was a businessman to the last. Most men would have crumpled the letter and burned it, not smoothed it out and filed it.

With a sigh, she stood perplexed, looking down at the open drawer. She knew she was right, but she would have to have evidence. Tremaine had begun to have suspicions right after the second debacle, even before he'd taken her off the job. She'd been so angry, but she saw now that pulling her out temporarily had been his way of protecting her. She closed the drawer and looked again at the bookshelf. If Fairfax had been paid to betray his country, why was he still sitting in an enormous empty Mayfair flat with only one housekeeper on staff? Had he collected the money and was he keeping it in a secret account? Had he gambled it away? His tipple was bad investments. There must be a file or something with his investment history. She began to pull the few remaining books out of the bookshelves and leaf through them. Nothing. And then one book triggered a "click," and a drawer revealed itself set into the wall behind the books. She shifted the books and hurriedly pulled out the narrow drawer that had sprung out an inch, and said, "Bingo!"

With a racing heart, she laid four letters out on the desk, all from the Reichsbank, all sent between 1941 and 1944, and all announcing amounts of money to be deposited into his account. She memorized the number of the account and contemplated taking one of the letters. They would want proof. She would have to take the risk. She selected one, folding it and pushing it into her pocket. The rest she put back into the file and she replaced the file in the drawer, pushing it shut. To her dismay it refused to latch. She tried several more times, felt around inside to see if something was stopping it, and wondered if she could just put the books against it.

She still had not found a file of his investment history. She was looking up at the rest of the bookshelf when there was a sound of a door closing somewhere in the house, causing her heart to jump. It wasn't the front door; that was close by. It must be the door below stairs, into the kitchen. She turned back to the problem of the drawer and gave it one last desperate push. It held. She closed her eyes momentarily in her relief, and then pushed the books into place. Any other material would have to wait.

Back in her room, feeling drained, she contemplated her next move. She would have to leave. Fairfax was clever. It would not take him long to figure out that someone had been in his office, as careful as she had been. If he was at all suspicious of her, he would have set some sort of trap: a hair, a pen tilted a certain way, something. He was already irritated at her presence, she could see. He maintained scrupulous politeness to her, but she'd overheard him telling Marisa that he didn't want her in the house. That was fine. Keeping the letter on her person, she went down to the kitchen.

"I'm going to pop out for a bit. The day has turned rather beautiful, and I should like a walk. Could you let

Marisa know?" She'd already prepared for this. Had packed her small suitcase and deposited it at Victoria Station in a locker. Tremaine would collect it.

"Certainly. You're right, there! If I hadn't the dinner to make, I'd be off to Green Park myself."

Outside, Diana strolled in the direction of Duke Street and then turned toward Portman Square. There was a phone box she used for her communications with Tremaine. Relieved that no one was using it, she closed the door, dropped a coin into the slot, and asked for a number. She let it ring three times and then hung up and waited. In seconds, the phone rang. She picked it up. "I have the proof," she said.

WHEN LANE ARRIVED at the Imperial, the concierge in the dark little foyer handed her a message along with her key. "This was called in for you. You'll have to use the phone box on the corner. The hotel telephone is not available to guests."

That kind of concierge, Lane thought, thanking her and not rolling her eyes. Lane opened the note, her heart compressing, but found to her surprise it was a message from Sandra Donaldson, along with a number.

Hurrying out to the phone box, she fished about for coins and put the call through.

"Lane? Oh, this is so thrillingly like old times! You must come over at once. He's sound asleep upstairs. He told me to wake him in an hour, but it seemed too cruel. He was absolutely all in, but seeing you when he wakes up will be just the ticket!"

Lane smiled happily. Sandra Donaldson, enthusiastic, generous, lovely Sandra, who always spoke in exclamation marks. "I will come as quickly as I can. My little basement room at the Imperial is tiny and looks out over the bins in the alley. I'm happy to be there as little as possible." When she had hung up, she turned her face to the greying sky and took a deep breath. An unexpected delight in this whole business, seeing Darling. She could cope with the missing Diana later.

CHAPTER FIFTEEN

"**M**Y DAD USED TO TAKE me fishing in a little outfit like this," Ames said, raising his voice above the noise of the motor and directing the little boat out into the lake. "It's funny, I remember the first time he let me take charge of the engine. I felt like I'd really made it." He sighed as the wind picked up. "Poor Dad. I feel like it was the only time he was happy."

Terrell, who was hanging on to both sides of the boat as it began to bounce across the waves, said, "Yes, sir. I know what you mean. My dad served in the Number Two Construction Battalion with the Canadian . . . sir, should we be going this fast?"

Ames turned and looked at Terrell and shook his head, smiling broadly. "Good grief. Have we found a weakness? I thought you lived by the sea in Halifax."

"Yes, sir, but my father was a porter, and my mom runs a little shop. We didn't really have time for recreational boating."

Ames slowed the motor. "Let's pull up to the Ardens' dock and see if his missus can tell us anything new that would be helpful."

Terrell, wearing his newly purchased rubber boots, hauled himself shakily out of the boat first, happy to feel the solid dock underfoot, and then held the boat while Ames climbed out. Mrs. Arden had come onto the porch above them and was watching them.

"Good morning," Ames called up. "We're going along the shore to see if there's any likely place your husband might have been going. We just want to ask if you have any ideas."

Mrs. Arden turned to look as a little boy in blue pyjamas came out onto the porch. She put her hand around his shoulder and said, "Sure. I'll be right down. Ben Junior is home from school today."

They waited, looking out onto the lake. "If you're going to live here, you're going to have to get used to the water," Ames commented to Terrell.

"Am I? I'm afraid I don't swim all that well."

"It must have been a trial shipping overseas, then."

"Yes, indeed, it was, though I was happy to find I didn't get sick. Some of the men were miserable the whole way."

"That will be useful when you want to take a girl for a romantic moonlight row on the lake."

Terrell was saved from having to respond to this bit of frivolity by the arrival of Mrs. Arden and young Ben, who was also wearing galoshes into which he'd tucked his pyjamas. He was shyly standing behind his mother, looking at them curiously.

"Sorry. He wouldn't stay inside. He's become a bit nervous since Ben left, and doesn't like to leave me."

"I gather you often go on the water," Ames said, giving the boy a smile.

"Nearly every weekend, and every day during the summer when the kids are home. Ben here likes to go out with his dad."

"Did he ever go on his own? Ben Senior, I mean."

"He did, yes. He said it made him feel 'whole.'" She frowned. "What a thing to say, now that I think of it. What's not whole about being with your family? Well, anyway. Off he'd go, rods, tackle, and all, usually early in the morning. He liked to see the sun come over the mountain. He said." She made it sound as if she hadn't quite believed him.

"Do you know where he went? Did he have a specific spot he really liked?"

"He might have. I've no idea."

"One time we went to a place where there was an old haunted house way in the forest. It was like Hansel and Gretel!"

The three grown-ups looked in surprise at Ben, who had come out from behind his mother and was pointing north along the lake's opposite shore. "There wasn't any candy, though, like in the story."

Terrell squatted down to look at Ben. "Do you remember where it was?"

"Over there. We only went one time. I was sorta scared, but it was okay with Daddy there. I wanted to go again, but he didn't want to. Maybe he was scared too!"

"Ben, darling, that's nonsense. I can't believe Daddy would take you there," Mrs. Arden said, frowning.

"He did. Don't you remember?"

Terrell smiled at him. "It does sound pretty scary! I think I'd feel nervous. Did you have to walk a long way from the shore to get there?"

"Yeah. When Daddy said he could show me an old house in the woods, I told him I could drop bread crumbs, like in the story, so we did. That's how we got back!"

"That was a very smart idea," Terrell said. "Was it a big house?"

"No. It was way smaller than ours, and it was all falling apart. I didn't like it. It smelled really bad. There was old stuff inside, like someone lived there a long time ago."

"Thank you, Ben. I think that is going to help us a lot," Ames said. He turned back to the boy's mother. "You said your husband would never take him there. Have you seen it?"

She shrugged. "A long time ago. I used to go there with my friends when I was a teenager. We all went. In fact, I'm the one who showed Ben. It's a godawful place—Ben Junior's right. Damp, smelly. At least it was when I was a kid. I've never been back. It gives me the heebie-jeebies. I don't know what we saw in it when I was young. I don't know why he'd ever have taken young Ben there. I'd have given him what for if I'd known! The truth is, we weren't talking much lately. I was beginning to look..." She glanced down at her son, who had squatted down to look at the rented boat, and dropped her voice. "I was beginning to look forward to the times he was away. I even think...but it doesn't matter."

"Think what?"

"No. It really doesn't matter." She looked down at young Ben and said, "Ben, could you run upstairs and find Mommy's glasses?" She waited until he'd clomped off and was well up the stairs before she turned to them and said very quietly, "I don't believe he's gone to that cabin. I just wonder if he's gone off with..."

"With whom, Mrs. Arden?" Terrell asked gently.

"There was this woman he used to know. Philippa Bentley. I always wondered if he ever got over her. I even wondered if he'd taken up with her again, that's all. He..."

Ames stayed quiet for a moment, wondering what more she had been about to say. He was surprised by how resigned she seemed to the idea of her husband going off with another woman. Should he tell her Philippa Bentley had gone as well? Perhaps she already knew, through gossip. He was about to speak when she turned to him.

"Before you ask, Sergeant Ames, I already know Philippa Bentley has run off, taken her boy with her. Everyone has been so very kind as to tell me." Her voice was clipped and angry. "I'm just suggesting that your ride across the lake will be for nothing."

Wondering if he should ask her how long she'd known about the missing woman, Ames said, "Well, thanks, Mrs. Arden. It's probably a waste of a boat rental, as you say, but we're running out of leads." Of course, they hadn't told her about the other things they'd learned about his war record. She'd have met him long after the war was over, though now he wondered if she knew about that as well. That was all to come, he guessed, when, and if, they

223

found him. "Can you tell me exactly where the abandoned cabin is?"

Mrs. Arden looked out at the water. "I honestly couldn't tell you exactly." She turned her mouth down. "Maybe a couple of miles up that way? It's a little cove, like a hundred others along the lake. I'm not sure I could find it myself now."

Ames nodded. "Thanks, then. As you say, it's probably pointless, but we've got to give it a try."

Ben had come back down the stairs holding his mother's glasses. He handed them to her and went to stand by Terrell, who was sitting on the dock, his feet dangling over their boat.

It was a risk, Terrell was thinking, considering Mrs. Arden's objections, but he'd ask it anyway. "Can you point to where you think the haunted house was again?" he asked Ben.

"I think maybe over there. There's a big rock sticking out. It was after that."

"Did it have a little beach nearby?"

"Yeah. You have to jump in the water to pull the boat up. It's really fun! It's not a very good beach, though. It's all full of little rocks. You can't walk on it with bare feet."

"Thank you. That's going to be really useful."

"Good luck, Officers, though I really don't see why you're bothering. I'm afraid you'll be disappointed. No one in their right mind would go there, if they could even find it now."

As they pushed off, they heard Ben ask his mother, "Are they going to find Daddy?"

"I don't know, darling. Come. Let's go inside and get you dressed and get to work on that colouring book."

OUT ON THE water again, Ames pursed his lips thoughtfully. "She already knows Philippa Bentley is missing. She might even know her husband had a dubious war record. But maybe not. He certainly seems to have been a normal sort of husband until he started giving all their money away and might have taken up with an old lover. I think she's right—this is going to be a waste of time. I bet he's just packed up and left because it all got too much for him. But we're here now. We might as well get it over with." He pushed the outboard to its limits, and the boat leaped forward and fell on the water with a loud "thwack."

Terrell, who had felt considerably less nervous because the wind had died down, now clutched the side of the boat convulsively with his left hand and pointed more or less to where they ought to go. "Okay. We're looking for 'a big rock.' That could be some sort of point, maybe? Should we slow down so we don't miss it?"

Ames steered. "If it was being used as a drop for money he owed, he wouldn't be going an awfully long way from home. It surprises me he took his son there."

Terrell shrugged. "Perhaps it was before he began to use it for that. Of course, we may be way off course, as it were, and the house might have nothing to do with any of it."

"I don't know. One cove looks pretty much like another. A secluded location would be a good place for a drop, but this is pretty elaborate."

Once along the opposite shore, they putted slowly, looking for Ben's "big rock."

"Do you get the feeling that Mrs. Arden is not all that sorry about her husband's disappearance?" Ames asked.

"I know what you mean. I wondered that myself. It makes me wonder if she knew more than she's said. She certainly doesn't make it sound as if her life's been idyllic. If you're happier when your husband is off somewhere, that suggests something, all right."

The morning was crystalline, and the air was warming up, putting them both into a better humour than their mission would suggest. Terrell was beginning to relax again, having got across the lake and finding himself still alive. If he stayed in this part of the country, he could almost imagine himself taking a little boat out onto the lake. "It's pretty nice out here when it's not windy."

"The wind can whip up pretty quickly. People have been out in the wider part of the lake, been caught, and never made it back."

"Thank you, sir. That's reassuring." Terrell looked up at the quiet blue sky with misgivings.

"Hey, how about this?" Ames said. He slowed the motor and pointed.

Terrell turned and saw an outcropping of rock that wasn't that high but could well be to a child's eye. They motored slowly past it and saw a tiny, curved beach tucked behind it. Ames angled toward it, ran the boat directly onto the sandy pebbled beach, and tilted the motor.

"Here's where those galoshes come in handy. Hop out and pull us closer."

Terrell stepped into the water from the wobbling boat and felt a wash of icy cold water sweep over the top of his boot. "It's deeper than it looks," he said, pulling at rope and bow until the boat was halfway onto the beach.

He found a log and sat to pull off his boot and empty the water out.

"Bad luck," Ames said, watching the cascade of water coming out of Terrell's boot, then added, "That could be a path." He walked to the beginning of the treeline and stopped where the yellowing grass had a look of possibly being trampled. "Mind you, it could just have been made by bears coming down for a drink." He grinned at Terrell's expression. "No need to worry. They're more afraid of us than we are of them."

"Somehow I doubt that, sir," Terrell said, following Ames into the dark shadow of the forest, his wet boot squelching unpleasantly. It took only a moment to realize any trampling was just on the edge of the wood.

Farther along the beach, they found a well-established firepit with several bottles strewn around it.

"A drinking spot. Certainly no cabin from what I can see. Should we go to the next cove?" Ames said.

"How many coves were you thinking of checking, sir?" Terrell asked nervously, when they were back on the water.

"The next one, then I think we give up. I really think this guy either went off with the Bentley woman or went off on his own."

"But why not drive off? Why the boat?"

Ames shrugged. "Wanted to leave his wife the car? She's got the kids, after all. For all we know, he went down the river toward Castlegar, where he could pick up the train."

"Wrong way for the boat to drift back, sir." Some minutes later, Terrell pointed past Ames. "There's another cove, sir."

"Let's check it quickly. When we've finished here, we can contact the station in Castlegar, see if anyone matching his description took the train anywhere."

This time Terrell managed to get out and pull the boat up without getting his feet wet. "This might be it. There's a path, all right," he said, pointing toward the dense wood at the edge of the rocky beach.

They'd gone no more than a hundred yards when they saw it: a squat log structure that the builder had tried to cheer up with some white clapboard, much of which was now hanging down or on the ground.

"If this is it, I can see why the kid thought it was scary," Ames said. "Who the hell would put a place like this in the middle of nowhere?"

They approached slowly and had gone some forty yards when Terrell spoke. "Little Ben is right about the smell, only this is much worse than what he probably smelled. I'm afraid we've found something dead."

Ames turned away, took a deep breath, clamped a handkerchief over his nose and mouth, and covered the distance to the cabin. He peered in the gaping doorway and then stumbled back to gasp in some clean air. "I didn't give it long enough to see who it is. He's face down."

Equipping himself with his own handkerchief, Terrell went to the door of the cabin. Whoever it was had been shot in the back. It looked as though the man had fallen forward by the way his body was splayed out. He looked up at the door and back to the body. Had the man even seen his attacker? The sickly sweet smell was overwhelming. Terrell took a quick look at the man's clothing. A pair of black pants, a blue shirt, suspenders, and a short brown leather jacket rent with the telltale bullet hole. He staggered out of the cabin and found that Ames had gone around the back.

"No sign of anyone leaving this way. It's pretty dense bush back here," Ames said.

By silent mutual agreement, they made their way some distance up the path toward the beach, and both stood gasping in fresh air.

"Damn. I should have checked his pockets," Ames said.

"He's still there, sir," Terrell said.

"Oh, very funny." On the principle that he would never ask an underling to do something he wouldn't do himself, Ames started back toward the cabin, but Terrell anticipated him and passed him.

"I'll go sir. I can hold my breath longer than you."

"Well, I can't let that stand," Ames said. "Now we both have to go, one side each. Ready? On three... Aha!" He held up a roll of cash triumphantly.

Outside again, Ames said, "Man, that does look like the photo of Arden his wife showed us. She said he had some clothes with him in some sort of rucksack, and a revolver. Finding those would confirm it."

Terrell was already circling the cottage, looking into the bush in case the killer had thrown these things out of sight. "Nothing directly around here, sir. I suppose he could have pushed deeper into the woods here to get rid of the stuff, but I'm wondering if he took them."

"And yet, he left this nice roll of money untouched in the man's trouser pocket," Ames said, holding up the roll. "Let's search around on the way back to the boat. It would be a nuisance if whoever it was took the stuff with him. Searching a dead man's pockets is not that much fun." He shuddered.

Standing at the edge of the water, looking at the boat they came on, Ames said, "She said he took the motor, but the boat came back without it. Did the killer take it? Did he throw it in the drink and push the empty boat into the lake to drift away?"

Terrell crunched along the beach looking into the water as Ames spoke. At the end, where the rocky point rose up, he turned and walked along the curve to the other end, bounded by deep brush that went right to the water's edge. He bent over and fetched out a bottle that had been lodged under the bushes. "An empty bottle. Some juvenile beach party, perhaps. It looks as if it's been here a long time. The label is faded and peeling. I imagine there is a lot of this sort of thing if this place was used for years, as Mrs. Arden suggests."

"Bring it along, I guess," Ames said. "Doesn't look like anyone has used this place since last summer, maybe. There are the remains of a firepit." He pointed at a slight indentation in the beach with a partial row of rocks placed around it. It certainly hadn't been used recently. "Good thing, too. If kids were here in the last few days, they would have found him."

Terrell made his way back to the boat, still looking in the water. He leaned over and, pulling up his sleeve, reached into the water and pulled up a rusty metal object. After scraping off the sand, he held the object up for Ames to inspect.

"That is an oarlock, landlubber. If we keep this up, we are going to find a garbage can full of old stuff. We need nice fresh prints and a discarded pistol," Ames said.

I STILL CAN'T get over it," Ames said, angling the boat back toward town. "It's almost certainly Arden. I've only seen a photo, but I would bet it's him. With two hundred dollars in a nice little roll and no sign of his rucksack. It makes no sense at all."

Terrell nodded, his mind no longer on his anxieties about Ames's handling of the boat. The money was wrapped in Terrell's handkerchief in his pocket, and the bottle and rusty oarlock rested on the floor of the boat. "It would certainly make more sense if it was not Arden. Let's say he's brought that money for a blackmailer. If that's Arden, and he was shot by the blackmailer to keep him quiet, his blackmailer would surely have taken the money after he shot him. And if dead guy is the blackmailer, and Arden shot him, he wouldn't leave his two hundred bucks in the dead man's pocket."

They had found nothing else in any of his pockets to identify the man. They would have to find out anything else about the man's death from Ashford Gillingham, a local doctor who had become involved in forensic work for the police. Ames said, "Gilly will enjoy this. He likes dead people."

NICE DAY ON the water, fellows?" O'Brien said when they came through the doors of the station.

"Hardly," Ames said, taking off his jacket and holding it away from him as if it had been tainted by what they'd seen. "Terrell got a boot full of water, and we found an old empty bottle of hooch, a rusty oarlock, and...oh, and a dead guy. Can you get Gilly on the telephone?"

"Well, well," said O'Brien, reaching for the phone. "The boss has only been gone five minutes and already you two are stirring up trouble. Where shall I say he's wanted?"

"Tell him to come here, and to wear his wellies. I guess I'd better get my equipment. If I'd known we were going to find a corpse, I'd have taken the damn camera with me in the first place."

O'Brien put the call through, and Ames headed toward the stairs but then turned to await the outcome of the phone call. Terrell was contemplating the roll of money on his desk, along with the bottle and the oarlock, wondering about fingerprints.

After a couple of brief exchanges, O'Brien hung up the phone. "You two had better go get a quick lunch down you. It's going to take him an hour to get here. He's finishing something up at the hospital."

"Good idea, Sergeant. One of your best. Put that oarlock down, Constable. I feel the need of a sandwich and a strong, sweet cup of tea, for the shock and all that. In fact," he said, bouncing back with the unabashed ability of the young to slough off unpleasantness, "I'm having two. I'm going to have to motor back along the lake to take Gilly out to see our little friend."

CHAPTER SIXTEEN

"**T**HAT'S PROBABLY HIM NOW," SANDRA Donaldson said, looking up toward the ceiling, where stockinged steps could be heard creaking on the floor above. "Listen, I'll go get things moving in the kitchen. His nibs will be home soon, and we'll have a nice dinner. I managed, don't ask, to get hold of a scrawny chicken. Unfortunately, we can whistle for spuds. They've been put on strict ration suddenly, after being the easiest thing to get during the war!"

Lane stood at the window, her heart beating unevenly, or so it felt. She chided herself for being nervous about seeing the man she loved—after all, they had only been apart a few days. Perhaps it was the distance. Seeing him far away from their home made it seem as if they'd been apart far longer. Outside, the street was quiet. She looked at her watch. Of course—kids would be in school. She still didn't have a clear sense of what time it was. She turned as she heard him coming down the stairs, and then heard

Sandra asking if he slept well. He had. "You'd better go along into the sitting room, then. I'll bring you a cuppa."

"You don't have to—" he began.

"No, really. Get along with you."

"Darling!" He stood in the doorway, surprised for a moment, and then came to her, folding her in his arms, breathing in the scent of her hair. "How did you get here?"

She pulled away and moved his hair away from his eyes and kissed him. "The usual way, on the underground. Sandra telephoned my hotel and told me you were out like a light. I thought I'd come and have a look. She offered dinner. Obviously, I couldn't turn it down. How was your flight?"

"Long. I think air travel is barely a step up from flying a bomber. Cold and noisy. I think they imagine the passengers are going to sleep, but I conditioned myself to stay awake while in the air all through the war, and it turns out not to be an easy habit to break." Darling had been a pilot on a Lancaster bomber.

There was a tentative knock on the door frame, and Sandra came in with a cup of tea, a couple of digestives perched on the saucer. "Please excuse me. I thought Frederick had better have a cup of tea to hold him till supper. There, I'm out of your hair!" She retired to the kitchen.

Darling and Lane sat on the sofa, hands intertwined. In her joy at being with him again, it seemed quite the coziest little parlour Lane could imagine. Worn furniture, a few books on a bookshelf pushed into insignificance by a massive wireless. Dark green curtains, the ornate gas grate in the fireplace. But it felt like a place where people who loved each other lived. "It's quite romantic meeting each other like this, so far from home," she said.

"You seem to be able to find romance in everything. Tomorrow, I go with the redoubtable CI Sims to Kent to have a look at a bombed-out house where the corpse was found. I suppose you'd find that romantic as well." He put his cup of tea down and kissed her again, and then took up the biscuit.

"Absolutely. I, on the other hand, must twiddle my thumbs. I had hopes about Major Hogarth being able to help me, but she claimed she had nothing whatever to offer."

Darling frowned. "Major Hogarth? Isn't she the woman at the War Office who helped you find my crew?"

Lane nodded. "I don't know what she does, exactly, but I suspect she was well in with the SOE. We never tell each other anything, you know, those of us who were involved. But somehow, we all seem to be in on the thing. But not this time. She said she'd never heard of Diana."

"I really hope you are not implying that you think your sister is a spy. That's a rat hole that contains that bounder, Dunn, right at the bottom of it."

"There's where you're wrong. He's been retired. I expect his utterly botching up getting you hanged to cover up his messes finally did for him. I'm sure the new wave of intelligence officers are modern and clinical. I can't say why I think she might be doing that sort of work, but I think it nonetheless."

Darling nodded, thirstily drinking his tea. "I don't really understand all that secrecy. Wouldn't it get in the way? You get that sort of thing among different forces because the locals don't want the Mounties in on their patch and so on. We're lucky in Nelson; we seem to get along just fine, but in general, secrecy is a nuisance, and I bet criminals love it when the police in different jurisdictions don't share what they know."

"I'm sure you're right. The trouble is the whole enterprise is steeped in it, and all the agents as well. I don't think it's good for people, especially people who are secretive by nature. And what about all the women who were in the field of battle or breaking codes? There are thousands of women right now whose husbands and families know absolutely nothing about what they did during the war. They live the lie every day of their lives that they did nothing important, that they are just ordinary housewives and not very clever because they are only women. It's monstrous, now that I think about it."

He took her hand and kissed it and said gently, "You have the most attractive frown. But you're rather secretive too—I mean, I can guess why. It's lucky for you I think you're brighter and far more clever than I am. And lucky for me I don't really know what you did in the war. It would keep me up at night." Lane had only ever told Darling a snippet about one of her missions, when a French Resistance fighter had been killed and she'd felt herself responsible; she'd only told him because she'd been grazed by a bullet on their honeymoon and the shock had caused her to think she was back in France. Even though she knew he would never reveal anything, she felt some guilt at even telling him that much, especially when she knew of all the women who would never talk about their wartime work.

She turned to look at him. "Do you? Think I'm clever? Do you really, or are you just talking nonsense?"

"I do, actually. I've always thought so. I suppose it's why you can't help interfering in my work. And look at all those languages you speak. I barely limp along in English."

She settled back, thoughtfully picking up the remaining quarter of his digestive biscuit and popping it into her mouth.

"Hey! That was mine."

"I don't think I agree with you. I mean, the biscuit, yes, sorry, but about the intelligence. I think we might be pretty equal. That's why the whole thing works."

He kissed her on the mouth lingeringly. "It's not the only reason, surely? Shall I come home with you to the Imperial tonight?"

"We can try. The manageress looks like a very stern 'no gentleman callers' type."

"I'm your husband," he said in mock outrage.

"She'll want proof. Did you bring proof? My passport is still under 'Winslow.'"

"Bother! Then let's pretend we're not married. We can go for long walks among the wreckage, and I can take you to supper in the evenings. And we can pine."

"I doubt there'll be time for all that. You'll be engaged with your pal Sims, and I may have to dash off at any minute. Seriously, I haven't a clue where all this business with Diana will go; I really do think she might be in danger."

Darling saw the worry in Lane's eyes and felt his own worry. If Diana was in danger, then it followed as night followed day that, sooner or later, Lane would be as well.

His thoughts on the matter lay unexpressed as, at that moment, Rudy came through the front door and didn't even bother to hang up his hat or Macintosh but came straight into the sitting room.

"How absolutely splendid to see you both again! I've been happy all day just thinking about it. Mrs. Darling! How lovely to be able to say that!" He kissed her on both cheeks and then seized Darling's hand. "Frederick. Splendid. Matrimony agrees with you, I see!"

"It does indeed."

"I'll just go see what wants doing, and then I want to hear all about what brings you both here!"

The evening passed with Darling sharing his mission, and Lane protesting that she was on a visit to her grandparents because her grandfather had been ill, and then the two men talking about their shared experiences as bomber pilots during the war. Lane and Sandra left them to it, and Lane insisted on doing the dishes.

"Are you really just here for your grandfather?" Sandra asked her.

"I really am. My sister is here somewhere as well. She was visiting them and then went off with friends and hasn't come back yet. I told them I'd track her down. The poor old dears haven't had us under one roof since '38. Gosh, that's ten years! Where does the time go? Never mind me. What's new with you?" Lane looked significantly at Sandra, who was sitting at the kitchen table with a cigarette, which she stubbed out after only a few puffs.

"I don't know why, I just don't have a taste for these things suddenly."

Lane smiled. "Don't you indeed? That's probably a good thing. When are we to expect good news?"

"I knew you'd squirrel it out of me. We've only just found out. Rudy is over the moon."

Lane sat down and took her hand. "And you're not?"

Sandra looked down and shook her head. "I am too, of course, and it surprises me. I can't seem to help being happy, though I would have told you before it happened that I would be a lousy mother, and I really had been secretly hoping to go back to work somewhere. After the war I've found it, I don't know, a bit boring keeping house. I was an ambulance driver, you know. It was absolutely beastly sometimes, with the horrible things I saw during the bombings, but I felt useful and important. What will I be like with a little kiddie? I won't even be able to wear red lipstick anymore."

"I don't know why not. I should think any child would be delighted looking into the face of a beautiful mother with interesting red lips! I know what you mean, about feeling useful. I think it's a real dilemma. I'm afraid I get terribly curious about Frederick's cases. I don't mean to interfere, but I enjoy—if that's the word I want for so ghoulish a pastime—the puzzle of human behaviour." She saw, of course, that this curiosity was how she combatted her own postwar ennui. "But that's neither here nor there. You will be the most wonderful mother. You will be generous and kind, and you'll think your child is the most interesting creature. And if it's a girl, you will make sure she can do anything she wants. I think whoever it is will be terribly lucky to have you two as parents."

"THEY ARE SUCH lovely people," Lane said as she and Darling set off for the Imperial, resolved that Darling was merely dropping her off. "They're going to be parents."

"That's splendid!" Darling said. "They'll be wonderful parents. I can't imagine being anyone's parent." He had her hand tucked into his coat pocket as they walked toward the underground station. "But I'm prepared to chance it, if you ever get the yen."

"I think I should find my sister first, and you should sort out the body in the bombed-out house. I wonder how Ames is getting on?" But her hesitation was about more than that, she thought suddenly. It was her own unsatisfactory upbringing. What kind of a mother could she be when she had so little experience of it? Even with the love lavished on her and her sister by their mother's parents, she and Diana were still fatally at odds with each other. She tried to imagine holding a baby in her arms and was about to imagine that she really couldn't see it, when an image flickered in her mind: herself as a little girl, holding Diana. She could almost feel the tiny form as she held her against her chest. How had Nanny even given her the chance? Nanny was such a stickler about the baby. No one had been allowed to touch Diana. Had she snuck into the nursery one afternoon and simply picked Diana up? Nanny would have had a fit. Feeling almost a glow at the physical memory, she turned to Darling, but he had fallen into thought.

"It's funny, you know," he said finally. "This body belonged to a woman named Renshaw, and a Major Renshaw, who died in the Great War, was the CO of our missing man. She was married to him—a very unsuccessful marriage, if his brother is to be believed. He said the baby she was carrying was not her husband's. There! Sink your teeth into that!"

Lane stopped, frowning, trying to recall something. "I'm just trying to remember. I'm pretty sure someone, either Eleanor or maybe Gladys, or the hairdresser, told me that she'd heard that that missing man, Arden, was a notorious womanizer. She'd said, 'He even made a play for his commanding officer's wife.' Remember? Could this dead woman be the one?"

"I do remember. It will go into the hopper, though it is just gossip, however interesting, and he could have had more than one CO. This woman has been dead for at least thirty years." He sighed. "Even when you are engaged in some dark pursuit of your missing sister, you still find a way to nose into what I'm doing."

SIMS CAME TO where Darling was standing at the window looking out at the foggy morning. "Inspector Darling. What a pleasure to see you again." He shook Darling's hand firmly and gave him a pat on the shoulder.

"Likewise, Chief Inspector. So, this is your domain."

"It is. Aside from the building having an attractively stripey exterior, it's crowded and noisy."

Indeed, the clattering of typewriters, doors slamming, people talking, and all the busy coming and going gave the place a rackety air of purpose. It suggested, Darling thought whimsically, that they would never be able to get at all the crime, no matter how hard they tried. "It's impressive. I imagine in a city this size the work never ends."

"It does not. And we're still sorting out crimes from the war. Come, let's get out of here. I managed to collar an interview room, and I'll tell you all about it. Or we could go to the canteen. The tea is thick and bracing."

"I'm staying with an Air Force buddy whose wife is feeding me as if I'd crawled in off a desert somewhere, but thanks."

They pushed their way through the busyness, and Sims showed Darling into a cramped room with a table and two chairs and very little else. "I brought what I have in the file. By the way," Sims said, waving Darling into a chair, "whatever happened to that wonderful woman?"

"I married her," Darling said simply.

"Lucky devil. And I should hope so, after what she did for you. She deserves a medal."

"I'm afraid all she got was me," Darling said, smiling. "Now then, the dead Canadian."

"Right." Sims opened the file and produced a photograph. "Here she is *in situ*." The photo showed a mostly exposed skeleton on what looked like an earthen floor behind a large conical structure with the narrowest part at the bottom, which Darling could not identify. The body had evidently been pushed into a small space behind it, against the curved wall. "This is, was, a smallish converted oast house. This structure here, which she'd been pushed behind, is the kiln for drying hops. She was exposed when the rubble was being carted away, preparatory to the building of a new farmhouse. The owner is fit to be tied because he's had to wait for us to finish the investigation."

Darling looked more closely at the photo. "What's going on with her hands?" He pointed at the image.

The skeletal hands were folded across her chest.

"Well spotted," Sims said. "We thought it unusual as well. As if the person who put her there had a sudden attack of conscience and wanted the body to look as though it had been respectfully laid out."

"Where is she now?" Darling asked, holding the photo close and then far to try to get it into better focus.

"We've pulled her out and put her in our morgue, as we would normally. We assumed she was a casualty of war, from the building being bombed, but we found the evidence of a bullet in the floor about five feet from the cottage door. Typical wartime ordnance for, say, a Webley MK VI. It doesn't tell us much. Everyone was issued one of those, officers and men alike. It might suggest she was shot by a soldier, but that isn't even sure because I imagine that type of revolver would not have been that hard to get. A leather satchel was under her head. We found some papers, more or less intact because they'd been wrapped in oilcloth. As you can see, there are remnants of a garment on her, and because it was blue, we wondered if she was Canadian. The papers confirmed it."

Darling put the photo back and was about to read the report when he picked up the photo again. "The bullet was in the floor? It suggests she was lying down when she was shot. That's a little unexpected. Did her assailant knock her down first?" Darling mused. He turned now to the police report. "Francine Elizabeth MacDonald, lieutenant. How did you conclude her name was Renshaw?"

"This." Sims picked up a photo and a folded, yellowed paper and handed them over. The photo was a wedding picture of, presumably, Lieutenant MacDonald, a pretty young woman with pale eyes and a very strong jaw, her hair hidden by her nursing cap, being married to an officer in a Canadian Armed Forces uniform. While she had allowed herself a little smile, the mustachioed man stood rigidly, his thick dark eyebrows drawn together as if he were being made to look into the sun. The paper indeed confirmed that Lieutenant MacDonald had married Major Richard Renshaw, on July 20, 1917, Boulogne-sur-Mer, France.

"So, not a coincidence," he said, almost to himself. "We have a missing person case I've left my men working on, and as it happens, Richard Renshaw was the missing man's CO. But would she not have been sent home? Canadian nursing sisters, as far as I recall, had to be single," Darling said.

Sims shrugged. "Yours to discover. Among the questions we cannot answer are: Why was she in England? The scraps we found indicate she was still in uniform when she was killed. Was she on leave? That suggests she continued with her nursing unit after she married. The post-mortem has been a bit hasty because there are more urgent current cases that need our attention. Oh, one immediate observation made by our man is that she was pregnant. And you can't see it in this photo, but just here"—Sims pointed at the middle of the remains—"there was evidence of flowers having been put on her, to go, presumably, with the crossed hands. A seed pod and dried stems suggested roses. Now, what do you make of that?"

Darling took up the photo and stared at it. "A killer with a guilty conscience? Or mad as a hatter? He strikes her, shoots her, and then arranges her with crossed hands and flowers." In the wedding photo, the young woman looked shy at first glance. Her head was tilted downward as if she were trying to look modest, but she was looking straight into the camera. She was in uniform, probably her parade uniform, as was Major Renshaw. But he looked more closely at her eyes, which he saw had a direct, almost challenging look. Had she challenged her killer with that look? Renshaw's brother had told him she was unsuitable, from a bohemian family. Had the murderer killed her and blamed her for his violence? Had the wedding been a hurried affair because of the pregnancy? He sighed. There was no need to suppose the wedding was hasty, though a wedding smack in the middle of a war zone seemed unusual. She certainly would have been no use as a nursing sister if she had been pregnant. And there was the glaring problem of her having been murdered and buried in an oast house in Kent.

"Whom did the cottage belong to back then?"

"We haven't sorted that one out completely. I thought you might like a drive out to have a look. I'd like to put that farmer out of his misery as soon as possible. There and back; I can get you back here by six?"

"Certainly. I'll just leave a message for my wife. We're meeting up at six and I can let her know I might be late."

"She's here as well?" Sims asked in surprise.

"She is. Visiting her grandparents and trying to find an errant sister. In fact, she came over before me."

"No wonder you were so quick to take up my invitation. You should make sure you get a nice holiday together out of the deal."

"I'm sure we will. Her grandparents are up near Peebles."

245

Sims shivered. "Scotland in the spring. You Canadians do live for pleasure alone."

August 1917

"IT'S KIND OF strange looking, isn't it? The agent told me it used to be an oast house, whatever that is. Like a miniature castle of our very own," Francine said. "Now that it's just the two of us, it will be plenty roomy." Another girl, Susan, who had planned to holiday with them, had accepted an invitation to stay with a friend in London. The little cottage with its brick tower and its peculiar white cowl was perched at the edge of a now sunny sloping field with a few large oak trees providing shade for a scattering of sheep. A stone wall climbed the hill behind the cottage. It had been a good twenty-minute walk from the village where the omnibus had dropped them off. They were pleased when they finally saw the cottage. The front had a lattice with actual roses on it, and there was a massive chestnut tree providing shade in a little grassy area outside. The garden was overgrown, as if the owner hadn't had time to tend to it, but on a beautiful August day it looked "quaint, with that round tower," Betsy declared. The inside of the cottage, however, was tiny and, in spite of its new renovation, dark. A heavy door into the tower was closed tight and would not budge when Betsy tried it. "It's quite cold inside, isn't it?" Betsy looked tentatively into the only other room. The tiny kitchen opened into a small sitting room with a dark couch and an armchair that had decidedly seen better days. Everything smelled of mildew. "We'll have to share a pretty narrow bed."

"We just have to open the windows and let in some air. It will soon warm up," Francine said. She put her bag and satchel down and surveyed the tiny dark space. "It's those thick walls. They keep the cool in. There must be some wood somewhere. Let's light a fire in the stove and have a nice cup of tea."

Betsy did not put her bag down. "It's the most depressing place I've ever been, and who knows what's in that thing," she said, pointing toward the locked door. "Why didn't we just decide to go to London and enjoy a bit of nightlife with Susan? She was right to change her mind. I wish I'd done the same thing. This place is like a morgue."

Francine, who had been longing for silence after the constant din of the big guns—and, if the truth be known, the tumult of her own feelings and growing sense of dread about her situation—looked at Betsy. "Look, I really do understand if you don't want to stay here. There's an omnibus to the train station at"—she looked at the watch pinned on her uniform—"two thirty. There's plenty of time for you to catch it. I don't mind at all staying here by myself. It's just what I need, honestly. I've got some books, I can get my letter writing done, and I can go for walks. Look at this countryside. I shall be as happy as a lamb."

Betsy finally put her suitcase down, but it was only to take Francine's hand. "I can't leave you here like this, in your state." She looked at Francine's belly.

"I'm fine! It's early days yet, nothing to fuss about. I just need some peace and quiet."

"Does he know? He doesn't seem like the kind of man who'd, you know..." She'd heard from some of the enlisted men what Renshaw was like.

Francine smiled. "You worry too much. If I told him, he might be upset. Anyone would, but I think he'd understand." How she hoped this was true. She'd begun to write him a letter before they married, to tell him about Ben, but then she'd torn it up. But she couldn't live with the dishonesty right into their marriage. He'd been cool and standoffish toward her and gone back to the front directly after their marriage. Had he already decided they weren't suited? She still wondered if Ben had said something, even hinted to the other men, if not to Richard. But the consequences for Ben would have been severe. It didn't matter. She had written him again just after the wedding when he was at the front, and this time had posted the letter. Her husband knew now.

Betsy shook her head. "I know you, Francine. You won't be able to live with the lie. You'll tell him, if you haven't already. You can't help yourself. I don't think you should, especially because of...the way it happened. He'd be liable to kill someone."

"Don't worry. I did write to him, yes. I didn't tell him who...he won't do anything rash. I'm sure...I'm sure he'll understand. Now, you go off back to London and have a good time. I'll see you back on the boat." Even in the short period she'd spent with her husband, the one thing she knew for certain was that he would not understand at all.

IT WAS NEARLY nine when Francine pulled herself away from where she had been sitting in the garden. The afternoon heat had finally begun to dissipate, and the light was beginning to wane. She pulled her shawl around her shoulders and wondered why she hadn't got out of her uniform yet. It was a kind of inertia, she supposed. She thought about the letter she'd written to Richard before they'd even left France. Looking back, she was astonished at her own rash behaviour. She had received no answer from him, and she told herself that it was because of the fighting, or perhaps the letter had never reached him. She had a feeling now as if her life was suspended, and she was waiting and waiting for something, she knew not what.

She sat on the broken-down sofa, her hands flat on either side of her as if she were trying to hold herself there. What happened with Ben was shameful. She could see that so clearly now. How had she not then? She should never have met with him. He had said he loved her, had always loved her—lies, of course—and she had been lost. She knew she had been vulnerable because she had discovered almost the moment she'd married Richard that he was the wrong man for her. She'd been lured by a desperate need to be looked after when she was at her weakest. The illusion of security and closeness had been broken almost at once. He'd been cold on their wedding night. She coloured at the memory of his "doing his duty" as if it were painful to him. She had been made to feel ashamed of her own desire. After what she'd done with Ben, her shame had become acute. It had been stupid to expose herself to danger like that. That was the trouble, really: she had always had the upper hand with Ben since they were children. Now she understood that that had been, was still, a kind of love, however unhealthy, and she had not been able to pull away from him.

She finally dragged herself off the couch and cleaned up after her modest supper of tea and toast and a boiled egg. She had hoped the walk from the village to the cottage would have tired her and she would sleep well, but even now, as she brought her teacup and placed it next to the washing-up basin, she wasn't sure how she would sleep. She had always been sure that things would work out in her life. Now she wondered if her luck had finally run out. She almost felt comfort at this. She didn't deserve luck.

After a brief moment of wondering if she should go outside and draw a bucket of water for the morning, she shivered and decided she'd best get into bed and try to get some sleep. She had just put aside her shawl and folded down the bedclothes when there was a knock on the door. Unconsciously she put her shawl back around her shoulders and, holding the kerosene lamp, went to open the door. Her eyes were wide with surprise when she saw who it was.

"Oh! What . . . what are you doing here?"

CHAPTER SEVENTEEN

"IT'S RAINING." ASHFORD GILLINGHAM, THE doctor who stood in for pathologist, glumly held his umbrella unsteadily over his head as the boat sped to the little cove where the cabin was, bouncing on the waves whipped up by the wind.

"Yes, sorry. Here, could you take this under there with you?" Ames, wearing a raincoat and a heavy felt hat, handed Gilly his camera case. "I'm sure you'll find it very interesting when we get there," he added.

"Why do you assume that because I have obligingly allowed myself to be roped in by the police to look at their messes, I actually enjoy it? I enjoy a good book and my evening pipe. Dead bodies are not all that amusing."

Gilly sat in the boat, refusing to move until Ames had pulled it well up the beach, and only then got out gingerly, like a cat avoiding a puddle.

The cool weather had dampened the smell of death slightly, but both Ames and Gilly wrapped handkerchiefs around their noses and mouths. Gilly stood at the feet of the body. "Judging by the bullet hole in his jacket, it's pretty close to the spine. I'll know better what's what when he's on the table. I wonder if the shooter was aiming for the general area of the heart and was just a lousy shot. No sign of a second shot to make sure," he said, as if he were talking to himself. He walked back toward the doorway, counting the steps. "I'm going to guess the gun was fired from here in the doorway. The gunman obviously did not announce his presence. You found the roll of money in his pocket?"

"Yes, the left one," Ames said. "What do you think that means?"

"Search me," Gilly said irritably. He really didn't like the rain. "I don't see a second shot taken, so the shooter might have thought he was dead when he went down after the first shot. Perhaps after having done it he was afraid and ran. You're the ones who look at peculiar human behaviour. I just figure out how they died. Do you know who he is?"

"No. It's either the missing man, Arden, or someone else."

"Well, that should cover every man in the known universe. When are they coming to get him?"

Ames, who'd been leaning over looking at the man's face, trying to place whether it was a match for the grainy photo he'd seen of Arden, stood straight and went to stand outside the cabin. "I think that's them now."

"Good." Gilly looked down at the man's feet. "That's interesting."

"What?" Ames, his disgust superseded by curiosity, moved closer.

"There's a bit of scraping here, as if he'd managed to

move a couple of inches before he succumbed." He stood back. "Has someone moved the body?"

"Definitely not. It was all we could do to check his pockets. Poor guy. You're saying he didn't die outright?" Ames imagined the victim felled, then instinctively trying to drag himself forward, knowing perhaps that he'd reached the end. He shivered.

Gilly nodded speculatively. "It's possible. Poor beggar."

"He had a rucksack, according to his wife, and a service revolver. We haven't been able to find either. We assume the killer took them."

"Very clever, Ames. I shall mention it to Darling when he gets back. I expect that's right. Now, can we get out of here? I can give you more answers when we've looked at him."

Outside, on the path back to the beach, Gilly pulled his handkerchief away from his nose and took a deep breath. "You'll have to get the missing man's wife to come have a look at him. That's a beastly part of the business, I imagine."

"You imagine right," Ames said, his heart sinking at the prospect. But all the way back, he wondered why the shooter wanted the rucksack.

AMES WAS LEANING against Terrell's desk with his hands in his pockets. "I telephoned her. She's coming in with her friend Mrs. Barnes, after they pick up the kids from school and drop them off at a friend's. I never know what to do with a weeping woman."

"A gentle hand on the back? A cup of tea? Grief is a solitary affair. The tea gambit is good because you can leave her alone for a few minutes to compose herself while you get it."

"SHE'S HERE, AMES," O'Brien called over. He stood up and pulled the door open. Mrs. Arden was with Mrs. Barnes, looking pale with anxiety. She was wearing a coat and a dull green hat that made her look older.

"Here goes," Ames muttered, scrambling up.

"Anything I can do, sir?" Terrell asked, also standing.

"Maybe get the tea makings ready." Ames went forward to greet the two women. "Thank you for coming."

"I hope you don't mind me coming too," Mrs. Barnes said. "I couldn't leave the poor dear to face this on her own."

"No, that's perfectly fine. If you'll follow me downstairs."

As they heard the descending footsteps, O'Brien shook his head at Terrell. "Never liked this part of the job," he said.

Outside the door of the small room that served as a morgue, Mrs. Arden turned to her friend. "Just wait here. I have to do this on my own."

Her friend looked as if she were going to protest, but Mrs. Arden shook her head vigorously and then nodded at Ames. Putting her gloved hand over her mouth, she followed him into the room and stood beside the draped figure.

Ames, trying not to breathe, moved the sheet off the body to reveal the head and shoulders, and stood aside. Mrs. Arden looked at the man. She did not move her hand, so her face was unreadable.

"How did he die?" she asked finally.

Ames cleared his throat. How much to say? "Dr. Gillingham said a bullet shattered his rib very near his spinal cord, and it's likely a bone shard severed the cord."

"I see." She leaned toward the dead man's face, looked at it for another moment, and then turned toward the door. "Thank you."

Ames stayed behind to replace the sheet and breathed a sigh of relief that she did not ask if he'd died outright or suffered. Once out in the hall, he found the two women talking quietly. Mrs. Barnes had her hand on Mrs. Arden's shoulder and was peering into her face.

"Are you all right? Please, sit down here." Ames turned a chair toward her.

"I'm fine," Mrs. Arden said brusquely. "It's him. Did you find the rucksack? He took some of his clothes." Her face was without expression.

"No. Not yet, I'm afraid. We found some money in one of his pockets."

"Money? How much money?" Mrs. Arden looked up at Ames in surprise. "It's mine, of course."

"Mrs. Arden, let me get you a cup of tea," Ames said, beginning to feel slightly desperate himself at her lack of emotion and the problem of the money. He knew she needed it, and it was technically hers, he was sure, but it was evidence.

"I don't want tea. I want to get out of here, and I want my money. How much was it?"

"Two hundred dollars, but I'm afraid we have to hang on to it. It's evidence in a murder."

"Two hundred dollars?" She collapsed into the chair. "Two hundred? It's money that will feed my children!" she said angrily. "How long do you need to keep it?"

"Um, I'm not sure. I will try to get it released as soon as I can, I promise."

"Let's get out of here," she said to Mrs. Barnes, standing up. She turned back to Ames. "I hope you didn't think I'd be distraught. He took every penny I owned, and he was planning to leave me and the children. Do you know what he told me right after our wedding? He told me he would never get over his first love. Can you imagine saying that to your new wife? I was devastated. I could never forget that, you know." She sniffed angrily, looking toward the closed room where his body lay. "Getting himself shot was the final straw."

O'BRIEN WATCHED THE two women confer on the street and then turn down the hill toward the Kootenay Feed Store. He looked to where Terrell and Ames were talking by the stairs. "There goes love's young dream. You planning to hang on to her money?"

"Oh, she told you," Ames said.

"Sure did. In no uncertain terms."

"It's evidence." Ames was feeling a bit defensive and, in truth, wasn't quite sure what he ought to do. He looked up as Terrell moved discreetly away and sat at his desk, taking up a sheet of paper.

"Constable dusted it for prints. Not much to show for it. I think we just make a note of it and give it back to her. Bastard cleaned out the bank account and left her with nothing. And she has those two kiddies."

"I wonder what the boss would do?" Ames mused, half to himself.

"You are the boss just at the moment." The phone rang, and O'Brien turned away and hoisted himself back onto his stool to answer it.

Needing a minute to clear his head, Ames went upstairs to his office, walking past Darling's unhelpfully closed door. He sat at his desk and rubbed his eyes.

Of course, he had made decisions on his own, several times now, when Darling had been away, but he had always felt there had been a good procedural basis for things. If he were to follow procedure, he'd keep the money with everything else until the case was solved. But Mrs. Arden's anger, both at her dead husband and at him, had rattled him, muddled his thinking—and, if he was being honest, his own sense of what was right. He wanted her to have the money; it was more than likely hers, and she and her children had great need of it. But what if it wasn't hers? What if it was money he took from someone else? It was only a slight possibility, but it existed. C'mon, his inner voice said, it's morally hers, regardless.

On the other hand, it was very relevant to the case because it was an anomaly. That money should not be there; the shooter should have taken it. He must have known Arden had it. After all, that was the whole reason they met there. But the shooter might have thought it was in the rucksack. Before he'd followed this bit of logic through, he was up on his feet and leaping down the stairs three at a time. He slid to a stop at Terrell's desk.

"What if the shooter didn't know?" Ames asked. "What if he had no idea about the money? Maybe the shooter wanted the bag for something else. Maybe Arden wasn't shot by the blackmailer! We have to take a thorough inventory of anyone who might want to shoot the guy."

Terrell nodded thoughtfully. "Everyone, so far, except maybe his mother, and I wouldn't bet my paycheque on that, either. Unless they had an argument, the person getting all his money got scared and shot him, then grabbed the bag and ran. It's a good idea, sir. We should expand our search."

O'Brien, who'd turned at the racket of Ames descending the stairs, said, "Oh, well done. You've added to the number of possible unknowable suspects. That's the sort of leadership I like to see!"

SIMS AND DARLING were greeted by an angry farmer who climbed out of a farm lorry when the police vehicle stopped in front of the debris of a stone cottage, mostly roofless and with the remains of what looked to Darling like a small round tower. The ruins sat in an unkempt garden at the base of a hill and lay within the boundary of a stone wall. Fat sheep were grazing in a clump along one side of the fence.

"When is this rubbish going to be over?" he asked by way of greeting. "I didn't fight in this bloody war to camp at my wife's harridan of a sister's house."

"Hello, Mr. Watler. We do appreciate your patience in this. Won't be too long now," Sims said breezily, sweeping past the farmer with Darling in tow. "This gentleman's come all the way over from Canada to see your oast house."

"If I'd known it was going to be all this trouble, I would have buried her under the foundation!" Watler called after them.

Inside, it was evident that clearing out had begun in preparation for the rebuilding of the cottage. Piles of charred and splintered boards were heaped against the wall. Wooden boxes were filled with red roof tiles, and all the doors had been removed. It was toward one of the empty frames in a curved wall that Sims was now pointing. Seeing Darling looking at the strange shape of the house, he said, "That's the kiln. Heat goes up into the tower where the hops are laid out." He pointed upward. They went inside, though with most of the roof missing, it might just as well have been outside.

Sims walked a few paces and stopped, pointing at the floor, which appeared to be tamped-down earth. "Here's where one of my men found the bullet. It's hard to know what happened, of course, but this would be consistent with, as you suggest, the woman being knocked over and then being shot. It's so close to the door, let's assume she answered the door to her killer, though he could have pushed his way in, I suppose."

Part of the floor above had been punctured by, Darling assumed, bombs, and a joist with a section of flooring from above hung down precariously, letting in light from the open floor above. He looked at the bullet hole and imagined the frightened woman backing up, pleading for her life. He was brought away from this grim picture by Sims.

"According to our impatient friend out there, he and his lads were clearing out the rubble and found her skeleton tucked behind the kiln just here. Somehow the tower wasn't damaged much, so she stayed put, more or less untouched. There was a broken and very rusted lock among the rubble. It's possible that had originally been on the door."

"Why would she have been here?"

"That's the problem, you see. Apparently, an old party who died in 1910 owned the place. Hadn't any descendants, so the place sat empty. The village council got hold of it, turned the storage area into a little living space, and let it out as a holiday cottage until it was damaged in a fire in 1917. Obviously, they didn't find her and must have abandoned any project to rebuild after the fire. Then it was bombed in '43. That did for it. Watler out there got it for a song."

"She could have come here on holiday. If she was in her uniform, it must have been sometime during the war. Did she come alone, or with her killer? You'd change into civilian clothes on holiday, so she'd not had time to do even that."

"We haven't had much time to go into all that. Now you're here, maybe you can throw some light on it. Canadians would have records of her going missing, I suppose, if she'd disappeared from her post and whatnot. I thought the family might want her back. We could arrange to have the remains repatriated if family in Canada want her." He kicked at a broken roof tile on the floor. "Not much hope of solving this at this late date, but she's worth whatever we can find out. And then she might as well go home."

"Let me call my men back in Nelson. I'll get them to track down what they can, and provide you with, I hope, an address to send the notice to. She has some family. Her husband's brother is the one who was so anxious for me to come here and put it to bed. He's of the opinion that you'll never find who killed her and that she should just be buried in one of your local military cemeteries. I assume you have cemeteries that have in the past accommodated Canadian service people."

"Brookwood in Surrey will do. Very nice place. I wonder that he's so anxious to have done."

"I do too. He suggested he was worried about a scandal if the thing drags on. He apparently didn't think much of her. Can I take you to lunch? You can tell me what you think."

"You certainly can." Sims walked over to Watler, who was watching them with the exhausted stub of a cigarette hanging out of his mouth, one hand in his pocket. "All yours. Thanks for holding off."

The farmer humphed his reply and threw his cigarette on the ground.

LANE HAD STARTED her day at loose ends. She'd hit a wall in her search for Diana. If Diana hadn't been working for the SOE, and if it were true that Hogarth knew nothing about her, and Marisa knew nothing about where she might be, she wasn't sure what more she could do. Over her cup of tea and boiled egg at a tearoom, she tried to let her mind loose to just follow its own inclination. All it did was think about when she could be on her own in a good country hotel with Darling, but back in a time when she didn't have any worries about her sister. Disgusted with herself for trusting her mind to come up with anything useful, she finished her breakfast and found herself wandering toward Horse Guards Road. She realized she was unconsciously turning her steps back to the War Office. Perhaps this was her mind delivering its idea. Instead of stopping, she walked onto Westminster Bridge, stopping in the middle as she had always done on any bridge in London, to look along as much of the river as she could see on either side of the bridge. She loved the spreading, regal magnificence of the Thames, seen from this vantage, going its own eternal way, as if oblivious of all the history that unfolded along its banks across the span of two thousand years. With a sigh, she continued across and stopped on the other side, looking back across the river.

She knew, she realized. There was no doubt whatever. Diana had been in some sort of intelligence role. And someone in that building knew about it. That is why she had found herself heading back to the War Office. If Hogarth really didn't know Diana or Tremaine, someone did. Who could she see in that warren of offices who would tell her anything? She had the tenuous connection with Major Hogarth from her dealings with her the year before, but the major certainly owed her nothing. Still, it was all she had. She remembered the wooden expression on Hogarth's face when she looked at the names, the way she'd shaken her head. Hogarth was practised. Lane knew that expression. She'd used it herself many times. It's what she'd have done in Hogarth's shoes. With a shakily confident determination, she went back up onto the Queenstown Road and across the bridge to try again.

"Full marks for persistence, Miss Winslow," Major Hogarth said to her when she had offered Lane the chair opposite the desk for the second time in as many days. "I still don't see in what way I can help you. We, I, have never heard of your sister. She was not involved with any organization through us." She hesitated. "I can say this with certainty because after you left yesterday, I did ask someone who might know, who used to have connections with some people in the SOE that I might not have. I'm afraid, as I'd suspected, that I came up with nothing."

"Thank you for trying, Major Hogarth. The problem, really, is that I'm not sure if I believe that. That is to say, you yourself may not know about her, but someone does. Did I tell you our father was a spy? He died in '43 in a German prison. He, like my sister and I, spoke perfect German. I used my Russian, I think I told you last year, in a minor translating role, but based on what I have seen, my sister would have been involved more deeply."

"No, I don't think you told me that."

"The thing is, Major, I know from a friend of my sister that Diana was recruited in South Africa, probably by this Major Alex Tremaine, of whom you have evidently not heard either. I wonder if you know of someone called Fairfax?" Lane didn't wait for Hogarth to answer, though she noted the major had glanced at her watch. She took a deep breath, contemplated the major for a moment, and then continued "I haven't met this man, Fairfax, but I was at his house because his daughter Marisa is the girl my sister went out to Africa with in '39. They stayed with an uncle, James Fairfax. I found my visit to the house quite interesting. Very large flat off Russell Square. That was a prestigious address when I was here during the war. I assume it still is. The funny thing is, the flat was nearly empty with only the barest smattering of furniture. Marisa told me her father had lost all his money, had sold everything off. It's not my business what a man has done with what might well have been a fortune, but in a situation like this, I find it all of possible interest. Another thing she told me was that Diana had come by to see her and stayed for about ten days, and then a few days ago she left quite suddenly. Marisa told me her father had been unhappy that Diana had come around. I should have thought that if Fairfax was known to anyone in this vast edifice, they might not know he'd lost all his money, and they might be concerned about what it might mean. But of course, if you don't know Fairfax, it's all moot." Lane smiled and rose, pulling on her gloves. "I must be off, but I thought you ought to know. Good afternoon."

This time Major Hogarth did not call up to Fairfax. She waited until Lane would be well out of the building. Then she rose, pulling her tunic down firmly, and went upstairs to find him.

"Had you thought of knocking?" Fairfax asked in his soft, avuncular voice when she walked into his office. She could see he'd moved a bottle unhurriedly into a bottom drawer of his oak desk. Broke and drinking, she thought. Splendid.

"I've had a visit from Lane Winslow again. She is being persistent. It's clear she has not accepted my assertion that I don't know of her sister. And she has done enough looking now that she knows her sister worked for us. I can hardly tell her after all my denials that her sister is, in fact, a murderer and a traitor!"

Fairfax leaned back and looked at Hogarth. He disliked her. Too mannish. And he disliked women doing this sort of work. He smiled. "This might work to our advantage.

Maybe she can find her bloody sister and save us the trouble. Diana's sister came to visit my daughter, did I tell you that? My daughter cleverly got the name of her hotel and of the friends her husband is staying with." He'd put some people on her, see where she went. "I'll keep an eye on her."

"What if she picks out your tails? She worked for us during the war."

"Nonsense. You worry too much. My people are excellent. What did she do for us?"

"Translation. Something to do with Russian."

"There you are, you see? She's at a hotel called the Imperial and has friends in Marylebone."

Only when Hogarth was making her way down the stairs to her own office did she wonder why she'd lied to Fairfax about what Lane Winslow had done during the war. She tried not to relish the little thrill of pleasure she got when she lied to him. If they really wanted to find Diana Winslow quickly, they ought to give her sister an added impetus.

CHAPTER EIGHTEEN

DARLING LOOKED AT HIS WATCH. It would be eight in the morning in Nelson. He'd returned to Scotland Yard in the morning and had been given a phone and permission to make a transatlantic call to get any information he could about the dead woman. O'Brien finally answered after nine rings. "Nelson Police. O'Brien speaking."

"About time. I need some information. Could you get one of those bone-idle men to find out anything they can about Francine Elizabeth Renshaw, née MacDonald, born in the '90s probably. Nelson girl. You might have to send Ames to the library to muck about in the old papers. He likes that sort of thing."

"Hello to you, sir. Neither man is all that idle at the moment. They managed to find the body of Benjamin Arden. God knows how. I wouldn't expect either one of 'em to find a red barn in an empty field."

"Have they, by Jove," Darling said. This was interesting. He would have put any money on Arden turning up as having murdered someone. "Drowned?"

"No, sir. Respectably shot in the back in an abandoned cabin. Big roll of two hundred dollars still on his person. The rucksack full of clothing and revolver he took with him missing."

"Well, I'll be. I wonder if he was shot with his own gun," Darling said thoughtfully, and then returned to proper long-distance mode. "Well, it'll give them something to keep busy with. I do need my information as soon as."

"Right you are, sir. I might undertake it myself."

Will wonders never cease, Darling didn't say. "Thank you, Sergeant. You can wire me at Scotland Yard, attention Chief Inspector Sims, when you've got something. I'll call you back. It might as well be on their dime, not ours."

"Sir."

Darling hung up and sat for some moments staring at the contours of the black telephone. He and Lane had met for dinner the evening before, and he had found the whole exercise unsatisfactory indeed. She had been worried about her sister, and didn't, she said, see how they would have time for anything until she was found. He'd asked her what her next step would be in the search, and she'd said she wasn't at all sure, and that she'd have to phone her grandmother to let her know she'd be longer. She hadn't been sure how she would tell her grandparents that it was going to be nearly impossible to find Diana, without giving them any details.

Darling now felt himself at loose ends. Sims was off following up some other case, and he had to wait to learn what he could from O'Brien's search. He wondered if he ought to go off on a lonely touristic exploration. Perhaps the Tower of London. Or perhaps he should ask to be shown the remains of Francine Elizabeth MacDonald Renshaw. Both prospects were depressing. He chose Francine.

AFTER HER UNPRODUCTIVE visit to Hogarth—though she hoped some sort of dropped seed would sprout along the way—Lane sought out a phone box and placed a call to Scotland. "Oh, Lanette, darling! I'm so glad to hear your voice. She's telephoned us!"

Momentarily nonplussed, Lane was about to say, Who? "Do you mean Diana?" she asked.

"Yes, of course I mean Diana! I was so relieved, I can't tell you. She was absolutely knocked over to learn you were here. I'm sure she can't wait to see you. I told her all about you going down to London to see her friend to try to find her. I must say, she sounded very upset indeed that you were going to all that trouble."

"Where is she? Is she going back to you?"

"Oh." Her grandmother hesitated. "You know, she didn't say. Well, I'm sure she'll be home soon. She did say that while you are in the south, you ought to visit a place called...now wait a minute, I've written it down. Sounds like something to do with chickens. Here it is, Cuckmere. I've never heard of it, but she says it's very nice at this time of year, especially just now. That's all she was able to say, I'm afraid, because she said someone was wanting to use the phone box."

Lane looked behind her and saw that she too was occu-pying a phone box a very impatient young man wanted to use. She gave him a little wave and a smile, to which he replied with a smirk and a wink, and she turned back. "How's Ganf?"

"Well, he's quite troubled by all this to-ing and fro-ing. He'd really like you all back, please. Of course, he's more cranky because he only gets one digestive with his tea."

"Give him my love. I've a very impatient young man fidgeting outside waiting for the telephone. I'll call again when..." When what? "When I can. And tell Ganf we'll all be there soon."

"No need to hurry on my account, luv," the young man said when she stepped out onto the pavement. "Why not wait for me? I'll show you a nice time." He flicked the remnants of his cigarette into the drain and grinned at her.

She gave him a wan smile and walked briskly away. She considered going to her hotel, but the prospect of spending any time in the poky little room with its basement window was unappealing. She had to think. She made her way along Sloane Street to Grosvenor Gardens and found an unoccupied bench. She took a deep breath and put her handbag beside her. There were not many people, but the weather was turning, so perhaps people were staying in. She watched an older man with his umbrella over his arm taking his constitutional. Londoners were never far from their umbrellas. What did Diana's message mean? Diana had not gone to her keepers, whoever they were, at any spy agency. She had phoned their grandmother. And why Cuckmere? That at least was obvious: It was so obscure a place that it could only mean that she was there, or meant to be there, and wanted Lane to be as well, and soon.

By degrees she calmed down enough to form a plan. She would go to the hotel and change her shoes and collect a couple of things, then go to Hatchards to buy a map, in hopes of finding out where Cuckmere was, and maybe find Darling. If not, she'd have to leave a message for him. Thus resolved, she walked the distance to the hotel, happy that movement absorbed some of her agitation.

"Message for you," the attendant said when she handed over the room key. This woman appeared as uninterested as possible in the affairs of the guests. Lane had a fleeting thought that she could sneak Darling past her with no trouble. The envelope was brown but had no markings to indicate whence it had come. Government, she was sure, and had a momentary passing memory of receiving just this sort of envelope during the war. She took it and went downstairs to her room and sat on the sagging bed to tear it open.

"Please come immediately when you get this. M. Hogarth."

This was a surprise. She changed into some comfortable lace-up shoes and slipped some money out of the envelope she had slid behind the tiny vanity mirror and put it into her handbag. She could feel herself moving calmly in spite of the wrenching alarm Hogarth's note occasioned. It was a familiar feeling. Outward calm, inner stomach-churning panic. It was the war all over again. Outside on the street again, she was about to hurry toward Victoria to find a cab when she noticed a man walking in the opposite direction. She didn't stop or look back at him, but she knew she'd seen him before. Furious, she picked up her pace. Hogarth had people tailing her!

She found a cab for the short distance to the War Office, an expense she wouldn't have indulged but for the terrifying brevity of Hogarth's communication. It took all her strength not to turn back to see if her tail had caught a cab as well.

"I'm glad you're here so quickly," Hogarth said, her face unreadable. She had evidently just put out a cigarette before Lane had been shown in, because a residual trail of smoke rose from her glass ashtray, to add its contribution to the darkened ceiling above the desk. "Something has come up. Rather serious, I'm afraid. Your sister, Diana."

Lane could feel her heart banging at her ribs. Had something happened to her? "The one you know nothing about?"

Hogarth ignored Lane's tone. "I'm not really sure how to put this. She's in a lot of trouble. She's murdered someone called Tremaine, who was her handler, and she's on the run. She's apparently playing for the other team."

Lane frowned, trying desperately to grasp what she was hearing. "She's what?" Her own voice sounded overloud.

"Look, Miss Winslow, I know it's shocking, but there's been no mistake. She was actually seen doing it by one of our most trusted people."

Lane wanted to say it wasn't possible, that Diana would never do such a thing. But she had no way of knowing if Diana would cross over or even kill someone. She hadn't seen her in ten years, and though she'd loved her, she hadn't liked her much then. She sat rigidly, staring down at the edge of Hogarth's desk, noticing a tiny splinter lifted off the surface of the oak, as though someone had meant to whittle a piece off the desk.

"So, the important thing is to find her before she leaves the country. We've alerted all the ports and Croydon, but there are a million places along the coast she could disappear at night if they sent a boat for her."

"Are . . . are you sure about all this? I can't believe it," Lane finally said. The idea of her sister flashing a signal at an enemy vessel off some cove somewhere was ludicrous spy-novel nonsense. But, of course, she herself had flashed for pickups many times to get back to England during the course of the war. But that was the point: there had been a war on. This was peacetime.

"As sure as we can be. Eyewitness sure. Now, have you heard anything at all from her, or about her whereabouts since we last spoke? I know you were off to try to track her down. I mean," Hogarth said after a pause, "there may be an explanation. The point is, we can't know unless we find her. It may not be all black." She sounded as though she was trying to persuade Lane of their essential benevolence.

"Why have you changed your tune?"

Hogarth ignored her question. "You have grandparents near Peebles. Have you contacted them?"

"Only to see how my grandfather is doing." She would have to find a way to call immediately when she was finished here, to warn them. Warn them of what? Her heart sank at having to involve them in any sort of subterfuge.

Hogarth leaned back in her chair and rubbed her chin. "It's a dreadful business. I'm sorry you've had to be involved. I just thought you ought to know what sort of trouble she's in."

"It's my sister. I could hardly not be involved. Though I don't see what I can offer. I've less than no idea where she might be." They wanted her to find her sister. That's what this was about. She had to find Diana before they did. She had to know the truth. Lane was lying to the intelligence services of England. She had never done it before.

Sitting with her hands folded on the desk, Hogarth knew she would have to tell Fairfax, and he'd ask why she deliberately went behind his back. She thought of saying, "Because you're stupid," and then formulated a more acceptable answer. Because, she would tell him, a woman like Lane Winslow would want to find her sister before they did, would want to find out for herself what happened, would lead them, if they were careful, right to Diana.

"Why are you having me followed?" Lane asked abruptly.

"I'm not having you followed," Hogarth said, frowning. "What earthly reason would I have?"

"To see if I get to Diana before you do," Lane said simply.

AMES WAS AGAIN among the newsprint in the library, with Mrs. Killeen, the librarian, delightedly engaged in finding him what he was looking for. "Why not try these, from '15?" She produced a pile of yellowing *Nelson Daily News* papers and put them next to him on the table. "How's your mother? It's shocking how long it's been since I've seen her. But the spring tea is coming up at the church. I'm sure she'll be baking something wonderful."

"She's very well, thank you. Sends her love," Ames said with a definitive nod he hoped would send Mrs. Killeen on her way. He wanted to get through the papers and be free to concentrate on his other concerns: the murder of Ben Arden and the picnic he'd like to surprise Tina with on Saturday.

"I'll leave you to these, Sergeant. I think I'll go through and see if I can find any mentions of her later on in the war. If she got any commendations and so on, it would certainly appear in the papers. Such brave girls!"

Leafing through the papers gave substance to the phrase "a bygone era." Modern, bustling Nelson appeared quaint in the old photos and newspaper drawings full of horses and wagons and a few old cars. A report on the tramline, he noted with interest, which had been bought by the city in 1914 because it was losing money, suggested it had been recovering nicely. It was probably losing money now, he thought, with most people having their own cars and bus service working some of the routes. April 1915. Here was something! There was a blurry picture of two young women in nursing caps, both smiling shyly at the photographer by the headline "Two Local Girls Get the Job!" *Two of our very own Nelson gals were among the 75 nurses picked out of nearly 1,500 who applied across Western Canada. They're off to France to help our boys win the war! Francine MacDonald, daughter of Frank and Irma MacDonald, near Balfour, and Elizabeth "Betsy" Edison, daughter of Dr. James Edison of Nelson, undertook the gruelling exam and interviews to become nursing sisters at the front. We're proud of you, girls!*

As Ames was making notes, it occurred to him he'd heard that second name before. Edison. Just at that moment, Mrs. Killeen came from her front desk, holding a newspaper aloft.

"I have something, I think. It's a small announcement about Miss MacDonald marrying Major Renshaw over there, in July '17. I'm a bit surprised it's such a little announcement.

The Renshaws are a fairly prominent family." She sighed. "I suppose there was just too much news of the fighting, and it got pushed out."

"Thanks, Mrs. K. I've found something from April 1915." He peered up at the date. "Friday the sixteenth. Miss MacDonald and a Miss Edison win prestige postings as nursing sisters."

"That is impressive. It was quite hard to do. You had to have impeccable training, and have high moral character, and I'm sure you had to be from a good family. They didn't just send anyone over."

"It's amazing they were so choosy, considering how dire things were during that war. Say, I keep thinking I know this name, Edison, but I can't put my finger on it."

Mrs. Killeen smiled. "Well, what about Dr. Edison over at the hospital? She did something during the war, as I recall. She was actually in charge of something. Air Force, maybe? She could be a relation."

"Yes," Ames said. "This Betsy Edison was the daughter of Dr. Jim Edison."

"Goodness! I remember him! A grumpy Scot. I was taken to see him as a little girl for something. He had an enormous beard and was rather frightening. He's long gone now, of course. I bet Dr. Edison at the hospital is related to him. Doctoring runs in families."

They both spent another hour over the papers. The only story they found was from October 1918: *Local Girl Elizabeth Edison Returns with Medal. Elizabeth "Betsy" Edison returns home after a long war bearing the Royal Red Cross Class 2 medal for her selfless work during the conflict.*

"Nothing here about MacDonald or Renshaw," Ames mused. "I'll pop up to the hospital and see if Dr. Edison can throw any light on things." Once on the street, he shuddered slightly, looking up toward the ridge where the hospital sat. He didn't like hospitals at the best of times, and he'd been in there himself as a patient with a gunshot wound much too recently to relish a visit there again.

"Sergeant Ames! What brings you here?" The girl at reception greeted him with uncharacteristic friendliness.

"I'm here to see Dr. Edison," he said a little nervously. Was that an actual flirtatious smile he detected? That was the trouble with a small town. Everyone knows everything.

"Certainly. How's the shoulder?"

"Fine, thank you."

His abrupt answer did not seem to have any effect on her. She gazed at him over the phone receiver, smiling brightly, even as she spoke with whoever picked up on the other end. "Go on up to the second floor, Sergeant."

With relief, he eschewed the wait for the lumbering elevator and bolted up the stairs two at a time.

"Sergeant. What brings you here? Not a setback with that shoulder, I hope." Dr. Edison smiled. She hadn't treated him, but a member of the local police down with a gunshot wound was something notable in the hospital.

"It's fine. Been healing really well." He'd skip the complaints about the twinges and aches, tempted though he was to succumb to her kind manner. "Inspector Darling has asked me to track down some information about a nursing sister who did not return to Nelson after the Great War, and the name Elizabeth Edison has come up.

I wondered if she might be a relation of yours. She was one of two nursing sisters that went off to France from here in 1915."

Edison, tall and angular and tending to seriousness, was kind and quick to laughter. "Goodness, I hope you aren't implying Auntie Betsy has committed a crime! She's practically bedridden."

"No, no. Nothing like that. But I'm hoping it's possible she might know something about the other woman. Does she live in the area?"

"Oh, dear. I wonder if that is her friend Francine. I know they used to be great friends. I've seen pictures of them, and Mother always told stories about them. But Aunt Betsy has never talked about her. Perhaps they had a falling-out or something. Aunt Betsy lives just across the lake near Willow Point. Her married name is Denton, though her husband has been dead some while now. She lives with her daughter. She's not that old, but she has a dicky heart. In fact, she was very ill last year. We thought we were going to lose her. But you know how plucky some people can be. She somehow managed to pull through and seems right as rain now."

"Do you think she'd mind talking to me?" The fact that she didn't talk about Francine MacDonald to anyone was not promising.

"I couldn't tell you, but she's very responsible. It's why she signed up in the first place—to do her duty. She may speak to you because you're a police officer."

Ames nodded his thanks. "I understand you served as well. Medicine and duty must run in the family."

"I love and admire my aunt. She was a great model for me. Both she and her brother, my father, went into the trade." Dr. Edison shook her head a little. "I always thought something in the Great War affected her more than she would ever say. The conditions were beastly, I know that, and I always wondered whether she, such a tower of strength, just saw too much." She shrugged. "In my experience, that isn't unusual from that war. I expect we'll see the same sort of thing beginning to manifest in people who fought this last war. Did you fight?"

This was a source of regret, and even some shame, for Ames, who had been required to continue his policing. He shook his head and looked down. "Had to stay back on the home front at the station."

Dr. Edison gently put her hand on his shoulder. "Now you listen here: Besides the old 'they also serve' business, be very, very thankful. You did important and necessary work here. War is a punishing activity that can knock the light out of people. You have nothing to reproach yourself with in the matter of duty and courage. The world needs people exactly like you right now. Now then, give my best to Constable Terrell."

He should have been comforted by this, but instead he felt as if he'd failed somehow. The old anxiety that he was different in some way from all his friends who went to war, that he hadn't held up his end, surfaced. His own father had died of the effects of his experiences in the Great War. What right had he to live a charmed life? It didn't help that Darling and Terrell were both war vets, and so was Tina for that matter. The thought of Tina, whom he would be seeing that very evening, depressed him even more. What on earth could she see in him, really?

CHAPTER NINETEEN

―――――――

"WHAT'S THE MATTER WITH YOU this evening? You're all broody," Tina asked. They were sitting in the car a little way down the drive to the Van Eyck garage. She had asked him to stop before they got to the yard. They'd had dinner provided by his mother and then gone to see *The Bishop's Wife* at the Civic Theatre. "I can hardly get a word out of you." She took his hand.

Ames looked down and entwined his fingers around hers. His heart was aching at the softness of her hand. Finally, he looked up. "Tina," he began, but she leaned forward and was kissing him.

"Whatever it is, it can't possibly matter to us," she said gently.

"But that's the trouble. I think it can." He sat back, pulling himself away from her. The movie had stirred a further unease in him. The bishop's wife found Cary Grant, unattainable angel though he was, much more interesting than her own husband. That jumbled together with Dr.

Edison's words to him. He turned fully toward her, looking at her worried face in the lingering light of the day. "I mean, you went over there. Maybe you weren't in the thick of the fighting or anything, except the bombing, I guess. But you never say, do you? And I didn't do anything. I was stuck here, nice and safe, out of the action."

Tina frowned and sat back. "What are you saying? I don't understand your drift."

Ames was beginning to be sorry he'd gone down this road. He wasn't good at revealing his emotions at the best of times, and he didn't understand exactly what he was feeling anyway. He had a sudden stab of fear that he was about to destroy his relationship with her, only for good this time. He'd nearly done it once over his jealousy of Terrell and his damn motorcycle. He hadn't understood his own feelings that time either, but she'd understood them in a jiffy, and would have no truck with them.

"It's just that, I don't know, you might eventually find me boring or shallow. Our lives have been so different."

Tina put her hands over her eyes, shaking her head, and then looked at him. "Daniel Ames, you really do take the biscuit, you know that? I love you—there, I've said it—because you are just who you are. Full of bubble and quite humble, unlike, believe you me, many another man, and you are very, very brave. Or have you forgotten you were shot recently in the course of your dangerous service in the police? When you're not being a silly idiot, I think you are a wonderful man. And anyway, Dad thinks you're the bee's knees. I don't need a man who's all depressed because of the war. One of us is enough. I was in some of the bombing, and it was bloody awful. To be at home again with someone like you is the most glorious thing in the world."

Ames was speechless but, for once, not powerless to act. He leaned forward and held her, kissing her forehead, her cheek, her mouth.

Eventually Tina said, "If we linger up here any longer, Daddy's going to demand to know what your intentions are."

He took her hand again. "They aren't that honourable just now. But they could be. I love you, you know that?" How surprised he was to find it wasn't hard to say, and how true and right it felt.

She smiled softly in the dark. "I know. But let's not think of intentions just now."

"YOU'RE IN A good mood," O'Brien said the next morning when Ames came down to take the keys for the car.

"Why does everyone think they're entitled to comment on how I'm feeling?" Ames asked in a direct imitation of his boss, though he was smiling broadly. "Constable Terrell, care for a drive across the lake?"

Terrell's chair scraped noisily as he got up and retrieved his cap from the hook by his desk. "Sir," he said, and made to follow him out the door.

"It'll be that Miss Van Eyck, I expect," O'Brien said to Terrell *sotto voce* as he passed the front desk.

"We're going to see a Mrs. Denton, née Miss Edison," Ames said as he got into the car. "She went off to France with Francine MacDonald. According to her aunt, your pal Dr. Edison—who sends you her best, by the way—Auntie

Betsy never likes to talk about the war, but I'm hoping she'll change her policy for us. I'm expecting a cable from the inspector soon, and I haven't got much to give him yet."

They turned up a road just past the little school and went about three hundred yards till they saw a short, rutted driveway leading to a large cheerful-looking white house. "That'll be the one," Ames said, turning. "I hate these roads. They're murder on the undercarriage."

The door was opened by a woman who introduced herself as Mrs. Grimes, who said she was expecting them.

"I'm Sergeant Ames, and this is Constable Terrell," Ames said, holding up his warrant card.

"I look after Mrs. Denton when her daughter is away. She is in the parlour, if you'll follow me."

The parlour faced the lake, just visible down the hill through the trees, and they found Mrs. Denton sitting in an armchair with a blanket over her knees and her feet up on an ottoman. A glass of water stood on the small table beside her, and her chair was positioned so that the light from the window illuminated the book she had been reading.

She looked up when they came in, her pale round face made endearing by a warm smile. "I won't get up," she apologized, "but please, bring those two chairs a little closer." She waited until they sat. "This is my favourite place in the whole house. Ah, Mrs. Grimes, could I trouble you for tea?" She looked back at them, from one to the other, as if she were memorizing their faces. "I so seldom get any visitors besides my wonderful niece. Have you met her, Sergeant? I know she's met the constable here. She was so full of your praises when you met earlier in the year," she said to Terrell.

"She's a wonderful doctor," Terrell said.

"She tells me you'd like to ask me about my friend Francine. You know, of all the dreadful things we were exposed to, I have the hardest time talking about her. But my niece tells me you need to know anything I can remember."

"We appreciate it," Ames said. "The inspector is in England now and"—he hesitated—"apparently they have found the remains of a woman that might be Francine MacDonald Renshaw." Ames took out his notebook and turned the pages. "In a bombed-out house in Kent."

Mrs. Denton put her hand to her mouth and then leaned toward Ames as if she might look at his little book.

"So, it's true. I so hoped it wasn't her. That's too awful. I always wondered what happened to her, and then a couple of weeks ago a friend sent me a newspaper clipping from an English paper. Are they sure it is her? She was pregnant, did they see that? It wasn't mentioned in the article."

Ames checked his notes. He hadn't written it down, but he remembered Darling mentioning it. "That's right," he said with a nod.

"But no one was bombing houses in the Great War. It was very peaceful there. We'd gone on holiday. I don't understand."

"I should have been clearer. The house was bombed during air raids in this war. The house was destroyed, and the man who bought the farm wanted to rebuild it. He found her under the rubble. She'd been there for a very long time." He did not tell her that Francine had been shot. That had no doubt been in the article. He suddenly wondered if she could have shot Francine MacDonald, but he could not, in all honesty, imagine this kindly woman shooting anyone. This thought was immediately followed up with Darling's injunction that you'd be surprised who could be capable of murder.

"I knew something must have happened. All these years I lived with the idea that she just left nursing and was living in England with her child. Her husband died in action, you know. She was such a free spirit in some ways, it would have been like her to just disappear and do that, especially after he died. But she was dedicated to our job. When she never returned from that holiday, I did wonder. The paper said she'd been shot. Is that true? I can't understand that. Who could have shot her? I left her alive and well."

"Tell me about the last time you saw her," Ames said.

"We signed up together, you know. It was very difficult to get into the Bluebirds—that's what they called the Canadian girls because of our blue uniforms. We were so excited to be going over. We didn't work right at the front, you know, but at stations behind the lines, but we saw some dreadful injuries and so many young men dying. One of our stations was bombed as well. We were given a nice long leave to England, and three of us decided to rent a little cottage in the countryside for the two weeks. The other girl changed her mind about the countryside and went back to London... what was her name? And, I confess, I was of her mind, but I thought I ought to be loyal and stick with Francine. Only I didn't in the end. I couldn't stand the thought of staying in that place for a single minute. You have no idea how much I regret my change of mind!" Mrs. Denton looked out at the trees and the scruffy garden and wrung her hands together. "You see, when I saw the place, it was just so dark and small and depressing. I didn't think I could stick it, I just didn't. The weather was turning bad, I remember, and the place was cold and dark, which in August is intolerable. She seemed delighted with the beastly place. She said she wanted some peace and quiet, and she urged me to go to London, said she'd be quite happy. God forgive me, I did leave. One is so selfish when one is young. I was only thinking of myself and my own comfort. And then I went back to France and she didn't return. I was quizzed by the major; she was our head sister. But I knew nothing. I assumed...I assumed..." It suddenly seemed difficult for her to carry on.

"Assumed what, Mrs. Denton?" Terrell asked gently.

"Oh, dear. I don't know if I can say. I mean, the poor creature is dead. What can it matter now, after all these years? Let the dead past bury its dead. What can be gained by all this dredging up?"

"Justice for your friend," Ames said. "Finding out what really happened to her. She told you on that holiday that she was pregnant?"

Mrs. Denton nodded. "She did, yes. I was worried about her because of what had happened, you see. She had just married Major Renshaw. He was from around here as well. I was surprised that she chose him. She was so light and cheerful in her outlook, and he was a very hard man. I'd heard from some of his men when they were brought in that he was a very good leader, but quite brutal in his ways.

But, you see, I knew there was something amiss even before that. She wouldn't tell me what, but she changed. She became unhappy and, I don't know, furtive. Just suddenly one day, as if the weight of the world had landed on her. It was only on the boat on the way over that I learned she was pregnant, and she as much as confided in me that she had got into that state with someone other than her husband. She said it didn't matter, that everything was going to be all right. She even went as far as to tell me not to worry, that the major was nicer than he seemed. But I could see she wasn't happy. If what she said was true, their marriage had been a hurried affair."

Terrell was writing. Ames was thinking of what more to ask. "You were friends before you left, weren't you?"

"We were, yes. Mother didn't approve. She thought Francine would lead me into sin, is how she put it. But I never thought of her as sinful; I just thought of her as too trusting. She was being brought up by her grandparents, on the mother's side, because both her parents were dead, and I'm afraid they gave her free rein. She was terribly bright. She had no difficulty in nursing school, where I struggled a bit. I think I hero-worshipped her, you know how you do. She was beautiful, bright, free. I didn't see then that she hadn't any judgment about people." Mrs. Denton shifted in her seat and sighed. "I loved her, I did. But I wouldn't have put anything past her. It didn't surprise me she had become pregnant. She did have . . . an affair, I guess you'd call it, with Ben before we shipped out. He was very young, barely twenty, I think. Local boy. They'd been friends as children. I knew him, but I never understood why she spent any time with him. Two years is an enormous difference in age when you're ten, but I suppose not so great when you're twenty. Even when we were children, she kind of took possession of him, like he was her pet or something. I remember she was still completely infatuated with him when we were twenty, and then I think she suddenly saw him for what he was: young, a bit stupid, for all he was good-looking. She came to her senses, thank heaven—at least I thought she had. But when he turned up at our station, of all the places, with a shoulder wound...well, I always suspected he was the man who made her pregnant.

"She could be impulsive, as brilliant as she was. I suppose the whole thing just started up again, even in that short time he was there. Though how they would have managed, I don't know. Matrons were very strict with us. Mind you, she never did tell me.

"She had a brother, did you know that?" Mrs. Denton looked at Ames, shaking her head. "He was in the Princess Pats as well, and when she disappeared, he stayed on after the war searching for her. He eventually married and settled down in the old country."

"That boy, Ben, do you remember his last name?"

"Oh yes, we were all such chums when we were young. Ben Arden. Of course, he's married and has children now. I still think of him as that young soldier, but he must be fifty now, if he's a day. I never see him, so I've quite lost touch."

Ames and Terrell exchanged glances. "Do you recall any investigation into her disappearance?" Terrell asked.

She shook her head. "Like I said, I was asked questions, but I don't think there was a real investigation. I just don't know. I asked the third girl who didn't go to the village with us—I do wish I could remember her name, but I suppose it doesn't matter. I asked her if she'd seen Francine in London at all, and she didn't know any more than I did. We were run off our feet at the station. I'm afraid I simply assumed it had all become too much for her and she'd run away or, being pregnant, resigned. But wait, now—I remember something. I remember someone coming to collect her things. I roomed with her, you see. I wasn't there, but when I got off my shift, I found everything gone. Someone said her husband asked to have it collected. Of course, they would never have allowed her to stay on if they knew she was expecting, so I assumed she had been sent home. I fully expected to see her back here. Her grandparents died shortly after the war, and her only remaining relative was her brother, and he hadn't come back either. He's back now. Bill. He works at the print shop. I called him and told him about the letter I'd gotten with the news about Franny."

"He didn't know?"

"No. He'd spent all those years looking for her, and she'd been dead the whole time. I think he was relieved, or maybe resigned, I'm not sure."

"Thank you, Mrs. Denton." Ames got up, and Terrell closed his book. "If there is anything else you think of, can you get hold of us at the station?"

"Certainly, Sergeant. It's such a long time ago, now. I've only talked about her once in all this time. I think it affected me more than I can say. I really loved Francine. She was such a magnetic person. You couldn't help it."

Just as the two men reached the door, Mrs. Denton called out, "Sergeant, I know this is a strange question: Are they sure about her being shot? I've had nightmares thinking she might have had a miscarriage and bled to death all alone in the dark little cottage in the middle of nowhere."

Ames turned. "She was indeed murdered, I'm afraid."

CHAPTER TWENTY

LANE SAW THE FULL EXTENT of her dilemma. She was certain now that she would be watched and followed because she might lead them to Diana. She cursed herself for giving Marisa Fairfax the addresses of all the places she could be found. She could not take the chance that the Donaldsons' telephone was already being monitored, and she could not even sneak back to her hotel to leave Darling a note. In Covent Garden, she crossed Bedford and darted through the gate and into the little garden at St. Paul's, the small church on the square opposite the market, and stood behind the wall and waited. No one came through after five minutes had passed.

Could she call Scotland Yard and ask to speak to Sims? Or even Darling? She tried to remember if Darling's business was finished. What if the War Office contacted Chief Inspector Sims? He would have no reason not to believe any appeal from someone in the War Office to keep an eye out for her. She would have to go to Cuckmere on her own;

she'd bought a map at Hatchards on Piccadilly and seen it was close to Eastbourne. Her heart sank at the thought of not telling Darling where she was off to. Disappearing without a trace to pursue a fugitive sister must be very high on a list of things Darling would not like. She looked out toward the market. Merchants filled the whole edifice and were doing a brisk business. An old woman was talking to a boy of about fourteen who looked bored. He should be in school, she thought. But it gave her an idea.

LANE GOT OFF the bus and looked out at a delta sparkling with the dying light of the sun. There was a small river snaking to the sea from the gentle hills just behind her. It too was catching the last of the evening twilight. Such a beautiful, quiet place. She tried not to think about Darling. She should be here with him, touristing, instead of on her own on a mad and hopeless pursuit. She told herself she would be back soon, the next day probably. It was unlikely she'd find Diana in this lonely, deserted place, so she could make the return journey first thing in the morning, and it wouldn't matter in the least who followed her because she could not lead them to Diana anyway.

A great chalk cliff rose on her left. It must be a popular walking place, she thought, because the pale marks of well-used trails criss-crossed and climbed along near the edge of the cliff and disappeared toward Eastbourne. The undulating hills were called, she knew from her map, the Seven Sisters. To her right, the bay curved inland toward the village of Seaford, which the bus driver had told her was at two miles' distance and might provide lodging. She wondered if she should have hired a car. The journey had taken so much longer than she had anticipated. It would be completely dark in another hour.

It was a bleak but beautiful prospect in the twilight, with no sign of human life. She might have been absolutely mistaken about Diana's intentions in that message. Why in God's name would she come here in the first place? Well, nothing for it. She pushed her hands into her jacket pockets and started down the path, making for a couple of whitewashed coast guard cottages on the right side of the river above the beach.

"You came."

Lane hadn't gotten yards when she heard the voice calling softly from a low rise above her. She whirled around in surprise and saw what she had not at first: a wartime pillbox. Diana was standing near the entrance, watching her. "Diana! Thank God!" Lane ran up the grassy, uneven slope and, driven by relief, embraced her sister. She held her out at arm's length and looked at her. Diana had become lean, lost the chubby pinkness of her adolescence, but more than that, Lane saw worry etched into her sister's attractive face. "My God, Diana, what are you doing here?"

Diana pulled away from Lane and folded her arms around herself, perhaps surprised or put off by the hug, and looked past her sister. "Were you followed?"

"No. I'm certain I wasn't." Lane looked around at the waving grass on the hillside and the darkening shoreline below. "How long have you been here? What's going on?"

Diana took her sister's arm and pulled her toward the dark entrance of the pillbox, a bleak reminder of the

Luftwaffe's attention to Britain's southern coast. "We mustn't be seen."

A wooden bench, perhaps left for ramblers in case of a sudden deluge, was just inside the doorway. A musty smell emanated from inside, and cold air seeped out. Lane sat down next to her sister, glancing back at the black interior, and shivered.

"I don't know if I can trust you," Diana said. "I don't know if I can trust anyone."

"You can bloody well trust me. I'm your sister. Out with it!"

Diana managed a wan smile. "Always the bossy older sister. You look well." She clasped her hands together and looked out to the darkening sea. "This is in deadly earnest," she continued. "National security earnest. If I get this wrong—"

"Look, I know you worked for intelligence in South Africa, and I'm going to assume you worked for our side. And I believe you stayed on for some reason. And now they're looking for you." She turned and took Diana's hands. "I can't believe what I was told, Diana, I just can't. Why are they looking for you?"

"It's not what you think."

"I don't know what to think. They tell me you've killed an agent called Tremaine, that someone saw you. They imply you have gone over to, I don't know, the Russians, I suppose."

"I didn't kill him. I loved him." Diana's voice was low and hard. "But I know who did."

"Well, for God's sake, tell them! What's the point of

all this cloak and dagger?" Lane was beginning to worry Diana would refuse to come with her even as far as the village so that they could have a decent supper and a bed for the night.

"How do I know they didn't send you to find me, to bring me in? If I go in, they'll find a reason to kill me too. You don't know what you're dealing with." Diana pulled her hands away.

"Diana, listen to me. No one sent me. Someone I trusted, called Major Hogarth, asked me if I knew where you were, and I told her I had absolutely no idea, that I'd been looking for you. Once I talked to Grandmama and thought you might be here, I came as soon as I could. Someone has had people following me, so I was very careful to lose them. Major Hogarth believes you to be a murderer. I knew at once that was wrong. I want you to tell me everything. Never mind the Secrets Act. Please trust me, or we'll both be for it."

"What do you know about the Secrets Act?" Diana looked sidelong at her sister.

"I've signed it myself. Right now, I have to know everything about what's happened to you, and then we have to make a plan."

"I've no one else," her sister said, resigned.

"FOR CRYING OUT loud," Fiona muttered, looking up from her newspaper. It was three in the afternoon, and she was having her well-earned break while the old people slept. The knocking began again, loud enough to wake the dead. A glance at the clock told her it could not be Dr. Mwangi, who said he would be by at a little after four thirty. She hurried through the sitting room into the hallway and pulled the door open. A tall man of some fifty years in a very expensive wool coat stood smiling at her. He removed his hat and held it in his hands. He had thick, wavy, pale gold hair.

"Am I right that this is the home of Mr. and Mrs. Andrews?" He had a warm, resonant voice.

"Yes, but they are not available just now. It is their usual time to rest."

The man nodded. "Ah. I see. The thing is, I've driven up from London on business, and I most expressly hoped to see them. My name is Gregory Fairfax." Here he smiled again and offered a hand. "You are...?"

"Fiona Dempsey. I do for Mr. and Mrs. Andrews." She paused. She could see his expensive black roadster out in their little driveway. She could hardly pack him off back to London. Why did that name ring a bell? "You'd better come through, then. I'm about to make their four o'clock tea." She pulled the door open and let him through.

Fairfax wiped his feet on the mat and unbuttoned his coat, revealing a double-breasted suit and a dark blue silk tie. Fiona took the coat, hung it on a peg, and led him through to the kitchen.

"Please sit down, Mr. Fairfax. Where do I know that name from?"

"Oh, that's easy," he said, settling comfortably on the chair and smiling again. "My daughter Marisa is a friend of Diana Winslow's. They went to South Africa together at the start of the war. I thought it best to keep my daughter away from it all, if I could, and she wouldn't budge without her best friend!"

"Oh, of course!" Fiona said. Fairfax's sudden appearance had set off a slight anxiety, which she now felt ebb away. "Oh, they'll be pleased to see you. Do you mind? I'll just get the tea things. They've been terribly worried about Diana." She filled the kettle and settled it on the stove, put out the teapot and spooned tea into it, and set it on a tray. When the cups had been organized, and the tray set with a little jug of milk, a bowl with a very spare amount of sugar, and a plate to which she added another digestive biscuit in honour of their guest, she said, "I'll just go wake Mrs. Andrews up now."

Fairfax watched her go, and when the door had closed behind her, he sprang up and walked around the kitchen, his hands behind his back, clenched, as though he were trying to still some agitation. He swung around as the door opened, and Fiona was there again in the doorway.

"I am sorry. I've been awa' with the fairies. You must come through. You'll have tea in the library. There's a fire there and you'll be quite comfortable."

Fairfax followed her through the sitting room, across the hall, and into a small, book-filled room with a murmuring fire in the grate. "This is splendid, thank you. You just carry on. I'll be perfectly happy looking at books."

When she had again disappeared, he looked along the shelves and wandered the short distance around the room, very lightly touching the tops of the occasional tables. He stopped at a small desk, pulled open the centre drawer, carefully lifted a few letters in their opened envelopes, and peered at them. He heard hurried footsteps and voices, and quickly shut the drawer and moved to the bookshelf, pulling out a book. It interested him that the books were in Russian, English, French, and German. The one he'd hastily pulled from the shelf was Russian. *Anna Karenina*. He read the famous first words, which he'd never been convinced were true: *Happy families are all alike; every unhappy family is unhappy in its own way.* He reshelved it and picked out a copy of *Also Sprach Zarathustra*. Nietzsche, in German. He turned to the first page and began to read, but hearing a hand on doorknob, he turned, the page still open.

Mrs. Andrews, plump in her green cardigan and tweed skirt, and in a state, surged toward him. "Mr. Fairfax, I am sorry we've kept you waiting. You are most welcome to our home. I must apologize for my husband. He's been a little indisposed and will take a few minutes longer to join us." She held out her hand and Fairfax, switching the book to his left hand, took it.

"Please, think nothing of it. It's the absolute height of bad manners to arrive unannounced. I had thought of stopping along the way, but the village I picked had only a broken phone box to offer. I thought I'd take my chances."

Mrs. Andrews waved a hand at a chair and sat down herself. "We are not in the least troubled. Do you read German?" She nodded toward the book he had set on the table beside him.

"Not a word. Wish I could." He smiled. "This is a lovely part of the country, I must say. Your view down the valley is splendid. I'm afraid I look down on one of those postage-stamp parks London is so famous for. It's only the trees in it that keep me from peering into the homes of my neighbours. I sometimes long for a great open view like this."

She smiled. "We've only been here a couple of years. Our house in Riga was taken over by Soviet troops. They were polite enough, but they crammed us into one room and dismissed our servants. I became very adept at handling a saucepan on an electric ring. But, Mr. Fairfax, why have you—" Her question was interrupted by the sound of the tea trolley being wheeled across the hall.

Fiona pushed it into the library and positioned it in front of Mrs. Andrews. Right behind her came Ganf, his leather slippers slapping softly on the carpet. He carried his cane but did not use it.

"We have a guest, I hear. Wonderful! No, no, please don't get up. I can manage quite well on my own." He slumped into his chair and set his cane on the floor beside it. "Women are apt to baby one. You're the father of Diana's friend Marisa. Wonderful. We've been a bit concerned about her—Diana, I mean—but maybe she just popped back off to London and you've come to tell us that. Or ask if you can send her off with Marisa to some other exotic part of the world."

In an effort to stem the flow, Mrs. Andrews said, "Yes, I was just going to ask him that. Sugar?"

Fairfax shook his head, accepted his cup of tea, and took a digestive from the offered plate.

"I'm sorry about the digestives. It's all he's allowed, and I don't want to make him unhappy by devouring cream scones that he can't have."

"Digestives are the only thing with a cup of tea," Fairfax said, lifting his with a smile. "The truth is, it is about Diana I've come. As you've guessed, Marisa *would* like to travel to

Argentina. She's always been fascinated by South America, and she wants Diana to come with her. When she couldn't reach her, she thought she'd delegate me to come see you, as I'm on a Scotland junket anyway."

"Oh, dear. I am sorry to disappoint her. I'm sure Diana would love it. She's always dashing off somewhere. We can't seem to keep either of them here with us."

"Either of them? Oh, of course, her sister. In Canada, I believe?"

Mr. Andrews said, "As a matter of fact, she's—"

His wife cut in quickly, "She's just sent us a nice letter. It's so interesting to get letters with foreign stamps. Of course, Canada's stamps feature our own dear King, so they're not much different."

"But..." began her husband again, and then stopped. "But, we wish she were here. They haven't seen each other in ten years, the two of them."

Trying not to show her relief, Mrs. Andrews asked, "So, did Diana visit Marisa in London?"

"No, sadly not. All the plans are held up. My daughter is a force of nature. What she wants goes. I'm ordered to find Diana and bring her back. Has she contacted you at all?"

"No, but I don't expect her to," Mrs. Andrews said hurriedly, to forestall her husband from any revelation about Diana's call. "She said she was off to Aberdeen to visit friends. She didn't say more than that."

"Miss Dempsey did mention you were concerned about her."

Mrs. Andrews smiled primly. "Only in that now that she's a grown woman, we can't ask her to be accountable to us. She has her own life to live." She sipped her tea, and then put her cup down and took up the teapot to offer it to their guest. He shook his head, and she turned to her husband. "For you, dear?"

He turned his mouth down. "It's not much fun without sugar."

She looked at the clock on the mantle. "I usually take my husband for a turn around the garden. I'm a bit worried about the weather..." She left the rest unsaid.

Fairfax jumped up, his tea unfinished. "Good heavens. You mustn't let me stop you." He reached into his inner pocket, pulled out a silver case, and opened it, extracting a card. "I'm expected at my friend's house before dinner, so I'd better make tracks, as our American friends say. Do call this number if Diana returns. Marisa would be so pleased!"

"Certainly. I'm sure Diana has never thought about going to Argentina. She'll be thrilled." She rang the little brass bell sitting in the corner of the trolley.

In a few moments, while Fairfax shook his host's hand and exchanged a few pleasantries, Fiona arrived.

"Ah, Fiona. Could you show Mr. Fairfax out. He'll have a coat, I expect, in this wind."

Ganf struggled out of his chair and joined his wife at the front window after the outside door closed. Fiona came in and stood beside them. They watched Fairfax going down the path toward the car, looking around the garden. Just before he got into his car he looked back at the house, first glancing at the upstairs and then at the window at which they were standing. They were well back and knew they could not be seen from that distance.

"He seems a nice enough fellow, but what was all that in aid of?" Ganf asked finally, looking at his wife.

"A bit well dressed, didn't you think?" his wife said. "I don't trust him. Too charming, and sleek in those expensive clothes, and he was lying. 'Not a word of German,' my aunt Nora! He was reading the damn book as comfortably as if it were the King's English. I learned something from the girls' father, you know."

"I didn't trust him either, after a couple of minutes," Fiona declared. "He sat in the kitchen and he fidgeted as if he would like to crawl out of his own skin. When I left him to come and wake you, I realized I should have put him in the library, so I went back and he was out of his chair roaming all over the kitchen."

Ganf shook his head. "If he is Fairfax, what's he want with our Diana? Perhaps we shouldn't believe that business about Argentina." He turned toward the door, waving his cane briskly. "I do want that walk. We might as well not be liars as well."

Outside, bundled in warm coats and wool scarves, the three of them began their walk. It took them around the vegetable garden outside the kitchen door, across the path behind the hedgerow that marked the edge of the property, around the side of the property onto the road, and back to the front of the house. They'd only just reached the hedgerow path when they all saw the quick flash of light from above them at the top of the hill where the road wound to the next village. It was gone as quickly as it appeared.

"Now what do you think that was?" Fiona said.

They waited only a moment and it was repeated. The flash of late afternoon sunlight off a glass surface.

"Birdwatcher," Ganf declared. "Field glasses."

They walked on, all three of them subdued by Fairfax's visit. Ganf shook his head. "She's in her father's line of work, isn't she?" The sound of a motor car approaching reminded them of the doctor's visit. He turned and started back into the house. "That'll be the good doctor. I can make a tremendous impression coming in windswept from a brisk walk."

"I wish Laneke would call again," Mrs. Andrews said softly, as if afraid the birdwatcher at the top of the hill would hear her. She turned to Fiona. "That's no birdwatcher. I just don't want to alarm poor Ganf." What she didn't say was that she feared Diana was in danger, and so was Lane. She turned back to the house and shook her head. "I thought we'd got away from all that when we left our beautiful house in Bilderlingshof."

CHAPTER TWENTY-ONE

May 10, 1948

THERE WAS A BARE SLIVER of a moon, but its faint efforts could not penetrate the wood, and Diana found herself having to peer at the ground to follow the path steeply upward. He had told her to bring a torch, but not to use it unless absolutely necessary. And a change of clothes. She stopped, cursing at the steep climb up from the edge of town. He was supposed to have picked up her suitcase, but now she wondered if he'd been able to. She hadn't packed much, but the bag gained weight with the steepness of the climb. During the day, the path would likely be full of dog walkers and ramblers, but tonight it had the power of darkness that she used to fear so much as a child in the woods near their house. She could hear her own breath coming heavily, and she stopped to take off her heavy cardigan and tie it around her waist under her leather shoulder bag. She had to decide. He'd asked her to leave with him. He must have set something up, perhaps a boat pickup somewhere below in the darkness. Now, with her satchel of clothes, stumbling about in the dark, she wondered if she would come to regret this decision. She'd wanted so badly to be finished with the whole thing, to retire to private life, whatever that proved to be. But she loved him, and she knew about Fairfax. Something would have to be done about that. She and Alex could come up with a plan together.

One thing was certain: she had to be as far away as possible. Fairfax would realize sooner or later that she'd been into his secret cubbyhole and taken something. She hadn't been sure at first about leaving with Alex, but it offered the chance to get far away where there would be time to work through what ought to be done.

She could just make out the end of the dense wood up ahead and picked up speed. A root caught her foot and she fell heavily, her torch flying out of her hand. She could feel that she'd skinned her hand, and she felt a burst of anger. Anger about being here, alone, in the dark, when she could have been in Scotland with her grandparents fussing over her. Anger that Alex still had the kind of hold on her that would bring her out to the middle of nowhere to crash about in the dark. She lay still for a moment, but hearing nothing but her own breathing, she got up, dusted off her trousers, and began to look for the torch. She found it four feet away, where it had rolled down a slight slope and come to rest against a tree.

She tested it and was relieved it worked. She hoisted the bag back onto her shoulder and scanned a short section of the path directly in front of her with the torch and then turned it off. Her watch with its phosphorescent numbers told her she was already late, and she picked up her pace. If she thought the opening in the wood meant she was close to her goal, she was disappointed. The terrain opened up after the wood, but it continued relentlessly uphill.

Her relief at finally seeing the figure just at the top of the hill was huge. She was going to call out, to let him know she was there, but something stopped her. What? It certainly was Alex. She'd recognize that stance anywhere. Why had she hesitated? Then she saw that he turned suddenly to look behind him. She waited, watching to see what he'd heard. She was standing in the darkest shadow of a high bank of shrubs. Something was not right. In the next moment another man came from somewhere behind Alex. He was tall, wearing a long coat, his hat pulled low. She felt as if she were watching a shadow play. She had the idea that his hands were in his pockets. He said something she couldn't hear. Perhaps this was why Alex wanted to meet her? They were to meet this other man? But that was . . . she couldn't believe what she was seeing. Why was *he* here? Horror froze her. The tall man burst forward suddenly, and in the next instant the two of them were grappling, moving toward the cliff edge, Alex was struggling, his back to the sea, and then he was falling backward, his arms flailing. He dropped like a stone casually tossed by a schoolboy, his scream filling the air.

How long did she cower in the dark, shivering with terror and shock? She could not take her eyes off the man who had pushed Alex Tremaine to his death. He stepped back from the cliff and shrugged as if to adjust his coat on his shoulders, and then he turned and walked a few paces toward where she was hiding. He looked into the dark of the wood as if he were expecting someone. It took a cold moment to realize she was the one he was waiting for. How had he found out? She looked hastily back the way she'd come, wondering if she could make her way back, and when she turned again, the man was calmly lighting a cigarette, his lighter flipped open, the bobbing flame illuminating his face for the briefest second. He stood, looking out to sea for a few moments, nonchalant, as if he had not just thrown a man to his death. Suddenly he turned, looking into the darkness behind him, and called out, "Diana, I know you're here somewhere. I know what you took. I will find you and I will kill you."

BETSY DENTON TOSSED and turned, unable to sleep. It was a condition she was used to. Normally she turned on her bedside lamp and read until she felt sleepy enough to try again. She only wished the nights were not quite so long. But this night had been longer than most. All this talk of Francine and that strange so-called holiday leave in England. The unease she felt as she lay in the dark turned into a kind of dread. Lord knows those days during the war had been bad enough, but now, thinking of Francine, murdered, she began to develop the terrifying notion that it was somehow her fault. The logical part of her knew that the middle of a sleepless night was when one was visited by guilt and a sense of one's own awful failures, but she could not shake the memory of Francine standing at the door of that peculiar cottage, watching her walk back to the village to take the train to London.

Why had she done it? Why had she left her alone? In all the years since the armistice, she had buried the whole business deep in her subconscious. She had returned to the nursing station in France and been overwhelmed by the work, long days, longer nights, and had assumed that Francine, pregnant as she was, had gone home. The major, her husband, would surely not have allowed her to stay on. And then he had died in action.

She jolted awake and realized that she must have finally drifted off, because she woke into the darkness with the sound of voices, urgent, whispered, angry. At first, she thought they were in the room with her, and she lay congealed with fear, but slowly, as the silence enveloped her, she realized they had been in her head.

She rolled over, turned on the light, and lay back, staring at the ceiling. What had she heard? Why had it seemed so real? A man and a woman locked in a furious whispered exchange. She closed her eyes, tried to recapture it. The shock made her sit up. It was Francine and a young soldier. They had been outside, in a little thicket of trees. He held her arm, and even from where she was, almost on the other side of the camp, carrying a bucket of bandages to be burned, she could see the force of it, could see the anger and desperation in her friend.

Why had she not intervened? She tried to pull anything out of the pit of her buried memories that could explain it. Someone must have shouted at her to get a move on, or maybe an ambulance with more casualties had pulled them all back into the new emergency. Betsy remembered now that when the rush had been over, and they finally got to lie down for a couple of hours of sleep, she had asked Francine, "Wasn't that your brother?" What had she said?

"SERGEANT, PHONE CALL from up the lake. A Mrs. Denton." O'Brien had to shout this up the stairs because Ames's phone was engaged.

"I'll call back. I'm waiting for this call to England to be put through."

"She says it's urgent."

"Drat." Ames listened. Just the silence of an as-yet-unconnected call. He looked at his watch. He could try again within the next hour and still get it through before quitting time. "All right," he shouted down. "Put her through."

"Oh, Sergeant Ames, good morning. I think I've remembered something. I mean, I don't know if it will make any difference, but I feel sure it might be very, very real."

"Go ahead, Mrs. Denton," Ames said. It struck him as a peculiar way to put it, saying it was "real." The two "verys" suggested that she was trying to convince herself that what she was about to say was real.

"All this talk of Francine and those old days must have put me in mind of it. I remember her having a violent argument with a young man, but I was too far away to see who it was. It was before that leave we took to England. We'd had an awful wave of casualties and she'd had to rush back in with me to work, and it was only very, very late when we were finally dismissed to get a couple of hours of sleep that I finally asked her who she'd been arguing with. She told me it was just her brother. It might be important because I remember him being quite a bully when we were children. Now that I think of it, of course it was, but I was too far away to see properly. She said to me, and I can remember it now, word for word, 'He never approves of anything I do.'"

"Her brother?" Ames was surprised and struggled to find the significance of this, and why Mrs. Denton thought it urgent. He imagined brothers were always disapproving of their sisters, especially someone like Francine MacDonald, whom her friend described as a "free spirit." But, if he had been a bully as a child, he might have been one still, as an adult.

"Yes. That's what she told me. She was upset about it and said he was always pushing her around. It's true. William was very bossy when we were young. She'd thought when she married Major Renshaw it would be the end of it. It wasn't till we were in England that I thought I understood. I was right. That baby she was carrying was not the major's, and her brother knew it."

DARLING PUT THE receiver back into the cradle and stared at the wall of the cubicle after his call with Ames. His anxiety about Lane hovered in the background where he had successfully pushed it when he sat down to make the long-distance call. He reread his notes, trying to give them a sense of order he could supply to Sims. It was nearly four thirty. He had resisted the temptation to call Lane's hotel earlier, but here now was a telephone at his disposal.

"May I speak with Miss Winslow?" he asked, his heart beating loudly, when he was put through. He knew already that she would not be there.

310

"I'm sorry," the voice on the other end said. He'd been right. "She's not come in or left any message. I can leave a message for her, if you like. I did leave one from the other gentleman."

"What other gentleman?" he asked.

"Oh, I'm sure I couldn't say. He didn't leave it. Just a note for her in an envelope. Whom shall I say is calling?" She said "whom" as if she was trying to sound ladylike. It grated.

"Ask her to call Frederick at the Donaldsons'. She has the number."

"Frederick, Donaldsons'," she muttered, writing. "Very good, sir."

Perhaps the "other gentleman' was someone who knew something about Diana. This certainly wasn't assuaging his increasing anxiety. He picked up the phone and dialled again.

"Oh, I am sorry, Fred," Sandra Donaldson said. "Nothing yet. But I'm sure she'll telephone just as soon as she can. Will you be along soon? I can put the kettle on."

Yes, he told her, he would. He knew he couldn't dash around the city looking for Lane. He was helpless before her antics as usual, he thought with a touch of bitterness. He stood out on the street now, having arranged to see Sims, who was out on another case, the next morning. Under normal circumstances his mind would be full of the tragedy of Francine Renshaw, but his unease about whatever the hell Lane was up to had pushed it aside. He walked grimly toward the underground feeling a mix of anger, fear, and even doubt, he realized, as he rode the wooden escalator down to the platform. Doubt that he could endure these episodes with Lane. The only real model of marriage he knew was that of his own parents. He remembered thinking when he was young, before his mother had died, how boring his parents were. The same routines every day: his father off to work with his lunch kit, his mother standing in the kitchen with her apron on, looking...he tried to think now how she looked and was distressed that he could not read her face from this distance in time. It was not happiness he'd seen, that was certain. Relief? Weariness? Of course, he was remembering her when he was in high school. Perhaps she was already ill with the cancer that killed her.

Had she ever had vitality? Even as he was trying to remember, it struck him that he was thinking of his parents as two completely separate entities, as if the life of one had nothing to do with the life of the other. Perhaps some people marry but never really become part of one another's lives. Well, their lives, yes, but not their minds or hearts. But there were Rudy and Sandra, who so clearly and palpably loved each other, and indeed were friends. But, of course, he thought glumly, Sandra wasn't disappearing to God knows where whenever she felt like it.

By the time he'd emerged from the station and was walking toward the Donaldsons', he knew that regardless of what a pain in the posterior she was, he missed Lane, loved her, felt her very existence change and lift his life. He wondered uncharitably if that were even remotely true for her.

"TELL ME WHAT happened," Lane said. They were sitting in a little cubby seat in the Feathered Bird with bowls of chicken soup before them, light on chicken. Rain pelted against the tiny windows of the pub. Diana had had a bath and looked somewhat revived, though still much too gaunt.

"It's such a long story. But it started in South Africa. I won't go into all the eye-wateringly wearisome details, but I had an assignment as a 'German' courier to this completely repellent Boer, who was the 'leader' of a rebel group called the OB. They were absolutely unbelievable! They spent the entire war sabotaging the Allied efforts. Well, eventually the authorities were able to disrupt their whole operation by getting to their targets before them and arresting them. They weren't that clever, really. They eventually lost the support of even their own people." She stopped and shook her head, lighting a cigarette, her soup untouched. "Do you know that when the war ended, a sympathetic Afrikaner government was elected and every one of those sabotaging bastards was let out of prison? After committing treason! They're probably all government ministers by now. I couldn't stick it anymore, I can tell you. I came back here to get out of the whole mess. Especially after that ridiculous business where I was 'stood down.' There was some cock-up in the works, and our agents arrived at a place I'd given them the coordinates for, a factory that was going to be blown up, only it was a trap and one of the agents was killed. Tremaine had the bloody nerve to think I'd betrayed them. Of course, it happened again when I was off the job, so they knew it wasn't me. We never did find out who the traitor was. We had most of the OB by that time anyway." She smoked and looked nervously around the empty room. "Until I figured out who had betrayed us, I couldn't even trust Alex."

"Diana, eat your soup. You look like you haven't had a proper feed in weeks." Lane watched her sister in the murky light provided by the low-wattage bulbs. Diana was clearly in a state, obsessing ... or was that fair? Perhaps decompressing would be a kinder description. Lane tried to trace the progress from the careless girl she had last seen to this brittle, cynical woman before her. It was hard for her to imagine that Diana too had been a spy. It is like a family affliction, she thought, and it's done none of us any good. She felt a stab of guilt. "So, it all started in South Africa, but what has that to do with why you're on the run here? Whatever happened?"

Diana finally took a spoonful of soup. "Not bad," she said, having a few more. She seemed to be thinking about what she could, or would, say.

"Alex, Major Tremaine, came back about a month ago, and he wrote me that he had a proposition that would allow us to go on working together, and that with my skills, I could be especially useful. I told him in no uncertain terms I was done with intelligence work. I only did it during the war because it was the right thing to do. I have no intention of making a career of it. I couldn't bear the thought of ending up like Daddy, beaten and left for dead. I thought the whole business had probably run its course, anyway—me and Alex, I mean. Then, I came back and went to stay with Marisa. It was a beastly thing to do to Grandmama and Ganf, I know, but I couldn't shake the idea that Fairfax, Marisa's father, had something to do with what went wrong in Africa. I suppose I thought that if I could just see him, talk to him, I might find out.

"Of course, he was furious about my being there, and that really made me suspicious. And then I found proof. He was getting money from the Nazis. I was amazed I hadn't seen it before, amazed that everyone hadn't seen it. I don't know who runs things over here I assumed Alex would know what to do. I contacted him in our usual way, and I told him I had proof. He just said something urgent had come up, that he was going undercover in Europe, leaving that night. He begged me to meet him at a place called Beachy Head because he wanted to say goodbye. Then he said he wanted me to come with him. He begged me." She put her spoon down and rubbed her hand along her forehead. "I don't know why I went. I still love...loved him, I suppose. I was certain Fairfax would find out I'd taken a document from his house, so I thought I should get away, lie low till I could figure out what to do. Even so, it was a bloody nuisance. I was to get to Eastbourne and then walk up along paths at the edge of the cliff until I saw the lighthouse below, and then I was to wait there. He said there was a long wooden stairway to get down to the water, and he'd meet me at the top and we'd go down together. At night, mind you. Luckily there was a bit of a moon so I could just make out the trail. There is a heavily wooded section before you get onto the cliff that is beastly, absolutely pitch black. He'd said not to use the torch so I soldiered on in the dark. He'd told me there was a boat and that we could leave together. I don't know even now if I would have gone with him." She sighed, pulling out her cigarettes. "When I arrived near the place, I saw a man standing alone on the cliff as I approached, and even in the dark I could see it was Alex. I was relieved, I can tell you, after crashing around in the dark, but before I had gone a few steps, another man came from absolutely nowhere and sort of strong-armed Tremaine and pushed him over the bloody cliff. I don't think I'll ever forget that scream." Her hands shook, and she clutched them tightly together.

"My poor Diana!" Lane exclaimed softly, putting her hand on her sister's arm. "But what did you do then?"

"What could I do? I dashed into some bushes and sat there, terrified, and tried to think through what had happened. At first, I worried that Tremaine might be alive, but I realized that he couldn't possibly be, falling from that height. Then, when I got my heart back out of my mouth, I saw that the very man I knew to be the traitor had killed him. He must have followed Alex, known that he was meeting me—or maybe he forced Alex to tell him who he was to meet before he...I thought at first I would race down to Eastbourne and alert the authorities, but of course, he would have put the blame on me, used his position to see me in prison, probably executed. Anyway, he moved between me and the path back down and didn't leave. He looked at his watch, put his hands in his pockets and paced, up and down, up and down, smoking, calm as you please. Then he called out that he knew I had something of his and that he would find me and kill me too. I had moved slowly back, away from the cliff; I was lying flat behind a small rise covered in bush, and I could hear him looking for me, I could see his flashlight moving closer and farther away. I don't know how he missed me, but he finally gave up. I think I stopped breathing the whole time. I wanted to get the hell out of there, get back to Eastbourne, and get to London. But I knew that's what he'd think, that I'd head back to Eastbourne. So, I began to slowly make my way in the opposite direction, well away from the cliff edge. I had no idea what a bloody lot of nothing there was over here! I walked what felt like hours, up and down over endless hills, and finally got here and found the pillbox. Then, when I'd slept a little, I came into the village and found the phone box and phoned Grandmama. When I heard you'd come over from Canada, I thought you must be my last hope."

"Tell me about Major Tremaine."

"He's dead. What more is there to say?" Diana's face hardened, and her lips pursed tightly; Lane recognized her sister's expression of disapproval and anger as something she'd done even as a child. "No. That's not the real problem. The real problem is that I know who the traitor is, and he knows I do." She put her hand on Lane's arm and held it tightly. "I don't know how high up he is, and who else knows. If he finds me, I'm done for. My only chance at safety is to leave the country."

CHAPTER TWENTY-TWO

TERRELL, MUCH TO HIS ANNOYANCE, found his mind divided. He was looking at the two things that had been lying near the cabin where they'd found Arden, and he was trying to imagine how the oarlock, in particular, had gotten there. He was also thinking about April. He looked at his watch. He'd come into the station early, even before O'Brien, because he was restless and wanted distraction. He had even contemplated an early morning ride out onto the Slocan road, but felt it was too early to importune his neighbours or his landlady with the roar of his bike.

He plunked the oarlock down with a clatter. It was iron, fairly rusty. Arden had taken a motor, leaving the oars, so it would have nothing to do with Arden's desperate nighttime journey across the lake. Mrs. Arden had called at the end of the day and said she'd been going through the papers in her husband's desk and found several other invitations to weddings and parties of people they didn't know. Two of these bore the number five hundred. She'd given him the names on the invitations, which he'd taken note of. He'd go along to the print shop when it was open, which wouldn't be—he looked at his watch—for at least another hour. He'd no doubt find that these invitations had been doctored as well. The return address on the envelope was the same as on the Spinks invitation.

Should he ask Mr. McAvity, the local fire chief, how his daughter, April, was doing in Vancouver? He thought about that lovely spring afternoon when he had taken her on his pillion and they'd gone along the Slocan road. It felt as if summer was just around the corner. She'd put her arms around his waist and exclaimed about the air whipping her hair out of the leather helmet. He'd driven carefully along the gravel road, conscious of his cargo, of the pressure of her body, of her father's stern injunctions not to kill his daughter on his damn bike.

And then she'd thanked him, her hair pulled about, her face flushed, her eyes looking into his for a long moment that he was sure meant everything. And that was it. Now he wasn't even on much of a letter-writing footing with her.

Coffee. At least the café was open and hard-boiled Marge could provide that. And breakfast. Sergeant Ames would be in soon. Should he wait? He heard the front door open and he turned to see O'Brien, lunch box in hand.

"Morning, Constable. What have you done with Tompkins?"

"I was in early, so I sent him home."

"You don't look like you've had much sleep. What's the matter?"

"Yes, sir. No, sir. I was just thinking of popping over for breakfast when you got here, but I'd better wait for Sergeant Ames."

"Why you two can't eat at home like decent people, I don't know. Any headway on your body?"

"It's all a bit all over the place. But it's very interesting that Arden could have been the paramour of the woman Darling is investigating over in England before the war, Francine Renshaw. And we learned yesterday that according to her friend, who shipped out with her, she was carrying a baby that was not her husband's."

O'Brien shook his head with complacent disapproval. "War seems to give people the permission to do all sorts." He stowed his lunch box under the counter and sat on his stool, ready for the day's crossword.

Terrell nodded and picked up a pencil to twiddle. Was it significant that there'd been a war on? The baby was not her husband's. Had it been Arden's, her previous lover's? Maybe, but that had only been Mrs. Denton's guess. Francine had never told her whose it was. Arden was reputed to be a bit of a gadfly; perhaps Francine had been too. Mrs. Denton had suggested that her friend might have taken up with Ben Arden when he turned up at their station in France. Or she'd met someone else, had a fling. The problem was that none of this had any bearing on Arden's death thirty years later and on the other side of the world.

"Morning, all!" Ames said, coming through the door.

"Morning, Sergeant. You'd better take Mr. Droopy over there across the way for a feed. He appears to be pining and unable to sleep." O'Brien had looked up from his work. "Now, what do you reckon he's losing sleep over?"

Ames beamed at Terrell. "I couldn't possibly say. Perhaps he's losing sleep over our little murder."

"Yup. That'll be it, I expect," O'Brien said. Neither sergeant winked, but Terrell couldn't help feeling they were barely controlling the urge.

Terrell began to feel a bit better after his cup of coffee, and now tucked into his scrambled eggs with some of his old vigour. "I've been thinking about the murder, sir." He shared his thoughts of the morning with Ames. "And there's that brother, William. I had a call from Mrs. Arden that there are other invitations with that same number, and two with the number five hundred at the bottom and the same return address. When I went up to the address written on the envelope, it was an empty house with a For Sale sign on it. A perfect place for a rendezvous to exchange money. All the signs point to William MacDonald as our likely blackmailer."

Ames nodded. "I'm sure that's right. He's gone off on a supposed vacation, but what if he's killed Arden and cleared out? After all, he might have form. Didn't Mrs. Denton say that Francine had been having violent arguments with her brother all those years ago? Maybe we need to factor him in for his sister's murder as well. Or at least the inspector might."

"It's tempting to connect the two deaths because the two victims were so closely connected." Terrell said, holding up his cup in the direction of April's irascible replacement. "And yet I'm wondering about Philippa Bentley. He's dead; she's gone. On the surface a simple equation."

"Well, one common denominator, if we must use arithmetic, between the inspector's case and ours, is the behaviour of Benjamin Arden himself. He was a womanizer when he was young, and he seems to have picked up on it with only a brief interlude of pretending to be a normal married man with children. Or something. Your equation might work, but for the blackmailing. If MacDonald was blackmailing Arden, what did he have on him?"

"And in the end, why would he kill Arden? That would be killing the golden goose."

"Except," Ames said, turning excitedly to Terrell, "what if Arden says, 'I've got no more money to give you.' MacDonald has almost no option but to kill him because he would never be safe from the possibility that Arden would expose him."

"That seems foolhardy to me. Being discovered as a blackmailer would be bad—it would involve a hefty prison sentence—but to add murder? It seems an awful risk."

"If we can find MacDonald, we'll at least be partway along. Let's focus on that," Ames said, getting the breakfast money out of his pocket.

Out on the street, Terrell pulled his cap down and said, "Arden is being blackmailed for something he's done—or for what someone *thinks* he's done."

"And whatever that something was, it's so bad that Arden has emptied his bank account, heedless of the effect on his wife and children. I still can't get over the fact that it's not the blackmailer who's dead." He pushed open the station door. "My office?"

"Yours, certainly, sir." Terrell said. "I'd just like to get to the printer and double-check this second invitation. I don't have the original, but French might have some copies around just to confirm that they were all printed without the added numbers on them. I didn't find Mrs. Spinks at home last time, so I'll go there to confirm whether they know the Ardens well enough to send them a wedding invitation."

"Righty-ho. I'll go up and start the list of Arden's blackmail-worthy activities, as we know them."

The front desk of the print shop was unmanned, and Terrell could hear the steady stamping of the machine in the back. "Hello!" he called out, but he received no answer. He pushed past the counter after some moments and went through the door into the workroom. He could see at once that there was a sense of frantic activity. He was still amazed at how work could get done in such a crowded space.

At last, the printer looked up and saw Terrell and stopped the machine, shaking his head, not so much at the police officer as at his own circumstance. 'Sorry about that, Officer. Run off my feet here today." He pulled a handkerchief from his pocket and wiped his forehead. "Wedding and a machinery auction at the same time, everybody wanting their stuff last week."

"Good morning, Mr. French. You're on your own here," Terrell observed sympathetically.

French nodded. "I owe Bill the time, so there wasn't much I could say, but it's been difficult having him away. He's not taken a day off since he started here three years ago. He's good, and it's hard to get experienced help. I told him, 'I don't pay enough for you to take long holidays!' That said, how can I help you?"

Terrell nodded. This could confirm their suspicion about William MacDonald. Perhaps he was on the run. "We had another call about invitations with numbers on them, including two with the number five hundred, like on the Spinks invitation. Here are the names of the senders." He handed over the list he'd made.

French shook his head. "That's three things now. Here, let me find the overrun for those." He disappeared around a shelf, and Terrell could hear him shuffling papers. He reappeared, holding up an invitation. "I usually toss these into the garbage, but luckily, without Bill, I haven't had time to empty the can. See, no two hundred or five hundred on any of these either. I really don't understand it. Who was getting these, again?"

Terrell demurred and thanked him.

"I mean, no harm done with the jumble sale," French said as he followed Terrell out of the print shop to the front room. "I was at that sale myself because my daughter was looking for a doll, and the place was standing room only."

It wasn't far to the vicarage, where the Spinkses lived next to the church, so Terrell thought he'd try again. When he knocked on the door it was answered by a harried-looking woman of middle years holding the plug end of a vacuum cleaner cord that disappeared into the murk behind her.

"Yes?" She looked at his uniform briefly and managed to smile. "Officer."

"Am I speaking with Mrs. Spinks?" Terrell had extracted his warrant card and was holding it up to her.

"Yes, that's right." She looked anxious.

"Ma'am, we are pursuing a matter, and you may be able to help. Are you familiar with Mr. Benjamin Arden?"

She shook her head, frowning. "No. Should I be?"

"Mr. Arden received an invitation to your daughter's wedding in December. That's why we wondered."

"Oh, dear. Wait now. Isn't he the man who was found dead? I saw it in the paper. We certainly don't know him."

"Is there any chance your daughter or her husband knew him?"

"No. I'm certain of it. We went over the invitation list together. I would have remembered. It was a very small wedding. Forty people. He most certainly was not on the list!"

Only forty people. Definitely not two hundred. Back at the station, Terrell put his cap on the hook and went upstairs to Ames's office and knocked on the door frame. The door was open and Ames was doing a very passable imitation of their boss, his chair turned toward the window, pencil in his mouth.

"Ah. Terrell. Any joy?"

"I'm wondering now, sir. Those numbers at the bottom of the invitations that were sent to Arden do not appear on any of the originals that French has the overruns for. I did find Mrs. Spinks at home; she didn't know the Ardens and said the couple didn't know him either. I guess I'd learn the same thing if I tracked down the other couple."

"I suspected as much, I must say, since Mrs. Arden hadn't heard of them, either."

"So. Bill MacDonald, our possible blackmailer, and possible murderer, is also the brother of the inspector's dead woman. It's funny, I could swear Mrs. Robinson said her son had come back from the war and his friend Billy hadn't."

"She doesn't look like she gets out much, so she might not even know he was back."

Ames nodded thoughtfully. "I think we've established it is him. So let's look at this. Why is Bill MacDonald sending Arden invitations to the weddings of people he doesn't know, and with those numbers added to them? Two hundred and five hundred are, interestingly, the amount of money that Arden is paying his blackmailer each time. Is that what those invitations are about? 'Here's how much money I want this time'?"

"At eleven at night," suggested Terrell.

"Okay, wait. What's MacDonald got on Arden? Now, let me think. Bill MacDonald, out there in France thirty years ago, finds out his sister is pregnant with someone's baby, has a fight with her, and she ends up dead. Shot. And now that same man is back here, blackmailing Arden, and Arden ends up shot. I think we're right. I bet we have our killer, on both counts!" Ames slapped his hand on his desk with satisfaction.

"And MacDonald called his boss just yesterday and told him he'd be away longer. Maybe he's on the run."

"I think we should get after him. Let me call our chums down at the RCMP." Ames suited his action to his word and then picked up his pencil. "All right. Let's see now. Okay, so back to the question of what MacDonald had on Arden. I've got a list here of Arden's sins and peccadilloes, and I'm damned if any of them amount to anything worth blackmailing over. Or murdering him, for that matter." He waved a hospitable hand to his extra chair and pushed the list over to Terrell.

> *-Affair with Francine Renshaw before she shipped out, and possibly at the front.*
> *-Affair with Philippa Bentley during his wife's pregnancy.*
> *-Desertion, apparently never followed up by Princess Pats.*
> *-Stealing a medal, possibly off dead soldier? Unless acquired at pawnbroker.*

"If Arden made MacDonald's sister pregnant, and her brother knew about it, that would make a lot of sense. Bill MacDonald has a very specific grudge against Arden. But even that last one could hold some promise, since they served together. Maybe MacDonald knows how Arden got his bogus medal. Maybe he would know if he'd actually killed some soldier to get it, for example," Terrell said.

"Yes. Good. The trouble is, we don't know enough gritty details about some of these things. For example, how long was Arden's pre-war affair with Francine MacDonald, as she was then? They both went over to France, met there, and possibly took up their affair again. She marries Arden's commanding officer in a hurry and, according to Mrs. Denton, was pregnant already. Arden's baby? And that's a long time ago, and both Renshaws are dead. Would Bill MacDonald knowing these things be enough for Arden to bankrupt his family? Let's look at the more recent possibilities: the Philippa Bentley business. Is MacDonald blackmailing him to keep the affair secret from Mrs. Arden or Mr. Bentley, or both? I could imagine small amounts, but two hundred dollars a time? If I were the victim, I think I'd throw up my hands and confess rather than destroy my whole family."

"It's something big that we don't know about yet. We need to talk to Bill MacDonald. What if Ben Arden killed Francine? What if she threatened to tell her husband, who was, after all, his commanding officer and a man with a temper?" Terrell suggested.

"Okay. It's possible, and Bill MacDonald knows Ben killed his sister. But wouldn't he be more likely to do something much more drastic? What's the point of blackmailing him if he could take revenge by killing him?"

"Gets all his money and kills him. Two birds," Ames said. "And that explains why MacDonald would kill him—not because he ran out of money, but because it was his plan all along."

July 1917

"WHY DID YOU come? I don't want you here." Francine stood with her arms folded tightly at her waist. Her brother was standing close to her, leaning forward angrily.

"Grandma asks about you in every letter she sends me. Why don't you write to her?"

"I don't have time. You can see what it's like here." Francine turned and looked back at the busy casualty tents.

"That's rubbish, and you know it. She deserves an answer. She's worried about you!" Bill flicked the cigarette he'd smoked down to the nub into the mud.

"What a surprise! She sends her golden boy to spy on me. I don't have time. I have to go, if you've nothing more to say."

Reaching out, Bill snatched her right forearm and twisted it upward. "I've got more to say. You think we don't hear things? It's all up and down the line. 'Major's wife, anyone's for the asking. Major's wife up the spout. Who's gonna tell the major about his wife? Ha, ha, ha. Hey, MacDonald, she's your sister. Introduce me. I like a good time!' Yeah, I've got more to say, all right! Is it true? Are you up the spout?"

"What I do is none of your bloody business." Fury almost choking her, Francine pulled away from him and turned to leave.

"Then it's true! It's that bloody Ben, isn't it? Isn't it, you tramp!" he shouted after her as she hurried away from him down the wooden walk.

An officer had heard the commotion and was almost upon him. "You! Unless your arm's ripped off, you can clear off out of here and quit bothering the nurses. Where are you supposed to be?"

Bill stood straight, saluted, and gave his identification. "Just chatting with my sister, sir. I got leave, sir."

"Well, you can bugger off back where you came from and quit bothering the help."

Francine sat on the cot in her tent trying to still her shaking, her brother's voice still boring into her. If the enlisted men were saying that sort of thing, her husband was hearing it too. She told herself it didn't matter. She wiped her eyes angrily. She had to get away. Her holiday leave was coming up. She could put off sorting it till then.

"Are you all right? I saw Bill being rough with you," Betsy said.

Francine sat up straight and pulled at her uniform. "It's just Bill being his usual bossy self."

"It looked a good deal worse than his usual! I bet he's left a mark on your arm. Here. Let me see." She took Francine's arm gently, unbuttoned the cuff, and pushed the sleeve up. "See?" There was indeed an angry red welt on her arm. "He hasn't changed, I see. Tell Matron next time that you don't want to see him!"

Pulling her sleeve back down and buttoning the cuff, Francine stood. "I have to get back. Captain Sanford was not happy about my leaving in the middle of his surgery preparation."

CHAPTER TWENTY-THREE

LANE LOOKED OUT THE WINDOW of the phone box and gazed at the sea, the water sparkling in the morning light. She felt her first moment of optimism, as if the sun itself had decided to take a hand in their affairs.

"Are you sure?" she asked.

"Absolutely, my dear. I'm pleased you thought of me. Do you remember how to get here?"

"Yes, I do. On Castelnau Road." Lane had gone out to Barnes to pay her respects when Timpson's wife had died in '44. Timpson had always had a soft spot for her, and she felt guilty about abusing his kindness now.

"That's right. Still here!" He chuckled. "It'll be like old times. I know it's not right to say, but it's been that dull since the war ended, and with my Liz gone."

In the snug, the tea had arrived and a boiled egg and toast were promised. Diana sat smoking, staring out the murky window.

"Well? Any luck?" Diana sounded skeptical. She had

been watching Lane think.

"Yes. It's someone I knew during the war. A driver. We won't take the train. I'll sort out a circuitous bus route."

"You can trust this man?"

"Implicitly." Lane stopped talking as the food arrived and thanked the cook. They were absolutely alone in the place. They had heard the usual noise of talking and laughing the night before until just after last call, but no one appeared to be staying there.

"I trusted Fairfax implicitly. I want to see Grandmama and Ganf. It's so unfair that I might have to leave."

"I know. Maybe it won't come to that. But we can't risk you seeing them now. I unfortunately told your friend Marisa the three places she could reach me, so there'll be a watch on my hotel and, for all I know, on the cottage as well. I can't even take the risk of telephoning. There might be some sort of listening device on their phone." Lane stopped and looked down at her plate. Darling would be frantic by now. What would he do? He'd certainly telephone her grandparents. She shook her head. Would he understand?

Diana, who had discovered she was quite hungry, sat now chewing the last morsel of toast and marmalade. They'd been limited to one piece each because of rationing. Potatoes and bread, the cook had said. "Lousy weather last year, crops ruined."

"I want to go for a walk," Diana said when she was finished.

"No," Lane said. "It's too dangerous. We can sit upstairs for the next hour and you can tell me all about your life in Africa. Whatever you can tell me, of course. For starters, you'd better tell me what Fairfax looks like."

"You wouldn't believe it. He's like everybody's favourite uncle. Very tall, and handsome for a man that age, soft-spoken, a gentleman. He's the most dangerous man I know."

With redoubled caution, now that she had a rough idea of what to watch out for—very tall, likely well dressed, thick, greying hair, holding his chin slightly high as if trying to avoid an unpleasant odour—Lane found the post office and went in, glancing around quickly to see who else was inside. Only a very old lady buying a stamp.

When it was Lane's turn, she leaned over and said into the window, "Can I send a wire, please?"

"Certainly, miss. Haven't seen you around here before. Come to tackle the Sisters?" The postmistress pushed a form and a pencil through to her.

Lane was confused for a moment and wondered if the woman could read minds, then remembered. The Seven Sisters. "Oh. Yes. That's right." She smiled. How should she word this?

"Nice day for it. Not above thirteen mile. You leave now, you can be there by tea time," the woman said companionably.

"Oh, quite," Lane said. Should she write it in Russian? She glanced at the curious postmistress. No. That would alert a woman like this instantly. *Home soon. Stop. Don't let her tall boss talk you out of anything. Stop. Ha. Stop. All love.* She pushed the message back, where the woman looked it over, counting words.

"That'll be one and six, please, luvvy. Answer?"

Lane smiled and shook her head. "No, none. Thank you."

She was littering the countryside with obscure communications. Would they know what to do with that message?

DARLING WOKE EARLY, feeling as if he'd spent the night tussling with the bedclothes. He was bleary-eyed and had come to fully in the grip of the same anxiety he'd gone to bed with. What was Lane up to? And where was she? Not in Liverpool, certainly. Maybe the opposite. What was the opposite of Liverpool? He rolled onto his side and took up the envelope he'd been handed by the receptionist on his last desperate attempt to get word of her at that miserable hotel. It was impossible to know if it had been read by anyone. Something about the receptionist told him it had been read by her at the very least. She'd looked slightly cagey, as if someone were lurking behind a curtain like Polonius, listening to them. Darling had not given them the chance. He'd taken the folded envelope with INSPECTOR written on it and gone back onto the street to read it. "Off to Liverpool for a couple of days to see Jane. It'll be fun having Sunday supper with them again! They were always terribly punctual. I'll have to be on my best behaviour. See you soon!" He could hear Sandra and Rudy downstairs talking quietly. It was Sunday, and he'd been promised a nice breakfast. Sunday! He swung his feet to the floor and looked again at the note. It was a bloody cipher! She'd be somewhere at suppertime . . . Liverpool . . . Liverpool Station? Whose suppertime? Theirs was at six. And why "Jane" for God's sake? They didn't know any Jane. A distractor. He'd have to get there without being followed. Well, my hosts would no doubt love to help with the enterprise, he thought, and I'm certain they'd like nothing more than to act as decoys. As he dressed, he thought he'd almost enjoy this, if he weren't so worried.

FIONA SAW THE boy on the bicycle first. He was riding as if trying to dodge the sparse but very large raindrops that presaged a storm. He leaned his machine against the low stone fence and ran up the steps and around to the kitchen door. She was ready for him and had swung open the door. "What brings you out in this?"

"Wire, miss." He handed her a brown envelope. "No reply." Then he looked past her at a cooling pile of oatcakes. She reached into her pocket and pulled out a couple of coins and then said, "Oatcake?"

"Yes, please, miss!"

She buttered two and handed them to him. "Get along home—it's really coming down now."

"Mrs. Andrews, there's a wire," Fiona whispered. She'd found her employer sitting in the library, knitting by the fire. The old man was snoozing with his feet on an ottoman.

"Thank God. It had better not be bad news."

Ganf woke with a start. "What's happened?"

"A telegram," Fiona said. She wasn't going to move until she learned the contents.

"Well, this has come a bit late. It's a good thing we were cautious. Something is up." She handed the wire back to Fiona, who read it out loud. "*Don't let her tall boss* . . . that must be that oily man who was here yesterday. I knew there was something not right about him."

"She is warning us that he might be dangerous, and more importantly, she is warning us that someone knows about this cottage."

"Some days I wish our poor daughter had married someone else," Ganf grumbled.

"She wasn't to know he was a spy. He seemed such a competent young man. One didn't like him much because he was not warm, but one felt she'd be looked after, didn't one?"

Ganf snorted and sat up, leaning forward on his stick as if he was about to tell a tale of the past to a group of children. "And then our darling girl died, and it is we who looked after their children while he was gallivanting around Europe playing at spies."

"All water under the bridge. You can't deny it was lovely having the darling girls, and there's been a war on. They only did their duty. I'm very proud of them."

"Yes. By aping their miserable father and going into the family business. How do we know they won't end up like him?"

In truth, Mrs. Andrews worried about this herself, but she wasn't going to magnify his worry by speaking it out loud. "We're not in wartime. I'm sure it's not a danger. The thing is, what are we going to do about this?"

Fiona looked again at the telegram. "I don't think there's anything you can do. One thing I'm sure of: Miss Lane will think of something. Now, I've got some lovely warm oatcakes."

At this Ganf sat up straight and smiled. "That's the stuff," he said.

His wife said, "One for him, no butter, if you please, Fiona."

TERRELL NODDED AT O'Brien and picked up the receiver. A call this early on a Monday morning?

"Hello? Constable? It's Dick French. I'm calling from the print shop." He did not give Terrell a chance to say anything. "I've been robbed. All the money I had. Five hundred dollars."

Holding back on his desire to blurt out "Five hundred dollars?" Terrell said, "All right, don't touch anything, Mr. French. We'll be right over." He stood up and grabbed his cap, and then ran up the stairs three at a time.

O'Brien watched this feat of youthful athleticism and muttered, "Why do carpenters bother building all those steps?"

"Sir?" Terrell said, stopping at Ames's door. "The printer's been robbed. Quite a lot of cash. Five hundred."

"Why is he keeping that much cash around? He's practically asking for it. We're not making any progress on Arden. Let's go."

"IT WAS IN the safe," French said. "I just put all my money into this box." He held up a wooden box, a little bigger than a cigar box, with a brass latch. "But I had a large order for a farm auction, so I thought I'd put the larger amount of cash in the safe. Only it was empty." He pointed at the small safe on the floor, with the door hanging open.

Ames bent down to look. "Any sign of how it was got to?"

"That's the thing. It was locked as usual. Hadn't been tampered with at all."

"Does anyone else know the combination?" Terrell asked.

"Bill, of course." He put his hands over his eyes and groaned. "I'm afraid I've been had." The printer sat heavily on the chair in front of his desk.

It didn't look to Ames like he would ever notice if anything went missing. The desk was piled with papers, in no apparent order, the top drawer of an oak filing cabinet behind it was hanging open, and it looked as though documents and records had been pushed into it apparently without resorting to any sort of system. It struck him as strange that the shop could be so chaotic, with the precision of the work he was required to do. He had a passing thought that the mistakes on the invitations and poster were the result of the chaos, and not some subterfuge by Bill MacDonald after all.

"He went off on holiday, didn't you say?" Ames asked.

"Well, yes. It wasn't really a holiday as such. He gets two weeks a year, and aside from a few days last November, he's never used the time. He just said he needed a few days off. Then he phoned—I don't know, yesterday, maybe the day before—to say he was in Alberta and he'd need a couple more days. I was annoyed about it, but he's very good at his job. Anyway, he said he'd be back soon. I guess he won't be back. Or at least, it looks like he's been back and got at the safe."

Terrell had taken out his notebook. "Do you know his address?"

"I...I don't know where he lives. I think he said he has a landlady."

"Do you have any documents from when you hired him? How did you pay him?"

"Well, no. I mean, I just gave him an envelope at the end of every week. Twenty dollars."

"And you took his pay from the safe? Did he leave on a Friday?" Ames asked.

His brow furrowed, the printer finally said, "Yes. I'm sure that's right. I would have paid him, and he said he needed to be away for a week."

"Is there any chance you might have left the safe door unlocked?"

"Oh, no. Not at all. I'm terribly careful."

Ames just stifled a skeptical "Oh?" as he gave the area a quick glance. "There's no chance someone else could have broken in, found the safe open, and stolen the cash?"

"No. I would have found the shop broken into. I'm very careful about locking up. There is a lot of valuable equipment here. No. I'm very sorry to say it must have been Bill." He sighed. "I'm sure I'll never see that money again."

Terrell said gently, "You don't use the bank?"

The man coloured. "I never saw the need, with the safe. My wife always wanted me to." His form slumped further. "I don't really trust them, if you want to know the truth. How do all those people get paid? Out of our savings, I'm sure. No, thanks. I'd like to keep all my money."

Ames bet he was now realizing he was going to have to tell his wife. Poor guy. He'd lost the lot. "Do you know of any family members of Mr. MacDonald? They might know where he'd go to."

"I don't think he has any. Like I said, he came back from England about three years ago because his wife died. That's all I can tell you."

Kent, January 1919

BILL MACDONALD GOT off the train in Chatham. Even at two in the afternoon it was dark and miserable, with rain-filled clouds hanging low. Aside from a few people at the station, the streets looked deserted. He asked the conductor where he could find an omnibus to the village of Hardale.

"You won't find one now, lad. It only makes one run, and that were at ten this morning. It's not but seven mile." He waved his hand vaguely in a southeasterly direction.

Bill looked where the man was pointing, and his heart sank. Seven miles was not a difficult distance to walk, but in this weather he was likely to arrive soaked and muddy.

"Is there a pub with rooms there?"

"They do have a small pub on the road just the other side of the village. Now, as to its having rooms, I couldn't say. Most do though. You American?"

"Canadian."

"Well, that's all right then," the conductor said. "Must get on." The doors of the carriages were closing, and his services were required to get the train on the move.

Bill pulled his greatcoat across his front and did up the buttons. Pulling his wool cap low over his face, he shoved his hands into his pockets and started down the empty street. He wondered at himself, setting out with not even his rucksack. All his asking among the nursing sisters who were breaking up the field hospitals had got him nothing. No one knew where Franny was. Everyone thought she'd gone home. They'd heard she was pregnant. Obviously, she'd not be able to stay on. When he'd finally found Betsy, she'd been standoffish, trying to brush him aside, saying she had work. She told him the same thing: she assumed Franny had gone home.

"But she hasn't," he'd said. He'd reached out his hand to take her arm and she'd pulled back. Exasperated, he'd said, "I've cabled my grandmother. She's not there. She's never written, nothing. She's run off with that bastard, and I mean to find them."

"Everyone died in that battle, you know that. Her husband, everyone."

"I know who died there. I was there! God, where is she?" he had shouted, felt his own tears falling down his cheeks. That, he reflected now, eyeing a bakery, was what finally seemed to frighten Betsy, and he'd managed to get out of her that the last time she'd seen Franny was at this cottage in Kent.

He pushed open the bakery door and saw at once that nearly all the shelves were empty. Everything would have been cleaned out by mid-morning. But there was what looked like a small pork pie under a glass lid. "Can I have that, please?" he said to a stout woman with a wool shawl wrapped across the front of her body and tied at the back. It was cold in the shop.

"Good day to you, too," she said with asperity. "Last one. I was just about to close and get ready for tomorrow."

He fished in his pocket for change and handed it over, taking the pie.

"And you're welcome!" she called after him. "Yanks," she added, shaking her head. She watched him push the pie into his pocket and start down the road. Should they just be wandering around the countryside like that?

The rain had begun at around the second mile, and the road, narrow and for long sections hemmed in by hedgerows, was becoming muddy. He stood under an oak and pulled the pie out of his pocket, looking glumly at the sheep huddling in a field opposite. The pie, at least, was good. He'd been hungry since a couple of buns in the early morning before leaving London.

His thoughts turned to his sister. After what he'd seen, he didn't even know what he'd do when he found her. What if Arden had survived somehow? But no. Not after what he'd seen. So, she'd gone off, hiding somewhere with that baby. How could she have done this, after everything their grandparents did for them, he thought angrily. She'd been spoiled rotten, allowed anything she'd ever wanted, sent off to study nursing while he stayed home. He could still remember his grandmother cupping his chin and saying, "You mustn't worry, my sweet. You'll have the army. She has such a facility. And nursing will steady her, give her a purpose."

Facility. Ha. Intelligence in a woman was unseemly. Marrying a man who kept her under strict control would have steadied her, he thought. The major came too late. And now look what she'd done. She surely got the last laugh. He threw the pie wrapper onto the ground, pulled up his collar, and started grimly along the road. He'd kill them both when he found them.

CHAPTER TWENTY-FOUR

"**A**T LEAST IT'S IN TOWN, and not in some godforsaken place in the West Country," Lane said. They were sitting opposite each other on the bed with Diana's map spread out between them. Lane pointed on the map to Castelnau Road just after the Hammersmith Bridge. "No one will find you there, and you can be safe until we think about what to do." Lane had proposed a plan of taking buses steadily in the wrong direction to Southampton, and then going by train to Waterloo. Barnes was across the river from Hammersmith. If one could get to Waterloo, the District line would take them to Hammersmith, and from there they could walk. Lane had never had the desire to live in such a massive city as London, but now it was infinitely desirable to lose themselves in that sea of humanity.

"And then what?" Diana asked glumly. She had shown no interest in Lane's elaborate detailing of the travel plans. "I can't hang about in a bedsit in Barnes for the rest of my life."

"It's hardly a bedsit. Timpson owns a lovely big house with a splendid garden, and he doesn't mind people smoking." Lane folded the map so the next leg of their journey was visible. "It's too bad about Major Hogarth. I thought we might have had some hope with her," Lane said.

"Oh, yes. The bright light that thinks I pushed Tremaine over a cliff." She stood up abruptly and went to the window, holding her cigarette away from her face. "I don't think Daddy would think much of all this."

Lane found it hard to imagine what aspect of the business Daddy would think ill or well of. He'd managed to evade his fate for thirty or more years. But in the end, he'd run out of luck and ended up dead in the road outside a Nazi prison.

"Listen, I hope you don't think this is your fault. Even he must have walked into traps from time to time."

"I should have quit the minute the war was over and we could see how things were going in South Africa. Tremaine was up to something. He told me he was leaving, and he couldn't say more. But I think he knew what I knew: that Fairfax was a traitor." She sat on the one chair provided. "I don't know what I would have done if he hadn't died. I expect I might have gone, I don't know. I certainly hadn't any other plan for my life." Her voice trailed off, and Lane could see now how miserable Diana was. She'd lost the man she loved, seen him die. It was unthinkable, unspeakable. Seeing death seemed to be part of some blurry past they'd all somehow stumbled through to arrive here, safe on the banks of peace. And now she saw what she had missed: Diana was rudderless. The war work had completely engaged her, leaving her no time to think about a future after the war, and now she was truly at loose ends. No time to develop any interests of her own, to grow up thinking about a future. She had no idea what to do with the rest of her life. She might well have set sail with Tremaine because she could think of little else.

"I loved him," Diana said, looking away and releasing smoke as if it were that very love dissipating into nothingness.

"Diana, I'm so sorry...I..."

Diana turned back to look at Lane, her face set. "It's quite all right. Please don't. Nothing to be gained by it." She spoke in her strangely clipped accent, and stood, brushing her trousers down as if to begin a job. "What time are we to catch this bus?"

On the bus finally, Lane looked out at the vast stretch of sea disappearing behind the rolling hills as they moved north. Of course, their father hadn't been inclined to any sort of emotional or personal expression. He discouraged it actively. How many times had she heard that "nobody was interested" in what she felt? She had felt like she belonged to strangers who were not burdened with the emotions that raged uncontrollably inside her childish breast. She wondered now if Diana had felt like that and had simply beaten back her feelings, or if she was truly their father's daughter and was never troubled by an excess of sentiment. She closed her eyes and thought how lucky they were in their grandmother, who had no constraints when it came to expressions of love.

What had their mother been like? If she was like Grandmama, would she have eventually been crushed by living with such a hard man? Though she remembered her grandmother saying he'd changed a great deal after their mother's death, that, she was sure, was just her grandmother being kind. Grandmama thought the best of everyone. Lane suspected he'd always been as she knew him. One thing was certain: she did not believe that Diana was immune to grief. She was simply better at pushing through and covering it up. The thing now, she thought, was how to help Diana. But whom could she trust? Not Hogarth—that much was clear.

MAJOR HOGARTH STOOD as Greg Fairfax appeared in her open doorway, hands in pockets, as if he had been casually passing by and stopped in to say hello. "Greg. Come in." She stood until he had closed the door and sunk gracefully into the chair, crossing his long, expensively trousered legs.

"At ease, Major. I just stopped by to see how we're getting on. Any sign of our fugitive?" He spoke with a soft upper-class drawl and reached into his jacket pocket for his silver cigarette case, leaning forward to offer it to her.

She shook her head. She had the odd sensation of being offered something that would compromise her. She knew what he was asking. It was not her job to engage in the search for Diana Winslow. It was her unspoken job to work Diana's sister, to keep her on a lead, to know where she was. To be her confidante until she led them to Diana. She wasn't sure what she could tell him. She didn't know where Lane was because Fairfax had bungled it by not having her followed the minute she left the War Office. He'd assumed she would go either to her hotel or to the place in Marylebone where her husband was staying. She credited Lane with intelligence. Fairfax had not. Lane had turned up at neither place and was now missing.

After a considerable struggle, Hogarth finally said, "She should have been followed from here."

Fairfax uncrossed his leg and brushed his trouser cuff, as if to control a sudden rush of anger. "She talked to my daughter, you know."

"Yes, she told me." She moved the ashtray, which held his smoking cigarette, farther away from her.

He looked up. "Did she? What did she say? My daughter's being a bit standoffish." His mild eyes were piercing, suddenly.

"Nothing really, I'm afraid. I didn't tell her who you are. She thinks you are just her sister's friend's father. Do you think Lane Winslow knows you work for us?"

Fairfax shook his head. "I don't see how. My daughter wouldn't have told her. She doesn't know herself."

Hogarth nodded. He'd returned to his scrutiny of the books on the shelf behind her and she watched him. Now she began to imagine the scene he'd reported about Tremaine's death. He'd known there was to be a clandestine—this was the word he'd used—meeting between Diana Winslow and Alex Tremaine. Both were agents. She knew Tremaine had been assigned to go into Germany. She'd had no idea, until Fairfax suggested it, that Tremaine might have been compromised by Diana Winslow. Was it a "clandestine" meeting, or were they meeting simply because Tremaine was saying goodbye? She knew they had been close after their work in Africa. Or had Tremaine wanted to persuade Diana to go with him?

"You were lucky you found them."

"You know, I got a bit leery of her in Pretoria. We had a couple of missions go wrong. That's how we found out. Enemy got the wind up sort of thing. Lost a couple of agents." He shook his head, smiling. "As to finding them, no luck involved, Major. I suspected Tremaine had been turned. I followed him. I suppose she saved us the trouble, pushing him over the cliff like that."

Nodding again, Hogarth waited. "Why wasn't she arrested?"

"What do you mean?" He sucked in a mouthful of smoke and frowned at her. He released the smoke in a cloud, as if he wanted to obscure her.

"Why wasn't she arrested there, in South Africa, if you knew?"

"Need-to-know, I'm afraid."

Well, that could cover a multitude of sins. She wanted to ask him how he'd lost Diana. How she'd got away when he'd been right there, had seen her commit a murder.

"It was beastly that I lost her," he said, as if he read her thoughts. "She melted into the darkness before I could reach the scene. Of course, Tremaine was done for, I could see that at once. No one could survive a drop of five hundred feet. He was a good agent in his day. A shame to lose him. I've got people out everywhere. I don't see how she can get away. We have a tail on her sister's husband. She somehow managed to leave a note for him, we believe. She'll have told him where she was going."

He tapped the top of her desk twice and turned toward the door. "Keep me posted," he said. "And try not to make a mess of this, Major."

Hogarth sat staring in disbelief at the closed door when he'd left. He'd cocked it up and was blaming her! He'd emphasized her title, "Major," with palpable condescension. And he'd left his beastly cigarette burning in the ashtray. She stubbed it out angrily and tried to shake her thoughts but couldn't. Too smooth, too lean, too facile, and a damn sight too well dressed, if what she'd heard from Lane Winslow and others was true. Botched investments and even a rumour of a breach-of-promise lawsuit. He'd not waited overlong after his wife's death, she thought. He'd been climbing inexorably up the ladder until the rumours began. And there was a sharp edge to his urgency to find Diana. Was he getting pressure from above? Had someone higher up told Fairfax *he'd* botched it and now he was trying to push the blame onto her? He was definitely rattled for some reason. Very uncharacteristic of him. Perhaps his personal life was closing in on him. She'd bet his daughter would be giving him grief about marrying again, if that rumour was true.

Why had Diana Winslow pushed her lover to his death? She tried to imagine the scene. Tremaine must have been stronger than her. How had he allowed himself to be overwhelmed? But of course, they'd been lovers. He trusted her. It must have happened quickly, before he realized. But if Fairfax was right and Tremaine had been a double agent, and so had she, they ought to have both got into the boat that might have been waiting and sailed away. She thought back to her last conversation with Tremaine. He'd been in charge of Diana from the beginning. Diana had told him she wanted out. He had been persuaded to take on one more job, then he too wanted to have done with it. He had told her he wanted to divorce his wife and move abroad with Diana. He had German contacts in the east. It was to be an in-and-out job to set up a network, and then he would be free.

Had Tremaine been crooked? Maybe Fairfax was wrong. He'd been killed because he knew Diana was crooked. She cursed the circuitous workings of the organization. Fairfax must have known, or thought he knew, and because she was junior to him, he'd never bothered to include her in the matter. She suspected he didn't think much of women officers. Well, nothing unusual there. A lot of men never adapted to the idea of women in "men's" jobs.

The knock on her door startled her. Was he back? "Come in."

It was the young man from the desk downstairs. He held aloft an expensive-looking envelope. "This came for you, ma'am."

She took it. "By hand?"

"Yes, ma'am."

"Did you see who it was?"

"A young boy."

When he'd gone, Hogarth put her letter opener to use and took out a thick card embossed with the British Museum logo, part of a note set. *Darling, so stupid of me. Can't meet as planned. Forgot I had a fitting. Can we change it to half six instead? I'll be dying for tea by then!*

No signature, not even an initial. Lane Winslow, she was sure, wanting to meet her near the British Museum. She looked at the clock on the wall opposite her desk. Five thirty. She would give herself half an hour to walk, and another half to survey the area to make sure neither of them had been followed. With a shock she realized Fairfax might follow her. It infuriated her that he might not trust her. She would give herself forty-five minutes to get there instead. Covent Garden would be quiet by then, except for the sweepers. She would look in the windows of the Floral Street shops, cross through the market, watch. She guessed Lane would try for the front steps of the museum, but she might not know it was a construction zone now because of the destruction during the Blitz. Then she'd most likely pick Great Russell or Bloomsbury. Perhaps there was a pub or tea shop across from the museum.

She pulled on her gloves, adjusted her cap, and surveyed her office before she stepped out the door into the hall. It was quiet. People had begun knocking off. The front desk was empty on the ground floor. She turned down a narrow corridor and slipped out a little-used door onto Whitehall Place. It was a pleasant evening, and she walked like someone without a care in the world, enjoying a stroll. When she reached Floral Street, she stopped in front of a dress shop that was just closing and looked in the window. The two mannequins were a study in how the well-dressed woman was spending her time: shopping all afternoon in a prim, dark-green suit and a fetching hat, and drinking cocktails in a long, sequined gown at a reception at some embassy in the evening. There was no one following her, she established with relief. She moved more quickly to Covent Garden and ducked into the market area. A few more minutes of waiting in the shadows still revealed no sign of anyone tailing her.

In the end it was Lane who found her. She stepped out of a doorway on Great Russell and fell in beside her, linking arms as if they were chums out for the afternoon.

"Thank you for coming," she said quietly. "There's a little restaurant just over here. I've got a table behind a potted plant."

Hogarth actually laughed. "Well done. I've always wanted to lurk behind a fern in the performance of my duty."

Lane resisted the urge to turn and look behind her. She certainly wasn't followed, and she was certain Hogarth would have made sure she wasn't either.

Once at the table, they fell into an uneasy silence. A waiter came with menus. "I'll just have tea and a biscuit," Lane said. "I'm being fed later." Hogarth asked for the same.

"You know where she is," Hogarth said. "It's your duty to bring her in. Sister or not. She is a traitor and a murderer."

Lane did not respond to this. "You have a problem," she said at last. She respected the major's ability to wait. "I believe Gregory Fairfax is working for...I don't know who. The other side possibly, himself certainly."

"What rubbish! You base this on what, exactly?"

"I visited his house, you know. He lives just nearby. He has a jumpy, unhappy daughter and an expensive flat with every valuable object gone. As I told you, he's in some sort of financial trouble."

"That makes him careless and imprudent. It doesn't make him a traitor." Hogarth reached into her handbag, and then withdrew her hand, empty. "I've been trying to quit. I developed the habit in university, and it got worse during the war."

Lane smiled momentarily. "You're all right with me, then. I never really took to it. I won't be tempting you." She folded her hands on the table. "People who are used to money often don't cope very well when they've lost it. I would say by the state of his furnishings, he's reaching the end of his rope. Bad investments? There are plenty of investments he might have made in Africa that could have gone belly up. But no, you're right. What *would* make him a traitor is killing another agent."

"I suppose you mean Tremaine," Hogarth said. She really did want a cigarette.

"My sister is in danger till he's stopped. So is the country."

Hogarth looked at her. "Did you find her?" She didn't expect an answer.

"You know, your previous director, Dunn, was stupid in the end. He thought he knew better than anyone else, so he harboured a dangerous rogue agent right under his nose. I think Fairfax is possibly a little similar but with more hubris and less brain. I think he banks on the belief that no one could possibly suspect him. The epitome of the British moneyed class. He's not motivated by a passion for fascism or Bolshevism or disillusionment with his King and country. He's motivated by money, and he's expecting a big payout for betraying and eliminating a double agent. And whoever is above him doesn't know."

Hogarth thought about this. If Fairfax was what Lane said, it didn't follow that his boss didn't know, or at least suspect. She said coolly, "You seem very sure. You haven't met him, I think?"

"I haven't, but I am sure of this: my sister didn't kill Tremaine. She saw Fairfax do it. He waited for a long time for her to reveal herself at the rendezvous. He suspected she might be there somewhere. He will eliminate her as well because he thinks that she might have seen him kill Tremaine. He can't take the risk of leaving her alive. She suspected something in Africa. She hasn't told me what, but he thinks she knows something about that as well. Perhaps that's why he killed Tremaine. I know you don't believe me, but if he finds her, he will kill her." She leaned forward. "And if he does, he'll get off scot-free."

Silence fell. Beyond their potted fern they could hear the clatter of utensils and the rising tide of restaurant noise as people talked increasingly loudly to be heard.

Hogarth tried to imagine that what Lane was saying might be true. Suppose Fairfax was a traitor, had killed Tremaine, and was now a danger to them all. She shook her head. She knew Fairfax was a condescending ass and always had been, but he was true blue; he'd been a war hero in the first show. No one doubted him. But, of course, she knew there were people who went over, and she knew that when they did, the agency clamped down so that the right hand might never know what the left was doing. Even if he were a problem, she'd be unlikely to ever know about it.

"It must be obvious to you that I can't accept what you are saying. She's your sister, so of course you are bound to believe her. But none of it is true, you know. Instead of this cat-and-mouse nonsense you should encourage her to turn herself in." Hogarth shrugged. "She might have had a reason that would mitigate her actions. We can't know until we have her." The tea had arrived in the interim, and she gazed at it now, her appetite gone. Bea would have dinner ready when she got home.

Lane picked up the teapot and poured tea for both of them. "What if I am right, Major Hogarth?" She spoke very quietly. "What if Fairfax is the traitor and my sister is innocent? You must at least consider it." She put her cup down and looked at her companion. "You're my only hope. I could see a year ago that you were a straight shooter, that you are honest, that you are trustworthy. I know in my heart you would not want an injustice done."

"You're asking me to shield a murderer. Anything else?"

Lane smiled and then became serious. "I'm asking you to help me keep my innocent sister alive. I'm asking you to consider that your real problem is not Diana. If you will not hear her, at least let me get her out of the country, and she'll be no more trouble to anyone." She wondered if she should cross her fingers. She couldn't actually imagine Diana being no trouble to anyone.

Hogarth, fighting the desire for a cigarette, tapped the table with her index finger and looked away. Then she said, "I'm surprised you can ask this of me, Miss Winslow. To let a traitor go, to look the other way?" She stood up. "I'm sorry you feel you could take advantage of a small favour I did for you last year. I had thought better of you. If you know where she is, and I suspect you do, the only right thing is to have her come in. Good evening."

CHAPTER TWENTY-FIVE

DIANA LOOKED AROUND THE DINGY parlour. She felt imprisoned here. She'd been happier in the bloody damp pillbox. Why had she allowed Lane to drag her here? And where was Lane now? She'd said she was going to see this Major Hogarth. She hadn't told Lane about the paper she'd taken from Fairfax. Looking into the dismal street outside, she wondered now why. Lane would get no joy from Major Hogarth, she was sure. These people stuck to each other like limpets on a rock. No one would believe her over a man like Fairfax.

The door opened and Timpson came in with a tray. More bloody tea, she thought, and then saw that he carried a bottle of sherry and two glasses. Well, that was something.

"Thought this might do us. I'm sure you could use a drink."

Diana stopped pacing and sat down. "Thank you. I hope I won't be imposing on you for long."

"Nonsense. You stay as long as you like."

Diana tried to calm the surge of desperation that welled up in her at the thought of having to stay here, trapped like a fox in a hunt. She managed to stutter out a "thank you." She accepted the sherry, clinked her glass with his, and sipped. "My sister tells me you were a driver."

"That's right. I took to her right away. She was always kind, you know. Some of the others treated me like a skivvy they could just order around. Nary a word of thanks, nothing. She always took an interest, asked about the family, gave us a little something at Christmas. Not that she'd have much. I don't think she had much of a job. Worked at Wormwood Scrubs."

Diana didn't ask how he'd had occasion to drive a woman around who had a lowly job at Scrubs. She wondered now if Daddy had got Lane some sort of higher-up job in intelligence. She pulled out her cigarettes and offered one to Timpson, who shook his head, smiling.

"Better hang on to those. You might need them."

When the telephone sounded in the hallway, Timpson got up, making a "stay put" motion with his hand. Diana didn't acknowledge this but leaned back in the chair, a movement that made her realize she'd been perched on the edge of the chair, as if she might flee then and there. She could hear Timpson saying, "I see. Of course. I see." She suspected it was Lane. At least there'd be an end to this purgatory.

"She said—your sister I mean—that she can't come back here, that what she tried hadn't worked, and she thinks she's being tailed. She's going to meet her husband in the hope that they can come up with a plan, and could you just stay on here."

357

"I see," Diana said, her heart sinking at the thought of staying in this utterly depressing house with this utterly depressing little man.

"I tell you what: I'll go to the shops, then we'll cook up a nice dinner and listen to the wireless. Tomorrow will be a new day," her host said.

LANE KNEW THAT she had almost certainly been followed. That was fine. She was leading them straight to Darling. She tried not to worry about Diana, but she had seen when she'd left her at Timpson's that her sister felt impatient and trapped. Would she stay as she'd been told? The last thing Diana had said to her as she'd left to see Hogarth was, "What's the bloody point? I might as well turn myself in now. It's where it will all end anyway!"

She could see that Diana's defeatism must be part and parcel of her sorrow at losing Tremaine. She'd barely had time to take in all that she'd been through and was feeling since she'd seen him killed. Diana's coping strategy was not unlike hers: bury unhappiness and pretend it wasn't there. As Lane got off the train and started up the steps toward Liverpool Station, she uttered a quick prayer that Diana would at least give her a chance, and then another that Darling had understood her note.

She saw the clock tower and went to stand under it. It was Sunday evening, when she'd expect people to be at home, and it amazed her that so many people were still out and about, hurrying along with suitcases, or coming out of the station and dashing down into the underground. She saw him at just the same moment that she located a

358

man leaning against a phone box as if waiting to use the telephone, nonchalantly reading his newspaper.

Darling enveloped her with an exclamation of "Thank God!" that was muffled in her hair.

He held her at arm's length to look at her. "Your hat's crooked."

She kissed him. "I'm not surprised, after that bit of manhandling."

"I've been here for an hour, slowly losing hope that I'd gotten the whole thing right." He took her hand. "Is the part about a Sunday dinner still on? I'm starving."

"Me too, actually. Let's see if we can find a restaurant or something open and have a proper meal."

"Should we get a table for five? How many people do you think you have tailing you? I've got one at least." He nodded toward the other side of Liverpool Street. "I expect your chums have a watch on Rudy's house, and they've been following me around like puppies. It must be very boring for them."

"I certainly have one. Let's try that restaurant over there. I doubt they'll come in. It will give us a chance to chat."

"Chat? Chat? I thought you might be dead, and you want to 'chat'?"

"It hasn't been particularly dangerous for me," Lane reassured him, ploughing past his skeptical expression and her own nerves. They went across the street and into a small restaurant called the Shepherd's Pie—a promising name. They were shown to a table where Lane settled into a chair facing the door, feeling somewhat better to be where she belonged, with Darling. She took off her gloves and hung her jacket on the back of the chair. With his hat off, Darling's rumpled hair had fallen onto his forehead. She wanted in the worst way to brush it back, to kiss that forehead. To forget about what they, no, she, was in the middle of.

"I was just thinking how nice it would be to kiss your forehead."

"You're cruel, you know that? Making me want something I can't have. Are our chums coming in?"

"No. Should we forget about dinner, duck into the back, put on disguises, and completely confound them?"

Darling shook his head firmly. "No. I've left my disguise at Rudy's, and I'm hungry. Being terrified is exhausting."

She reached across the table and took his hand. "My poor darling. All we have to do is think of a way out of it, and it will be over."

"You *are* joking. I'm not pitting my intelligence against the whole of the British war machine without something to eat. Do you think they actually have shepherd's pie?"

They did. "Not bad, considering the conditions," the waiter told them.

"I shudder to think," Lane said when he'd gone. "Let's talk about something else. How is your, or rather Ames's, case going?"

"I bet you don't think we can solve it without you."

"Obviously. I'm sorry that I haven't been able to give it my full attention. I suppose Ames is getting along all right?"

"He is. He found the body of Ben Arden, you know, the missing man. He thinks the blackmailer did it, only there's a problem. The dead man was found with two hundred dollars rolled up in his pocket. Oh, and he thinks the blackmailer is Francine Renshaw's brother."

"Aha. So maybe not the blackmailer—we've decided it's blackmail now, I suppose—because he would have taken the cash. Now, let me see." Lane tilted her head back a little to look at an imaginary list. "We have the blackmailer, the lover from up the lake, the lover's husband, and the wife, obviously. A lover can be tiresome and want eliminating. Oh, and of course the ghost of the dead girl they found in Kent, and her brother, who might also be the blackmailer."

"Oh?" Darling said. He wanted to lean in and kiss her, feel the warmth and generosity of her lips. "When this is over—"

"When this is over, we are going to Scotland so I can finish my original mission, seeing to Ganf. He's dying to see you again. He thinks you're the cat's pyjamas. Now stop it, the waiter is watching."

"Poor man has had nothing else to do. It's the least I can do for him. Tomorrow, I have the pleasure of another transatlantic chat with your friend Ames. I will share your theories with him."

"About Diana: I have her stowed with a friend from the war. No one knew where either one of us was, but I thought I'd break cover and make one more attempt to get them to see reason, through Major Hogarth. Nothing doing, I'm afraid. She's obdurate. She really does believe that Diana is a traitor and murdered her lover. We just need to buy a little time till I can think of something. There must be some way to prove I'm right." Lane had given Darling a précis of all she knew about the situation. "I believe her. She didn't do this. There has to be a way to prove that Fairfax did."

361

Darling felt a rising tide of rebellion. He took her hand off his and placed it on the table, shaking his head. He looked at the other diners, as if one of their followers were at one of the tables, and growled in an undertone, "I don't like this and I don't want this. Why can't your blasted sister get out of her own messes?"

By the time they'd finished eating, they'd agreed to separate, she back to her hotel, and he to the Donaldsons'. As long as the watchers were kept busy following them, they were far away from discovering where Diana was.

The last thing Darling said to her rang in her ears as she descended into the underground. "You're on the horns of a dilemma, then. As long as she's hiding, she can't prove her innocence, and if she comes out, she could be dead before she has a chance to try. Your best hope is to catch Fairfax red-handed trying to kill her!" Even knowing he was engaging in dark sarcasm, she wondered if he wasn't right.

WHEN DARLING WAS in the cab, he asked the driver to set him down outside the Yard and sat back to think. He had secrets on his mind, and he was struggling not to be angry about the whole business. He hadn't meant to sound so harsh. But he realized he was probably right. Tomorrow they would meet again. Perhaps a good sleep, now that he knew where Lane was, would show them the way. He settled grimly against the seat of the cab, thinking of the secrets inherent in a murder like that of Benjamin Arden, but he was distracted from this line of thought by the changing view outside his cab window. He became fascinated by how the cabby negotiated the bewildering labyrinth that was London streets. He had the sudden whimsical notion that secrets in a case were a tangle of circuitous streets and dead ends, and that it would take someone with a mind like this driver's to find a way through. Arden's death was certainly not the work of a long-dead ghost. But was it the work of a long-dead secret?

ACROSS WATER AND continent, Ames was wondering much the same thing. The blackmailer knew something so powerful about Arden that his victim was prepared to give him everything. What was it? He turned a piece of foolscap on its side and wrote names in a line along the long edge. Under each name he listed what he knew, in the hopes that something he hadn't given enough thought to would suddenly leap out as significant.

He had just finished the first part of his list—blackmailer, Bentley, Mrs. Bentley—when Terrell came in. "Nothing yet from the Mounties," he said.

"I can't believe French would keep five hundred dollars in his safe," Ames said, leaning back in his chair. "Too bad he doesn't believe in banks."

"Yes, sir. Well, I mean, he probably believes in them, since there's one just up the block as evidence, but he doesn't trust them."

"So, MacDonald," Ames said, smiling at Terrell's customary precision. "A blackmailer, a murderer, and a thief."

"I think I'll telephone Betsy Denton to ask a couple of questions. I don't think she's deliberately withholding information or lying, but she might have important information about this without knowing."

Ames leaped up. "Good. I can finish this list later. I'll go along to the rooming house and see what I can learn. There's a nice strong thread developing here connecting Arden to Bill MacDonald through Francine, who was murdered thirty years ago in England. In fact"—he took up his pencil and drew a triangle on the paper, putting each name at a corner, and held it up—"a triangle, I'd say," he said with satisfaction.

"You're convinced MacDonald is our killer."

"Why not? It's just a question of finding the motive. If Arden knocked up his sister and she died, that may be enough."

"After all this time? What about the blackmailing?"

Ames shrugged. "We can fit it into this triangle. We just have to know where. Or maybe it's a separate thing altogether. I mean, we're assuming from the doctored invitations that it must be MacDonald, but, at a stretch, it could be someone else. Mrs. Bentley, say. She blackmails him for everything he's worth by saying she'll spill the beans to his wife and uses the money to get away from her horrible husband, and Arden."

Terrell nodded thoughtfully.

Watching Ames, still in a buoyant mood, bid a cheerful farewell to O'Brien after securing the address of MacDonald's rooming house, Terrell turned to his telephone and asked the exchange for Mrs. Denton's residence. The receiver was snatched up at the other end on the first ring.

"Yes? Denton residence, Mrs. Grimes speaking."

"This is Constable Terrell of the Nelson Police. May I speak briefly to Mrs. Denton?"

"She's not well. I wouldn't like to trouble her."

Terrell wouldn't like to either but needs must. "Listen, could I come out and see her for only a few moments? Perhaps I can pick something up for you?" He imagined that if she'd been caring for her patient during a relapse, she wouldn't have had time to shop.

There was a long hesitation and then she said, "We have run out of a few things. I just haven't had time. I usually order what I need and it's delivered. Would you mind? If I order now, we wouldn't get anything until tomorrow, and I'm out of milk and eggs. Could you find some sort of cookie? She does like a little bit of sweet with her tea. But you can't stay long," she warned. "All these visits are wearing her right out."

"I won't, ma'am. I'll be out there in under an hour."

TERRELL HAD REASONED that a woman who liked a bit of sweet with her tea might think it a treat to have a chocolate bourbon, so he had bought a packet of these and a bottle of milk, along with a dozen eggs, and he now presented them to Mrs. Grimes.

He was shown into the same room where they had met with Mrs. Denton on the previous visit, and she did look a little paler. Watching her sitting in the slant of light through the window, he conceived the idea that she was like a flower that had been placed in the sun, its petals fading until it was no more.

"Hello, Mrs. Denton. I bought you some chocolate cookies." He smiled. "Of course, I'm hoping I'll be offered one myself."

She gave him a tired smile. "You're so kind. I shall insist you eat at least two. Please, sit down. It's this business again, isn't it?"

"It is." Terrell slid into the chair opposite her. "You mentioned Francine's brother. I think you said he had visited her behind the lines where you worked."

"Bill, yes. In France."

"And you knew he was back. You mentioned telling him about the newspaper article."

"Yes. I'm not sure how I heard he was there, but last fall, early, at the beginning of September I think it was, because we could still sit in the garden, I invited him to come and see me. I was so surprised he had turned up here after all this time. Almost thirty years. I was anxious to learn if he'd ever found Franny. I never stopped thinking of her. When I came home after the war and she still hadn't come home, it became a bit of an obsession. I spent the first ten years after I returned writing to various Bluebirds and even a few English nursing sisters we worked alongside, but no one had any idea about her whereabouts."

She looked up and smiled as the tray of tea and bourbons was placed beside her. She poured tea for him and then offered the plate of cookies. "Help yourself, Constable Terrell. Have as many as you like. I won't get through all those."

But he took only one. "I was under the impression you didn't think much of Bill MacDonald."

"I didn't. He was always a bit of a bully, especially toward Franny, and of course instead of cowing her, he seemed to have the effect of making her more rebellious and outrageous. I think she relished the fact that he seemed powerless to stop her. Still. It has been thirty years since I last saw him, that day he visited her at the nursing station. Water under the bridge. I assumed he would have matured as he got older, and I was right, I think. He seemed well-mannered and took his job very seriously. He talked of taking over the printing shop one day, buying it when he had enough saved up."

"You talked about Francine, and he hadn't found her."

She sighed heavily. "Poor girl. I shall always think of her like that, her uniform still on, making the best of things as we all abandoned her." Mrs. Denton turned away and said to the window, "I couldn't bear to stay even long enough for a cup of tea. I mean, she was pregnant, for God's sake! I don't think I shall ever really forgive myself for leaving that day."

"You weren't to know what would happen, Mrs. Denton," Terrell said gently. He waited a beat. "What else did you speak about?"

"I caught him up on people we knew. Who'd died, who'd married, and so forth. Of course, I told him about Ben, with his wife and children. We'd all been friends when we were children. We all went to the same school, Willow Point."

"How did he react to that news?"

She shrugged. "He seemed fine, happy to hear about everyone. He was surprised about Ben because he hadn't realized he'd survived the war. He laughed, saying that considering what a scamp Ben was, it was amazing that he grew up and had a family. He asked me where he lived so he could visit him. I didn't hear from him again after that. I suppose he was trying to settle back in. He'd lost his own wife to some sort of cancer a couple of years before

367

and didn't have children; that's why he decided to leave England and come home."

"He didn't say anything about Ben during the war, maybe?"

"No. Nothing. Just that he was surprised to hear he'd survived."

Terrell nodded, taking notes. He stopped and took a sip of tea. Mrs. Denton looked sad suddenly and took a handkerchief out of the sleeve of her thick sweater and held it in her hands.

"Then I got that letter from one of the girls from Quebec. She told me she'd been sent an article in the *Times* or somewhere, an English paper anyway, about a body that was found somewhere in the south of England. She said, 'Look what's happened to poor Franny.' She told me there was no mistake because her leather satchel had all her papers in it." She shook her head and put the handkerchief to her nose. "I left her there to die."

Terrell wanted to reach out. "No one could have known."

"I kept asking myself, How did whoever it was know where to find us? Were we followed? We never would have suspected such a thing. Mind you, we didn't keep it a secret. All the other sisters knew where we were going. Or was it just some local madman who saw me leave and knew he'd find her alone?"

Shaking his head, Terrell wondered if this weight of guilt was taking a toll on her health. "I know it feels as if you could have done something, Mrs. Denton. You couldn't. As I recall, she was shot. If you'd stayed it's likely you'd both have died."

"I know. Of course, you're right. But she was so full of life. I can't get over the idea that she should have died, and not me." She sighed and shifted on her chair. "I confess, I always wondered if he might have killed her himself because...because of the baby. Some sort of family shame or something. It's a terrible, wicked thing to think that about someone I knew at school."

"Did he say anything else about Ben Arden when you told him he was alive?"

Mrs. Denton pulled her lips into a thin line in an effort to remember, and then shook her head. "I honestly can't remember. He might have wondered if Ben knew, I suppose. You don't think he has anything to do with Ben's death?"

"We're gathering as much information as we can right now, Mrs. Denton. You've been very helpful. Thank you."

She took his offered hand briefly. "I like the new Bill. He seems kinder than he used to be when he was young. I'm sure he couldn't be involved. If he had been, he would have run off, wouldn't he?"

Alas, he might well have run off, Terrell thought.

CHAPTER TWENTY-SIX

"I REALLY THINK WE DON'T HAVE to look much further,"
Ames said. He and Terrell were in Ames's office.
Terrell had related his conversation with Mrs. Denton.
"MacDonald's landlady was mighty displeased to see the
state of his room. He owed a week's rent and left the place
a pigsty. She said she had no idea it was this bad, and that
when he first moved in three years ago, he was quiet and
clean. She used to clean his room once a week, but in the
last year what she called 'the rheumatics' kept her from
doing it, and he agreed to take over for a small reduction
in the rent. It was all I could do to get her out the door so
I could give the place a once-over."

"Did you find anything?"

"I found a place that looked as though it had been
hurriedly abandoned. Also this." He held up a scrap of
paper. "His landlady had kindly provided a wire trash can
that contained mostly beer bottles, but this was wedged in
the bottom. If this was a Sam Spade, it would be a clue.

As it is, it's probably just trash."

Terrell took the paper between his thumb and forefinger. "'At the house.' Hmm. I guess we can put it in the file with all the scraps of paper that seem to be part of this. It's not paper from the print shop, anyway. Pretty ordinary notepaper. The words look hurriedly scribbled." He placed the note in the file, which was sitting open on the desk. "'Drop the order off at the house'? 'Come over for a drink, we'll meet at the house'? It could be anything."

"It could. I'm feeling pretty bullish on MacDonald. For starters, we know he's a bully, or at least we know Mrs. Denton thinks he is, or was. We also know he's been away for thirty years, apparently some of that time looking for his sister, and then he suddenly comes back, settles into the print shop. He meets up with Mrs. Denton, who tells him their old friend Ben is happily settled with wife and family. Within a few weeks, Bill starts to blackmail Ben Arden. He uses the wedding invitations to tell Arden how much money he has to give him. We find Arden dead, and Bill has absconded with all his money, plus the money from his boss's safe."

Terrell nodded thoughtfully. "It looks very possible..."

"I know, I know. You're going to ask what he was blackmailing Arden about."

"His affair with Mrs. Bentley is certainly a possibility," Terrell began.

"Ha! What if the lovely Mrs. Bentley and he were working this together and have gone off together? That takes her disappearance into account."

"I don't know, sir. If I were a woman leaving an un-satisfactory husband like Bentley, would I trade him in

371

for a bully of a man who's been living a slovenly life in a rooming house?"

"A slovenly man with a lot of cash," Ames said, picking up the receiver of the ringing phone. "Yes? I'll be right down. Oh, all right. He'll be right down." He hung up. "O'Brien said there's a mail call for you."

"Excuse me, sir."

Ames waved his hands in a friendly dismissing gesture and put his feet up on his desk, feeling the first shreds of satisfaction the case had so far offered.

"NO PRIZE FOR guessing who this is from," O'Brien said, holding out a cream-coloured envelope.

Terrell took the envelope and, retreating to his desk, sat down with his back to O'Brien and tapped the envelope on the desk a couple of times.

"That letter won't open itself!" O'Brien called out.

It wouldn't. Terrell just wasn't sure he wanted to open it. He felt O'Brien across the room watching him and tried to will him to go back to his crossword. It would be April reporting about the course, perhaps asking him a question about something. With this resolve, he slid his thumb under the flap of the envelope and took out the several pages.

> *Dear Constable Terrell,*
> *I hope you are well and have something inter-*
> *esting to work on. I must admit, as interesting*
> *as it is to be in the city, I do miss Nelson and*
> *the café. I hope Marge is treating you well.*
> *She used to work there, you know, before I*

did. We brought her out of retirement. I don't think she was happy about it.

The course is very interesting, and I'm not the only girl, thank heaven. There are three others. Did you know that the Vancouver police had the first two women officers in Canada? What I see from the women police officers here is that they are mainly used in the jail dealing with women prisoners, or in domestic disputes. And plenty of typing. They aren't allowed to have any guns to train with. In fact, they don't do a thing that would put them in competition with the male officers. I haven't asked, but I bet they get paid a lot less, too. I confess, I'm finding it a little bit discouraging. Especially after everything women did during the war. I bet Miss Winslow would never put up with being told to type and fetch coffee!

Anyway, I committed to it, so I'm going to stick it out. Maybe on a small force like in Nelson a girl would get a little more action!

I'm looking forward to another ride on your motorcycle. I really enjoyed the last one, and Daddy didn't get too anxious because he thinks the world of you.
Yours faithfully,
April McAvity

He nearly jumped out of his seat when he heard O'Brien right behind him. "'Daddy thinks the world of you.' What good is that? I'd like to know! Unless it's code." Did he wink?

"Sergeant!" Terrell exclaimed, folding the letter quickly.

"Keep your shirt on. That's all I saw. Mrs. Arden just called. She wants you two to go out and see her right away. She sounded upset." O'Brien handed the paper he'd written the message on to Terrell, who snatched it out of his hand, glowering. Chuckling happily, O'Brien went back to his desk and heaved his substantial person onto his stool. "Young love," he said contentedly under his breath, opening the *Nelson Daily News*.

"WE'RE NOT GOING on that thing," Ames declared as Terrell gestured toward his Triumph, offering the option. Safely in the car, and at the wheel, Ames asked, "I wonder what Mrs. Arden is upset about? I guess we'll soon know. You got a letter from your gran?"

"No, sir," Terrell said. "I wonder if she found something—maybe another card?"

"So, not from your gran," Ames persisted. "Mother?"

"No, sir," Terrell said. He could feel the flush in his cheeks.

"Not gran, not mother. Hmm. That only leaves April. Your relations send letters to your home. Only April would send it to the station."

Terrell maintained a polite but dogged silence. "She was just letting me know how training is going. She thinks women are being given short shrift. I'm sure that's true," he said finally.

"Listen, don't get me wrong. I think it's swell. You two would make a perfect match. I just worry about what

374

people...well, not so much what they might think, because people think a lot of nonsense, but what will they say, how you'll be treated."

"I believe you are getting ahead of yourself, sir." Terrell sought to change the direction of the conversation. "Times are changing, though. Look at Miss Van Eyck. She does a job anyone would say is a man's job, but people have come to accept her. And I bet she doesn't give a damn if they accept her or not. She's very admirable."

Ames glanced at Terrell and smiled. "That she is, and so are you, diverting me off to Miss Van Eyck like that! It's funny, really. I never much thought there was anything wrong with what she does. Unusual, yes, but she has me beat all to hell where a car engine is concerned. She could be quite handy to have around the place."

Terrell wanted to ask him if he planned to ask Miss Van Eyck to marry him, but knew it was much too personal a question to ask his superior officer.

"But seriously, I can tell April is quite mad about you. You'll have to cross that bridge one of these days, how people will react to it and all that sort of thing."

"You know, sir, I came out here to get away from all that sort of nonsense. Where I come from, there are actually laws about where a Black person can sit. Our schools are segregated. It was lucky for me the Canadian Armed Forces don't practise the same sort of thing, though my father wasn't so lucky in the Great War. About a year and a half ago, this woman called Viola Desmond went to the pictures and decided she wasn't going to sit up in the balcony where she was supposed to. She sat down in the front and brought the place to a standstill. Of course, she got tossed out and had to go to court over some silly tax thing. Here I can buy a ticket at the Civic Theatre and sit anywhere I want. There may be a rule I don't know, but they don't enforce it. Maybe because I'm the only one, or maybe because the owner is a decent man. I really admire Mrs. Desmond. Maybe one day people like her will make a difference."

Ames whistled. "Do you ever think the female of the species is a lot braver in some ways than the male? In fact, isn't that even a saying of some sort? 'The female of the species is more something something than the male'? I'm pretty sure Tina is braver than me."

"I believe the word you're looking for is *deadly*. From what I've seen, though, that's not actually true. The male can be pretty deadly, especially where the female is concerned. But if they were more deadly, it would be because they have a lot more to put up with."

"You're right there. That poor dead nurse in England being bullied by her brother and maybe her husband, and Ben Arden for all we know. And that angry man Philippa Bentley is married to. It seems sometimes like it's always women who have to be the responsible ones, put up with all sorts to make sure the kids are all right. My mother did. She used to say my father 'wasn't well,' but I knew he drank a lot of the time because he never recovered from the war. It was a bit of a relief when he died, honestly. I felt very sorry for her. I could see how hard she had to work to make things right."

As they pulled up next to the driveway that led down to the Ardens' lakeside house, Terrell was thoughtful.

He and Ames had something in common. Not about their fathers—Terrell's had been a very responsible, sober man. A strong member of the Sleeping Car Porters Union, for which he'd fought. Religious. But he'd died young of a heart attack. Both he and Ames had been surrounded and cared for by strong women. Perhaps that was what made them so sensitive to the plight of women.

Mrs. Arden pulled open the door as if she'd been waiting behind it and held an envelope toward them. "This came." She wiped her hands on a dishtowel and had an apron on. She held the towel up to her mouth. "I'm frightened."

Ames opened the envelope and pulled out a single sheet of folded paper. *I wouldn't stay in that house if I were you. You could be next.* He passed it to Terrell and looked again at the envelope. "Where did you find this?"

"It was dropped through the slot in the door. What does it mean? Am I...are the children in danger?"

Ames shook his head. He'd love to say no, that everything would be all right. But he had no way of knowing. This letter came right out of left field.

Terrell spoke suddenly. "This looks like the handwriting on the envelopes the wedding invitations came in."

Ames took the envelope and looked at it again. Terrell was right. If MacDonald had sent those invitations...but why would he be threatening his victim's wife? There was no demand for money.

Mrs. Arden had hurried to the desk and she pulled out an envelope. "Sorry, I found this when I was cleaning up." It was indeed another invitation. Ames didn't bother looking inside. He knew what he'd find.

He compared the two lots of handwriting. They certainly appeared to be the same. What could they tell her about the man they suspected? They didn't even know where he was. Close enough to have snuck into his boss's shop and stolen his money. He could have dropped this off in the night on his way off with the stolen money.

"I understand your concern, Mrs. Arden. I don't know if it represents any real threat, but you could bring the children and come into town for a few nights. Or stay with your mother-in-law?"

"When hell freezes over. Why can't you find this guy? Am I to be threatened in my own house? I'm not going into town with the children. They need their own beds, their own things. Who is this man, anyway? You have a suspect, I know you do." She sat down abruptly on the sofa and looked out toward the lake as if she were deciding something. "I'm not leaving. It's ridiculous."

The two policemen stood, undecided. Terrell finally spoke again. "Let me go through the house, make sure everything is secure. When you pick the children up from school, only use the front door, and make sure it's locked at night."

"Oh, would you, Constable? That would make me feel better."

Ames nodded at Terrell, who said, "Do you have a basement door, any other side doors?"

"Yes. Downstairs, over there in the kitchen. It opens out to the beach down below. And there's a door at the side down there into the laundry room."

When Terrell had disappeared into the kitchen and they could hear him going down the stairs, Ames turned to her.

"No Ben Junior today? He feels all right about going to school again?"

"Yes. He finally felt safe enough, I guess, to go. Poor kids. They just can't understand why their father is gone. At least the older one knows about death, but Ben keeps expecting he'll come back, keeps asking me when Daddy is coming home. Audra knows that her father is dead, but she's being strong and kind for little Ben. It's remarkable: you'd think children have to be protected and can't handle terrible news, but my daughter has been a support even to me. I don't know what I'd have done without her." She looked down at her hands. "Of course, I wouldn't want to tell them about this."

"The note," Ames said.

"Yes. It's terrifying and so unfair to them."

Ames nodded, and then took the card out of the envelope he was still holding. "Wedding day is for October of last year. Is this the first one that was sent? It has '150' at the bottom." This matches what the bank manager said, he thought—that amounts of $150, $200, and $500 were being drawn out of the account. Did the blackmailer start out with demands for $150 and then increase it gradually? Had she reached the conclusion that he was being blackmailed? "You think he was being blackmailed?" he asked.

She nodded. "I don't know what else it could be. This reminded me of something that Ben said last fall: he told me he'd run into an old friend from when he was a boy who he didn't even know was still alive. When I asked him who it was, he just brushed it off. But that's when he began to act strangely, now that I think of it."

"Strange in what way?" Ames took his notebook out.

"Well, hiding things like this." She held up the invitation. "Going out more. Jumpy when the telephone rang. I felt like he was keeping secrets."

Ames nodded. "Did you ever find out who the friend was?"

"Not from him, that's for sure. I finally got up the gumption to go visit his mother up the hill on some pretext. It wasn't easy. I don't like her, and she sure doesn't like me. I asked her if Ben had a friend who might have come back after a long time, and she told me his best friend had been Billy MacDonald, but he'd never come back. You could see she was pleased as punch that he told her something he hadn't told me, the old bat! She didn't know this Billy had come back, though."

"So, this new invitation suggests something to you?"

"Well, Bill MacDonald works at the print shop, but I didn't think a thing about it till I found this. I think Bill was sending them. Why would he send invitations to Ben for weddings of people we didn't even know? I think there was some code or something. Here I was thinking Ben was having an affair with that woman again, but now I'm wondering, if they are old pals, maybe he knew something he could hold over Ben's head. Maybe he's the one who got all our money. Or is it something else? Why would he send a frightening note like this?"

Ames was about to speak when she whispered, "Oh my God, maybe he's the one that killed Ben!" She gulped and put her hand to her mouth as if she was going to cry but pulled herself together. "And now he's after me!" She turned to him, her face contorted. "Have you even thought of him? You find him—you find my husband's killer!"

"I'm not sure we can jump to that just now, Mrs. Arden, but if he was the one blackmailing your husband, we'll get to the bottom of it." He added cautiously, and, he realized, in complete opposition to his own theory, "It would be unusual for a blackmailer to murder his victim if there was still something to be got."

"But there was nothing to be got! He'd bled us dry! Five thousand dollars of mine he got! You mark my words: he decided he couldn't leave Ben alive in case he revealed who'd been blackmailing him. I wish Ben had gone to the police. He'd still be alive." She looked around her living room. "He must think there's more to get! That's what this means. He wants me out of here so he can come here." She wheeled around to Ames again. "What if Ben had something of his? Something he wants back? I wouldn't put it past Ben to have something that wasn't his. Not after everything I've learned about him."

Ames nodded. "You may be right." Of course, the blackmailer had something on Ben Arden. Arden couldn't risk going to the authorities without potentially being exposed.

Mrs. Arden stood up and went to the window, looking out to the lake, and then reached into her pocket for her cigarettes. "I've started smoking again. I try not to do it when the children are home." She blew smoke at the pane of glass and then turned the latch to open the window. The smoke drifted out and disappeared in the warm spring air.

Ames watched her, his pencil poised, and wondered why all the windows had been closed on a day like this.

Perhaps she'd begun to shut everything when she found the threatening note.

She finally turned. "I don't know what he had on my husband. I'm guessing it has something to do with the Bentley woman, or some other woman, for all I know. I think when his back was against the wall, and all the money was gone, he would have told me everything. Only that man never gave him the chance."

"WHAT DO YOU think, sir?" Terrell asked on the trip back into town.

"She has the same idea we do: the blackmailer is Bill MacDonald, and he ran his victim dry and then killed him. A third card increases the likelihood that he was using the cards to say how much money he wanted each time. And I must say it's what I call supporting evidence that he's absconded with all his boss's cash, as well. This last card was from October—that's about when the bank records show the withdrawals began. Looks like he started with the $150 and then ramped it up. How much money did Arden have in his savings account?"

"It was around five thousand dollars, according to the bank manager."

"So, he's been blackmailing Arden since October, say, because he learns he's alive in September, so that's about eight months. Maybe he meant it to be a once-a-month demand but decided to increase the amount and the frequency. He could certainly get through the Ardens' savings in that time."

Terrell nodded. "And the threatening note? Honestly, sir, I'm not sure I understand it. It's out of character, maybe.

I mean, we haven't met MacDonald yet, but it doesn't fit in somehow."

Ames glanced across. "Why? What do you think? You're not saying much."

"Yes, sir. I'm just anxious not to mix my apples and oranges, as it were. MacDonald is likely a blackmailer, and certainly appears to be a thief. It doesn't absolutely follow that he's also a killer."

"It's good to be cautious, Constable. But as my mother would say, in for a penny, in for a pound. Trust me, I think what we have here is a fruit salad, apples and oranges all together."

"But then, why not take that last two hundred dollars? And why in the middle of nowhere? And why threaten Mrs. Arden like this, when you could take your money and run?"

"Yes, well, you have a point. I'll give Mrs. Arden a call tonight and again tomorrow morning just to make sure things are all right. And I'll alert Tompkins that there could be a call at night."

CHAPTER TWENTY-SEVEN

HOGARTH LOOKED AT THE YOUNG woman sitting on the bench. The Serpentine sparkled in the morning sun. She looks like a young girl wearing grown-up clothes, Hogarth thought. Thin and fair-haired, an air of youthful resentment about her, though she must be at least twenty-six. She was Diana's friend, and it was critical that Diana be found.

"Miss Fairfax," she said, approaching the bench. The girl started to rise, but Hogarth waved her back. "You wanted to see me."

Nodding, Marisa Fairfax glanced around the nearly empty park. A couple was sitting on a bench about thirty feet away, the woman's head resting on the man's shoulder. Marisa stifled a sigh of longing. When had she decided that her job was to look after her father? In return for what? It should have been in return for security and wealth, the prospect of the good match these would have secured for her. Not this. "I want to talk about Daddy," she said. "Miss Winslow, Diana's sister, said I should talk to you."

Hogarth sat beside her watching the wind stirring the lacy lower branches of a weeping willow hanging near the water. Lane Winslow again. Such maddening tenacity! This was not what she was expecting, or hoping for. She wanted to find out about Diana. "How can I help?" The girl, to her surprise, burst into tears and pulled a handkerchief out of a small, elegant red bag.

"I doubt you can. It's too late, you see. I knew all along. I didn't even tell Diana when she and Tremaine were working in Pretoria. Daddy started losing money even before the war. He thought he knew everything, he couldn't go wrong. Men at his club would oil up to him with fail-safe investments, and Daddy fell for them." She looked up suddenly, directly into Hogarth's eyes. Hogarth could see now that worry was already wreaking damage on the delicate face. Lines creased her forehead and the sides of her mouth. "He used to gamble when Mummy was still alive, but somehow it wasn't so bad. After she died... I had no way of knowing. Some of his so-called pals got him into investing in the 'next big thing.' My uncle, in Africa, tried to warn him. He lived there, you see; he knew which investments were bogus and which were good. We stayed with my uncle all through the war, Diana and I, so I didn't know what was happening at home.

"I came home to find the house stripped. He'd had to sell everything, including the jewellery Mummy left me. He wouldn't tell me at first—he lied and said it was in the bank.

"I never told anyone this before. Daddy used to come out to Africa, after they declared war against Germany. I know he did something for you lot. By then, Diana was keeping secrets from me, and Daddy was keeping secrets from me. Then I saw them one day, in the garden, arguing in whispers. He was furious, I could see that, and I was so surprised. I didn't think they knew each other well enough for that sort of argument. Does that make sense?"

Hogarth nodded.

"At first, I wondered if they were having an affair. It was horrifying to think of someone my age, a school friend for God's sake, having a fling with Daddy. But I knew she was completely taken up with Major Tremaine, so I decided it must be something else. Something to do with the work they were doing.

"Then one evening, I came home early from one of these parties we threw to entertain the British officers. I had a pounding headache. I told my uncle, and he got a car to take me home. He told me to let Daddy know, and he'd make sure I was all right.

"I got home, and the lights were on in the study. The door was open. I was trying to decide if I should just take some powders and go to bed or let Daddy know I was home, when I realized someone was in there with him. A Boer. I could hear his accent. I was stopped in my tracks. I was shocked. Why would Daddy know someone like that? We were practically at war with them because they supported Herr Hitler and were making all kinds of trouble. I wanted to go upstairs, but I was worried. The Afrikaner was a big man. I began to wonder if Daddy owed him money or something and he'd come to collect. But I was surprised. They seemed to be getting along perfectly well. I heard my father say something like 'Don't worry. It'll go off without a hitch. Leave the thing to me.'" Miss Fairfax stopped and looked down, as if to take a breath.

"So, you thought there might be something wrong about this?" Hogarth asked quietly.

"That's the thing. I did right away. I knew there was something very wrong with it. Diana never talked about anything she did, but I remember several times right around then when she'd be angry at what she read in the papers about the sabotage by this one group of Afrikaners. They'd blow up railways and bridges. Anything to disrupt the government effort for the war. But of course, it was Daddy, so I couldn't tell anyone what I heard. I suppose I thought someone else would catch him, or he'd see sense. I just put blinders on, and when the war ended, I thought it was over, that none of it would matter."

"And it wasn't? Is that why you're telling me now?"

"I don't know if it was over or wasn't. We're still poor. We'll have to sell Grandmama's flat, I expect. But it was the way he suddenly took against Diana. He told me she wasn't to come around anymore, and I was forbidden to see her. What rubbish! Forbidden things at my age. I don't even know where Diana is, anyway. But he seems desperate, always disappearing and coming back at all hours. Near dawn recently. He shut himself up in his office and wouldn't talk to anyone. When he finally came out, he was all smiles, artificially sunny, if you know what I mean. He said to me, 'Everything is going to be all right.' That's when I knew."

"What do you think you knew?"

"That he'd found a way out of his troubles." Marisa turned to face Hogarth. "I know it's wrong because it's

Daddy, and I should be loyal, I suppose. But I haven't seen him that relieved and happy for years now. I feel as if he's...he's got rid of his problem, and I'm terrified."

Hogarth took a big breath in, watched the couple on the other bench get up and walk along the grass to the path hand in hand. How simple life was for some people. How complicated for this young woman. She put her hand on Marisa's and patted it. "Listen, I can't explain, really, but I want to reassure you that your father has done nothing wrong. I think the best way to put it is that everything you have described to me is part of the work he does for the diplomatic corps. Please, go on as usual, and don't worry. Can you do that?"

Marisa nodded and took a deep breath. "You must know, I suppose. I am relieved. I've been so worried that he's involved in something he shouldn't be. We're in such a mess with the house and the money, I...I just jumped to conclusions."

"It's an easy thing to do. I'm glad you've come to talk to me. Don't worry anymore, and...perhaps don't talk to anyone else."

Marisa gave a grim smile. "There's no one *to* talk to. There's only our housekeeper, and only because she refused to abandon ship when we couldn't pay the servants anymore. Daddy's gone away somewhere again."

Stifling a momentary desire to say, "There's a good girl," Hogarth said, "Thank you, Miss Fairfax." She got up and smoothed her skirt. She made as if to leave and then turned back. "Miss Fairfax, can you tell me where Diana is now?"

Marisa shook her head, her expression bitter. "I've no idea. Abandoned ship like everyone else. Some friend."

Damn, thought Hogarth, making her way toward Belgravia. Damn. Damn. Damn.

"THIS IS FOLLY," Diana said. "You shouldn't get involved." She was smoking again, her arms crossed against her waist, a cardigan hanging on her shoulders. They were in the dark and little-used parlour. Timpson, living alone, spent almost all his time in the kitchen. It was early, but Diana wanted her tea. "I'm going to clear out and leave you in peace."

Timpson looked distressed. "Oh, I don't think you should! I don't know what sort of trouble you're in, but if Miss Lane says you should stay, you ought to stay."

"Of course, that is very kind of you," Diana said, struggling not to sound rebellious and disagreeable. After all, none of it was this man's fault. "But I think I'll be better off finding someplace else. I don't want to bring the authorities down on you."

"At least wait until you hear from her. She's very good, your sister. She'll think of something."

"Of course, you're right," Diana said, smiling suddenly. "Now then, I'm looking forward to that supper. What can I do?"

Timpson found the note and the envelope on the kitchen table the next morning. He picked it up and tapped it on the edge of the table thoughtfully. The War Office. Well, he certainly knew his way there. It'd be like old times.

LANE ARRIVED EARLY at St. Martin-in-the-Fields. It was one of those wonderful London mornings when the air was surprisingly clear after a night of dense and stifling smog, because of the breeze coming up the estuary. A warm sun appeared to be successfully keeping a roll of dark cloud along the southwest at bay. The sun winning the battle made it feel as if the day might be lucky, she thought. Confirming the idea of its being a lucky day, she heard the organ inside strike up. She had about fifteen minutes until Darling was to arrive, so she pushed open the door and sat at the end of the second-to-last pew. The contrast of the ancient dark wood and the light pouring in the windows of this airy space provided a momentary lift to Lane's spirits. The organist played a scale, and then to her absolute delight began Bach's Toccata and Fugue.

She'd almost lost track of time when she felt Darling slide into the seat next to her.

"This is nice," he whispered in her ear over the music.

"I wish we could stay till the end. Perhaps when this is all over we can come back, before we go home."

"What are we doing, then?"

"We're going back to Rudy and Sandra's, we're going to have lunch, and then wave an obvious and fond farewell to them on the street. We'll take a cab to Euston; you will buy us two tickets to Edinburgh, and thence to visit my grandparents. They'll be so happy to see you."

"This fugue offers the best possible cover. I almost thought I heard you say we are going to Scotland. What about your sister?"

"Ah. I'm going to sneak to a phone box a bit later.

I want to make sure she stays put." She turned to look at him. "I had a good think about what you said. Of course, I can't put Diana in danger, but some version of catching Fairfax red-handed *is* what's needed. I suspect when he sees I've gone north and he follows me, we'll find him up there. Perhaps I can get him to threaten me."

"Oh, what a good idea! Maybe one of your best. You rile him up, he attacks you, perhaps kills you, your sister is no better off, and I am a widower. And before whom would this charade be played? You've already said the people at the War Office believe Fairfax and are themselves looking for Diana to bring her to justice. The local bobby in the village? No, my dear. I'm afraid not. I'm putting you on a ship and sending you home. There. I'm putting my foot down on this one."

Lane smiled. "You're quite attractive when you're putting your foot down. Masterful. Commanding. And I do understand your concern. But, of course, I won't be in any danger. Fairfax is hardly going to kill me in front of my grandparents and Fiona. Fiona wouldn't put up with it, for a start. And you'd be there. You're a policeman."

"What you are saying is that you don't have a plan at all." He was relieved that Lane apparently wasn't in earnest.

Lane sighed and said, seriously now, "I think my plan ultimately is to get Diana to someplace safe. I don't like how restless and unhappy she is. She won't stay long at the place I've left her. I'm worried she might bolt and do something foolish. We need more time. There must be a way to clear her. I think the only way is for me to have her tell me everything she can about her work. I might be able to find just one thing that could implicate Fairfax. He's been losing money for a long time, according to Marisa. Maybe he's been betraying his country for a long time. Maybe he did something in Africa that Diana might not have seen the significance of then. If there's anything at all, I'm going to have one more go at Hogarth, ask her to interview Diana. In fact, I'm beginning to think Diana might be on to something; if we can find any hole in Fairfax's version of things, Diana might be safer turning herself in and going to jail than being out somewhere with Fairfax after her."

He settled back in the pew and sighed. "Your plan now is to get her to give herself—" The music stopped suddenly, and Darling, feeling as if he was shouting, finished, "Up?"

The sudden silence reverberated in the vast expanse of the room. Lane nodded and tilted her head toward the door. Outside she looked across Trafalgar and then back at Darling. "Yes. I think it is the best way. Don't move. I'll find a phone and tell her. I know she suggested it, but she won't be happy, I expect. I just can't think of another way to keep her safe from Fairfax."

Darling was not about to stay put. He stood outside the red phone box watching the buildings and St. Martin's Lane. He didn't doubt they were being followed, but it didn't matter. Everyone who passed looked suspect to him. They wouldn't have a listening device on every booth in London, and they didn't know where Diana was. He turned when he heard the handset being put back. Lane was standing with her back to him, looking down. He pulled open the door.

"What's the matter?"

"She's gone. She left a note saying 'Thanks for your kindness. If Lane asks, I've gone to Scotland.' She's walking into a trap! She knows there's a watch on the cottage."

"When did she leave?"

"He doesn't know. Last night sometime, or early before he woke up." Lane tried to keep her breathing calm.

Darling took her gently by the arms. "Okay. Let's think through this logically. There are surely no trains in the middle of the night, so she will have taken an early one." He took her hand. "Come on." They hurried on to Charing Cross Road, and he waved at a passing cab.

"Euston Station, please, as fast as you like."

THE EARLIEST TRAIN had been the 8:20 to Edinburgh. The next was at 1:30.

"Should we tell Rudy and Sandra? They'll wonder where you are," Lane said.

"I think they'll have to just wonder. I've been watching the ticket window. Any one of the people buying tickets just now could be an agent flashing a badge and asking where I bought tickets for. Or I might have got away with it. If Rudy's phone is being monitored, they will know immediately." Darling had purchased their tickets on the principle of his being less immediately recognizable than Lane.

DIANA SAT IN the rocking train looking out the window, seeing nothing. The momentary release she had felt from being free of the stifling protection of Mr. Timpson had waned, and now she had the sensation of being empty. Her decision to go to Scotland had been unconscious, but as she thought it through now, she began to understand it. It was over. Of course her grandparents' house was being watched. She would turn herself in there. She knew she could walk into the War Office and do it, but she felt this aching desperation to be with them again. It would be the last chance to see the people who brought her up, who loved her when she had no mother, who were there when Daddy was away so much. She knew it had been unfair to rush away practically the minute she got there when she came back from Africa, after almost ten years. Now at least she could have a proper goodbye. She was certain Fairfax wouldn't be there. She would be arrested by whoever he put up in Scotland and be taken back to London. Once there, he wouldn't be able to get rid of her so easily. His plan would be based on wanting to get her alone. He wouldn't be expecting this gambit. She would tell the authorities the truth, and if they didn't accept that, so be it. She didn't want to run anymore. That horrific moment of Alex going over the cliff came to her unbidden. She could never win against a man like Fairfax, and without Alex, what would be the point?

THE AFTERNOON HAD turned cloudy, but the warmth of the earlier part of the day lingered. Hogarth stood at the window looking down Horse Guards Road toward the little corner of the Thames she could see. Was she making a mistake? If she was, it would be the costliest of her career. No, of her life. She turned at the knock.

"Greg. What is the state of things?"

Fairfax sank into the chair he was offered and pulled out his cigarette case. He extracted a cigarette, without offering her one, and lit it. "No sign of Diana Winslow still," he said, smoke pouring out of his mouth. "We've got ports and airfields alerted. She won't get away. Now we have our eye on the other one, the sister. We have someone at her hotel and at that friend of her husband's. I expect they will be off to the grandparents' place. If they are, we have people on hand there. I was there, in Scotland, did I tell you? It should be over soon. I'm quite sure they have arranged to meet Diana there. I'll be there to make the arrest."

Hogarth gazed at him, frowning. How certain he seemed. "Are you sure? Lane Winslow did work for us. I can't believe she'd do anything so obvious. I think you should not underestimate her."

He shook his head, smiling indulgently. "And you shouldn't overestimate her. She has no idea she is being watched. It's remarkable we didn't lose the war, introducing all those bloody, I beg your pardon, female agents into the business." He looked up at her, a smile playing on his lips.

"You know, her old handler, who became our director, thought very highly of her work," said Hogarth.

He barked a laugh. "Yes, and look what happened to him. She was his lover at one time, I hear. That's what it always comes down to, doesn't it? It's a new world now, Hogarth, a man's world, a new sort of agent needed for a new sort of war. Women, thank God, can go back to what they do best and stop playing at being grown-ups. You're démodé, Hogarth. You should retire to your garden. When this is over, I intend to go after that top job. You won't catch me being hoodwinked by a pretty girl. They need someone at the helm who knows what the bloody hell he's doing."

Don't they just, thought Hogarth. "You're off in pursuit?"

"Why don't you come with? You can see how it's done. I pull off the arrest of a traitor, I should think my whole future is in the bag."

"And the sister? Lane Winslow?"

"It depends if she gives any trouble. We can kick her out of the country and keep her out, and her husband. Do you know he's a police inspector? The Yard tells me he's here on some cold case from the Great War."

"I don't think I'll come with you, thanks all the same. There are things to attend to here. I've briefed everyone who needs it. Would you like me to prepare an interrogation team?"

Fairfax, surprised, looked at her with raised eyebrows. "No, I would not. What I need from you when I get back is a written report about both of them. Anything you can tell me. Neither of them is even from here. From somewhere in Russia, for God's sake. What was Dunn thinking, recruiting her in the first place? Tremaine too, for that matter. He must have known Diana wasn't English. He paid for that mistake in the end. I'm surprised they let them stay as long as they did. The service is usually pretty good at rooting out people with dodgy backgrounds."

"It's not true that they aren't English. They are to the core. And it isn't really Russia, it's Latvia."

"Same thing. What did Lane Winslow do for us? Some sort of minor work in communications?"

"That's right. Translation, that sort of thing. She's clever with languages. There's really not more I can say. I met her once a year ago, and once again just now, when she came looking for help to find her sister." And outside the British Museum.

Fairfax nodded. "Two of a kind, then. That's what Diana did for us. Our fault it fell through, I suppose. I didn't do the work on the ground. Don't speak German. Left it all up to her. More fool me. Hoodwinked the lot of us. We'll need the report with their background. It will confirm everything."

"Tell me about what she did. Diana, I mean."

Fairfax glanced at his watch and reached over to the glass ashtray on the desk to stub out his cigarette. "My team *in situ* has been alerted. I'm off up in my motor. Suffice it to say, she was going straight to the bastards and telling them everything, then lied to us about where the rebels would be bombing. Turned double agent. Don't know what inducement was offered. Money, I suppose. It's the usual. Or they told her she was pretty. Doesn't take much. Poor bastard Tremaine was drawn right in. Had no idea."

"You didn't think to tell him, when it became evident?"

"Couldn't take the risk. He might have been in on it too. By the time we knew, it was too late. And now she's killed him." He stood up after this self-satisfied recitation of Diana's treason and Tremaine's murder. "Right. I'm off. Sure you won't come? You might like to see the whole lot unmasked."

"Thanks. You go ahead. I suppose we'd better involve the Met, for the murder."

"We'll involve the police when I say so, and not before."
His voice was steely.

When he'd left, Hogarth sat rigid. The combination of vanity and stupidity infuriated her. Fairfax had an unimpeachable reputation in the service. There was his war record, and he'd been an agent, using his cover as a wealthy businessman travelling back and forth to South Africa, pretending to sell his services to the highest bidder, unmasking countless plots by the Boer underground. That's what his assignment was, anyway. That's what he told people. Using, she remembered now, his facility with German. She frowned. Now, why would he lie to her about that? She suspected that Tremaine had been the brains behind the operation, and Diana Winslow. And then she'd turned. Why? Perhaps she'd got sick of his male arrogance too, she thought rebelliously.

She looked at the time, then opened the shallow cupboard built into the wall and took out a small bag, opened it, checked the contents, and then picked up the phone. If she got there early enough, she could do the arresting. "Can you have a car ready in four minutes?"

CHAPTER TWENTY-EIGHT

AMES HUNG UP THE PHONE. Mrs. Arden reported nothing unusual, though she said she thought she heard noises. "I'm not sure I can stay here after all," she said. "I've got to get the kids ready for school." He shook his head. It must be awful to be on your own with two children with this sort of thing going on. His thoughts were interrupted by his phone ringing.

"They got him!" O'Brien shouted. Terrell was out of his desk in a second and standing by O'Brien. "I have good news. Your missing printer has been found."

Ames didn't bother answering but sprinted down the stairs. "Where?"

"I don't know when I've been more popular," O'Brien said, holding up his notebook to his two eager colleagues. "He was caught trying to cross the border at Nelway. They have him locked in the woodshed till the Mounties fetch him. He should be delivered in three hours' time."

Ames pounded his fist into his hand and then winced. His

shoulder still gave him trouble. Undaunted, he said, "Ha! Case closed. Blackmail, murder, robbery, threats. Wrapped up, tied with a bow. This ought to make Mrs. Arden feel safer as well. MacDonald has no intention of following up his threats. He was on his way across the border."

Upstairs, Ames pulled out his notes and showed them to Terrell. "I think he's our man. Opportunity, motive, the works. And just for starters, we certainly have him on robbing the printer and very likely have him on the blackmail."

"I'm interested in how all this started. It would make me feel better if we could build an edifice of things leading up to this," Terrell said.

"'Build an edifice'? Sometimes I forget you went to university, and then you go and say something like that. Well, build away. What have you got?" Ames leaned back, his hands clasped across his middle.

"Thank you, sir. What interests me is that MacDonald comes back from England three years ago, goes to work at the printing shop and leads a quiet, law-abiding life. Then, seemingly out of the blue this last fall, it all starts to come apart. He, let's assume, begins a campaign of blackmail against a childhood friend, if Arden's mother is to be believed. Let's say he didn't know Arden was here until Mrs. Denton told him. It's possible. Nelson is a small town, but Arden didn't live in town. He worked down the hill at the feed store. Or had they met earlier and restarted the friendship, and then did MacDonald lie low, knowing a secret of some sort about Arden, and then pounce when the time seemed right?"

Ames nodded. "They are—were, in Arden's case—both in their fifties. I could see if Arden was going home to his family up the lake right after work, they weren't hanging around at the Legion drinking. And Arden might have been busy with his old flame, so he wouldn't have much time for socializing. I can see how they might have missed each other for the first couple of years," he mused.

Ames leaned forward, took up his pen, and began to write. "So, the blackmailing begins in the fall, and that's when Mrs. Denton said she told MacDonald about Arden being here."

"Another factor is that he learns that his sister's body has been found. But that's only recently, so maybe nothing to do with the blackmail. Mrs. Denton said he was calm when she told him about the newspaper article she'd been sent. 'Resigned' was how she put it."

Nodding, Ames let his pen rest where he'd scribbled "dates correspond." "Does he put those two things together somehow? For example, does he think Arden killed his sister?"

Terrell shook his head. "He may think that, but the dates aren't quite right—and anyway, for blackmail to work, you have to know, you have to have practically seen him do it. He spent twenty-seven years looking for his sister, so he must have believed she was still alive somewhere. If he had seen her murdered, he'd have gone after Arden long ago."

"Granted. So, it might not account for the blackmail, but thinking Arden had killed his sister might be enough for murder. Maybe when they met, Arden said something that made MacDonald think he did it. It might not take more than that. Unfortunately, we'll never know what Arden said. I wonder if I should telephone Mrs. Arden and tell her she might not need to worry. No. Better wait till we've talked to him."

"I know what you mean, sir. It would be good to be able to reassure her."

IT WAS LUNCHTIME when Ames and Terrell had exhausted their various theories and written them down, so they went across to the café, hoping Marge was in a good mood. She wasn't.

"Well?"

"Grilled ham and cheese and a coffee," Ames said meekly.

"For me as well, thank you." Terrell hoped a smile might work, but he hoped in vain.

"I miss April," Ames said, leaning across to Terrell when Marge had gone. "I may start bringing a big metal lunch box from home like O'Brien does rather than face that every day. When is she coming back, anyway?"

"I'm not sure, sir. Sometime in August, I think."

"Oh my God. That's ages! What do we do till then? What do *you* do till then?"

Terrell ignored the implication in Ames's last question. "Lunch boxes, as you say, though I consider it a personal challenge to see if I can get Marge to smile just once."

The sandwiches were brought and plunked down, followed by two cups of coffee.

"Could I have cream and sugar?" Ames asked. "Please." He also tried smiling. Marge only shook her head as if she was very put out and produced both off the table behind them, eliciting a "Hey!" from a man lunching there.

Ames turned and looked over the back of the seat apologetically. "I'll send them right back."

Finally settled, Terrell asked, "How is Miss Van Eyck, sir?"

"At least Al is still slinging the hash. These sandwiches are as good as ever," Ames said, wiping his mouth with his napkin. "She's all right." He hesitated after this. "Say, how long do you think a person ought to date a girl before moving things along?"

"Oh, you are going into territory I have no experience with, sir. Do you want to move things along?"

"I don't know. I've made a mess of most of my relationships. I'm worried she's waiting for me to pop the question, and if I don't do it soon, she'll toss me over. I've had that happen once."

"I must say, sir, she doesn't seem like the kind of woman who would toss someone over that easily. I believe you mentioned she'd broken the whole thing off before you got shot, but she's been very dedicated since then. I mean, she may have broken it off, but it was clear she didn't stop caring about you."

Ames nodded in acknowledgement. "Shall we annoy Marge again for some pie?"

"I think we should." Terrell caught Marge's eye and waved, turning on his winning smile again.

"What?" Certainly no smile.

"What is your pie today?" Ames asked.

"What do you care? It's pie, with fruit in it. Do you want it or not?"

"That sounds delicious. We'll have two of those, oh, and coffee refills if you'd be so kind." Ames produced his jauntiest grin. "She must have got up on the wrong side of bed today. I think we did it. She is definitely more annoyed now."

"Congratulations, sir. Are you worried that she might say no?"

"Who, Marge?" Seeing Terrell's expression, Ames said, "I suppose you mean Tina. I don't know if that's what I'm worried about. For all I know, I'm worried she'll say yes."

"I wouldn't ask until I felt sure about what I wanted," Terrell suggested.

"That's the problem. I do want to. I can't see being without her."

"Maybe she can't see being without you. Why don't you discuss it with her? Find out what you both want."

"That's not very romantic. Don't girls expect the surprise, down-on-the-knee proposal?"

"I'm not entirely sure what girls expect. But Tina is a very practical person. Have you talked to your mother about it?"

Ames looked aghast at him. "To my mother? Not bloody likely! Anyway, I already know what she thinks. She thinks no matter what I do, I'm bound to ruin things. I will say this: she likes Tina. She hasn't liked any other girl I've ever seen."

"In my experience, mothers know. I think if I was in this position I'd talk to mine. Or my grandmother."

"Splendid, has either of them got a telephone? Anyway, I can't see it," Ames objected. "What could a mother possibly know about stuff like this?"

"Your mother knows you, sir, better than anyone."

But the mention of his mother brought up another

consideration. Both he and Tina lived with aging parents. He would have a hard time leaving his mother on her own, though he knew she would probably be fine, but Tina might feel the same about her father. None of it was looking promising. Maybe that was a relief.

AN HOUR INTO their three-hour wait for MacDonald to be delivered, a call came through from Victoria and was shunted up to Ames by O'Brien.

"Sergeant Ames."

"I understood I was to speak to an inspector."

"He's away just now. How can I help?"

"I'm calling from the RCMP. Sergeant Deacon. We've picked up a woman that you were apparently looking for. Someone called Bentley. She's not happy. Says she came out here to stay with her sister and doesn't know anything about the missing Benjamin Arden. Hasn't seen him since last summer. Do you want us to hang on to her? She has a child she has to get back to—a twelve-year-old boy. She says he's with her sister, but her sister's not well."

Ames considered. She was still a potential suspect, even though it seemed less likely to him because she had a child. Still, she could have arranged a meeting, killed Ben, and then gone to her sister. On the other hand, if she arrived there before Arden was killed, she'd be in the clear. "How long has she been with her sister?"

"I'll ask."

Ames heard muffled voices, as if the officer at the other end of the line had put the phone receiver against his chest while he asked the question.

"Says she's been there since May 4. Drove across and then took the ferry onto the island."

That would put her in Victoria the day before Arden's disappearance. If that was true, she'd be in the clear. "Can you get her to provide her ferry receipt? You can let her go back to her sister's, and if she can provide it, she'll be fine."

"Right. I'll give you a ring when I've gotten the receipt."

"Thanks, Sergeant Deacon."

Ames sat back and put his feet on the desk. They had stopped thinking about Mrs. Bentley when the body of Ben Arden had turned up. However, she did fit the bill in one respect, which his current favourite, MacDonald, did not: she wouldn't have known he had money in his pocket if she killed him in a jealous rage. If the child was not Bentley's, something Bentley himself seemed sure about, Arden could be the child's father. That made it less likely she'd killed Arden. Also, she was unlikely to send threatening messages to his wife from Victoria.

There was still the business of the rucksack, so maybe it wasn't true that the killer didn't think he had money. The killer just assumed it was in the rucksack. MacDonald, on the other hand, who more than likely arranged this rendezvous to get the blackmail money, would know Arden had money on him. And he was clearly in the process of amassing money. He fit the missing bag theory. Otherwise, why shoot him and leave money there? And wouldn't he immediately have gone through the rucksack and found no money? The killer/blackmailer would have gone back and searched Arden's pockets. And it's likely they would have found the contents of Arden's bag strewn everywhere.

He didn't like to admit it to himself, but he could see now it put a definite kink in his idea that MacDonald was the killer. If Mrs. Bentley was proved to be in the clear for the time of the murder, and MacDonald seemed less than likely, who did that leave?

With a flourish of wingtip and trouser leg, Ames swung his feet off the desk gracefully and smiled. Who had simmering resentments against Arden? Well, lots of people, but who also had the temperament for it, and wouldn't have known about the money? Who would have taken the rucksack just to see if there was anything worth taking? Bentley himself, of course!

His delight was interrupted by a call from O'Brien. "Sergeant, call from the army with a message for you. He said he went to a lot of trouble and that you owe him one. That medal number you gave them belonged to a Major Richard Renshaw, and is a Distinguished Conduct Medal issued during the Boer War."

DARLING, WHO HADN'T been sleeping all that well since he'd arrived in Britain, was dozing with his head tucked against the serviceable brown British Rail curtain that hung over the carriage window. Lane watched him with a mixture of affection and guilt. Trains always made one ruminate. She ruminated now on the extraordinary stroke of luck that had put Darling into her life, and on whatever fate it was that allowed her to love him so freely. She was not partial to psychology, but she supposed that she would be a very unlikely candidate for being able to love anyone. Trickcyclists always seemed to be saying that childhood held the key to the psychology of the individual, and her childhood had not been an auspicious grounding for adult happiness. Her mother had died when she was four, her father had been a cold and forbidding man, and she had been at war with her sister for as long as she could remember. These factors had intensified her tendency to solitariness. She was someone who kept herself away from any messy feelings. The war had certainly added to her reclusive and introverted ways, what with all the secrecy required—secrecy that had never been particularly hard for her to maintain. She'd had very few close friends from the university, and, as it happened, had a responsible and focused disposition when it came to her work.

Of course, it had all been shattered when she'd allowed herself to fall in love with Angus Dunn, but even then, she had never been tempted to reveal any aspect of her war work. The disastrous and tragic ending to that romance, if anything, pushed her further into herself. And then suddenly, when she had imagined a long, self-contained, and solitary life for herself in King's Cove, there was Darling. So like her in so many ways, and so different in his willingness to trust in love. He had made it possible for her to trust.

But it was guilt that caused her to turn away finally, and watch the countryside, greening now, occasional gleams of sunlight making everything beautiful. She still had to keep secrets. A whole six years of her life, certainly the most intense period of her existence, could never be revealed to him in full. She knew that he knew something of her life. Angus Dunn had made sure of that when he demanded

Darling let her go back to England with him when she'd been arrested two years before. And she herself had already said more than she ought; when she'd been shot on their honeymoon, she'd revealed she was still trying to come to terms with her guilt over a contact having been shot during the course of a mission.

She was very lucky. Darling had known never to ask, though she could see that her secrecy must infuriate him sometimes. And now, here they were. She was dragging him into a dangerous situation, about which she could reveal very little.

She closed her eyes and tried to imagine what they were walking into. Confident that they were being followed, or that watchers were waiting at the other end, she wondered if they could get there in time to prevent anything happening to Diana. If Diana was planning to turn herself in, why would she have gone to Scotland? To see their grandparents one last time before she was arrested? If that happened, she'd have to break the news to Darling that she'd have to stay on and continue the fight to free Diana through legal channels. If Fairfax was lying in wait for her, he wouldn't be alone. It would be difficult to prevent an arrest if that was the case. But more terrifying, Diana said she had seen Fairfax throw Tremaine off Beachy Head. Would Fairfax arrest her but arrange to have her killed on the way back to London to face trial? He could say anything: a car accident, or that she attacked him, or tried to escape.

She had entertained the mad idea that Diana should flee, come to live with her in Canada, but, of course, she would be tracked down there. In any case, Diana, still exhausted and depressed about her lover's death, had put the brakes on any ideas of flight. It worried Lane that her sister had seemed to be giving up. Diana had said to her that the whole thing was ridiculous. She was going to be arrested, and there would not be much doubt about the outcome. It was as if, Lane thought, Diana felt she had nothing to live for.

Darling opened his eyes and reached across to take her hand. "Are you all right? I'm sorry I've been asleep. I could have been trying to be cheery and helpful. You look like you need it."

Lane smiled. "You looked so lovely and so peaceful drooling away on that curtain. It made me think for quite a few miles how lucky I am."

"Then what happened? That expression does not say 'Lucky me!'"

"I've been thinking about Diana. I can't make out how defeatist she is. She never used to be like that. In fact, she was always rather a trial because she always seemed to have everything worked out in her life. Nothing ever daunted her. She was always fearless."

"And you're certain, I'm sorry to ask you this, that she is not guilty of something?"

"Not what they're saying. She told me what happened—she shouldn't have, but I suppose desperate times require desperate measures—and I believe her. I don't think it would be in her to push someone off a cliff, for starters."

"The way you've described her to me, she seems perfectly capable of it."

"Yes, but that's just me being horrible about my sister. Something I should have got over a long time ago. I wouldn't have thought it possible, but she seems to have lost some coping skill that somehow I have, against all probability."

"I suspect your mean father toughened you up. I should make a mental note, should we ever have children."

"You wouldn't be capable!"

"Oh, thank you very much!"

She smiled. "Not the children, you goose, the meanness." She fell serious again. "But it might be in Fairfax; if he arrests her, he could arrange to push her off a cliff as well."

"First, we don't know he's going to be there, and if he is, whether we will prevent him from getting her. Now. You need distraction. You've become fatalistic. We've hours to go. Let's talk about Ames's troubles. For starters, it is remarkable. The man they think did both the blackmail and the murder is the brother of my dead Canadian nurse here. He's on the lam, apparently, with all his boss's money. Naturally you will have an opinion about all this." He looked at her expectantly.

Lane leaned forward, falling in with Darling's plans to distract her. "The dead man was the girl's lover, and her brother is the blackmailer and possible killer. And the girl herself was murdered. That fairly shouts, doesn't it? The killing of the lover is revenge for the killing of the girl. There!"

"There are problems with your theory. What hold did the blackmailer have over Ben Arden? Not that Arden had killed this man's sister. Big brother spent the last thirty years in England looking for her, we are to understand, so he didn't know she was dead, much less who killed her."

Lane nodded and screwed her mouth into a thinking shape. "Yes, I see what you mean. If he'd seen Arden kill his sister, he'd have taken his revenge right away, and wouldn't spend the next thirty years wondering what happened to her. Nevertheless, there can't be all those coincidences and the two deaths not connected *somehow*. Would you like to have a little wager on that? A shilling?"

Darling harrumphed. "What's that in proper money?"

"Let's see...six shillings to the dollar...about fifteen cents. Can you run to that?"

"I forgot what I'm betting on now."

"That the murder of your nurse in 1917 and the murder of her lover, Ben Arden, in 1948 are connected," Lane said.

CHAPTER TWENTY-NINE

A MES SAT WITH HIS HANDS folded, twisting his mouth and looking at Terrell. "That beats everything, doesn't it?" MacDonald had been delivered and was waiting in a cell downstairs.

"It is startling, sir. How on earth would he have come into possession of his CO's medal, especially one from the Boer War? It takes real boldness to swipe your commanding officer's medal and pass it off as yours, but especially if it's from the wrong war."

Ames stood up. "Just one more crazy thing about this case. We'd better get to MacDonald."

MacDonald was surly and sat in the sparsely furnished interview room with his arms crossed, leaning back in the chair. He reminded Ames of a teenager, for all his fifty-odd years. "Who are you to be interrogating me, anyway? I haven't done anything wrong."

"Running off with the contents of your boss's safe is considered wrong in some places. Here, for example."

"You can't prove that."

Terrell sat to one side of Ames, ready to take notes. He wrote something now.

MacDonald turned angrily. "Hey, what are you writing down? I didn't say anything. You're trying to frame me!"

Terrell leaned over and showed MacDonald what he had written. "May 17, 1948, 3:45 PM. Interview with William MacDonald. Present Sergeant D. Ames and Constable J. Terrell."

"Let's stop this rigmarole," Ames said. "According to your boss you were the only person who knew the combination for his safe."

"Doesn't mean I took the money."

"It narrows it down somewhat. And you had that money on you when you were picked up by the RCMP." Ames held up an envelope. "In fact, this envelope contains nearly six thousand dollars. We have some questions about where you got the rest of it. But one thing at a time. You left your job for a holiday on May 8. Told your boss you were going to Alberta. Telephoned your boss, supposedly from Alberta, to say you needed a couple more days, and then you're picked up today right here in BC at the Nelway border crossing. Where have you been this whole time?"

The prisoner tilted back on his chair, lifting the front two legs, and looked recalcitrant. He gave no answer.

"I'm writing down the questions," Terrell said suddenly, causing MacDonald to look at him.

"No? Okay. Let's go at this another way." Ames took out the scrap of paper they'd found in his wastebasket. "We found this in your room, which you left a pigsty, by the way. I don't think your landlady will rent to you ever again. It says, 'At the house.' We have been wondering what it means, you see. We think it might be something like 'Meet me at the house.'"

MacDonald was now watching Ames, his brows beginning to furrow, as if he was surprised by the turn of the questions.

"We believe you were meeting your victim, your pal Ben Arden, at an old log cabin at a deserted cove up the lake, to pick up the money you were blackmailing him for. Now he's been found shot dead, leaving us to assume you received this from him, went to meet him, and killed him."

If Ames wanted this summation to have shock value, it worked. "What?" MacDonald's front chair legs crashed down and he fairly shouted his question. "What? Ben? Shot dead? You're bluffing! Trying to trick me!"

"I'm not bluffing. Not at all. I can show you his body. It's up at the morgue now. I'm happy to take you there. Tell me about it, why don't you?"

"Look, I had nothing to do with that! I had no idea he was dead! Yes, that note was from him. He usually left the money under the bottom stair of the porch. No one lives there. He...he owed me money, so he told me it would be there like usual. I went and he didn't show up. I swear it! I waited. Then I got scared. He was always there. I knew something was wrong. I thought it was a trap. That's when I told my boss I had to leave."

Ames nodded. Terrell wrote. "He owed you money?"

MacDonald returned to looking stubborn. "Yeah. What of it?"

"He seems to have owed you close to five hundred dollars every few weeks since some time in the fall. Why'd he owe you so much money?"

"Look, I know what you're thinking, but I didn't kill him. I don't even know anything about a house on the lake."

"You cleaned him out. There wasn't a cent left in the bank because of your blackmailing scheme. Very clever about the use of the invitations and posters to tell him amounts and times, by the way. You left his wife and kids with nothing. I figure once you knew he'd run out, I guess he told you that, begged you to stop maybe, maybe threatened to go to the authorities—after all, he had nothing left to lose. I figure you got panicky and shot him. And there was that threatening note to his wife."

MacDonald shook his head in confusion. "What note? I never sent any note to anyone! Look, okay, I did get some money from him, but I never shot him!" MacDonald leaned back again, his face grim. "Not that he didn't deserve to die."

"Oh?"

Leaning forward now, his hands clasped in front of him on the table, MacDonald appeared to have given up the battle. He looked like a man who wanted to tell a story.

"We were in the Princess Pats together. Last show. We'd been friends all our lives. I suspected over the years that he'd been fooling around with my sister, though it would be hard to tell if she didn't start that herself. Anyway, then she went over to nurse, and he started it all over again out there, even after she was engaged." He shook his head. "I don't know what hold he had over her. She was smart and stupid at the same time. I told her I'd tell her fiancé if it didn't stop. He'd

416

find out anyway. She was pregnant. I did the sums. It couldn't have been her husband. She was separated from him because we were on a long campaign. Mind you, Renshaw—that's who she married—wasn't any great shakes either. I hated him. He was our CO." He stopped and took a breath.

"You were blackmailing Arden because he got your sister pregnant?"

"My sister died. Someone shot her. Left her for dead. Someone gave me a copy of an English newspaper from a couple of weeks ago. That's how I found out." He slumped back, shaking his head. "I looked for her for thirty years. I wanted to tell her I was sorry. After a few years, I knew none of this fighting was worth it. I just wanted her back, and I wanted to meet my nephew or niece. Our parents and grandparents were dead. There was no one else. The war changed me."

Not entirely for the good, Terrell thought.

"You gave up and came back here three years ago," Ames said.

"Yeah. I was married over there, and when the wife died, I came back. I didn't have any kids."

"What do you think happened to your sister?"

MacDonald leaned on the table and looked down. After a pause he shook his head. "I don't know. I've thought and thought about it. My first thought was that he did it—Ben, I mean. Maybe he wouldn't leave her alone and she threatened to tell her husband. He coulda done it. Or maybe Renshaw did. Maybe he found out about the baby and shot her. He was the type, all right. That would explain what happened after."

"What happened after?" Ames asked. He had hoped to find, somewhere in this story, a solid admission that MacDonald had killed Arden.

"Ben Arden shot Renshaw in the back right in the middle of a scouting party near a place called Commotion Trench. *That's* what happened after. August 26, 1917. I can't remember much detail of that war, but I remember that, all right. It's burned into my brain." He tapped his head violently, his eyes flashing at Ames.

Ames and Terrell both looked up at MacDonald. Terrell leaned forward, frowning, and gave a little involuntary shake of his head.

"Are you saying you actually saw Ben Arden shoot his commanding officer? During battle?" Ames asked. This shocked him to the core.

"That's what I said, didn't I? Shot him dead, leaned over to check. Even felt in his pockets. Then all hell broke loose, and I was one of the few to get out alive. I assumed Ben was dead with all the rest of them, then I find him here, living a normal life like nothing ever happened! He was always a weasel." He leaned back and shook his head. "I blame his mother. She's a real piece of work, too, but this was beyond anything I would have thought him capable of."

"You didn't think to report it to someone when you saw your commanding officer murdered in cold blood?" Ames struggled to believe the story—but then again, there was that medal.

"Can I have some water?"

Terrell looked at his watch, wrote down the time, and stood up. "I'll get it, sir."

Ames also wanted to get out of the interview room, which now felt claustrophobic, if only for a little break. He wanted to think about what MacDonald had been saying, figure out how he should proceed, but he didn't want to have MacDonald clam up. In any case, he couldn't leave him alone. He sat silently while they waited for Terrell. The prisoner seemed to have sunk into himself.

When Terrell came back with a glass of water, MacDonald looked up and thanked him. He took a small sip and put the glass down.

"You ever been in a battle, Sergeant? It's not like anything else. It's dark, noisy, you move like an animal. I don't mean that in an insulting way; I mean you're moving on instinct. I was near the tail end of the party, but I had my eye on Arden because I'd been thinking about him, what I could say or do because of my sister. Then I saw him lift his pistol and shoot Renshaw. It was like some sort of horrible dream. I couldn't believe it. I wanted to shout, to see if anyone else saw what I did, and in the next moment a shell hit almost directly, and most of the party was wiped out. I woke up in sick bay myself. My war was done. You ask why I didn't tell anyone? I was told everyone else was dead, and I had my own troubles. I won't say I forgot what I saw, but it seemed like a dream afterward, if you know what I mean." He sighed and took another drink. "After armistice, I went to where I knew my sister had gone for her leave the year before. I never went back to my unit, so I didn't really know who died and who lived in the shell blast, but when I heard from my grandmother that Franny never made it home, I thought maybe Arden had lived somehow and she'd run off with him. Of course, I didn't find them. Someone in the village remembered a couple of Canadian girls renting the cottage, but that was it. I went to the cottage, but it was abandoned and locked up tight." He put his hands over his eyes. "To think she was lying there the whole time. I never really stopped looking for her after that, even though I got married and settled down myself. When I came back and found out from her friend Betsy that Arden was alive and well, living his life as pretty as you please while my sister was still missing, I wanted him to suffer. I wanted him to know I knew about Renshaw. After all that time, I'd begun to wonder if what I'd seen at Commotion Trench was just a bad dream, but when I told him what I saw, his reaction showed me that it was true. He was terrified. He didn't even try to deny it. He and I both knew that if it ever came to light, he'd be finished. It was easy getting money out of him after that. But before you ask, I didn't want him dead. I never really took to killing, even in the war. But yeah, I did take his money. Hell, I took my boss's money. I figured I'd earned everything I could get my hands on. I was going to go somewhere else, start again, forget about Arden and every other damn thing."

Terrell had been writing steadily, turning pages in his notebook. He stopped now and looked at Ames.

Finally, Ames spoke. "You're saying you did blackmail him, and you did rob Dick French at the print shop, but you did not kill Arden or send Mrs. Arden a threatening note?"

"That's about the size of it."

LATER, IN A booth at the café, Ames and Terrell sat over coffee and a couple of hard-won slices of blueberry pie.

"Maybe she just doesn't like the police," Terrell said. "It shouldn't be that hard to get a piece of pie in an eating establishment."

"I have a feeling she's like that to everyone. I don't see as many people in here as we used to. I don't think she liked coming back to work, and maybe she's hoping she'll get fired. I bet when she was young she was sweet as pie."

Terrell shook his head doubtfully. "I'm not sure about that, sir. Do people change that much?"

Ames thought about the girl he'd dated before Tina. Violet Hardy. He could well imagine her becoming like Marge. "I think they start out the way they end up, only when they're young and pretty you don't notice it so much. What do you think of our friend in the cell?"

"I'm inclined to believe him, I must say. He seemed genuinely surprised about Arden being dead, and about the house across the lake. And I think the medal supports MacDonald's story. He said he saw him lean down to check he was dead—or look in the man's pockets."

"Yes," Ames said. "And he did confess to the rest of it. I suppose, threatened with a murder conviction, he thought he'd better come clean with the other stuff."

"It was a good tactic, sir. I saw what you were doing when you shifted away from the robbery to the murder. It flushed him out, as it were."

"Thank you. But before you say it, we're still looking for our murderer. And now we don't know about the threatening note, if MacDonald didn't send it. I'll wire Darling at Scotland

Yard the latest on his dead nurse, and then I think we'd better interview Bentley. If what MacDonald says is true, we need someone with a motive to murder Arden, and Bentley seems promising. Looks like his wife had been continuing her affair with Arden. He could have lured Arden to the cabin with a note claiming to be from his wife."

Terrell nodded. "Or Bentley could have thought his wife was going to meet up with him, not taking a trip to Victoria like she claimed, and he followed her to catch them together." He sat back and shook his head. "No, that's no good. She's got her child with her. She's not going to go to some abandoned cove to meet Arden. It works better if Bentley sent the note to get Arden to the cove. Arden left with a rucksack of clothing and a roll of money in his pocket, thinking he's going to meet her, but instead all he finds is Bentley, who shoots him."

"Why would Bentley take the rucksack?"

"Good point. And when you think of it, why would he go to all that trouble to shoot him at all? He doesn't have any real proof they're going off together. The whole thing is a set-up, after all, to get Arden alone. Is he just—"

"You two done?" Marge was suddenly upon them, hands on hips, as if there were a lineup at the door and she needed their table.

Ames reached hurriedly into his pocket to put the necessary coins on top of the bill. Terrell beamed at her and slid out of the seat, cap in hand. He put this on and tipped it at her.

"Thanks very much, it really hit the spot," he said. She glared at him and then at Ames, looked at the change in her hand, gave a grudging nod, and slipped the money into her apron pocket.

"Why am I absolutely terrified of that woman?" Ames asked when they were safely out on the street. "It's not like she could physically harm me, but I'd rather face a raging bull holding a revolver than her."

"I know what you mean, sir. Perhaps it's the psychic damage."

"Don't you start! Now then. Fancy a trip up the lake?"

"A TRAIN CHASE lacks some of the urgency of a car chase," Lane said, sighing. "And once we get to Edinburgh we have to hope for a bus to Broughton. They go twice a day, I think. It will take ages because it will stop at every little hamlet. From there, we still have to get out to the cottage, but that at least is only about four miles' walk."

Darling settled further into his corner. "Delightful. A rambling holiday. I'm glad we aren't in a hurry."

"I know. I'm beginning to think it might have been better to try to hire a car. But it's a very long drive from London, with plenty of opportunities to get lost."

"What if your sister isn't there at all? What if she is taking this opportunity to get lost herself and her note was a decoy?"

Lane nodded. "I see your point. It's just, I don't know. It makes a strange kind of sense. Isn't there an instinct to be home when the chips are down?"

"Scotland isn't really her home," Darling pointed out.

"No, but my grandparents are."

LANE, STANDING AT the counter where bus tickets were sold, turned to Darling, a look of frustration on her face. "There's no bus to Broughton till tomorrow morning! We'll have to stay in Edinburgh overnight. This is really bad luck!"

"Should we see if there is someplace to hire a car?"

"Excuse me, did I hear you want to get to Broughton?" A man in a cloth cap and a tweed suit had stopped at the sound of Lane's exclamation. He had a deep voice and soothing brogue.

Lane and Darling both turned to look at him. "I'm off there myself just now. My son is picking me up. We could give you a lift."

"Are you sure?" Lane asked, daring to hope. The fate of her sister was really beginning to frighten her. Of course, she thought ruefully, this offer of help from a perfect stranger ought to frighten her as well. "Perhaps you know my grandparents. They live in a cottage outside the village."

"You're never one of the Andrewses' granddaughters! They are proud of the two of you, I must say! Talk of nothing else! John Dickerson." He reached out a friendly hand. "Come along. He'll be outside, waiting. You've no baggage?"

"No," Darling said, shaking Dickerson's hand. "Frederick Darling; my wife, Lane Winslow. This is really kind of you. We do have to be there sooner rather than later."

"American are you, then?" The man smiled broadly and began to walk with them toward the street.

"Canadian," Darling replied. "My wife, as you can hear, is English."

"Ah, well. We won't hold that against her! Here we are.

My son, Douglas. We're giving these nice folks a lift to Broughton," he explained.

Once they were in the car and tooling through the city to the outskirts, Dickerson leaned over the seat. "Were you stationed in England in the war?"

"That's right," said Darling. "Air Force. I flew a Lancaster. A couple actually; one went down."

"Splendid! Douglas here wants to fly. He was able to sign up just as the whole thing ended, so he never got airborne. Is that how you met your wife?"

"No, she came across to Canada after the war. We met there."

Dickerson turned to Lane. "Very adventurous. Your grandparents are delightful. They come into the village often. Small place. You come to know everyone, and they're interesting to us all because they came out from Russia. Lovely people." He settled back, facing the road again. "We'll have you at the farm in two shakes. I'm delighted to have found you!"

"What do you do in Broughton?" Lane asked.

"I'm a solicitor. I have a little practice that just keeps body and soul together. I did the conveyancing on your grandparents' farm in '45."

"But that's extraordinary!" Lane exclaimed.

"Not so much. I'm the only solicitor in town. The Andrewses attracted lots of attention, simply because they bought the old Simpson farm, and were considered quite exotic, what with coming from so far away. I think we all expected they'd be Russian, and they turned out to be very British indeed." He chuckled. "I expect people were a bit disappointed at first because we've come to see ourselves as a bit exotic by comparison to the usual borderland village. Our doctor hails from Kenya, for example. People were doubtful about him just at first, but he's proved to be a splendid medico."

"Oh, yes, he's my grandfather's doctor. They seem to love him."

"Here we are. A few minutes more!" Dickerson announced from the front seat. Douglas turned the car off the main road and up a dirt road that curved toward the east and they drove past several small, neat farms.

Lane and Darling stood for a moment looking at the cottage as the Dickersons continued down to the village. It looked quiet and peaceful. How Lane longed for it to be just a normal day and a normal visit. The door flew open, and there was Lane's grandmother, coming down the stairs, waving, exclaiming.

"I didn't know you two were coming! It's too wonderful, at last! Diana is here, did you know that? Ganf is over the moon."

In the midst of her grandmother's embrace, Lane asked softly, "Is everything all right?"

"Yes, he's right inside, just waiting for you. Fiona is making our supper." Mrs. Andrews held Lane at arm's length to look at her, and then her gaze encompassed Darling, but only after looking very pointedly left and right. "Inspector, how thrilling to see you again! How lovely that you got a lift right to the door!"

Lane nodded, acknowledging her grandmother's hint that they were not alone. Did that mean Fairfax himself was here somewhere, or just his watchers? "A lovely man called Dickerson was at the station and heard us trying to get a bus to Broughton, so he offered us a lift."

"The solicitor," Mrs. Andrews said, nodding. She led them up the path toward the steps. "Lovely chap. He helped us get settled when we first arrived." Inside the house, she continued her exuberant tone. "Look, love, who has arrived to complete our little party."

Ganf struggled to his feet, and Lane was so intent on his efforts that it took a moment to see that Diana was there as well, standing now, helping him up. She looked a question at her, and then was enveloped in his embrace.

Darling had been divested of his hat and coat by Fiona, who offered to show him where he would be sleeping. "Oh, good. Though I've been sleeping most of the way up here!"

When they had settled, all performing normality as if in a play, Diana said with a slight drawl, "So that's him. He is good-looking. Fancy you landing that." She was back in her seat, beginning to light a cigarette, and then stopped at a look from her grandmother.

"And he doesn't at all mind being spoken of in the third person," Darling said, coming into the room. He approached Diana and held out his hand. "Frederick Darling. How do you do? I've heard so much about you."

"Have you, indeed," Diana said, glancing at Lane. "I bet it was all marvellous, too."

"Diana, why…" Lane looked uneasily at her grandparents.

"Oh, it's all right. You can ask me anything. I've told them everything. I understand there are people watching the house. They will have seen me arrive earlier. I suppose they are waiting to pounce on instructions from their overlord. We've been discussing what I ought to do. I still think turning myself in is the best plan. I've not unpacked my bag, just in case."

Mrs. Andrews shook her head. "This whole thing is appalling. You have to talk sense into her, Laneke! She can't hand herself over to that man. I wouldn't trust him as far as I could throw him. There must be another way."

Lane watched Diana's face. "No, she can't, not if what she says is true. How many people do you think have been watching the place?"

"Two at least," Ganf said. "I've had my eye on them. They seem to be very stupid, thinking we can't see them."

"So," Lane said, "they will have notified Fairfax. He might simply order an arrest, or, more likely, I think he will come here himself. He won't have taken the train. I expect he'll have flown or taken a motor. The question for me is, are his henchmen in on his deceit, or do they believe they will be making an arrest for God and country?"

Diana shook her head impatiently. "Why don't I turn myself in to one of these idiots in the shrubbery before he gets here? I don't believe for a minute they are in on what Fairfax is up to. His survival depends on no one knowing. His survival depends on getting me alone. If I go now, I have a chance of getting back to the authorities alive."

Lane set her mouth in a grim line. She desperately wanted to say, "Then why did you leave London? Why did you come here bringing danger to our grandparents?" She was furious at Diana's carelessness. Typical, bloody Diana, not thinking about anyone but herself! A sound at the hall door made her turn.

Fiona had been leaning on the door jamb, her arms folded, listening in. "This whole thing is ridiculous. Surely among us we can overwhelm one man," she said.

"It won't be one man. It will be at least three, and they'll be armed," Darling said.

"Yes, my dear Inspector. You have experience with this sort of thing. What do you suggest?" Ganf asked.

Darling smiled grimly. "I had no experience with this sort of thing before I met your granddaughter, I assure you. Most of my work has been common or garden criminals or the intoxicated who mostly don't own weapons, and those who do are bad shots. My one experience of coming up against the might of the British Empire found me woefully inadequate." He stopped and looked toward the window, thinking. "I mean, we don't actually know how it is going to unfold. I assume Fairfax will be coming because he's been having me and Lane watched and he's put heavies here. I think Diana is right. We must at all costs avoid her being alone with Fairfax. I can imagine he will insist she be handcuffed and put in his vehicle. We must not allow this. And no," he said, turning to Lane, "we will not all offer to ride along. If he is planning to kill her, it will be the work of a moment to include us in the fun. Anyway, there is a good chance he will arrest us as well, for harbouring her, and we'll be handcuffed in the back of whatever car those men came in. What we have to do is focus on keeping Diana out of his clutches."

They all turned at the sound of a car stopping in front of the house. Lane darted to the window and stood just behind the curtains, looking out. Diana was with her in a moment. "Is that him?" Lane asked. A tall man in an expensive overcoat and charcoal-grey fedora had stepped out of a sleek black Bentley. He pushed his gloved hands into his coat pockets and gazed at the house.

"Expensive car for a man who's broke," Diana observed wearily. "Yup. That's him."

BENTLEY SAT ON his front steps, drinking. A half-empty bottle of scotch stood next to him, and he leaned forward with his elbows on his knees, holding a glass in both hands.

"Not working today?" Ames asked when he got out of the car.

Uttering an expletive, Bentley said, "What do you want?"

"We'd like to ask a few questions about your wife and Ben Arden."

"And I'd like you to go hang yourself. Any chance of that?" He gulped down the last of what he had in the glass and then lifted the bottle toward them.

"No, thank you," Ames said. "Had your wife renewed her relationship with Arden recently, do you know?"

With a mirthless laugh, Bentley poured himself another drink and lifted the glass in a toast. "She could have renewed her relationship with half the valley, and I wouldn't have known, being a working man."

"Where were you on the night of May 5?" Ames decided on a more direct approach.

"I killed him, now? That's the best you can come up with? I had a blazing row with my wife, and she stormed off." He attempted to touch his nose with his index finger and succeeded on the second try. "She left that note, pretending she and Eddy were going off on their own, but I knew they were going off with him. She told me, and I quote, 'At least he's a gentleman, and he has money.' Clever of her to get in that dig about how my wage is just not enough to keep her in the style she thinks she deserves."

"She told you she was leaving to meet Arden? What time of day was this?" He still hadn't heard if she could prove when she'd gone to Victoria.

Bentley hung his head and was silent for a considerable length of time. Terrell, who'd been writing in his little book, shifted his weight to the other foot. At last Bentley shook his head. "You know, I don't know. Not in so many words. Maybe she did, maybe she didn't. She just liked to throw him at me. No, wait. She told me I was an idiot if I thought she'd go off with him. She said he tried to get her to run off and they had a big row about it. Then she got in the car and drove off. Maybe five in the afternoon? That's the last I seen of her." Putting his bottle down, he shaded his eyes and looked up at Ames. "You know what she told me? She never loved me. That's when she told me the boy wasn't mine. But I already knew that." He nodded vigorously and looked out across the garden, moving his hand to pick up the bottle, and then thought better of it. "It's like my whole life has been a joke." He waved a hand at the space where his car might normally be parked. "And now I have to hitchhike into town for my shifts. I'll probably lose my job because I can't always get there on time. Doesn't it beat all? They clean you out when they go. She thought I was poor before. She better not try to get anything outta me in a divorce!" He hiccuped and tried to laugh.

Ames was reminded of Darling's injunction that there was no point in trying to interview a drunk person.

"Are you sure he's not your child? Not just something she said to upset you?"

"Yup. I always blamed her because we couldn't have kids. I see now, it was probably me. I had mumps when I was a kid." He shrugged. "I guess I always knew it was my fault."

"Did you try to follow her?"

"In what? I told you, she took the car. I was too drunk to stop her, if you must know. That's why we had the fight. She said I drink too much. What would you do? I had fellows at work telling me they'd seen them together. This guy never lets me down." He held up the bottle and gave a messy chortle.

"Do you have a boat?"

"What's that supposed to mean?"

"A rowboat, or any kind of boat—do you have one?" Ames insisted.

He frowned. "Just over there. There's a dock at the bottom of the road. The fellows around here hook up to that. What's that got to do with the price of tea in China?"

Perhaps Bentley hadn't known that Arden was killed across the lake. He seemed genuinely puzzled. But just about anything would puzzle a man in his condition. "What's it called?"

"*Philly*. I named it after her, believe it or not. It's no wonder I never catch anything."

Ames turned to Terrell and gave him a nod. Terrell pocketed his book and pencil and went off toward the lake.

"Do you own a firearm?" Ames asked.

"Don't you need your little sidekick to write down my answer?"

"I'll probably remember it," Ames said amicably, "because after you tell me I'm going to ask you to show me around inside, just so I can check."

"I own a .22 rifle. You got a warrant?"

"I don't, but we can sit here and chat while my sidekick goes off to town to get one. Two hours at most?"

Bentley pulled himself off the step with effort. "Don't bother. I got nothin' to hide. Come on in, make yourself at home." He swayed slightly as he climbed back up to the porch and opened his screen door.

ON THE WAY back from this very unsatisfactory interaction, Ames gave the steering wheel a little frustrated pound. "Not much to hang on to there," he said. "If what he says is true, Mrs. Bentley might well have renewed her relationship with Arden. I can see them having a fight over it, and I can see her leaving him and throwing at him that the boy wasn't his. But she took the car, or at least it's not there now, and he seemed genuinely puzzled about the boat. It's either true or he's weaving an incredibly roundabout lie to throw us off."

"Well, '*in vino veritas*,' sir. Maybe he's too drunk to lie to us," Terrell said. "The boat was there, turned over on the beach. The oars were underneath. No sign of an outboard." When Terrell had got back from his visit to the beach, he'd looked into the outbuildings—a shed and a now-disused chicken house—while Ames had been inside patiently asking

433

Bentley to open all his cupboards and drawers. "I wonder if we should stop at Mrs. Arden's on our way back and see if she can go through his papers again. Maybe there's a note from whoever lured him out there."

"It's a good idea."

Mrs. Arden didn't prove to be home, and rather than leave a note, Ames decided he would try to phone her later. He took a quick look in the window by the door and was about to turn away when he stopped. The house appeared to be in some disarray. "Constable, come look at this."

Terrell stood up from where he'd been leaning on the car and joined Ames. "Spring cleaning? Though it looks like more than that. All that stuff in piles. Perhaps she's planning to get it all to a jumble, or is she planning to move?"

Ames shrugged. "I wouldn't blame her. I'd probably want to move after everything. But there's something a little desperate about it."

Back on the road, they resumed their exploration of the possible murderer.

"You know that case of Inspector Darling's?" Terrell asked, changing tack. "It also involves Arden and MacDonald, and their commanding officer, Renshaw, whom Arden apparently shot and stole a medal from. And years later Arden ends up shot himself. Could someone be taking revenge for that? Or maybe whoever killed Arden believes he killed Francine, and it's revenge for that."

"Yes, but that could only be Francine's brother, and while he's no saint, we don't really like him for this," Ames protested.

"So not Bentley, not MacDonald. Mr. X, then."

"Mr. X for the inspector's case too. MacDonald didn't even know Francine had been dead all this time. Arden apparently loved her. So much so that Arden kills Renshaw, who took her from him. Would you shoot a man just for that?"

"With Arden, who knows?" Terrell said. "It doesn't seem sufficient motive to risk killing your own co, though jealousy has been the force behind many a murder."

The traffic coming the other way cleared enough for Ames to pass a tractor that had been holding them up. He pressed the gas and made the car leap forward as if suddenly freed from a trap. In that same moment he had his idea. "The army. It keeps every damn kind of record there is!"

CHAPTER THIRTY

"**Y**OU'VE LED US ON A merry chase," Fairfax said, trying for nonchalance. He'd let himself in and now leaned on the window ledge looking at Diana, who was seated, her legs elegantly crossed, a cigarette at the ready. Ganf was standing, holding the back of the armchair his wife sat in. Darling and Lane were standing behind Diana. "And you have your whole cast assembled, I see."

"Listen here, you can't barge in here throwing your weight around. It's like bloody Russia!" Ganf said.

"Oh, surely not," Fairfax said, smiling. "They burst in on the innocent. I am after the guilty. I am after a traitor, whom you are shielding. I have all the power of the law behind me, I assure you." He turned to Darling. "Now, let's see. You must be that Canadian police officer married to Miss Winslow's sister. You'll back me up, of course—about the law, I mean. Unless you don't have laws out in Canada?"

"What you're doing would require a warrant in Canada. I believe that's true here as well," Darling said neutrally.

"What are you planning to do?"

"Take Miss Winslow into custody. My men are in the hallway, in case you're planning any interference. I should warn you, we are all armed," he patted his pocket. "So, I expect we can carry on with a minimum of fuss and leave these nice old people to get on with their dinner, with you Canadian guests, of course." He bowed at Darling. "The British government has nothing against you. I urge you to keep it that way. Miss Winslow—Diana, I mean—you have something of mine. I'd like it back at once, and then we can be off. I will, of course, leave one of my chaps here to ensure no one gives chase. Rogers!" he called behind him. A man in a dark coat with incongruously ginger hair just visible under his hat appeared at the door. "Did you check on the vehicles?"

"I don't, you know," Diana said suddenly. "Have anything of yours, I mean. Not with me, anyway. It's someplace safe."

Fairfax wheeled and glowered at her but turned his attention back to Rogers.

"Sir. There are no motors here. Just a trap in the barn."

Lane, who'd been wondering what property of Fairfax's Diana had put away safely, looked at the new man with interest. He looked no older than Sergeant Ames. She could see that he was nervous. She wondered now about the other one as well. She had just thought of them as "watchers." Nameless, dark-souled men with hard, shadowed faces under the brims of their hats. But like everyone else, they were human, or at least this one was. How had he got into the business? she wondered.

She spoke up now. "What did you have of his, Diana?"

Diana shrugged. "Just a communication from the Reichsbank. It will be delivered no matter what happens to me."

Lane looked at Fairfax. "I don't see how you'll get away with this, Fairfax. You, in fact, are the traitor, if what Diana says is true. You murdered Major Tremaine yourself, and you were seen to do it. Is it your plan to drive off with Diana and get rid of her? Certainly, if I were in your shoes, that's what I would do."

Darling looked at Lane, frowning. Why was she waving a red cape at this man just now? But then he saw what she had seen: the red-headed watcher turn to look at his boss, for just a moment, his brows pulled together in a split second of indecision. Darling came out from behind the chair and approached Fairfax, talking before Fairfax could respond to Lane's challenge.

"This is all rubbish, of course. I'll ask you to show me your warrant." He drew nearer to Fairfax, holding out his hand.

The young man, unnerved, pulled his gun out of his pocket, but turned at a noise in the hallway behind him. Diana leaped forward with her grandfather's cane and swung it, striking the young man hard on the back of his knees so that he lost his balance and fell over.

Fairfax pulled his pistol out of his pocket and bellowed, "Get back, all of you. I'm quite prepared to shoot." He grabbed Diana by the arm, causing the cane to fly out of her hand, and began to pull her toward the hall, waving his gun at the onlookers.

Rogers was pushing himself back to his feet, looking for the gun he'd lost as he fell. Fairfax gave him an irritated kick that knocked him over again, dragging the protesting Diana across the sitting room toward the door. Lane darted forward. At that moment she caught a glimpse into the hall behind Fairfax.

"You're not taking her without me!" she said in as commanding a voice as she could muster.

"Spencer!" Fairfax shouted at the second man, still in the hall, without looking behind him. There was no response. He turned back to Lane, who now was trying to pry his hand off Diana's arm. "My God, woman, you're as bad as she is. Get the bloody hell out of my way, or I'll kill you both!" He raised his gun hand across his face with a view to a downward strike at Lane. As the pistol came down, she ducked, receiving a glancing blow, and Darling surged forward and struck Fairfax on the chin with his fist, so that Fairfax overbalanced and fell backward. Lane rolled sideways to get out of the way, saw that his revolver was still firmly in his hand, and, righting herself, plunged forward to snatch at it.

Diana, free now, found the cane and raised it toward Fairfax, who was struggling to get up, his progress impeded by his heavy wool coat.

"That won't be necessary," said a commanding female voice. "We'll take over from here."

The effect of that voice momentarily stunned everyone, except Fairfax, who was still grappling with his coat, trying to get to his feet. He finally made it up, only to find himself looking into the barrel of his own gun, now held by Darling. Then he saw Major Hogarth, also armed. "Hogarth! Thank God!" He dusted off his coat and held out his hand for the revolver in Darling's hand. "I'll have that now, Darling. This has gone far enough. Keep this rabble at bay, Hogarth, while I get this bloody woman out of here."

TERRELL SIGHED AND stretched out his legs under his desk. He had the note Mrs. Arden had received and two of the wedding card envelopes spread out on the desk in front of him. If MacDonald said he had nothing to do with the notes, then they shouldn't look so similar. Then he picked up the note and looked more closely at it. He shook his head. It wasn't enough. Upstairs he knocked on Ames's office door. "MacDonald said he never wrote the note to Mrs. Arden, so I've been comparing the handwriting on the threatening note and the wedding envelopes. There is a tiny discrepancy in the way the *e* is written. But the rest looks pretty close. It could have just come about because the note writer was in a hurry, but if MacDonald didn't write the note, then something's wrong, because he confessed to writing the wedding envelopes."

"Someone forging the note to make it look like MacDonald's?" Ames shook his head. He was flicking his pencil repeatedly into the air and catching it. "We're no farther ahead," he said. "It's been thirteen days, the boss will be back, and what have we got?"

Terrell drummed his fingers quietly on the open file on the desk and was about to say something when the phone rang.

Ames, relieved perhaps by the distraction, gave his pencil one last flick that sent it flying past Terrell's head and onto the floor, and grabbed the receiver. "Ames."

"Mrs. Robinson, a little overwrought if I may say so, is on the line for 'the person in charge.' I thought I'd let you take it."

"You're a laugh a minute, O'Brien. Put her through." He waited. "Sergeant Ames here."

Overwrought didn't cover it, he thought, as her voice squawked down the line at him. He looked at Terrell, who was just sitting back down after corralling Ames's rolling pencil, and raised his eyebrows.

"You've got to stop her! She can't do this!"

"We've got to stop who, ma'am?"

This seemed to momentarily stop the flow. Then she spoke again. "Are you in charge, or not?"

"Yes, ma'am. Can you start at the beginning? Who has done what?" Ames said. He took up the rescued pencil, nodded thanks to Terrell, and got ready to write.

"My son's so-called wife. She's moving away, she's taking the kids, and she isn't telling me where she's going, that's who. She's got to be stopped!"

"They are her children. She isn't breaking any laws if she moves. I'm afraid there's not much we can do," Ames said, using his most pacifying tone of voice.

"That's outrageous! I demand to speak to someone else. That inspector with the ridiculous name. This must be against the law."

"I'm afraid the inspector is away and won't be back for another week. But I assure you, what Mrs. Arden is doing is quite within her rights. Now, I can understand why you feel badly about it, because of the children, but there's nothing we can do, I'm afraid. Have you tried talking to her?"

The old woman faltered and then dropped her voice so that Terrell could no longer hear what she was saying. "They're all that's left of my darling boy. If she takes them...I just don't know how I could live."

Terrell took the pencil, turned the writing pad around, and scribbled, "Why is she leaving?"

Ames swivelled the pad back, and said, "Did Mrs. Arden say why she was leaving?"

"She said 'to start a new life.' She said she was sick of this place. But you know she means she is sick of me. She's always hated me." Mrs. Robinson began to cry, which caused Ames to hold the receiver away from his ear.

"All right, all right, Mrs. Robinson. I'll try to find out what's going on. Yes, I promise I'll call you back." Ames hung up the phone and shook his head. "Whew. You never know how long a person in that state is going to keep you on the phone. But it is interesting. Why does Mrs. Arden suddenly want to pick up and leave? Is she that scared?"

"It will completely disrupt the life of the children, leaving everyone they know. Did Mrs. Robinson say where she was going?"

"No. Only that Mrs. Arden wouldn't tell her. And what is she using for money? She's only got the two hundred bucks we gave her back."

Terrell moved his head in a sort of shrug. "Could be she is selling her house, the boats, her husband's things. That could give her a start, anyway."

"I'm surprised she didn't tell us. I'll call her. You'd think she'd want to tell us because she's been waiting for us to find out who killed her hubby." He picked up the telephone and put the call through. Terrell could hear the unanswered ringing.

Ames slammed the receiver down. "I think we should take a little ride and find out what's going on. There's something about it I don't quite like the feel of."

EVEN FROM THE outside, it was possible to see the house was in turmoil. Every door appeared to be open, and there was an accumulation of things on the ground by the stairs that looked, by the way they were tossed willy-nilly, like they were bound for the dump. They could hear a banging noise from inside. Ames knocked and called into the house. "Mrs. Arden? It's Sergeant Ames and Constable Terrell."

Receiving no answer, he started into the hallway. The banging was coming from the sitting room. Mrs. Arden was hurling things into a box. The room was in disarray, with furniture moved, books in stacks, and knick-knacks piled on surfaces and in boxes.

Noticing they were in the room, she wheeled around and clutched the carriage clock she was holding to her heart. "You startled me." She put the clock down and wiped her brow. "Do you have any news? Have you charged that man yet?"

"We're still sorting everything out," Ames said. "We just heard you were leaving and thought we'd come out and see if you were all right."

"That old bat, I suppose. She wants to get her hands on the kids. I'll burn in hell before that happens." She sat down in an armchair that had been moved out of position, but she offered no explanation about why she was leaving.

"Selling up then, are you?"

She looked irritably at him. "It will be good to be away from here. I put on a brave face, but the truth is I'm too frightened to stay now. Now, do you want anything else? Because I've got to get on. There's a van coming this afternoon to take the stuff to the dump."

"You've sold the house already?"

"I don't see that it's any business of yours, but yes. What?" She looked up at Terrell.

"Sorry, ma'am, but I wonder if I could get myself a glass of water?"

"Yes, yes. In the kitchen. I've left a couple of glasses out."

"Thank you." Terrell went into the kitchen and turned on the water tap, and, while it was running, took a quick look around. Here, too, there was a sense of a hurried removal. Food had been partially pulled out of cupboards and then left on the counter, as if she'd been unable to decide if she should take it with her. Crockery was piled into boxes without being wrapped in paper. One box was already taped up and a note about its contents was taped to the top. He breathed a sigh of relief. He wouldn't have to sneak through any drawers. He carefully took the list off the box and put it in his pocket. He returned to the sitting room, where he found Mrs. Arden on her feet now, arms akimbo.

"If there's nothing else?" she said.

"How will we reach you?" Ames asked.

"I'll reach you. I don't want everyone knowing my business. I'm leaving tomorrow morning early."

Ames nodded and thanked her. He saw now, as she walked them toward the front door, that three suitcases and several boxes were stacked inside by the door. "I can help you get those into the car, if you like," he said.

"You can help me by leaving," she said testily.

"You do have a lot to get through, ma'am," Terrell said.

"Aren't you the observant one! Goodbye." It was plain that if she could have closed the door after they left, she would have, but for the piles of things in the way. Boxes of clothes, skis, boots, a few books.

Once in the car, Terrell asked, "What did you think, sir? Did anything about that look like an organized leave-taking to you?"

"Nothing. It looked more like she'd been tipping the house, not packing it up. She'll never get done in time to leave tomorrow," Ames said thoughtfully. "What's she up to?"

"I wonder if we should be worried. Why the hurry?"

Ames nodded. "Blast. Ferry's just left. I'm starving. I was thinking we should risk Marge and get some lunch. Perhaps Mrs. Arden might just be in a hurry to get away from her mother-in-law."

"She's not going to pack up the house by tomorrow. She's taken what she wants, she'll leave the rest, and clear out with the children in the morning. I'm wondering, sir: You said she seemed desperate. What if she did it? Now that we've arrested someone, she's hoping we'll charge him, but she's not taking any chances. She may feel we're getting closer. She wants to get clean away." He pulled a piece of paper out of his pocket. "I might have proof here, sir, that funny way of writing the *e*. I think she wrote that note herself."

"Wow!" Ames looked at the list of crockery Terrell had swiped. "Good work, Constable!" He rested his elbow on the window, a thoughtful hand on his chin. "I must say, she is the one person I wouldn't have suspected."

"I know. What's puzzling is that I'm pretty sure she didn't know her husband was being blackmailed, but I guess she had her reasons."

Ames shook his head, still incredulous. "Now, looking back, she certainly wasn't the grieving widow in the morgue—more like happy to see him dead as a fish on a slab. She couldn't even bother to pretend. In fact, MacDonald blackmailing her husband played right into her hands! She figured we'd think the blackmailer would be the obvious killer. And"—Ames turned to Terrell—"it answers that one nagging question about why whoever killed him didn't take the money in his pocket. What we need is some sort of proof, or she'll be off." He pulled the car over and stopped. "How well did you search the boathouse?" he asked Terrell.

"I was just looking for oars, really. I see what you're saying. You're thinking of the rucksack and the gun."

"I'm thinking she did one thing too many. Without that threatening note, you might never have noticed the handwriting. I think she's been lying to us all along. Just to be sure, we ought to get a search warrant the second we get back."

"Do we have probable cause?"

"We'll have to hope the judge thinks so!" Ames said. "Thank God, the ferry."

"IT WASN'T EASY," Ames said. "To quote the judge, 'The fact that you've run out of likely suspects is hardly sufficient.' He was only persuaded because I told him she was preparing to leave in a hurry. I told him about the handwriting. He snorted and asked if we were handwriting experts now. He warned me we'd better find something concrete."

Terrell nodded. They were on their way back out to the car. "If we do find something, one of us had better go and get the kids if we're going to arrest her. Why don't we go in two cars? I'll see if the sergeant will lend us his." Terrell hurried back into the station. To Ames's relief, Terrell came out a moment later holding up O'Brien's car keys. "See you there, sir."

Ames wished that they weren't doing this on an empty stomach.

MAJOR HOGARTH KEPT her gun trained on Fairfax and shook her head. "You're out of shape, Fairfax. I seem to have arrived a little late. All my work's been done. Just hang on to the gun, Inspector Darling. The Miss Winslows can stand down. Spencer!" This time there was a response. A tall man, much more like the watcher Lane had imagined, came in. "Time for your bit," Hogarth said to him, nodding at Fairfax. Spencer pulled Fairfax's hands behind him and clamped handcuffs onto his wrists.

Fairfax, outraged, struggled momentarily with the cuffs, and then glared at Hogarth. "Absolutely bloody marvellous! You've got it all wrong, as usual. You're protecting a known traitor, aiding and abetting. Your career is finished!"

"Oh, shut up, Fairfax," Hogarth said impatiently. "We don't need any of these dramatic scenes. Spencer, get him out to the car. Rogers, pull yourself together, for God's sake. Get your bloody weapon and go help. Miss Winslow,

447

could you give it to him, please. It's all right, he's with me."

Diana, who'd found the pistol half under the settee, looked at it for a moment and handed it back. "You should find an envelope waiting for you when you get back, Major Hogarth."

IN THE QUIET that descended with the sputtering Fairfax gone, Major Hogarth accepted the glass of brandy offered by Ganf, as indeed did they all.

"You were like the goddess Athena, appearing suddenly like that," Lane said. "I thought you—"

"Frankly, I was certain Diana was guilty. There was no reason not to think so. Fairfax has been working with us a long time. There'd been trouble in South Africa in the campaign Diana was working. Fairfax had scrupulously managed things so that it looked like she'd been betraying us, when it was him all along."

"What made you change your mind?" Diana asked.

Major Hogarth twirled the glass of brandy, the fire catching the facets of the cut crystal. "Your sister, in part. I was quite sure you were guilty, but I was familiar with Miss Lane Winslow's work and trusted her completely. I was quite shaken by how certain she was." Diana glanced at Lane, her eyebrows raised. "And then Fairfax's daughter asked to meet with me. She provided the proof. I cannot, of course, share that with you, but it throws considerable doubt on your guilt. There will be an investigation, and I will want you to come down to London to talk with us. Everything that happened out in Africa will be gone over. That communication from the German bank will help, I expect, and we'll go through Farifax's apartment to find the rest of his papers. Then I think you can carry on with your life." Hogarth smiled, bolted down the last of the brandy, and stood.

"You'll stay for supper, surely!" exclaimed Mrs. Andrews. "And you must stay over. You can't possibly dash off back to London now."

"That's quite all right. I have an aeroplane waiting for me at the Edinburgh aerodrome. Spencer is taking Fairfax there. He and Rogers and I will get him back to London. Diana, can I count on you to come down to town in a couple of days? I imagine you'd like a bit of time to recover from this day's work."

"I'll come down as soon as you like. Getting on with my life sounds very appealing," Diana said. Whatever that turns out to be, she thought.

The sitting room felt still in the aftermath of Hogarth's departure. Diana had stirred the fire, which now crackled soothingly, and the five of them sat silently watching it.

Lane asked, "Where was Fiona the whole time?"

"Making our dinner, I hope. People still have to eat, even during an invasion," Grandmama said.

Fiona herself came through the door with a tray of glasses. "I know you've had brandy, but that was entirely medicinal. I thought some sherry might be in order before dinner," she said. "Or something stronger. I've been working on my cocktail skills. I believe I could make a passable martini. I'm sure Dr. Mwangi wouldn't mind, just this once?"

Ganf and Diana both looked up hopefully at this.

"Not on your life," Grandmama said. "Sherry is splendid. And just this once, mind, because it's a special occasion.

Fiona, what on earth were you up to while all this commotion was going on?"

"Ah," said Fiona. "I saw which way the wind was blowing and popped out to attend to that man's car. If he couldn't drive it, I reckoned he couldn't drive away with Miss Diana." She pointed toward the front window. "My handiwork is out there."

This caused a surge to the window that looked out to where Fairfax's car sat in front of the house, listing slightly.

"You can't see so well from here, but I drove one of my best boning knives into his front right tire."

"WHAT ARE WE going to do with that?" Ganf asked after supper. He was again looking out at Fairfax's car.

"That's all right. I'll change the tire and move it to the patch next to the field where we won't have to look at it." Fiona, having revealed her unsuspected talent for sabotage, was standing with the rest of them. "I'm glad now I didn't give full vent to my feelings and puncture all the tires!"

"It was a brilliant thing to do, Fiona! Fairfax would have had a hard time limping away with Diana in that," Lane said, smiling at her. She felt a warm glow knowing her grandparents were in the care of this resourceful woman. Then she turned and saw Diana. "You look as tired as I feel."

"I've no idea how tired you feel, but you're right enough. I think I'll have an early night, if no one minds."

Lane rose as well, signalling to Darling that she'd like a minute with her sister. "I'll come up with you. I have to get a jumper. It must be all the excitement today. I'm feeling the cold more."

At the door of her bedroom, Diana turned to Lane. The light in the hallway was very dim. Somehow the shadows emphasized the thinness of Diana's face. "I should thank you," she said.

Lane shook her head, touching her sister briefly on the arm. "No need. You've had a beastly time. I just want to make sure you're all right."

"Perfectly fine, thank you." Diana tensed slightly, as if she wanted to pull away.

"Diana, when this is all over, why don't you come out to us for a while? We'd love to have you." Would they? Yes, Lane decided, under these circumstances where her sister was so in want of distraction and a new outlook.

Diana leaned against the wall and crossed her arms, as if to guard against any further outburst of feeling. How alike we are, Lane thought.

"Thank you, but not just now. I scarcely know who I am anymore. Does that sound strange to you?" Diana spoke quietly, looking down.

Lane shook her head. "Not at all. The war has divided us all from ourselves in some way. It takes...well, it took me time, to begin to right myself after everything."

"I want to stay here with Ganf and Grandmama for a bit. Something familiar where I can try to piece myself together. You never told me what you did, but I expect it was something along the same lines. The family business, eh? I was barely eighteen when I started. I can scarcely imagine who I might have become. I can scarcely remember who I was, or what I wanted from life. The war just took me over, so that there was nothing else. I think that when you are in the thick of it, you just think it will go on forever. You don't think about after." She trailed off and looked up, giving Lane a brief, then retracted, smile.

Nothing else but sorrow, Lane thought. And love.

"You've done all right, haven't you? Landed on your feet," Diana continued, pulling herself up, speaking briskly now. She nodded toward the stairs into the sitting room. "He's a bit of all right as well."

Lane wanted to say that she *was* all right, and that it wasn't because of him, that he was the consequence of finding her own feet, but it might come across as lecturing and that was not what she intended. "He is," she said finally, smiling. "I don't deserve him."

"Oh, I doubt that," Diana said. She took a breath and put her hand on the door handle. "Good night, then." And she was gone.

Lane went to her bedroom to find the jumper she'd claimed to need, and instead sat on the bed looking out into the darkness. She thought about what it must be like to be Diana now. The once-confident, overbearing Diana was now floundering, lost, having to retrace her life and pick up familiar threads to find herself again. Lane felt sadness pooling in her chest, and acknowledged that she and her sister might never be close. But right now, at least, they had something they'd never had before. And Lane knew that she, against all odds, was the confident one, the one who felt love, the one who knew, with or without Darling, who she was. Diana would have a whole new war ahead of her.

DR. MWANGI LISTENED to Ganf's heart and then smiled broadly. "He is doing very well. It is good that you have managed to keep him quiet and resting." Diana and her grandmother glanced at each other. Diana raised her eyebrows and tried not to laugh.

"Keep up with the regimen, and I think we may allow you to enjoy the excitement of a little piece of cake soon." Mwangi was pushing things back into his leather bag.

"I'll walk you out," Diana said.

By the car she said, "I was out in Africa for the whole war. I'm sorry I never made it to Kenya. I heard there was quite a colony of British people."

He nodded. "So many that I thought, If there are this many in Kenya, I might as well go to Britain to live. I didn't go home when I finished my studies."

"Don't you feel like a fish out of water here?" Diana asked, her arms crossed.

Shrugging, Mwangi shook his head in a way that suggested "maybe." "I feel very comfortable here. It was the villagers that had to get used to me. I have taken up activities I used to enjoy. I ride, for example. My uncle had a few horses on his farm in the Protectorate. These beautiful animals are the same everywhere, are they not?"

"Do you keep horses here?" Diana asked in astonishment.

"I have one only that is stabled in the home of a local bigwig. I dress in hunting pink and ride to hounds with the best of them."

"I was never off a horse as a child," Diana said, almost wistfully. "I don't know. The war." She shook her head. "I've rather forgotten what I used to do—or be."

"Then we must help you remember, no? I am sure the bigwig would be happy to lend a mount to so experienced a rider. We should go out one afternoon."

"I'd like that," Diana said.

SHE STOOD BY Fairfax's car, her bag in hand, coat over her arm. It was still early, but the weather looked as if it might turn fine. Ganf leaned on his cane, clutching the handle with two hands, looking worried.

"Are you sure you'll be all right? It's a long way to go on your own."

"Perfectly," Diana said briskly. She pulled open the door and stuck her bag and coat on the passenger seat, and then held her map aloft.

"Be sure you stop and rest, and don't drive too fast. Oh, good, here's Fiona with the basket," Grandmama said.

Fiona handed Diana a basket covered in a grey linen cloth.

"Blimey, what's in this? It's only me. I'm not feeding an army."

"Just a couple of sandwiches and a Thermos and a few biscuits," Fiona said. "You should hurry back, Miss Diana. These two will fret until you do." She gave a nod at the old people.

"I promise. The minute this is settled I'll be back," Diana said. "Though not in such handsome transport as this." She kissed Lane on each cheek and then offered her hand to Darling. "She's lucky," she said.

"The other way around, I think. I hope you will come out to visit us in Canada one day."

"Thank you, perhaps I shall. Now I really must be off. There's nothing more maudlin than a lot of goodbyes."

Lane and Darling stood arm in arm at the gate long after the car had gone off down the road, winding toward the village and away to the south.

"Did you mean that," Lane asked, "about her coming out to visit us?"

"I shall by then," Darling said stoutly. He leaned in to kiss her. "I must find a suitable time to put in a call to Ames. I expect Sims is tired of having the remains of Mrs. Renshaw in the Scotland Yard morgue. Perhaps Ames has more to impart, and then we can bury her. Apparently, there's a cemetery in Surrey where Canadians are buried. I'll go to that when it's arranged. And then I'm afraid I must begin to think of going home, in spite of the mayor's kind offer of holiday time."

"I have an idea, if you'll be going back to London soon. We could walk the Seven Sisters. I'm assured it's only thirteen miles or so. A nice woman at the post office said if we left after breakfast we could be in Eastbourne by tea time. After the funeral, perhaps." She looked back at the house. "I think they'll be fine. They have the wonderful Fiona, and Diana will come back and stay for a while. I'm longing to be home."

"Are you sure?"

"Completely and utterly sure," Lane said.

CHAPTER THIRTY-ONE

August 1917

"THANK YOU, SIR," MAJOR RENSHAW said, saluting briskly. "I'll be back in two days."

"See that you are. I can't think what possessed you. You should have sent her home at once." The general was impatient. "Why do you have to go chasing after her, again?"

"She's disappeared, sir." How far could he lie and not have the situation sound absurd? "I'm worried she may have met with a mishap," he added.

To his relief, the general grunted something he didn't hear, turned away, and focused again on his lunch and newspaper. Renshaw saluted again and left, back out into the afternoon, where at least there was a cooling breeze, if not shade.

The night boat crossing was smooth and the air warm. He stood on the deck for most of the trip, leaning on the railing. How had he become entangled? She was charming and pretty. His brother would be pleased to see him settled. He'd send her home as soon as the summer campaign was over. He knew she was needed here, but the rules were on his side: no married women in the nursing corps. Little had he known that he would have to send her home to rid himself of a scandal. The letter she'd sent was burning a hole in his tunic pocket. He still remembered the blinding hot fury he'd felt, the utter outrage at the words "I pray you won't think too ill of me." What he was to do with her when the war was over, he could not begin to think about.

He lit a cigarette and tossed the match into the churning water below. He knew he wasn't popular. It's what he intended, but the gossip, ditties, even, he'd heard about his wife's behaviour were undermining discipline. It was too much. He'd have to put a stop to it.

He borrowed the touring car of a London friend who supplied military equipment, and by afternoon he was on the road to the village in Kent where his wife and her friends had told their commander they were going. He thought about what he would say to her. He saw himself taking her by the arm and dragging her to the car, her friends watching fearfully from the door. She'd be on a ship for Halifax by week's end. She would not dare disobey him. He blew a stream of smoke into the air, uncertainty seizing him. Would she try to defy him? It alarmed him that he didn't know what she'd do. He didn't know her at all, that was the truth of it. He could feel his own anger mounting just at the thought of that uncertainty.

It was almost dark by the time he stopped the car, about a hundred yards away from the oast house he'd been directed to by someone in the village. He wasn't sure why, but he didn't want them to hear the car. He walked along the rutted road and stopped in front of the cottage door. The place felt abandoned, as if the women had changed their minds and gone somewhere more cheerful, but he'd seen the thin wisp of smoke curling out of the chimney. Drawing in a deep breath, he rapped on the door.

He said nothing when she opened it but looked in surprise at the tiny dark interior behind her. She was alone.

"Oh! What...what are you doing here?" She seemed almost too exhausted for surprise.

The man outside, who was coming for her, had hidden himself in the hedgerow at the sight of the car. He was too far away to hear the argument, or to hear her cry when she was struck. But he was not too far away to hear the gunshot, or to see starlings fly out of the trees, screeching their alarm at the blast. He ran then, saw the man come out of the cottage. Even at this distance, even without his uniform, he knew that man.

"HOW ARE THINGS in jolly old England, sir? What time is it there?"

"This isn't a social call, Ames. Do you have any more information on this woman I have here?"

"Yes, sir. As a matter of fact, I do. I'm quite proud of myself, if I do say so."

Darling exhaled impatiently. "Someone has to be, I suppose. What is it?"

"Well, sir, I had an idea about her husband, Renshaw, and it occurred to me that there might be a record of when commanding officers took leave. And I was right!" Ames stopped.

"It's a long-distance call, Sergeant. We don't have all day."

"Yes, sir. Anyway. It turns out that right at about the time the Bluebirds—that's the Canadian nurses, sir—had their leave, Major Renshaw was given two days' leave. Fifteenth August, 1917. The record said something like 'Two-day leave, England, family business.' That suggested to me, sir, that he could be added to a very small list of suspects for her murder. He had cause, as I'm sure he saw it. Mrs. Denton, the nurse Mrs. Renshaw went on leave with, told me that Mrs. Renshaw told her she had written to her husband about the pregnancy because she 'didn't want any lies between them.' She may not have bargained for his response."

"That's as good a theory as any. Well done."

Ames continued. "I suppose we'll never know, really, but our prisoner Bill MacDonald told us that he saw Ben Arden shoot Renshaw during a battle. In fact, it was what he was using to blackmail him. It suggests that Ben Arden himself might have suspected Renshaw of shooting Francine."

"Well," Darling said after a moment, and then he slapped the desk the telephone sat on. "Why, that bastard—he knew! Renshaw's brother. He must have known. That's why he was so keen to have me over here to hurry up the burial of his sister-in-law, trying to avoid a scandal."

"Do you want me to go find out, sir?"

"No. I'll handle him when I get back. Crack on, Sergeant."

"Oh, and sir?"

"Yes?" He tried not to sound impatient.

"You know that medal Arden's mother kept on the mantelpiece? You'll never guess—"

"Long distance, Ames," said Darling in a warning tone.

"Yes, sir. The medal, sir, it belongs to Major Richard Renshaw."

"What?" Darling frowned at the phone. "That one on the mantelpiece? Renshaw's?"

"Yes, sir."

"I will be well and truly damned. It gives credibility to the idea that Arden shot Major Renshaw. Could you collect it from Arden's mother? I'll be able to return the medal to the man's brother when I see him."

"Yes, sir. Give my best to—"

"Yes, yes. Goodbye." Darling hung up the receiver. Lane, he was certain, would be interested in this distracting discovery of Ames's. He would tell her in the morning on the train back to London.

LANE STOOPED DOWN and placed a small bouquet of asters she'd found at Covent Garden in front of the white cross. "Inspector, can you take a picture of us by the grave? Her family, if any, or her friend, might like to know she was laid to rest in this lovely place." She handed him the camera she'd brought from home.

Lane and Darling stood arm in arm by the cross, the rows of white crosses from other military burials behind them, the lost of two wars. "Thank you, Chief Inspector Sims," Lane said, taking back her camera. "Brookwood is truly beautiful. Thank you for suggesting it and making all the arrangements."

"Not at all, madam. We're just happy to have some idea of what might have happened to her. There are hundreds of unsolved murders on the books, so it's good to think of at least one cleared up."

"Or partially, anyway," Darling added. "We'll never really know what happened."

Later, in the restaurant at their comfortable hotel off Leicester Square, Lane twirled her glass of wine thoughtfully. "It was a good idea, this, getting a hotel together. It makes it feel almost like a holiday. Good thing the manager believed we are married in spite of the paperwork."

"I'm full of good ideas. I'm having some now," he said, taking her free hand.

Lane smiled briefly, but said, "I wonder how such a woman would fare today."

Sighing, Darling released her hand and leaned back to drink his own wine. "Yes, go on. I'm sure you have a theory."

"Well, I mean, think about her. It's tempting to say she's ahead of her time, but I'm sure there've been women like her all through history. She's bright, bohemian, free-spirited, takes lovers as she wants, seeks adventure, but at the same time feels she must somehow meet the expectations of her family to settle down and behave. She marries someone they'd approve of and ends up dead for her troubles. That same free-spirited, oats-sowing behaviour in a man would be par for the course, expected even, and he'd live out his life admired by all who knew him."

"I'm very much afraid she'd not fare much differently today. People think it's a question of morality. The expectations for women are different, I suppose."

461

"And I suppose you think that's quite all right, do you?" Lane said crossly.

"No, I do not, as a matter of fact," Darling said, realizing that he meant it. "My experience as a police officer has not endeared me to the idea that women must keep to a different standard. It's not fair, for a start, and even now we live in a society where men feel entitled, obligated even, for the sake of their masculinity, to correct women's behaviour. I expect that's why Major Renshaw might have shot his wife."

"You'll do, you know," Lane said, collecting his hand in her turn. "I think I feel sad for her, and all the unfairness, but lucky for me."

"You are lucky, but no more than me. Should we get an early night?"

"Quite right. We should get a good sleep so we can be ready to head down to the Seven Sisters bright and early."

"I wasn't thinking of sleeping," Darling said.

November 1947

YOU SHOULD KNOW. *He's been around again. He wants to go away with me and set up house with Eddy. I've told him to leave us alone. Don't worry. I wouldn't take anything from you and your children. P.*

Mrs. Arden let the hand holding this note fall into her lap. She could feel her heart banging, a pain radiating out of her chest. The house was so quiet that she could hear the faint ringing in her own ears. The gathering of grey clouds that hung over the lake muted the colour of the water, now leaden, and the forests on the rising mountain opposite were a dull green, so that the afternoon had all its edges rubbed off and languished in a permanent twilight. It would be like this all the way up to Christmas, she thought, unless it snowed and covered everything up.

Philippa meant nothing by it, she told herself. Indeed, she probably meant well. A warning. He's been around. Had she really sent him packing? Who knows what they did? Continued to do. She could feel a dark rage begin somewhere inside her. "He wants to go away with me and set up house with Eddy." Of course. Would she say anything to him? No. She hadn't known at first who she was marrying, though perhaps that first meeting with his mother should have tipped her off, but now it was clear. She'd married charm, self-interest, lies, betrayal, weakness. But she'd also married a good father, against all odds. You had to think hard about upsetting something that worked. She set her lips in a grim line and considered making herself tea. She felt the rage settle in, as if it was planning to stay.

She remembered the initial shock of his affair with Philippa, which had started when she was pregnant with Audra. She'd seen them together. He was working a Saturday because the feed store was busy, she'd driven up the lake to visit a friend in Balfour, and they'd walked along the curved beach. Her friend had suddenly said, "Let's go back. I didn't bring a sweater, and you shouldn't be doing this much walking." She'd pulled Maude Arden by the arm to turn her.

"But we were going to take that path; you said it goes through a patch of forest and loops back to your house." She could still remember how she turned to point toward the little wood with its path and had seen them. Holding hands, kissing where they might not expect to be found. In the shadows of the trees.

She'd pretended to see nothing. And then she'd almost convinced herself it hadn't happened. She had not spoken of it to her friend, either that day or since. But she'd never got over it. It had hit her like a blow to the chest. In her mortification, she hadn't talked to him, confronted him. She'd gone instead, weeping, to see his mother. It seemed like madness now that she had thought that deranged old woman would talk sense into her son, that she would understand and help her.

"How dare you go see Mother?" He'd been red-faced with fury after.

"What's her name?" she'd countered. "I saw you, so no need to deny it. How long has it being going on?" Was this the woman he'd said he never got over?

"Philippa and I have been friends for years. I was visiting her, that's all." He'd softened then, taken her in his arms. "You don't think I'd go off with her when I have you and the little fellow here?" He'd rubbed his hand on her belly.

She'd seen it all in that moment. Philippa, Ben, his mother; they formed an alliance, a triangle, with her on the outside.

She'd finally found out who Philippa was, where she lived, and had gone to see her just before Audra was born. "I want you to leave my husband alone," she'd said, standing on the doorstep of the Bentleys' house. She'd been nearly silenced, shamed even, by Philippa's beauty. "We're going to have a child."

Philippa had been surprised, had asked her in, had

explained that Ben had told her he was unhappy, that his wife turned a cold shoulder to him. She'd confessed that she wasn't too happy herself, and they'd just kind of fallen into it. Even then, Mrs. Arden thought now, even then that woman had not disavowed him, had not promised not to see him, but that afternoon she'd been convinced Philippa meant to drop him. Philippa must have been pregnant too. She tried to imagine this little boy. Was he blond like his mother, or did he look like Ben?

She stood up and folded the note, pushing it into the pocket of her apron, and looked around the little breakfast area in the kitchen. She saw it in a new light. She saw it as hers. She would have to make sure it stayed that way. With the house and her own money in the bank, it wouldn't matter what he did. But of course, Ben would not leave. He would stay. He loved his children too much. She went to where Ben kept his papers in the desk in the sitting room and riffled through until she saw the stationery from a law firm in town. She read quickly through what was in the letter, but it meant nothing to her. She'd not been involved in the purchase of the house, or the banking, or looking after the car. She'd have to learn all that. She searched for anything that looked official—a mortgage paper, car purchase, anything, but found nothing. No matter. She folded the letter and put it back. She'd start with this lawyer.

May 1948

MRS. ARDEN SAT down hard, as if her legs had buckled, when Terrell and Ames came through the door. She had a child's sweater in her hand that she'd been about to pack. She said nothing when Ames held up the warrant and said they would need to search the house. Her head felt hollow, as if there were a wind blowing through it that made it hard to hear what he was saying. She watched Terrell go out the kitchen door and onto the back steps, heard him descending. She could hear Ames opening and closing drawers. The children would be out of school soon. Audra would be walking home holding little Ben's hand. They would expect milk and bread and butter with jam, and she'd wipe their hands when they'd finished and send them off to play.

No, of course, that's not what would happen. She'd get them into the right clothes for travelling so they could leave. She'd better finish packing the car.

She only looked up, only felt the gale in her head subside, when Terrell put his head in the door and called Sergeant Ames.

IT WAS A depressing business, Ames thought. Mrs. Arden had finally shown emotion only at the thought of the children. She'd begun to cry when she thought of them going to their grandmother. Their grandmother would poison them against her, she had said from the back seat. And then she'd fallen silent. Ames and O'Brien had settled her into a cell, asked if she needed anything to eat, and then left her in peace when she said all she wanted to do was sleep. Terrell had driven back in O'Brien's car because it had been too early to pick up the children, and he'd need to make arrangements with Mrs. Robinson.

"MARGE WAS ALMOST civil," Ames said as they waited to cross the street back to the police station. By mutual consent, they'd agreed they should go to the café to have a bite and clear their heads.

"I didn't find that, sir. I think you are giving her too much credit for not throwing your sandwich at you."

"When is April back, again?"

"August, sir."

"God, we have to put up with this for another couple of months. And you'll be pining the whole time."

Terrell shook his head and pushed open the door, saying, "What makes you think she'll go back to the café? She'll have training and will want to use it. Anyway, I'm not pining."

O'Brien looked up and winked at Ames. "He is. Nothing from Mrs. Arden down in the cell. You've had a call, Sarge. A legal firm down by the bank. He's asked you to stop by at your earliest convenience. Name's Paget. You planning to sue someone?"

"Yes. I'll be starting with you. Did he say what it was about?"

"Something to do with the Ardens."

"Hmm," Ames said. "Wanna come along, Constable?"

"No, sir. I think I'd better phone Willow Point School and let them know we'll be collecting the children a little before end of day."

Mrs. Arden hadn't exactly confessed, but she'd allowed herself to be arrested, as if she could see no other option. What would the lawyer have to say? They had the remains of the rucksack. Terrell had thought he'd find it in the boathouse and was disappointed. But then he'd seen the barrel behind the boathouse. Of course. Everyone out in the country burned garbage. There in the bottom were the charred heavy hemp woven straps and bits of the canvas body still unburned. It would be hard for her to argue her way out of it.

Terrell had fished out the remains of the burned rucksack, and he told Ames that he'd been about to leave when he looked back at the boathouse. He knew it was a whim, but he'd gone back in and found the box with the oarlocks. "I saw that there were two different kinds. Some newer brass ones, and some rustier iron ones. I counted them. The brass oarlocks were in pairs, but there was a missing iron one." Terrell had also told him that he'd noticed this time that there was only one bracket for an engine. And there was one engine hanging there. Had she lied about their having two?

Not proof, Ames thought, but something. Maybe the lawyer had found something that would be the final proof. Or perhaps he'd found something that would deepen her justification for having killed her husband—maybe it was just what Terrell had said: jealousy.

"Thank you for coming, Sergeant Ames. I should have contacted you earlier. I don't know why I didn't think of it, especially in light of the poor man's murder. Please, sit down."

The law office fit every imagined idea Ames had of a law office. Dark bookcases full of leather-bound volumes, a thick carpet, a hushed atmosphere, a plump and officious secretary of uncertain years outside the inner office. He sat and, even at his height, felt small in the deep chair opposite the lawyer's desk.

"I was reviewing the dossier this morning and making a few concluding notes. Mrs. Arden came in yesterday to ask about the terms of the will. It was a bit later than is usual because of the circumstances of the man's death, and she had asked me to wait until she felt she could cope. And now I've been contacted by a realtor with regard to the house, and it reminded me of something that occurred early in December. I made notes and I can give you the gist. On December 5, Mrs. Benjamin Arden came in to inquire about the ownership of the home. She wondered, she said, if it were in both their names, as she had contributed toward its purchase. I was very surprised to see her, I can tell you. Her husband, as is usual, conducted all such business. I was able to tell her that it was in her husband's name, but that as his wife, she was, in effect, a partner, as it were, in the ownership of the house, and that if he predeceased her, the house would, of course, revert to herself."

"I see. Did she say why she was concerned about this suddenly?"

"You use the right word, Sergeant. It felt a bit sudden to me. As I said, I'd never laid eyes on her before. She asked me further, if she were to come into the house, as it were, would she be at liberty to do anything she liked with it—sell it, for example? I assured her that the property would be entirely, under the circumstances outlined, at her disposal."

Ames made a few notes. "Did she ask you anything else?"

"Well, yes, as a matter of fact. She asked me about his will, if he had made one. I said he had. Though I could not read her the full contents—he was my client, not she—I said that it contained nothing surprising and that the bulk of the property went to herself and then to the children, should she herself die, with a couple of legacies left elsewhere. She commented about what she termed the 'twilight' existence of a wife, who has legal rights, but not the ones that matter, and then asked me who the legacies were for. I felt put on the spot; I couldn't divulge the details, of course, but I did say they were left to his mother and to an old friend. At which point she said something like 'Have you told her?' I asked if she meant Mr. Arden's mother, and she said, 'No, the friend.' I could answer that in the negative as well. I wished immediately I hadn't answered at all."

"Who was the friend?"

"Oh, yes, I see. Of course, I may divulge that now. It was Mrs. Philippa Bentley."

"But you didn't give that name to her?"

"No, but I wonder if it alarmed her that he should have a female friend to whom he was leaving something in the event of his death. She demanded to know how much, but of course I couldn't give her an exact number. Instead, I said she'd nothing to worry about as she would be coming into over seventy-five percent of his assets."

"And what was he leaving Mrs. Bentley?"

"He left her something on the order of twenty percent of his assets. There is a child involved, you see," the lawyer added with a little clearing of his throat. "He did not say in so many words that the child was his, you understand, but one was led to assume it must have been. I believe that explains the size of the portion he wished to leave Mrs. Bentley." The lawyer clamped his hands together on his desk and looked down. Finally, he said, "I really wish I hadn't said even as much as I did. She left here very angry."

Ames was very little acquainted with the legal profession, never having cause to use its services, but the size of the portion surprised him, even with a child involved. "Twenty percent? Isn't that a little high, considering he had a wife and two children? And I also wonder what he would leave, after all. It was my understanding that the only real money in the family was money she'd brought in from her own inheritance. Surely, he would not be entitled to give away twenty percent of the money that was hers?"

"I'm afraid so. Money that comes into a matrimonial union can become joint property, unless it is specifically protected. He could, I regret to say, have been entitled under our current system to give the whole lot away on his death. As his legal adviser, I strongly advised against such a move, but he was insistent. And there would possibly be some basis for a legal appeal if he had left all his money away from her, should Mrs. Arden wish to pursue it."

"It's moot, I suppose," Ames said, "because there is very little money left. He was being blackmailed and handed the lot over to his blackmailer." He did not tell the lawyer that they had recovered most of the money and that she herself was at that moment in a police station cell.

"It's an appalling state of affairs, Sergeant Ames. Appalling. I feel very sorry for Mrs. Arden. I'm afraid the laws do not always protect women as they ought. She told me about it on this last visit, and while she was upset that there was no money, she was satisfied that neither Mr. Arden's mother nor his other legatee was to receive a dime, and that she retained control of the family home as the one solid asset."

"I THINK," AMES said to Terrell on their drive to the school to collect the children, "that not only did she commit the murder, but she'd been planning it for some time. Jealousy, just like you said."

They were approaching the school, perched just above the road. It had a fenced gravel playground surrounded by slender maples and black birch, with a grassy area on the north side of the school and pine forest on the south. Terrell took a deep breath. "I hope it's not too much of a shock to them. I did call Mrs. Robinson to tell her. I thought she'd be happy, after the fuss she made this morning, but she seemed resentful that she was going to be put upon. I wanted to tell her it was temporary, but there's no guarantee of that, the way things stand."

"None at all," Ames agreed.

WHEN AMES AND Terrell and their prisoner were settled in the interview room, the first thing Ames did was reassure Mrs. Arden that her children were safely with their grandmother. Terrell expected her to protest, to demand she be let go so that she could go to them, but she did neither. She sat completely still, her hands folded in front of her as if her whole being were locked in a battle that immobilized her.

He pushed a glass of water toward her.

Ames waited for her to drink and then said, "Can you tell us what happened, Mrs. Arden?"

She finally looked up, wiped her mouth where water had dribbled down the side of her chin. "You can't know what he was like," she managed.

"THIS WAS ONE of those arrests that gives me no pleasure," Ames said later, when they were leaning against O'Brien's counter, looking out at the street. People were going home, and Baker Street was busy with homeward-bound cars and the streetcar competing for space, and pedestrians piling up at corners, waiting to cross.

"She did kill her husband," O'Brien said complacently. "I find it hard to believe she couldn't have found another way. His paramour had no intention of running away with him."

Ames shrugged regretfully. "I know. But she didn't know that, and then she learned he had a child with Mrs. Bentley. She saw that he'd taken some of his clothing and assumed the worst. She took his revolver out of his desk and followed him, in the second boat. She knew where he was going the minute she saw the direction he was headed. She rowed out to the cove where the cabin is, certain she'd catch him with Philippa Bentley, only he was alone. I don't think he even knew she was behind him when she shot him. Of course, she threw us off in the first place by saying he'd taken the gun.

"She panicked at what she'd done and grabbed his rucksack and ran back down to the beach. She pulled the oars out of the boat she'd come in and tossed them into the boat he'd used with the motor, and then pulled the second boat into the middle of the lake so it would drift off. She threw the gun into the deepest part of the lake and motored home. She must have been horrified to see that boat float practically back to her own dock."

"I wonder why he even went there?" Terrell asked. "And why just then?"

Ames sighed and shook his head. "I expect he knew he was down to his last two hundred dollars and didn't want to meet his blackmailer as usual. He decided to run away. I suppose he thought no one would find him. He could lie low, wait till any search died down, and come up with a plan. I suppose he had ideas of maybe changing his name and just starting all over again somewhere. Mrs. Arden probably would have done away with him anyway, when she found out he'd been doling out all his money to a blackmailer, even if he hadn't run off. He turned out to be a lot worse than even she knew."

"Has anyone told her all the rest? About the stolen medal and the murder of his CO?" Terrell asked.

Ames shook his head. "Paget's with her now. We've filled him in. I imagine it will be part of his defence. He seems a little sweet on her."

"Or, like you, he feels sorry for her. No, I'm sorry. If we let wives off every time they did in their husbands, where would we be?" O'Brien asked. He had very firm views about this sort of thing.

IT WAS A subject Ames discussed later with Tina. She'd invited him to dinner, and they'd left her father cleaning up, at his insistence, while they walked down to the water and sat on the picnic table, enjoying the warm spring evening. "O'Brien is pretty adamant that she is a murderess and should be treated as such. I feel kind of sorry for her. She married someone she thought was sweet and loving, and he turned out to be an absolute cad. Worse, a murderer."

"That's the trouble, isn't it? The way things are, everyone expects women to be looked after by men. If the man is good, they're lucky. If he's bad, they have little recourse," Tina said disgustedly.

"Divorce?" Ames suggested. "She could have divorced him."

"Ha! Have you tried to get a divorce lately? A woman has to have grounds or it's nothing doing."

"He was having an affair," Ames pointed out.

"A lawyer would argue he wasn't. That he'd had the affair before and had reformed since his children were born. Nuh-uh. The judge would look at that charming man, saying how much he loved his children, and either wouldn't grant a divorce—or worse, would grant it and give the children over to him because the lawyer would have argued that she was a harridan who made his life miserable. If she tried to leave, she'd lose her children. The laws do nothing for us."

"Are you saying she had no alternative?" he asked with growing alarm.

She laughed and punched him gently on the arm. "Don't be an idiot! I'm not planning to murder you. And I'll tell you why." She was serious again. "Because I intend to make sure I don't have to."

"And how will you do that?" he asked, risking putting his arm around her. In her current mood, she might not like it.

"I'll make sure that I have resources. This may sound a little mercenary, but I have my job, I have my savings. I'll keep my own bank account. I've handled the banking in this family since I got back from overseas. I know how things work. If any husband of mine tries to pull any stunts, I won't have to kill him; I can just leave him and be perfectly fine." She leaned in and kissed him.

"Charming, I'm sure," Ames said. The truth was, he'd never thought about what marriage might entail in the way of legalities.

"I know it's not very romantic," she said, "but it's practical."

"It would make that husband a bit redundant," he said regretfully, bending over to pick up a rock and toss it into the lake.

"Well, if his only function is to make money to clothe and feed a wife, then yes. But if the idea is that husband and wife could be friends together, and companions, and, you know...then neither one has to be redundant." She shook her head. "I've often wondered about straying men. My mother always had some friend who was having that sort of trouble. I will say my dad wasn't at all inclined, and he and my mother always seemed to have a laugh, even over the ironing. I would say they were real friends. I think it outlasts everything, even death. Dad would never marry again. He once told me that no one would seem right after Mom."

"I never thought of marriage as having anything to do with friendship. I wouldn't have said my parents were friends. I guess they might have been once, but Dad was a bit of a mess after the war." He wondered if he should ask his mother about this.

"The goggle-eyed romantic bit can't last forever, can it?"

"Well, no, I suppose not. But you are making it sound like a business arrangement when all is said and done."

"Just think about how alluring it is to kiss a woman who has her own money." She turned, pulled him close, and kissed him again in a way that made his breath catch.

"YOU MUST BE very proud of them," Lane said, her head resting on Darling's shoulder. They were on a bus, taking the winding road to Seaforth. There was a light rain, but the sky out at sea had a late afternoon luminescence that uplifted the heart. Darling had called Nelson and learned about the outcome of the Arden case.

"They're police officers. They do their job. It is surely the least one can expect. Anyway, I'm not their father. It's not my office to be proud of them."

"I knew it! You are proud of them!"

He kissed her. "You're talking nonsense, but it is rather endearing. What's not so endearing is your insistence on a forced march across the countryside."

"You'll love it. All that fresh air. Anyway," she said, suddenly thoughtful, "I'd like to see where Diana's lover died."

"My God. Fresh air and unhealthy curiosity. I certainly hit the jackpot."

"Quit fussing. We'll have a lovely night in a tiny room in the pub in Seaforth and awake ready to tackle anything. Remember, Eastbourne by tea time. You like tea. It will motivate you."

Lane woke early and went to look out the little window in their upstairs room. It was a magnificent morning. The

477

sun had set the sea to sparkling, and she felt herself almost giddy with anticipation.

"Upsy upsy, darling!" she said, sitting next to her husband and giving him a gentle shake. "Time and tide wait for no man!"

"Do they not? I'd heard that in some circumstances they do." He pulled her toward him and wrapped his arms around her, nuzzling her neck.

She kissed him and pulled herself back upright. "And our breakfast is waiting for us. I asked for it to be ready at eight."

"Breakfast? Why didn't you say so at once?"

BY THE TIME they were on the first rise and looking out to sea, Darling had begun to feel the attraction of fresh air. "Chalk cliffs," he said, looking along in the direction they were going. "Even at night, coming back from raids, they seemed to glow. I never lost the elation I felt that we'd defied death yet again when they came into view on the homeward journey."

"I know." She hesitated.

He cut in. "I'm pretty sure you do know. How old will we be when you finally tell me? In our seventies? We'll be like the Armstrongs with a Westie and our gardening and baking, our house falling into decrepitude around us."

"Never mind that. Let's push on."

When they had reached Beachy Head, sometime past lunch, Lane went as close to the edge as she dared and looked down at the lighthouse. Darling had thrown himself onto the ground at a safe remove from the precipice and was eating the remains of a sandwich.

"Seven Sisters?" he said. "More like eleven! I've never been up and down so much in my life. I feel dizzy. Come away from that edge, you're giving me vertigo."

"You should get more exercise," she called back. "This is a terrible place to die, or maybe I mean it's a lovely place but a terrible way to die."

"I mean it, Lane. Please don't demonstrate by going over yourself." He was sitting up now, looking anxiously at where she stood, peering over the edge of the cliff. "These cliffs are chalk. Chunks just fall off. I'm sure people are always going over—now come back."

Realizing that she was feeling slightly dizzy, Lane went to join Darling, accepting the biscuit he offered her. "Our appetite will be spoiled for tea in Eastbourne," she said.

"My appetite is spoiled with not enough to eat. How long have we been walking?" He looked at his watch. "Four hours. Never mind tea when we get there. I'll want a massive plate of fish and chips."

"Just imagine Diana here, in the dead of night, expecting to see her lover and instead having to watch him being thrown over that appalling cliff. It's no wonder she's a mess. I do hope she's going to be all right."

"Your grandparents will be the best balm possible."

"Yes, of course. But in the end, they can't do anything but cheer her on. She'll have to decide what to do with her life." Lane ran her hand along the short tufts of grass where they sat. "We were brought up to be quite useless. I see that now. We had servants who did all the cooking and cleaning. I don't think my father had the least idea how to instill ambition or encourage our natural inclinations. I think he just assumed we'd be married one day and off his hands. After all Diana's done, I can't imagine her being happy as a secretary or something. She'd go mad with boredom. It's the war, really. It gave us both something useful to do and—though I hate to dignify war at all—it was exciting. Now we're set adrift."

"You're not adrift. You're firmly entrenched in interfering with my work. Maybe she'll find an obliging policeman to marry so she can do the same. Or maybe she'll continue with the agency. Look at Major Hogarth."

"Well, it's not up to me, I suppose. I think I underestimate Diana because I always thought she was silly. That determined, brave, intelligent sister of mine is the furthest thing from silly."

"Perhaps you should tell her what you really think of her."

Lane turned to him smiling. "Oh dear, no. That sort of expression of real sentiment is not done in our family."

He reached out and pushed the windswept hair from her eyes. "That's too bad. I was about to tell you what I really feel about you. I won't bother now."

"No, go ahead. Let's see how I tolerate it. Perhaps I'll learn by your example. It's ridiculous to have come from a family where no true expression of feeling was encouraged."

"You're very lucky in your grandparents. You'd be an absolute gorgon if it weren't for them. They love both of you excessively and are most certainly not afraid to say it."

"You're right, of course. I should tell her. I'm worried she will think me patronizing."

"You are underestimating her again. She has been through a lot. You may have it in your power to help her on her way to recovery."

Lane said nothing but felt acutely the truth of what he said. She wondered at her courage in jumping out of an aeroplane, and her absolute fear of telling Diana what she felt about her. She pointed out at the sea. "It's beautiful, but I'm longing for the lake and our beautiful house."

"I'm longing for a bath and an enormous supper. Shall we get a move on?"

THEY ARRIVED BACK on a Thursday afternoon, much to the delight of Ames, who offered to drive them home since he was going along to Tina's anyway. They had taken the extra week by sailing the Atlantic, and consequently were only moderately exhausted from the train journey home from Montreal. Lane pushed open the front door and stood for a moment in the silence, drinking in the afternoon sun pouring in the sitting room window and down the hallway, motes hanging lazily in the beams.

She remembered her very first glance at the inside of the house two years before. She'd stood right here and knew it to be her own. She turned to Darling. "I might love this house even more than I love you."

"I wouldn't be at all surprised. I'm going out to look at the garden. We can unpack later."

Lane pushed her suitcase into the bedroom, thought about unpacking, and then dismissed it as a foolish way to spoil her homecoming, and went instead to the kitchen. Of course, there was a note from Eleanor with a tin of cake and a fresh loaf of bread. "Welcome home. Here is your mail, and there are a few things in the fridge just to have on hand till you've settled back in. Alexandra has been pining for you, and Kenny has turned into a sergeant major, lording it over those poor children in your garden."

Lane looked in the fridge and found a chicken, ready for the oven, some milk, and a jar each of beans and carrots from Eleanor's root cellar. She was about to fling open the French doors when she noticed a folded piece of paper on her little typewriter table. Curious that she would have left anything out, as she normally shoved all her attempts at poetry into the drawer where they wouldn't be disturbed, she picked it up.

She was surprised to see it was an endearing sketch of a pot of flowers, each one with a disagreeable expression on its face, and a label: WOMANIZER, DESERTER, and so on.

She pushed open the French doors to air the house and went to stand on the porch. Darling was below her in the garden, his hands behind his back, looking at the progress. "Well?" she called out, her face wreathed in smiles.

"I can't tell. There's a row of tiny somethings coming up. I don't think I'm one of life's gardeners. Though I did have fun digging in it before I left. It might be peas. Kenny said they had to go in early. Come down here and give your expert opinion."

Lane came down and stood next to him, her arm around his waist, his over her shoulder, his sketch in her pocket. "Those are peas, silly. I was afraid you were only suited to being an inspector, but I see you have been planning the flower border." She unfolded the sketch and held it up. "Where are you planning to put these? Someplace sunny, I hope. It might make them happier."

"Ah," he said, taking it. "I was experimenting with

organizing my thoughts along the lines of *Les Fleurs du Mal*. What do you think? Has it a future?"

"You'll never know. Ames and Terrell solved it without a pot of flowers. It's novel, I'll give it that. You must try it again on your next case. Now then, I'll throw the chicken in the oven, and we'll have a drink on the porch."

Settled happily at their metal table with glasses of scotch, Lane lifted the envelope in her hand. "I've had a letter from Diana. Shall I read it to you?"

His eyebrows rose. "That was quick. Yes, you shall."

> *Dear Lane,*
>
> *I hope this finds you well and that you had a good trip home. My situation here is exactly what one might have predicted. Fairfax was found guilty of the treason he accused me of, and my endless testimony, the document I pinched from him, and God knows what other proof and material they have, demonstrates my innocence. He will stand trial for the murder of Tremaine, and I shall be chief witness, I suppose. My recent brush with being accused of a heinous crime myself is bound to raise doubt in the jury, and he'll get off. You can just see they all look askance at me. "No smoke without fire," you can see them thinking.*
>
> *They dragged me through all the weary facts of my work during the war, dwelling in particular on the parts where our network fell apart and our plans were discovered and thwarted,*

since it was these episodes he attributed to me in his accusations. I discovered, much to my amazement, that I have a near photographic memory for detail, which I think impressed a couple of the duller members of the panel. By the time it was all over Major Hogarth seemed satisfied, as did the director.

She offered me a job, you know, and I had thought of staying on—it seems to be the work I'm suited for, but I'm not sure, really. I don't like most of them as human beings, and more than anything I'd like to feel fully human again. In any case, it would be tiresome to work with people who I suspect would never entirely trust me.

One's fate is so dependent on things one can't control. My friend Marisa, for example. We've fallen out completely. I think she holds me responsible in some way for her father's downfall. Even so, it was her testimony that ultimately put the seal on my innocence. She'd seen her father in the very act of betrayal. I suppose if he hadn't lost all his money and sold her jewellery and everything that mattered to her, she might have gone on covering up for him till doomsday, and I'd have been hanged.

As to Tremaine, well, I'm lucky, really. I had my chance at love, and like for so many others, the war put an end to it. It will have to be enough. And in the meantime, I've taken to horses again. Ganf's doctor is quite a horseman,

as it turns out, so we go out from time to time.
You know me—it's all I really need.

Thank you, then, for my life, at any rate.
It was Ganf who encouraged me to try to get
you to help. You didn't have to come, but you
did. I won't soon forget it, though, of course,
you must read nothing into it. You are still
annoying and patronizing.
I remain your loving sister,
Diana

"Your grandfather's doctor," said Darling. "That could be something. What could that nice man have in common with your sister?"

"Africa and horses, I should think. Relationships have been built on less." She put the letter on the table and gave the kitchen a "Now, then" look. "You go unpack, have a bath, and the chicken will be ready. Maybe I'll write a reply."

Having pushed Darling out of the kitchen, Lane busied herself with checking the chicken and then went to her neglected writing corner and took up some paper and fished around in her handbag for her pen.

Dearest Diana,
Thank you for letting me know how your
interviews with Major Hogarth et al. went.
I'm absolutely positive you underplayed how
impressed she, and all of them, are with you.
I am sure, knowing what I know of you, that
they were bowled over by your precision,

intelligence, and clear-headedness—and, of course, your courage. I certainly am impressed with you. You really are the bravest person I know. You have everything it takes to recover your balance and joy in the world.

Having found someone to love myself during the war, I know the devastation of losing him. But much to my amazement, I discovered that, having been able to love once, I was able to do it again. And in my case, at least, I made a much better choice the second time. I am sure, you know, that that is down to our having the most wonderful grandparents in the world. Do you know—but of course you do—that they tried to love our father no matter what? I have always thought it was for our mother's sake, and for ours. I feel sure it was unrequited. I don't think poor Father was capable of love. Perhaps I'm wrong. He must have loved our mother. But I have realized after this last visit that they have taught me the most important thing of all: to forgive. And I do try to think more charitably of him.

I would not like you to get the impression from this missive that I do not think you the most annoying nuisance. Please give a big hug to Grandmama and Ganf and the horses—and, of course, warmest regards to Dr. Mwangi. With much love,
Lane

"What do you think?" Lane asked. "Of course, I can never send it."

Darling, in a loose cream-coloured shirt and smelling newly of soap, said, "It's charming. And true. You must send it."

"If I did, I would never be able to see her again after this embarrassing outpouring of slosh."

"You're ridiculous, you know that?" He punctuated this judgment by taking her in his arms.

May 9, 1948

ARDEN WAITED HALF a block away. He had to be sure MacDonald would be there, waiting. He took a deep breath and felt the pocket of his jacket. His means of deliverance was there, solid, ready to free him. He had tried this in the daytime and knew that the porch of their usual meeting place would be visible from where he stood. At last, he saw the flickering of a flashlight going up the stairs.

He raced forward, keeping his footfalls quiet, and stopped breathless behind the boxwood hedge that wound around the neighbour's yard. MacDonald hadn't bothered to turn off the flashlight. He was sitting on the steps waiting. He could see him looking down at his watch, pulling out cigarettes and putting his flashlight beside him to light one. The match flared up and lit MacDonald's face. He looked complacent, unworried.

Arden watched him, and then sat back, looking away into the darkness that descended all the way to the water, suddenly in the grip of doubt. He'd been a good shot during the war, Arden thought. Hell, being a good shot is what had got him into this trouble. He shook his head, as if to convince himself. He would never regret shooting that murdering bastard. Or this one. He could get him from here. He turned and lifted his pistol and balanced it on his other wrist, focusing on his target. He'd get him, then he'd leave for good. His life was a mess anyway.

He gave his head a little shake to try to sharpen his focus, but his supporting hand was shaking. He tried to steady it, but the revolver felt slippery with nervous sweat. He couldn't risk two shots. That would bring everyone out. And then he knew. He didn't have it in him. MacDonald had wrung him dry, had threatened his very family, but he hadn't shot Franny in cold blood. Renshaw had. Renshaw had deserved to die.

He closed his eyes and brought his gun down. He heard MacDonald finally give up, swearing under his breath. He saw the flashlight heading down the hill. He had two hundred dollars left. MacDonald wouldn't get his hands on that, anyway. He looked at the gun he was holding. It felt at once familiar and alien, something from another life. He would leave as he'd planned. His rucksack was packed and hidden in the boat shed. But he would leave this behind. It frightened him that he had thought of using it again, and he sat down suddenly, feeling light-headed. Tomorrow, he would be away, far from all his troubles. He closed his eyes, saw himself as a logger in some vast wilderness, changed, lost, free. And then he thought of the children he would never see again, and felt his eyes well up.

DARLING MADE IT his first job to drive out to Slocan to see Mr. Renshaw. He carried the photograph that had been taken of the grave of his sister-in-law, Francine Renshaw, and he had the medal. He was not happy, and was mulling over what he would say. He felt, he decided, used. He did not like it. He was greeted by the same curtseying maid and shown into the office where he'd sat before.

"Inspector Darling. It's so good of you to come." Renshaw waved him into a chair. "Drink?"

"No, thank you," Darling said. He did not sit. He put his hand in his pocket and pulled out the envelope with the photograph. "This is a picture of Lieutenant Francine Renshaw's grave. I thought you would like to have it."

Renshaw, slightly wary because Darling was standing, took it and looked at it. He nodded. "Thank you. I appreciate what you did for me there."

"I fear you were not honest with me, Renshaw. You know exactly what happened to her. I believe you knew before you asked the mayor to send me out there."

Renshaw shifted and looked down but said nothing.

I'm right, Darling thought. "My sergeant contacted the Princess Pats for records and learned that your brother had been given leave to go to England from the front in August of '17. This is what you didn't want coming out. Major Renshaw, I suspect, murdered his own wife. The thing that is galling is that you knew that. Did he tell you himself? Send you a letter perhaps?"

Renshaw looked up finally. "In the papers it said she was found with her hands folded, and flowers...he...he must have..."

"Oh, that wasn't him." Darling felt his voice go cold. "That was her lover. He got there in time to see what your brother had done. In fact, he must have seen your brother do it, because he didn't forget it. I have a witness in custody who saw him murder your brother on the battlefield. The man who killed your brother has himself been murdered. It's all a kind of justice, I suppose." Darling stopped and took a deep breath. Renshaw had collapsed into his chair, his head down. Darling shook his head. "Oh, and you needn't worry. There'll be nothing in the English papers. No one over there was able to find out how Francine Renshaw died. I've brought you back a medal, which your brother's murderer took from his body. Unfortunately, he managed to sand the name off, but he kept the numbers. That's how it was traced." Darling did not want to hand it to him. He was angry at being used by this entitled man to cover up the family scandal. He placed the glass case on the desk, rested his hand on it for just a moment, and then turned to leave.

"A medal?" Renshaw twisted around to look at Darling, and pushed himself out of the chair. Away from the window, the room was cast in shadows. He moved to the desk and picked up the glass case. "Good God! He always kept this on his person, even in battle. He said it brought him luck. How...?"

"It was not lucky enough," Darling said, and turned to go.

"Look here, Darling," Renshaw began, but Darling was out the door.

It took the entire drive home for Darling to shake off the melancholy vision of Renshaw standing alone in the shadowed room, holding his brother's most unlucky medal.

THE EVENING BROUGHT a drop in temperature that finally drove them away from the little French table where they had eaten their dinner, and indoors to sit by the Franklin.

"I'm happy to be home," Lane said contentedly. "I'm glad we sailed. I feel less wrung out. I suppose the rise in air travel means that a time will come when people are dashing back and forth any time they like, but it still feels to me like such a faraway place. And a faraway time; I felt as if I was flying backward to my girlhood. I expected everything to be the same—my grandparents, my college, my sister. It's as if life is only real here."

"You don't think you'll change your mind and want to go live there one day?"

"Everything I want is here," she said, leaning over to kiss him. "I wonder how Ames is getting on with Tina. Wouldn't you like to see them married?"

"I have no interest in Ames's marital state. In fact, I don't want anything to interfere with his work. He has the makings of a decent policeman. Married life will only soften him."

"Hypocrite! Anyway, I'm amazed you think he'd be more indulged with Tina than with his very indulgent mother."

"You're right. Tina's another one like you. We'd better push this wedding along, then. I'll tell him tomorrow he's got to marry her. Will that do? And don't try to divert by talking about Ames. You're mailing that letter."

ACKNOWLEDGEMENTS

As WITH EVERY LANE WINSLOW there are so many to thank, and more and more often, people with extraordinary specialties who are unstinting, generous, and enthusiastic in sharing their knowledge. Thank you to Dr. Jeff Fine for excellent advice on the matter of gunshots. *To Track a Traitor* owes a special debt to Crispin and Jan Elsted, whom I was able to visit at the wonderful Barbarian Press nestled in the forest near Chilliwack. I thank them for their inspiration and for initiating me into the fascinating world of the small art press.

The team at TouchWood Editions, the loveliest indie publisher in existence, continues to nurture, laugh with, and support me in sharing these stories. Thank you to Tori Elliott, publisher extraordinaire; Kate Kennedy, editorial coordinator, whose support is unequalled; and Curtis Samuel, lovely publicist, planner of epic trips, and most excellent cheerer-upper. A special hug of gratitude to owner Pat Touchie, who is always so very kind when we meet.

Editors Claire Philipson, Renée Layberry, and Meg Yamamoto helped to make a real book out of what I provided, and I am eternally grateful for the care and commitment each of them brings. The covers continue to delight everyone who sees them, and we have the wonderful Margaret Hanson to thank for these.

A special thanks to my wonderful first readers, Nickie Bertolotti and Sasha Bley-Vroman, who warn me away from disasters of language or fact before I expose them to anyone else. And of course to my family, Biski and Tammy for their enthusiastic support, my two grandsons Teo and Tyson for, well, frankly, just existing, and most especially my husband Terry, who must put up with every inconvenience occasioned by having a writer in your actual home. The elation, the hand-wringing, the endless sessions of "Let me just bounce this off you," the Zoom calls, the lost notebooks, the desperate calls for tech help. All of it borne with equanimity and kindness and not a little amusement. He claims to enjoy it. Thank you.

IONA WHISHAW is the author of the *Globe & Mail* bestselling series The Lane Winslow Mysteries. She is the winner of a Bony Blithe Light Mystery Award, was a finalist for a BC and Yukon Book Prize, and has twice been nominated for a Left Coast Crime Award. The heroine of her series, Lane Winslow, was inspired by Iona's mother who, like her father before her, was a wartime spy. Born in the Kootenays, Iona spent many years in Mexico, Nicaragua, the US before settling into Vancouver, BC where she now lives with her husband, Terry. Throughout her life she has worked as a youth worker, social worker, teacher, and award-winning high school principal, eventually completing her master's in creative writing from the University of British Columbia.

WEBSITE: IONAWHISHAW.COM

FACEBOOK & INSTAGRAM: @IONAWHISHAWAUTHOR

DISCUSSION QUESTIONS: TOUCHWOODEDITIONS.COM/LANEWINSLOW

THE LANE WINSLOW MYSTERY SERIES

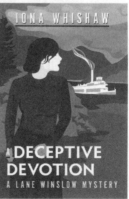

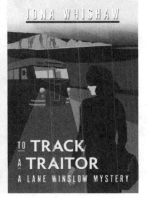